Trouble in the Valleys

Francesca Capaldi has enjoyed writing since she was a child, largely influenced by a Welsh mother who was good at improvised story telling. She is a member of the RNA and the Society of Women Writers and Journalists. Francesca currently lives in Kent with her family and a cat called Lando Calrissian.

Also by Francesca Capaldi

Francesca Capaldi

Trouble *in the* Valleys

hera

First published in the United Kingdom in 2022 by

Hera Books
Unit 9 (Canelo), 5th Floor
Cargo Works, 1-2 Hatfields
London, SE1 9PG
United Kingdom

A CIP catalogue record for this book is available from the British Library.

Print ISBN 978 1 80032 995 9
Ebook ISBN 978 1 80436 901 2

Printed and bound in Great Britain by Clays Ltd, Elcograf S.p.A.

To Carmela, Peter, Giovanna, Jack, Luca, Phynn and Seren.

To the men of the 13th Brigade (2nd Rhondda) of the 114th Battalion of the 38th (Welsh) Infantry Division, and all those who fought on the various fronts, in the sea and in the air, in the Great War.

Shall they return to beatings of great bells
In wild trainloads?
A few, a few, too few for drums and yells,
May creep back, silent, to still village wells
Up half-known roads.

—Wilfred Owen, 'The Send-Off'

Prologue

12th March 1919

Dorcalon railway station

'Not long now,' said Henry Austin, excitement filling his heart as the train's brakes hissed and squealed to bring it to a halt at Rhymney station.

'The quicker the better,' said Douglas Ramsay. He leant forward, smiling. 'I can't wait to see Susan and actually start our married life properly. It's not like we had much time after we married before I enlisted.'

'No one marched you to the enlisting office at the point of a gun,' Maurice Coombes retorted, the London twang still evident in his Welsh accent, even after years of living in Dorcalon. 'Voluntary it was when we went.'

'Let's not argue,' said Henry, noticing glances of appreciation at his intervention from the other five men in the carriage who'd all got a little weary of Maurice's touchy mood.

When the train finally came to a halt, doors clicked open and several men alighted on the platform to a welcoming throng. Music started playing. Henry stood and pulled the open window down a little more. He leant out to see a small Silver Band at one end of the station.

'Wonder if they'll send our Silver Band to welcome us,' said Douglas.

'Least they could do,' said Maurice.

After a minute or so, and the sound of several doors being slammed shut, the train chuffed on its way once more, through the Rhymney Valley, passing hills and Pontlottyn colliery on its way. Henry put the window up and sat down.

'I 'ope Susan's over that cold she told me about in her last letter,' said Douglas. 'It'd be nice to take her somewhere for a coupla days, before starting work again. Barry Island, maybe.' He scratched the scar on his eyebrow, the only indication now of the injury he'd sustained in battle three years back. 'I presume she got my letter saying we were due back today.'

'If she didn't, I'm sure word's got round,' said Henry.

'Reckon we should all take a few days off before starting work again,' said Teilo Brice. 'If we can get work again.'

'Course we will,' said Maurice. 'We're blinkin' heroes. Got to give us work, isn't it?'

'Dunno why I got sent back to the Front when I was on leave in November when the war ended,' said Daniel Williams. 'Ridiculous. I could have just stayed put. What have we been doing these last four months that's so important anyway?'

'Clearing up,' said Alun Lloyd, the farmer's son. 'Someone had to. And I suppose they had to make sure things wouldn't kick off again. There are some poor buggers still abroad, so we should think ourselves lucky.'

Daniel didn't seem impressed with this argument.

'Well, here we are at last,' said Henry as the train started to slow down once more. He stood to get his knapsack from the parcel shelf above him. Others followed suit slowly, those whose bags were on the floor leaving them there until the train finally ground to a halt.

There was a bustle of men and bags as several doors opened and the fifteen surviving Dorcalon men from the 13th battalion of the 114th Brigade of the 38th (Welsh) Division, known as the Rhondda Pals, and three from the 14th battalion, alighted from the train into their own part of the Rhymney Valley.

'They don't look very 'appy to see us,' Maurice mumbled.

Henry looked at the huddles of families coming forward only slowly to greet their returning lads. Smiles were muted.

He spotted Polly Coombes and her parents, who'd come to greet Maurice, whose wife Mabel and daughter Lily were also there. Idris Hughes, who'd signed up with them but who'd been medically discharged, stood with William Griffin, who'd lost a leg at the Battle of Mametz Woods and was now sporting a false one. Amelia Bowen, a young woman he'd long admired, was standing with Teilo Brice's wife.

Time seemed to slow down for Henry as he stepped onto the platform. He had a feeling of impending doom, that something bad was about to happen, like he'd had so often in the trenches in his latter days in the army. His hand started shaking, so he hid it behind his back as he heaved his rucksack up higher.

He spotted the blonde hair of his sister, Gwen Meredith, who was standing with their parents. They surged forward to meet him. Their expressions were more anxious than happy.

Henry spotted Douglas's parents coming towards their son, who'd alighted behind Maurice.

'Mam, Da! Where's Susan then?' said Douglas. 'She still unwell with that cold?'

They looked grave. Henry's parents lowered their heads. The muted chatter ceased.

'Douglas, it weren't a cold,' said his mother. 'It were the Spanish influenza. And well…'

'Son, she died yesterday evening,' his father finished, his voice low.

Henry's vision went blank for a couple of seconds. In his head he could hear gunshots and people shouting, a bomb exploding. He could smell the burning stench of charred ground. Then he was in the present again.

'Henry?' His father came forward to take the knapsack.

'I'm all right, Da.'

'But, she can't have,' said Douglas. 'All that time fighting, and I managed to survive the horror. I can't have survived only to come home to this. It don't make no sense. And I thought the influenza were on the wane.' A slow whine came from his lips before he threw the bag on the ground and sobbed.

The guard slammed the doors shut and blew his whistle. The train began its slow chugging as it left the station. A murmur went up among the soldiers, as word went around about Douglas's wife.

The train's tail end had passed the end of the platform before anyone stirred. Then they seemed to shift as one, like a slow river, towards the exit. Only Douglas and his parents didn't move.

On the road on the other side of the station, the returning soldiers and their families trooped in a long, weary line up Station Road, away from the colliery.

'The Silver Band was going to come and play to greet you.' Henry's mother's voice was barely audible. 'Didn't seem appropriate once we heard about poor Susan.'

The imposing structure of the McKenzie Arms came into view at the crossroads ahead. Henry had fancied a pint in there this evening, to have a chat with friends he hadn't seen in a while. He'd lost the heart now. As if they hadn't been through enough. Poor Douglas. His eyes shifted from left to right to take in the scene. Here they were, back in this small, unassuming village. Most of them had been relieved to get here. But what was in store for them? He only hoped this tragedy wasn't an indication of things to come.

Chapter One

19th July 1919

Peace Day

'That were a lovely wedding,' said Polly, pushing a stray wisp of her dark blonde hair back under her straw hat as she sat on one of the wooden benches in Jubilee Gardens. 'Or should I say, weddings. Gwen and Miss Elizabeth looked so pretty.'

Her son, thirty-four-month-old Herby, wriggled onto the seat beside her and gave her an appealing smile. 'Pretty ladies.'

Polly's sister-in-law, Mabel Coombes, sat next to her, watching as her five-year-old daughter, Lily, skipped with her rope.

'They was beautiful,' said the little girl.

Mabel looked wistful. 'Such lovely dresses. I believe they made them theirselves. I had to make do with second-hand, or probably third-hand when I married your Maurice.' She frowned slightly.

'Come on, Herby!' called Lily. 'Let's play chase.'

The little boy jumped down enthusiastically and followed her.

'Be careful of the plants, mind,' Mabel called, considering all the blooming flowers and the well-kept trees around the small bits of neat lawn.

'At least you got married at the chapel. We could only do the registry office, what with me being, you know…'

'Pregnant? I supposed you'd have had to.'

Polly looked at her left hand, where the cheap ring still sat, for Herby's sake only. 'I just wore my best dress. Gus didn't even own a suit, so wore black trousers with a jacket his next-door neighbour leant him.'

'I'm sorry,' said Mabel, shaking her head. 'Here's me moaning, after all you've been through. You didn't deserve a nasty piece of work like Gus. I don't suppose you've heard from him lately.'

'No. He only wrote from gaol the once, to tell me not to contact his mother and sister back in Surrey. Oh, and he warned me not to get any ideas about trying to divorce him. As if I could afford it.'

'I reckon you should save up for it. Stealing from houses and demanding money with menaces must be unreasonable behaviour. You read of divorces every week in the *Monmouth Guardian*. Times have changed.' Mabel nodded. 'Look at the law allowing women over thirty and all men to vote.'

Esther Williams, the village gossip, entered the park, eyeing them suspiciously. She sat on the seat at the top of the gardens, the opposite end from them.

'Better keep our voices down,' said Mabel. 'I was going to say, if you did win, Gus would have to pay you money.'

Polly laughed. 'From where? He can't earn in gaol, and he'll be in there another… three-and-a-bit years. I'm just thankful that Mrs Bowen were willing to take me back on after Gus and his brother-in-law were arrested. Especially since I was sent away to Surrey in a rush and left her in the lurch.'

'She's a good sort, Mrs Bowen.'

'By the way, we had Maurice round the house this morning, to borrow a saw. In a right mood he were. Is everything all right?' She asked this cautiously, not wanting to pry, knowing how much she disliked it when people tried to interfere in her life.

'He's often in a mood these days,' said Mabel. 'Finding it hard, he is, adjusting to being back here. Goodness knows why, after the awful time they had in the trenches. He spends a lot of time with the Pals, as he still calls them. Doesn't even mix with his old mates anymore.'

'Poor Maurice. Poor all of them. What a time they had. And poor Douglas in particular, going through the war like that, only to lose Susan the day before he arrived home. His sister's done a good job of looking after the kiddies though and keeping house for him.'

'I do feel sorry for the men, I really do.' Mabel bit the corner of her bottom lip, and Polly could feel a 'but' coming.

'Go on.'

Mabel huffed out a long sigh. 'Well, everyone knows it's hard for them, coming home, adjusting, but it's hard for the wives too, those of them what's married. We've got used to running things, see, making decisions, even if money was short for some. Now here we are, being told what to do by our so-called Lords and Masters again, having the money controlled by them and giving us what they think we should have. Not that I'm running Maurice down, look you, but the war's not been kind to him. He has a new kind of – hardness.'

'I – I had noticed that.'

'Oh, I shouldn't moan, least of all to you, struggling on your own. What an ungrateful wife I am! At least, working in the munitions, I had a bit more money than most of the army wives, and have saved a good bit. Looking to our future, I am. It'd be nice to rent a bigger house. A shame I couldn't stay at the munitions, but the men have returned and want their jobs back.'

'You can moan to me, Mabel. You're family.' She took her sister-in-law's hand. 'I know Maurice is my brother, but I also know how difficult he can be. He's always liked his own way. Suppose I was like that once. And don't worry about me. I'm lucky to have Mum and Dad, and I'm certainly better off without the husband I had.'

'Yes, you are.'

Esther Williams chose this moment to get up and walk past them, looking at Polly with a sneer as she came close.

'Who're you lookin' at?' Mabel called after her. 'Thinking you're better than everyone else when your husband's in gaol too.'

Esther didn't reply.

'Mabel!' said Polly. 'Just leave it.' Polly had suffered the same treatment from several people in the village. She hadn't got used to it, but she'd learned to ignore it.

'Well, who does she think she is with her scornful glares?' Mabel stood up and stretched. 'I'd better head home to make dinner before Maurice comes looking for me. Are you going to the Peace Day carnival this afternoon?'

'Oh yes. Herby will love all the noise and spectacle.'

'I've got to go as Maurice will be marching with the old Pals, and the Silver Band. I think it'll be fun though, with the kiddies' parade and the floats. Lily'll be dressing up.'

'Lovely. I'll look forward to seeing her.'

'Come on, Lily!' Mabel called. 'Time to get home.'

'Ohoo!' Lily skipped to them, her bottom lip sticking out. 'Bye, Herby,' she called back at her cousin.

'Bye, bye,' he called sadly, giving a little wave before joining his mother and leaning against her arm.

As they walked away, Polly considered how things had turned around in her relationship with her sister-in-law. She'd never been close to her, finding her a little dowdy. But that was in her younger days, when she always had to dazzle and be flattered by others. Polly'd loved to be noticed. No wonder other women had thought her a show-off. They probably thought she'd got her just deserts.

Her heart sank at the thought. Perhaps she had. She'd been shocking at school, after they'd moved here from London when she was eleven. She'd felt awkward, different, with people saying they couldn't understand her when she spoke, the girls particularly. That's probably why she'd become quite mean towards them. But she'd always been popular with the boys. That had annoyed the girls even more.

She shook her head. The events of the last three years had made her grow up, shocked into it by motherhood and a bullying husband. She avoided people's attention now. Mabel was a good person, kind, and always had been. Polly wanted to be like her.

'Come on, Herby, let's get home. Your mamgu will be getting some dinner for us.' She took the boy's hand as they stood.

If only she hadn't been so naïve. Yet she had Herby, who she adored, and couldn't imagine life without him. She picked him up and cuddled him before setting off home.

–

Polly made sure to get her parents and Herby out in good time for the two o'clock parade that afternoon. The village was a blaze of colour, with flags, festoons of ribbons and fairy lamps, hung all around Jubilee Green, the triangle of houses and shops in the centre of the village. Polly and her family found a good place on one corner, by the gardens, opposite the bookshop on one side and the McKenzie Arms on the other, and from there could survey four roads. Already the Silver Band and other participants of the procession were getting into place.

Mabel and little Lily soon joined them, and it wasn't long before Polly's sister Connie, with her husband, Sioni Gower, also found them, squeezing in to enjoy the advantageous position.

'Found a good spot here, you have,' said Sioni, his arm half around Polly because of lack of space. Already he reeked of beer and cigarettes, and she wished he'd gone to stand the other side of Connie. She turned towards her father, who was holding Herby in his arms, and started a conversation with him to avoid the smell as much as possible.

A little after two o'clock, the Silver Band struck up with 'It's a Long Way to Tipperary', and set off, followed by the men who'd served in the army. Tom Meredith, one of today's grooms, and Henry Austin, his bride's brother, had evidently slipped out of the wedding reception at the McKenzie Arms Hotel to join in.

'There's Maurice!' Mabel squealed. 'Look, Lily, there's your da.' She pointed to where he was marching, in the line behind Tom and Henry. After the soldiers, in a line on her own, they were surprised to see Elizabeth Owen, marching in her wedding dress, in her place as a former Voluntary Aid Detachment nurse. Behind her marched the Boy Scouts, led by their diminutive scout master, Twm Bach Breckon.

Polly heard the music of the band alternately rise and fall as the parade travelled halfway down James Street, went up Bryn Road, turned left onto Edward Street, took the route across the top of the Jubilee Green triangle, in front of the Workmen's Institute and carried on to halfway down Alexandra Street. From there, it came back down the side of the chapel onto Gabriel Street and headed back to the bottom of Jubilee Green, now playing 'Keep the Home Fires Burning'.

'That was a treat, that was,' said Polly's mother, Delia. 'Come on now, we need to get Herby to the children's tea at the chapel.'

'I excited about tea, and clowns,' he said, clapping his chubby little hands.

'Clowns?' said Delia. 'Oh, you mean the Pierrot troupe at the Workmen's Institute. Yes, I am too.'

'We'll see you there later,' said Sioni, placing an arm around Connie's shoulders.

'I wanted to see the kiddies eating their tea,' said Connie.

'Course you don't. Boring that is. Save us a seat if you get there first.'

'Righty 'o,' said Jim.

As they turned to go, Sioni flicked his head back to wink at Polly. It made her shudder. Daft, that was. It was probably only a result of having had too much beer already, like no doubt a lot of the men had. She wondered how the McKenzie Arms was managing with the copious number of patrons today, and a wedding reception. She was only glad she wasn't one of the staff having to work there and miss the Peace Day celebrations.

–

What a day it had been. Polly had thoroughly enjoyed it, and all the more because Herby had. She was standing with her family in a field beyond West Street now, looking at an overcast night sky. At least it hadn't rained yet.

'Look, Herby,' said Connie, holding the child in her arms, where he was half-asleep. 'They're lighting the bonfire. That means the fireworks won't be long.'

'I always wanted see fi-works,' he said.

'It's been a long time since I've seen any either,' said Polly, 'with them not being allowed during the war.'

They watched the fire of old branches and bits of donated demolished furniture grow across the hill. Polly was mesmerised by the flickering flames and the crackle of the wood as it burned. The odour of the blazing wood took her back to bonfire nights here as an older child, when life was simpler.

Connie had just moved away a little with Herby, to talk to a friend, when Polly felt warm breath on her neck. She turned to see who'd stepped so close to her, only to come face to face with her brother-in-law, Sioni, her cheek brushing his shoulder. The stench of alcohol was worse now than it had been earlier. She stepped back, peering around for her parents, but couldn't see them.

'Looking forward to this, I am,' he said, his salacious grin lit by the fire.

'Um, yes. Me too. Have you seen my mum and dad?'

'They're talking to the Austins, over there.'

Through the throng she spotted them as they chatted to Ruth and Albert, who lived a few doors up from them on James Street.

Sioni began a review of the day they'd just had, as if she hadn't been there, all the while standing too close to her. He'd always been a little too familiar, ever since Connie had married him, five years before. She'd wondered whether his whole family was like that, but since they lived down in Bargoed she'd never got to know them.

Polly was relieved when her parents and Connie returned, just as the fireworks began. Four of them stood in a row, with Sioni behind, between Connie and Polly. Jim was now holding Herby, who was shouting and giggling as each firework was set off.

'Look, Mummy, lully fireworks!'

'He's a bit different to me as a child,' said Connie. 'I didn't like them at all.'

'Like a lot of things,' Sioni muttered.

'I remember you covering your ears,' said Polly. 'I've always loved them.'

'I can imagine,' said Sioni.

Polly jumped and gasped as a firework whizzed into the sky.

'That's not like you,' said Jim.

'No, it's not normally.'

But it hadn't been the firework that had made her jump; she was sure someone had poked their fingers against her posterior. And the only person in a position to do that was Sioni.

It might have been an accident. Perhaps it had made him jump and his hand had shot out. But just in case it wasn't, when the next firework went off she poked her elbow backwards, catching him in the stomach.

'Oh, I'm so sorry, Sioni,' she said. 'I don't know what's wrong with me tonight. I'd stand well clear of me as I'm rather jumpy.'

'Duly noted,' he said, standing on the other side of Connie.

Chapter Two

Henry had tuned out of what Maurice was saying as he and the Pals stood in a circle in the corner of the small hall on Sunday. They were having their post-service cup of tea at the Ainon Baptist Chapel. Amelia Bowen was standing close by, chatting with the pastor's wife. Henry's eyes kept darting in her direction. Had she become even more attractive in the last four years, or did he feel like that because he hadn't seen her?

He'd always loved her dark copper hair and the way it contrasted with her green eyes. She was sylphlike, reminding him of one of the fairies in a book Gwen had owned as a child. Her dress was loose, stylish. It was green too, setting her hair off beautifully. Over one arm was hooked both a small handbag and a parasol.

It had surprised a few people when she'd turned up at the chapel recently. She'd told Gwen she preferred it to the parish church, which she'd long attended with her mother. His sister had been a little scathing in the retelling, wondering whether the attraction had not instead been some young man she wished to court. That being the case, how he wished that young man was him. Amelia had always seemed a little out of his reach, with her mother owning the dress business, but now his sister Gwen and his friend Gwilym Owen had married the mine manager's offspring, Tom and Elizabeth, who knew?

Maurice said, 'What do you think, Henry?' just as the pastor's wife moved away, leaving Amelia on her own.

'Um, I'll discuss it later. Excuse me a moment.' He placed his cup on the nearby table and hurried away, not wanting to question his hasty decision.

'Hello, Amelia.'

She turned in surprise. 'Oh, hello.' She looked him up and down. 'Um, Gwen Austin's brother, is it?'

'Gwen Meredith now, but yes, that's right. Henry.' He smiled, though his insides shrivelled a little. She didn't even remember his name. 'You and Gwen was in the same year at school.'

'That's right.' She gave a brief smile. 'I remember now. You were a couple of years ahead. Later, you courted Jane Probert, and her father said you were too young. Poor Jane.' She turned her head, looking solemn.

'Yes. Poor Jane.' He'd been eighteen and Jane sixteen, and her father had made plans for her future as a teacher. But she'd married young anyway, then died of the consumption shortly after giving birth. It had been a lucky escape for him, though he wasn't proud of himself for thinking like that.

'So, how have you found it, back in Dorcalon, after being in France for so long?' she asked.

'It's good to be back. It were certainly no picnic out there.'

'I would think not.' She leant forward to consider his army mates. 'They're not very sociable.'

Maurice, noticing her looking over, did a little wave and raised his eyebrows.

Amelia gave Maurice a stern look and turned away. 'Anyway, I sat in on Gwen's and Miss Elizabeth's weddings yesterday. Lovely dresses they were wearing. Where did they get them, do you know? For they didn't come to my mother.'

'They made them, with Anwen's help, and her mother, I believe.' He felt awkward, not wanting to mention their new business venture in case she felt it was a rival to her mother's.

'I'd heard they were doing the odd bit of sewing for customers.' Her face was neutral, so it was hard to tell if she was cross or not.

'Does your mother mind?'

'She probably doesn't see them as any great competition. And she's also, well, got her mind on other things.' She pinched her mouth in and looked away. 'So, where have the happy couples gone on honeymoon?'

'Gwen and Tom went to Swansea, to a guest house near the Mumbles. Gwilym and Elizabeth went to Talybont, to walk the Brecon Beacons.'

'Goodness, walking doesn't sound like much of a honeymoon. I'd certainly pick the Mumbles out of those two.'

'Me too, though Elizabeth and Gwilym both like walking, so I guess it suits them. I like spending time by the sea.'

He pictured himself with Amelia, walking along the footpath at Bracelet Bay, as he'd done once as a child with his parents.

'My goodness, what a dowdy piece Polly Coombes has become,' she said in a lowered voice.

He wondered at the change of subject, until he noticed her close by, with her parents.

'She comes to work looking like she needs a new wardrobe, which doesn't say much for our business now, does it? She used to be so colourful, and I had some admiration for her bold choices.'

'I reckon Gus Smith knocked it out of her, poor thing. I heard about it from my parents. She used to be so confident and chatty. And as you said, colourful.'

'Maybe a little too colourful, especially as she ended up, you know.'

Henry guessed she was referring to her pregnancy, which nobody was convinced was down to Gus. His stomach flipped as he embarked on a sudden plan. He had to do it now, or not at all.

'Amelia, do you fancy going to tea at Perilli's Refreshment House one afternoon, maybe over the bank holiday, the weekend after next?'

'Perilli's? I'm sorry, Henry, but we've an awful lot of sewing on and my mother has plans for catching up with it all the next two weekends.' She seemed to hesitate, looking over at the Pals once more, her brow creased as if she was deciding something.

Henry felt stupid. She wouldn't want to walk out with him, a stylish woman like her. What had made him so cocky as to think she would? Yet he'd been popular with the girls in his younger days, with his floppy blond hair and dapper suits, before fighting in the war had wearied him.

'But – but I could make Sunday, the seventeenth of August, if that would suit you,' she said.

His mood lifted several notches. 'Oh, yes, yes it would, if you're sure.'

'Absolutely. It's been a while since I've been to Perilli's. It will make a nice change. I have to go now, to get on with all this sewing I mentioned.'

'Yes, of course. I'll pick you up at two o'clock on the seventeenth, and we'll take the train in. I'll pay, of course.'

She smiled. 'Thank you. Henry.'

'*Hwyl fawr*, Amelia.'

'Good day, Henry.'

He let out a small sigh as she walked off. He wasn't in the mood to rejoin the Pals, with their brooding conversations. He'd find his parents instead. But as he set off, a voice called his name. It was Maurice.

'Oi, Henry, where're you off to now?'

Henry twisted round. 'Thought I'd find my parents and get home. Why don't you lot go and talk to old friends? People are starting to say we're being unfriendly.'

He considered them. William Griffin had joined their throng, with his false leg. Douglas Ramsay barely spoke to anyone, even in their group, except to mention the injustice of his situation. The only ex-soldiers not with them here were those who attended other places of worship, and Alun Lloyd, who was busy on the farm.

'Friendly were she, Amelia?' said Maurice, looking put out.

The group had started to feel oppressive, like a prison they weren't allowed to stray from.

'Aye, friendly enough.' He wasn't going to tell them about their trip to Perilli's. Not yet. 'It's good to talk to other people.'

'They don't understand what we've been through,' said Teilo Brice.

There was a mumbled agreement. Henry was about to encourage them once more, when there was a clatter. Several cups and a tray had crashed to the ground.

Henry yelled and jumped, before bending forward to put his hands on his knees. The room became silent. He closed his eyes, not looking up, but sure everyone must be staring at him.

'Calm down, mate,' said Maurice, patting his shoulder. 'You see, that's why we stick together,' he whispered. 'This lot don't understand.'

Slowly the chatter started up again. Henry opened his eyes and stood up to find his mother, Ruth, by his side.

'Reckon it's time to get home for dinner,' she said, taking his arm, which was trembling.

He was grateful for her intervention. 'See you later, lads,' he said, giving them a wave, wondering what he could do about his pals.

Chapter Three

Gwen Meredith stepped out of the house a little early for her meeting, keen to see how her sister-in-law, Elizabeth, was getting on with the two allotments on Edward Street she had rented from the coal company. It was a beautiful morning, the August sun's rays coating the houses with a golden hue.

Sister-in-law! She still couldn't quite believe she was married to Tom Meredith, the colliery manager's son. Mrs Meredith she was now. The name still made her laugh, given it was the name of her former employer, for she'd once been maid at McKenzie House. Well of course it was: she was Tom's mother!

She walked to the last house and took the path up past the end of two rows of houses, at the edge of the village, to get to Edward Street. The pit wheels were grinding their usual metallic whine. Tom worked there now as a clerk, having given up his place at university after the loss of his left forearm in the war.

Reaching the field, she soon spotted Elizabeth hoeing a patch in front of her.

'*Bore da*,' Gwen called as she approached her.

Elizabeth stopped and looked around, her honey-coloured hair dangling over her face. 'Good morning, Gwen! Are you off to your meeting?'

'Yes, but I thought I'd pop over to see how you're getting on first.'

'Things are growing very well thus far.'

'I've washed the steps and floors, blackened the grate. And I've got the vegetables ready to put in the pot for the cawl for dinner – lunch.'

Elizabeth laughed. 'Whatever you want to call it. We called it dinner when I was young. It was my mother who decided on lunch – or luncheon, as she calls it. And supper became dinner.'

'It's always confused me!'

'I hope you had time to do some of your sewing too.'

'A bit, but I can continue later,' said Gwen.

'I'll do my share of whatever needs doing when I return.'

'I'll put the food on to cook when I get back from this meeting, so it'll be ready for Gwilym when he gets back after two, and for Tom later on.'

'I think maybe we'll have to change things, so we eat our main meal for supper, with Tom and Gwilym doing different hours.'

Gwen sighed. It had made mealtimes a little complicated.

'I know it's not ideal, Gwen, us renting a house together, but at least it means none of us has to live with parents and we can share the bills and so on. It hopefully won't be forever. Maybe once you get your clothes business going, and I get my market garden profitable, we'll be able to get our own places.'

Gwen had found it a little stressful living with Elizabeth and Gwilym, even though they'd only been sharing the house a week so far. But it did have its advantages. 'At least we can share the housework, which does help with running our own businesses.'

'On that note, I had a further order from James the Veg today. That's who those are for.' Elizabeth pointed to the cabbages. 'And I've a greengrocer in Pontlottyn interested.'

'That's wonderful! We've had a couple of enquiries about wedding dresses since people saw yours and mine. Who'd have thought our lovely day would have a business benefit too?' Gwen examined her wristwatch. 'I'd better get going for this meeting. I'll see you later.'

Gwen walked between the allotments, waving to old Abraham, Gwilym's grandfather, as she passed him. Elizabeth's grandfather-in-law, she supposed. How strange it was, the way things had turned out. She went round to the path at the back of Edward Street, to get to number eight, the house her friend Anwen and husband Idris Hughes had started renting a couple of months back.

She opened the door to the scullery and called, 'Hello?'

Anwen soon came from the kitchen, calling, '*Bore da, cariad.*' Her tiny baby, Hope, was in her arms. 'Come in. Violet's already here, having a sewing lesson with Mamgu, and I've just put the kettle on.'

Gwen sat down at the table, where their other friend, Violet Llewellyn, was peering at the fabric she was sewing, her tongue poking out a little. Baby Gethin, nearly a year old now, was asleep in a pushchair placed behind her. She looked up to say, 'Hello, Gwen.'

'How are you getting on?' Gwen asked her.

'She's doing splendidly,' Anwen's grandmother, Cadi, replied in her stead, plonking her round body onto a dining chair.

'Isn't Enid coming?' She hadn't seen Anwen's mother so far.

'No, she has things to do, what with the two lodgers and taking in laundry. She said I could represent her and she'd be happy with anything we decide.'

'Hello Gwennie!' Sara Fach, Anwen's baby half-sister, who she'd adopted, popped her head out of the front room, a teddy bear clasped to her chest, before disappearing back inside.

'She's growing fast,' said Gwen.

'Thirty-one months old now. I can't believe it!' said Anwen. 'Right, first of all, I'm wondering: if we're going to expand our business, how are we going to do it without annoying Mrs Bowen? I don't know how aware she is of our little venture.'

'Henry were talking to Amelia at the chapel,' said Gwen, 'and it seems she does know, but doesn't seem particularly worried. Amelia also said she has other things on her mind,' Gwen added. 'Whatever that means.'

'Wellll,' Cadi started. She leant forward, and the others followed suit. 'I did hear – and it is only hearsay, look you – that she's courting a gentleman from Tredegar way. Has his own house and business.'

'Ooooh,' they all chanted at once.

'Bit old for courting, isn't she?' said Gwen. 'She's been widowed years and it's not like she's short of cash with her business being successful.'

'Well good luck to her, I say.' Cadi gave one firm nod of her head. 'I'd have done it myself if I'd ever found someone to match my Delwyn, God rest his soul.'

'Would you have, Mamgu?' Anwen asked as she spooned the tea leaves into the pot.

'Certainly. And if your mother has any sense, she will too.' When Anwen was about to interrupt, Cadi continued with, 'Oh, I know what you're going to say, that she's still married to Madog, but I've no illusions about my son. Your father's a badden, and no mistake. Your mother should be looking at divorce, as should Nerys Moss at the public house, what with her Reg turning out to be no better than Madog. It's not so difficult for women now as it were in my day. Oh, and that Polly Coombes, Polly Smith, whatever. Got a whole life ahead of her, she has. Nice looking girl. She don't want to be saddled with that Gus Smith when he comes out of gaol.'

'She made her bed and she's having to lie on it,' said Gwen, unsure of how sympathetic she felt. 'I know she were treated awful by him, but if she hadn't had a baby out of wedlock…'

'It can happen to the best of us, *cariad*. We're not in a position to judge,' said Cadi. 'I wonder who the father is? No one never said.'

Gwen shrugged and glanced at Anwen and Violet. They all knew it was Gwen's father-in-law, Herbert Meredith, but had agreed to keep it to themselves.

'Anyway, back to this sewing business,' said Anwen, placing a colourful cosy on the teapot. 'I reckon we could get hold of some good second-hand clothes from jumble sales and get a start on that end of the business. Mrs Bowen only deals in undamaged goods that she buys directly from people, but if we could get cheaper clothes that are repairable, or adaptable – especially with Gwen's eye for style – we could make a go of that.'

'That's a good idea,' said Cadi. 'Been mending all my life, I have. Reckon I can make a good job of most repairs.'

'I agree,' said Gwen. 'But we do need to advertise, otherwise who'll know about us?'

'Yes,' said Anwen. 'We can't not promote our business, just because there's a similar one. All right, who's for a cuppa tea?'

'Thought you'd never ask,' said Cadi. 'Gwen, how's your Tom getting on at the mine? He's been in that job about a year now, isn't it?'

'He's doing all right, but I'm worried it's a bit boring for him, working as a clerk in an office.'

'Then he's no different to them working underground,' said Anwen. 'Digging coal must be boring too, not to mention jolly hard work.'

Gwen felt embarrassed that she'd made Tom sound privileged. 'I'm sorry, you're right. I guess that – well, he were raised to expect more. He were doing a law degree at university. He may well have been a lawyer. And he's frustrated, with his false arm.'

Anwen put her hand on her shoulder. 'Of course he is. It's a crying shame, and no mistake.'

The other two nodded. Gwen sensed the atmosphere had become a little bleak and didn't want to make everything miserable. 'Come on now, let's get some ideas written down.' She pulled a notebook and pen from her handbag. 'Elizabeth gave me these, so I'll take notes.'

'Ooh, very fancy,' said Cadi as they all settled around the table.

Henry came out of his front door at a quarter to six as the sun's rays began to appear over the hills. It was promising to be a nice day, and here he was, heading underground for the next few hours. It was still strange being in his work garb, the moleskin trousers, singlet, flannel shirt, waistcoat and jacket, rather than the khaki uniform. Instead of his peaked cap he wore his flat cap.

He headed off along James Street towards the colliery, his tin box and bottle under each arm. There'd been a bit of a scrap at the pit yesterday, with some of the ex-soldiers who hadn't been re-employed coming back once more to ask if there were jobs. John Bowen, the undermanager, had said that they didn't need to employ so many miners now, as they didn't have to dig out so much of that 'good steam coal', with the war being over.

As he was approaching number four, Maurice came out and called, 'Morning Henry. You've got a face on you.'

'I was just thinking about the trouble yesterday, when David Keir and the others came to ask for jobs again. It doesn't seem right, after all they've been through.'

Maurice slammed his door shut and they headed off. 'Who cares? As long as *we* have work. Keir and his two mates asked for it, walking out of the job after it had become a reserved occupation. Dunno how they was allowed to enlist.'

There was no point arguing with Maurice. As they turned onto Station Road, Henry said, 'Did you have a good bank holiday yesterday?'

'We went to Barry Island. First time since Lily were born. Having a child hampers you a bit. Mabel weren't keen on me going off to have a pint. So all in all, a bit dull. Like the weather.'

'At least you got away. You should be glad you have the opportunity. Not like those what didn't come back.'

'No point thinking like that for the rest of your life, mun. We're survivors. We should be looking to get as good a life as we can, not put up with things just because others have lost the opportunity.'

Henry didn't reply, pondering what opportunities there were for the likes of them. His chance with Amelia maybe?

They met a few others from the Pals on the way, each adding their own account of their bank holidays. Other men passed them by, some looking back at their little group with curiosity.

Through the gate, among the church-like edifices of the colliery, they headed to the lamp room. Here they each collected their lamps and queued to get into the wooden cage that would take them into the abyss. As he entered the cage with seven other men, Henry felt the usual panic, like he was plunging into a trench that was going to be blown up and bury him alive. He steadied his breathing and closed his eyes as they descended, ignoring Maurice's chatter.

The cage reached the bottom with a slight jerk. Now they'd arrived and stepped out into the dusty, low cave, a kind of peace overwhelmed him. It was a relief to be away from sympathetic nods and looks of sorrow. His lamp was checked by the deputy, and he collected his pickaxe. Maurice went ahead, down the pitch-black tunnel, holding his lamp aloft. He was still yapping.

The roof of the tunnel became lower and narrower. Henry's right hand began to tremble, so he put his lamp in the other. At least down here, in the dark, his shaking was less obvious. He and Maurice were the last to reach their spot, both hanging their lamps on hooks in the wooden props. They divested themselves of some of their clothing, becoming naked from the waist up.

And so started their seven-hour shift of hewing.

-

A waitress at Perilli Bros Refreshment House seated Henry and Amelia by the window, looking out onto Rhymney High Street.

Amelia picked up the menu and perused it. 'It's such a relief to see they have more than just scones, fruit buns and biscuits now.'

'Is that all they had during the war?'

'Not to begin with, but by about halfway through the menu was getting very sparse, so my mother told me. I'd stopped coming here by then. What am I thinking, complaining about a menu! You'd probably have been glad for scones and biscuits at the Front.'

'We did have biscuits. Probably not as fancy as in here, mind.' Henry looked around the tearoom. 'It's the first time I've been in here, though I've fancied trying it a few times. It's rather elegant, with its neat white tablecloths, red napkins and little pots of greenery. And these green tiles are rather special.' He pointed at the floor.

'The Italian flag.'

'I beg your pardon?'

'The colours. Red, white and green.'

'Oh, of course. Though it could represent the Welsh flag too.' He laughed.

'I guess it could. The younger Perilli brother, Antonio, his son went back to Italy you know, to fight with the Italian army. Lorenzo he was called. He was killed in northern Italy in 1916. My mother knows Mr Antonio's wife quite well.'

'I didn't know about his son. How sad for the family. It's easy to forget, having been on the French front the whole war, that there was a lot of other places where we and our allies were fighting… I'm sorry, I'm becoming maudlin. So, when was the last time you came in here?'

'September 1915. With William.' She examined her hands and pursed her lips.

'William?'

Amelia let out a long, weary sigh. 'He was my fiancé at the time. He was an overman at Pontlottyn colliery.'

'What happened to him?'

Another waitress walked over with her pad and pencil at the ready.

'Hello, Loretta,' said Amelia.

'Oh, hello, Amelia,' she replied in a broad Valleys accent. Not what Henry had expected since she was clearly of Italian stock.

'How is your mother? We haven't seen her for a while,' said Amelia.

'She was quite ill with the influenza, but she's recovered now,' said Loretta. 'I dare say she'll be contacting your mother about an outfit or two when she's feeling up to it, or some more waitress uniforms.' She brushed her hand down her own short white pinny that covered a black dress with white collar and cuffs.

'Sorry to hear about your mother. Is your father not here today?'

'No, only Uncle Giuseppe. Papa's gone to the wholesalers.'

'Ah. Send my best wishes to your parents.'

'I will, thank you. Now, what can I get you?'

'Tea of course,' said Amelia. 'Unless you'd prefer coffee, Henry?'

'No, tea's just fine.'

'Lovely. And I'll have a scone with raspberry jam and a piece of the lemon cake. If that's all right?' She looked up at Henry through her long eyelashes, with her head tipped slightly to the side.

He smiled. 'You have exactly what you want.'

'And you, sir?'

'The same, please.'

'Very well.' Loretta picked the menus off the table. She grinned at Amelia and twitched her eyes towards him. Amelia grinned in return.

'I think she approves of you,' Amelia said as Loretta walked away, adding a little giggle.

The new Sunday suit he'd bought had cost a bit, which Da had lent him, but what else did he have to spend it on, except the rent to his parents? His old suit had been eight years out of date. He'd given his hair an extra wash, to make sure there were no black smuts among the dark blond strands. He'd had it cut last week, and it was now combed into a side parting.

'And do *you* approve?' he asked.

'Indeed. You look very – dapper.'

'And you look very pretty too.' He admired the light blue velvet dress with its high waistline and pointed collar. 'I guess being a dressmaker gives you an advantage in having the latest fashion.'

'It helps. Your Gwen has always been very fashionable too.'

'She does love her clothes, does our Gwen. I think the large wage she earned at the munitions came in handy for that.'

'Those days are gone for women, sadly. Not that working in the munitions turned out very well for Gwen, with her illness.'

'True enough. It could have killed her… Amelia, I'm sorry to go back to this, but did William die in the war?' It had been on his mind since she'd mentioned him.

She was silent for a while. 'No, he didn't go to war. He just, well, he jilted me for another woman. A widow whose husband had died in the war. We were engaged for three months. Mother had even bought the fabric for my wedding dress.'

'I'm so sorry, Amelia. Terrible that must have been for you.'

'To begin with. Now I consider it a lucky escape. He was a weak man. And, well, he was killed in a rockfall in Pontlottyn pit.'

It was said so matter-of-factly, as if she'd been speaking of someone she hardly knew. At first, he felt appalled by the coldness of her words, until he remembered Jane Probert. Hadn't he used those very words, 'lucky escape', to himself about her only recently?

'I'm sorry, that sounds heartless,' she said.

'No, I was thinking about a past, similar relationship.' He told her the story.

'Then we already have something in common,' she said.

The tea arrived, and, not long after, the scones.

'How is your business going, by the way?' Henry asked. 'Has it picked up, post-war?'

Amelia's expression was between a pout and a grin. 'Are you gathering information for your sister?'

'N-no,' Henry stuttered, feeling his cheeks redden. 'Sorry, it were just conversation.'

'I was only teasing.' She put her hand on his briefly.

Henry's heartbeat quickened, and he felt bewildered for a moment.

'Anyway, it's not *my* business, it's Mother's. And I wouldn't want to take it over, even if I had the chance. I don't mind keeping the workers in line, especially that silly Polly, but I wouldn't have the patience to run the whole thing. I don't want to be poring over account books, like Mother does. Which is just as well.' She pulled her lips into a thin line.

'I'm rather inclined to agree with you. I admire my sister and her friends for having the courage to start a business.'

'Not that Mother's been so occupied with the business recently, since she's found other *interests* in her life.'

'What do you mean?' he asked, though he had an idea what was coming.

'She's been seeing this distinguished gentleman, as she likes to refer to him. Lives over in Tredegar in a big house and has a business in ironmongery. It's worth quite a bit, I understand.'

Henry had heard the rumour from Gwen but didn't admit as much since he'd been told firmly to keep it to himself.

'Honestly, at her age! Fifty-three, she is. You'd think she'd be past such nonsense.'

'Plenty remarry at that age,' said Henry. 'Is she thinking of—?'

'Yes! And that's the thing. They've only gone and got a licence, without telling anyone, and plan to marry on the sixth of September. She's going to move into his house.'

Henry felt the dread creep up his chest. Would Amelia be leaving the village, just when he'd started to get to know her? Tredegar wasn't far, but it wasn't like having her close by.

'They say I'm welcome to live there too, but I don't want to play gooseberry, no thank you. Besides, there are attractions in Dorcalon to stay for.'

The way she smiled at him sent a wave of warmth around his whole body that was disturbing.

'What's happening to the business?'

'Closing down, I suppose. I've got a job teaching sewing at a school, and another at evening classes for adults. So, that's the answer to your original question, about the business. You mustn't tell anyone, not even your sister. Promise me.' She leant forward, looking him in the eyes.

'Yes, I promise. But they'll find out eventually.'

'Of course, but my mother wants to be the one to tell people.' She took a sip of the tea and cut the scone in two, ready to butter.

'That's understandable,' said Henry, following suit. He felt privileged that she'd let him in on the secret. She must trust him at least. 'If you're staying in Dorcalon, where are you going to live?'

'With Uncle John and Aunt Matilda. They have two spare rooms since both my cousins have left home.'

John Bowen, the somewhat confrontational and rather sly undermanager at the pit. Not someone he'd want to be under the same roof as. He wondered if Amelia's late father had been as objectionable as his brother.

'Confessions over for the day,' said Amelia. 'Let's eat up these scones so we can move on to the delicious cake.' She rubbed her hands together in anticipation. 'Then maybe you can tell me what the trenches were like.'

His initial instinct was to say no. He didn't want to appear rude, or odd though. He could tell her about the everyday life, about what they did in their weeks away from the front line. Hopefully, that would be enough for her.

Chapter Four

Polly stood in the queue at the butcher's, grateful that Herby was at home with her mother, not getting bored waiting.

She could hear Amelia, two people behind her, moaning to Pastor Thomas's wife, Anabel, about how dull the sky was again today. Anwen was ahead, talking to Gwen's mother, Ruth Austin, about the house she and Idris had recently moved into.

Nobody ever talked much to Polly, not since she'd brought back Gus and his family to Dorcalon. She probably wouldn't have talked to her either, even though she liked to think she'd be kinder than that. To be fair, Anwen did often pass the time of day with her, as did her friend Violet, but not many others did.

Stanley Pritchard came out from the back of the shop with a tray of what looked like lamb. That's what her mother had sent her for. It had been a treat seeing the variety of meat available grow in the last few months. Not like the monotony of pigeon, rabbit and offal that had become the staple of the war years.

'Ah, Anwen,' said Stanley. 'Don't suppose you ever get to see your father up at the gaol these days, do you?'

'I most certainly do not. Don't see him, don't write to him,' she replied firmly.

'Can't blame you, but thought I'd check. You might have been able to throw some light on why the old butcher, Iolo Prosser, is still sending letters here for his wife, Eileen. I presume they're from him. They've an Usk postmark and the writing's like that in the old account books. He is in the Usk gaol, isn't he?'

'Next!' called Gertie Pritchard, prompting Ruth to go to the left of the counter.

'Aye, he is,' said Anwen. 'He was part of the racketeering like my father. And Reg Moss, the old landlord at the McKenzie Arms. And a few others.'

Stanley rubbed his chin. 'I thought that's what I'd heard. You'd think he'd have found out his wife had left.'

Polly, drawing up all her courage, said in a small voice, 'To be honest, being in a similar position to Eileen, I wouldn't have told him I'd gone.'

Anwen twisted round to face her. 'I agree. I'm sure if my mother moved, she'd feel the same.'

Polly was thankful to Anwen for sympathising with her situation.

'Aye, reckon you're right,' Stanley conceded.

'Next!' cried Cyril Davies, the butcher's boy, and Anwen stepped up to the counter in front.

Polly's heart sank. Did that mean she'd end up with Gertie, who was always sour faced, and particularly mean to her. To her great relief, Stanley took his place in the centre of the counter, and she was served by him.

Outside, Anwen was waiting on the pavement, and smiled when Polly appeared.

'How are you getting on?' she asked. 'I hope Gus isn't bothering you from prison, with his letters. My father did that for a while to my mother.'

'No, luckily. He wrote once, a veiled threat, but getting no reply from me, he never wrote back. He never were much of a writer. Didn't do much school, see. I do wonder, though, what'll happen when he leaves prison in 1922. If I'm still legally married to him, would I have to live with him again?'

'I don't suppose so, but you'd be better off getting a divorce. My mamgu, Cadi, is trying to persuade Mam to do that.'

'From her own son?' Polly was astonished.

'She knows what he's like. She saw how he'd have killed the lot of us, given the chance.'

'Not sure Gus'd do that, but he were pretty unpleasant to live with. He gave me the odd slap, as you know, but never beat me up, nor threw me down the stairs, like your father did your mother.'

'Even a slap shouldn't be acceptable, though it still seems to be. Why did you marry him, Polly? I know he were a neighbour of your aunt's when you was sent to Surrey, and you needed a father for Herby but, well, he were a nasty piece of work.'

'He was all right to begin with. Considerate even. I was desperate to remove the shame. I thought we'd have a nice life in Surrey, him being a carpenter. Until I realised he'd only married me to use me as an excuse to move back here and get a reserved occupation so he wasn't conscripted. Told the authorities here I was going doo-lally, he did, after having Herby, and needed to move home, so that's why he'd got a miner's job.'

Anwen shook her head. 'I knew most of that, but not the bit about him saying you was doo-lally, as you put it. That's awful.'

'Suppose I was lucky not to get locked up in an institution.'

'You shouldn't say it like it's your fault. Look at all the trouble he and his family caused in the village, stealing, threatening Mr Schenck, and then setting his bookshop on fire. Well, you definitely shouldn't have to put up with his nonsense anymore… I'd better get this lamb home and start dinner.'

'Of course. And thank you, Anwen.'

Anwen's forehead creased in query. 'What for?'

'Talking to me. Many still don't.'

'Then that's their loss. You're a decent person now.'

Now, so presumably not before. It was fair enough. She'd been a bit of a madam, as her mother had once referred to her.

'Thank you for thinking so, Anwen. *Hwyl fawr.*'

'*Hwyl fawr.*'

She watched Anwen trudge up the road and was about to set off herself in the other direction, when Amelia emerged from the butcher's.

'Ah, Polly, I'm glad I've seen you. Just to let you know that my mother will be giving you notice when you come in tomorrow.'

Polly felt sick. 'But what have I done? My sewing's skilled and I always complete garments in good time.'

'Yes, of course, so you shouldn't have trouble getting work elsewhere. My mother will explain tomorrow, but I just wanted to prepare you, so it wouldn't be too much of a shock.' Amelia stretched her mouth into an approximation of a smile, the way she always did on these occasions.

'Right, thank you,' said Polly.

'Don't tell anyone else yet, mind, not even your family.' She shook a forefinger at her.

'I won't.'

Amelia headed off, towards her house a few doors up.

Polly felt a mixture of shock and resentment. There she was, Miss High-and-Mighty, trying to make out she was kind and thoughtful, but Polly knew her better than that. She could tell by her expression that she'd got a good deal of pleasure imparting that bad news to her.

The question was, what was she going to do for work now?

–

'Shall we put it by the door, near the window or on the other wall?' asked Gwen as she and Anwen manoeuvred an old bookcase they'd acquired into Gwen's front room.

'On the other wall, maybe. If we rent a sewing machine, it would be better to work by the window.'

'True.'

They lifted and shuffled until it was in place, then lowered it down with huffs of relief.

Elizabeth walked through the door, her gardening garb of men's trousers and a shirt on. By the mud on the front, it was evident she'd been at her allotments. 'My, what's all this then?'

'We acquired this bookcase from old Mr Morgan next door, this morning,' said Gwen. 'Said he'd be glad for us to take it off his hands for nothing. We thought we'd put our fabrics and bits and pieces on it.'

'What a good idea.' There was a knock at the front door. 'I'll get that.' Elizabeth hurried away.

She was soon back with Mrs Bowen, sporting a smart suit and a large hat. Gwen's mouth went dry, dreading some sort of showdown. By Anwen's widened eyes, she felt the same. They were surely in trouble for taking some of the other woman's work.

'Is this the room you're setting up for your business?' Mrs Bowen asked with no preamble.

'It – it is,' Gwen replied. 'We've mostly only done repairs at the moment, and a few alterations.' She didn't mention the two wedding dresses and some other orders they'd secured in recent days.

'Well, we all have to start somewhere, much like myself.'

Gwen exchanged a confused glance with Anwen. Mrs Bowen didn't seem even remotely bothered.

'We're hoping not to tread on your toes,' said Anwen, 'as I'm sure there'll be enough work for us all.'

'Oh, quite possibly, but it's not something you need to worry about anymore. You see, I'm giving up the business, to get married.' She beamed widely, obviously thrilled by the prospect. 'My intended is a modestly wealthy man, with his own business. Since we'll be living in Tredegar, it would be hard coming back here every day to continue, or start again over there, so, I'm retiring.'

'Isn't Amelia carrying on the business?'

'No, no. She doesn't have much of a business head and has no wish to anyway. So, if you've need of rails, hangers and a whole lot of other equipment, it's yours for the price of moving it out of the house. That will save me having to dispose of it somewhere or waiting for a buyer. I'm keen to be cleared out by the sixth of September, when we're getting married.'

That was one of the last things Gwen had expected to hear but she was thankful for the turn of events. 'Congratulations,' she said. The other two added their own good wishes. 'I'm sure we'd be very grateful to take them off your hands. Anwen?' She looked at her friend.

'Yes, of course. And although Violet, my mam and mamgu aren't here, I'm sure they'd be thrilled. It's very generous of you.'

'Now, there is a condition. Of course, I won't be employing anyone anymore.'

Gwen knew there had to be a catch, and she was sure it was going to be that they had to hire Amelia. Despite Henry's keenness on the woman, Gwen was ashamed to say she'd never taken to her. What could she say though?

'You want us to employ Amelia?' said Anwen, reflecting her thoughts.

'Amelia?' said Mrs Bowen. 'No no. She's secured a job teaching needlework. No, it's Polly Coombes. She's not well off as it is, and with all the misfortune with that dreadful husband of hers, I would hate for her to be out of work.'

Polly Coombes. With Herby, Tom's half-brother. That was even worse, thought Gwen.

'Of course,' said Anwen. 'I feel so sorry for her too. And I know she were largely responsible for altering the wedding dress I bought from you – and a good job she did too. I'm sure we could give her some work, couldn't we, Gwen?'

Did Anwen guess what she was thinking, and wanted to agree before Gwen could say otherwise? What a turnabout, since it used to be Anwen who disliked her the most! Gwen had felt sympathy for Polly when her husband had first been hauled away by the police. Then she'd found out that Mr Meredith was Herby's father. Now she wished Polly would move away and not remind her of the disgrace of her husband's family every time she saw her.

'I'm not sure we could employ her full-time, but we could sort out some hours for her, I should think.'

'As we get more work, we'll probably be able to employ her more,' said Anwen, giving Mrs Bowen a reassuring smile.

'Thank you. That's all I ask. Now, I'm not sure what your plans will be for shifting the items. I've just a couple more jobs to finish off, as I've not taken on any more work recently.'

That might explain the increase in orders. 'All right, Mrs Bowen. We'll have a talk and see what we can sort out,' said Gwen. 'It'll probably be just the group of us trooping up and down with the items.'

'I'm sure I could borrow the motorcar if there's anything heavy to shift,' Elizabeth volunteered.

'I'll leave you to discuss it,' said Mrs Bowen. 'I'll see myself out. Good morning, ladies.'

'Good morning,' they all echoed, with Anwen adding, 'And thank so much for giving us the equipment. It will be so useful.'

When she was gone, Elizabeth said, 'There's a stroke of luck for you. And to think you were all afraid she'd get annoyed at your competition.'

'Yes, but – Polly Coombes,' said Gwen. 'I'd rather not have employed her with her son being Tom's and your, you know. It makes it very awkward.'

'It sounds like a good reason to employ her to me,' said Anwen. 'She's a mother on her own and, well—'

'I think what you might be trying to say is that maybe the Meredith family owe her some kind of support?' said Elizabeth.

'Sorry.' Anwen looked down and pursed her lips before continuing with, 'But yes. Something like that.'

'It's all right,' said Elizabeth. 'I agree with you. I know it's not my sewing business, but I feel it would be the right thing to do. If my business were bigger, I would employ her, though she probably has no inclination to gardening.' Elizabeth gave a little chuckle. 'I'll get us some tea. It's what I came back for.'

When she'd left, Gwen said, 'I suppose we should ask the others first though. And it might be better if she worked in one of the other houses.'

'She can work in mine,' said Anwen.

'Fine,' said Gwen, though she didn't feel it was. Elizabeth might be sympathetic, but it could still reflect badly on her and Tom if people found out. And maybe on Gwen too. 'Let's get these shelves sorted out.'

Chapter Five

Polly looked around the small study of the McKenzie Arms, where she'd been deposited by Nerys Moss while she sorted out a delivery of beer that had just arrived. The study's tiny space was filled with shelves on which stood files and ledgers. In the corner sat the heavy oak desk.

She really didn't want to be here, but where else could she get a few more hours' work in the area? Apart from the colliery, sorting coal. No thank you. As grateful as she was to Anwen for taking her on to do sewing, she was only working there from nine in the morning till two in the afternoon on three days a week.

Polly had been existing on the fifteen hours' work a week since the end of August, her last day at Mrs Bowen's. So that was… nearly four weeks, she calculated. Her parents had been good about her poor contribution to the household, but how would she ever be independent if she couldn't find a full week's employment? Being a barmaid at a public house wasn't ideal, but it was better than nothing.

Mrs Moss finally returned to the study and sat down. She was wearing a large cream apron over her plain but clean skirt and blouse, while her dark hair, peppered with grey, was pulled up into a tight bun.

'Sorry to keep you waiting, Mrs Smith.'

The name always made Polly shiver. If only she could have returned to her maiden name, though goodness knows enough people still referred to her as Polly Coombes.

'That's fine, Mrs Moss.' She felt overwhelmed by this firm and efficient woman.

'Now let's see. Yes, the position of barmaid. I only need someone on Monday and Tuesday lunchtimes, from twelve noon to two thirty and then from Wednesday to Saturday evenings, six till nine thirty. Would that suit you?'

'Yes, perfectly, as I only have sewing work from Wednesday to Friday, during the day.' It really couldn't have suited her better.

'You wouldn't find it a problem, working all these hours with a young child? I don't want you not turning up on odd days. I can't run a business like that.'

'No. My mother will look after my son while I'm at work. And sometimes my sister, Connie.' She wanted to emphasise that there would be someone else in the wings should her mother be indisposed.

'I see. Well, that's something. I need someone pretty sharpish like, as my full-time barmaid, Elsie Thomas, wants to cut back on her hours.'

'I can start straight away, that is, tomorrow, if you like.'

'Do you have any experience serving customers?'

'Only those what came to Mrs Bowen to buy second-hand clothes, or order something new.'

'Mm.' Nerys pursed her lips, as if in thought. 'I suppose I could give you one month's trial, see how you get on.'

What could she say? She'd just have to make sure she picked the job up quickly and did her very best. 'Fair enough.'

'If you start tomorrow, and work with Elsie while she's still doing those hours, she'll show you the ropes.'

'All right.'

'I need you to become efficient quickly, mind. Going to improve this place even more than I have, I am, return it to its former glory, before Reg let it go to rot. And I'm going to build up the hotel side again, especially now the war's finished, for proper guests, not just the odd lodger. Its name is the McKenzie

Arms Hotel: I'm going to get the old signs renewed to remind people. It's not just a public house.'

Polly perked up at this news. Perhaps if she could tell people she was working at a hotel, it would look more respectable.

'So, you'll take me on?'

'I will.' Mrs Moss stood. 'I'm not going to judge you for what your husband did. It's not like I'm in a position to. A right rotter Reginald Moss turned out to be, what with making money on the side from his stealing and racketeering. Not money I ever saw, for he knew what I would have said about it. And now I know why he'd never let me go down the cellars. Too dangerous for a woman, he said. Huh! Just hiding his ill-gotten goods there, he was.' The landlady had gone into a brief world of her own.

'That's awful,' said Polly, lifting the older woman out of her reverie.

'Yes. Well. Seems to me we wronged wives of villains should stick together. So, I'll see you at five to twelve tomorrow. Thank you for coming.'

It was a dismissal. Polly stood. 'Thank you for giving me the chance, Mrs Moss.'

'You know the way out.'

With this, Polly walked to the door and let herself into the hall. Soon she was on the street, breathing the cool air in relief. Mrs Moss being in the same position as her, with a husband in gaol, had at least worked in her favour.

It wasn't the work she wanted, but it would tide her over for now.

-

Henry and Maurice stood at the counter of the public bar, to get a round in for them and three of the Pals who'd come out with them. Maurice's eyes were narrow as he peered at Polly, serving Idris at the other end.

'What's wrong with you, mun?' said Henry.

'Would you want your sister working in a public house, with the kind of customers it attracts?'

'We're the customers it attracts.' Henry laughed. 'It's become a more decent place since Nerys Moss took over. It's no different from serving in a shop.'

'Of course it is, mun. Men don't respect women what work in public houses. They think they're loose pieces what they can take advantage of.'

'Not all men.' Henry wondered whether that was how Maurice thought of them.

'Polly's already gathered herself a reputation, thanks to Gus Smith.'

And the rumour that Herby couldn't be Gus's child, but Henry wasn't going to say that to Maurice.

'Fights break out here every now and again. I don't want my sister involved in that.'

'The last time I saw a fight here, you started it,' said Henry.

Maurice humphed. Polly finished with Idris and came over to serve them.

'Hello, Maurice, Henry.' She nodded at him, and Henry nodded back. 'What can I get you?'

'Don't know why our mum's let you work here,' said Maurice.

'Oh, don't start,' she said under her breath. 'I'm a grown-up, and our mum has a great respect for Mrs Moss.'

Henry could see some of the old Polly, the one who'd speak up for herself, before she got involved with Gus and wouldn't say boo to a goose.

'It ain't respectable,' said Maurice.

She kept calm, which wasn't like the old Polly, who was likely as not to snap if someone said something she didn't like.

'Do you want to give me your order, or shall I fetch Mrs Moss and tell her I have an awkward customer? After that fight you started, you're lucky she still lets you in. I think she only made an allowance because you were fighting for the country at the time.'

'Five half pints of the GHB,' Maurice said reluctantly.

'Coming up.'

Henry and Maurice conveyed the beers over to Douglas, Teilo, and Alun Lloyd from the farm.

'Perhaps we should go and sit with Idris, Gwilym and Twm Bach,' Henry suggested.

'Nah,' said Maurice, not waiting for anybody else's opinion. 'Better to keep ourselves to ourselves.'

'I agree,' said Douglas. 'I dunno what to talk about with them anymore.'

'Nor me,' Teilo agreed.

Henry pushed his lips out on a long breath. 'But we'll—'

He got no further before the door was pushed roughly open, banging against the wall. The room went silent.

Through the doorway walked Reg Moss.

People around the room looked at each other, eyes wide or brows raised in surprise.

'Didn't know he were coming back here,' Maurice muttered.

'I doubt Nerys Moss knows either,' said Henry. He glanced over at Idris's group, where he saw them glance over at them in turn.

Polly's eyes were wide with shock, confirming to Henry that his arrival was unexpected.

Reg lifted the lid on the counter, shouting, 'Where's my wife? And who the hell are you?'

'I'll get Mrs Moss,' said Polly, walking backwards.

'Out of my way, I'll get the bitch myself.' He shoved Polly, who disappeared from view as she fell over.

'The boss is back,' Reg announced, the same time Maurice leapt up and cried, 'You leave my sister alone, you weasel!'

Henry, fearing the inevitable, jumped up and followed Maurice, arriving at the bar alongside Idris and Gwilym. At the same time, Nerys Moss appeared through the door to one side of the counter.

'What on earth is all this – Reg!' she shouted, her mouth pinched and eyes dark with anger. She surged forward, forcing Reg back out from behind the counter, causing him to bump into Maurice.

Henry took the opportunity to run behind the counter to help Polly up. She rubbed her arm vigorously.

'Thank you,' she said, then stepped back, looking agog at the ensuing trouble.

'Push my sister, would you,' said Maurice, his fists up, ready.

Reg had lost weight and didn't seem the challenge he'd once been when ejecting troublemakers from the public house.

'What are you doing here?' Nerys asked in a low, menacing voice.

The remaining men sitting at the tables, which were three-quarters filled, looked on, as if viewing a film at the picture house. Idris and Gwilym remained in their places by the bar.

'This is my public house. I'm the landlord and I'm back to take it over.'

'You're no such thing,' she growled. 'The coal company has allowed me to take over the leasehold. Check with them, or my solicitor, if you don't believe me.'

'How could you do that? You're just a woman.'

'The coal company weren't keen on having a convicted criminal, and a thief to boot, on the leasehold.'

'Bloody rubbish. A woman can't run a public house.'

'She's done a good job so far,' Twm Bach called over as he stood and came a few steps closer.

'Yes, a better job than you, I reckon,' said Idris, pulling his tall stature even higher.

Several other men stood and came forward, encouraging Henry, Idris and Gwilym to close in on Reg.

Maurice, fists still raised, jogged a little on his feet. 'Come on then, you want to try us?'

Reg looked from one to the other, his mouth stretching into a sneer. He gave a slight growl. 'You'll regret this. I'll let the coal company know I've returned, and they'll soon change things back, you'll see.'

He gave them all one more menacing glare, before stamping towards the door into the entrance hall. 'You'll all pay for this,' were his departing words, before he pulled the door open and slammed it shut behind him, causing the glass to rattle.

'Good riddance!' Maurice shouted after him.

'Reckon you should let Sergeant Harries know what's happened,' Henry said to Mrs Moss.

'Don't you worry, I've already thought of that.' She turned towards her barmaid. 'You all right, Polly love?'

'I am now,' she replied.

'You see, that's why I don't want you working in a place like this,' said Maurice as the men who'd stood returned to their seats.

'You have some respect, look you,' said Nerys, pointing her finger. 'I'm grateful to you for coming forward and standing up to Reg – it makes up for that trouble you caused before – but I'll stand no inference that I'm running a disreputable business, for I'm not a thief and I'll also tolerate no shenanigans here, you understand?'

Maurice bowed his head, saying, 'Yes Mrs Moss,' as if she were their teacher back at school.

'Good. Now. Who's next?'

Henry and Maurice joined their army Pals once more.

'Reckon we'll have to look out for him,' said Henry.

'If he's got any sense, he'll bugger off somewhere no one knows him,' said Maurice, who picked up his pint and took a long swig.

But Henry wasn't sure good sense was in Reg's nature.

–

Polly entered the butcher's, stopping at the end of the queue which reached the door. There were the usual mingled odours of sawdust, feathers and blood. It used to bother her as a child, but not anymore. Recalling last night's rumpus at the McKenzie Arms, it reminded her of when she was in here, a few weeks back, speaking up for Eileen Prosser's decision not to tell her husband she'd moved. Now Reg Moss had turned up back in the village, and it might only be a matter of time until Iolo did too.

She thought back again to the evening before, when Henry had come to help her up at the bar. He'd always had a kind face. At school he'd been a cheerful boy, and one whose fair good looks and blond hair had attracted some attention from the girls. The war had slimmed the rosy roundness of his face and added a wariness to his expression.

Now, what was it her mother had asked her to buy? Some bacon for breakfast, and a little chicken for dinner. She looked at the feathered birds hanging from hooks. She didn't want a whole bird, just part of one Mr Pritchard would already have plucked and cut into portions. Enid Rhys was being served by Stanley Pritchard, further along.

'Come on, move up,' said Florrie Harris behind her, giving her a little shove in the back.

Polly moved up to where Cyril, the butcher's boy, was grinning at her.

'Sorry,' she said to the lad.

'That's all right, missus,' he beamed. 'Looked miles away, you did.'

'Don't be so cheeky, lad,' Stanley called over, 'and just serve the lady.'

'Huh, lady!' Florrie murmured behind her.

'Could I have four rashers of the bacon, please?' said Polly, pointing to the streaky variety.

'Well, well, well,' said a booming voice from the direction of the door.

Polly, recognising it instantly, twisted her head around, as did the other customers. In the doorway, still as tall, but a lot thinner, stood Iolo Prosser. His face had many more lines than it had done, giving him a haggard appearance, while his bald head had wrinkled around his ears.

'Good to see the wife's been keeping the business going in my absence,' said Iolo.

Oh no, not again. Polly stepped to the right, closer to the wall and further away from what would surely end in another showdown.

'But who the hell are you?' He pointed a long, sausage-like forefinger at Stanley, where he stood in his bloodied apron.

'I could ask you the same,' said Stanley, 'except I'm guessing you're Mr Prosser, the former owner of this establishment.'

'Former?' Iolo boomed. 'Former and now current. Eileen can step down now. I don't need no wife leading the reins. Where the hell is she anyway? Lazy mare, getting in staff to do the work she could do.' He stamped forward, causing the women in the queue to follow Polly's lead and flee to a wall.

Florrie Harris, however, left the shop altogether.

'Oh dear,' said Stanley, who matched Iolo in height, but was a good ten years younger and looked a lot fitter. 'I'm afraid you're under the same illusion as your gaol mate, Mr Moss, who apparently marched back into the McKenzie Arms last night.'

'Reg did? He's back already? Thought he said he'd be a coupla days. And what do you mean, same illusion? You're an employee so don't go giving me no lip, see. Now fetch my bloody wife!'

At this point, Gertie Pritchard came marching out through the door behind the counter. 'What's all this noise?'

'Get my bloody wife!' Iolo repeated.

Gertie, with no apparent fear, came from behind the counter and stood right in front of Iolo. 'Get your own bloody wife, whoever or wherever she may be!'

'I own this shop, and you two are fired!'

Gertie threw her head back and laughed. 'So, you're the great criminal mastermind, Iolo Prosser, are you?'

'Don't you give me lip, woman.'

'Give you lip? I'll throw you right out of here if you don't shut your trap and get gone. *We're* the owners of this business. Your Eileen sold it to us and is long gone. Didn't you realise when she didn't reply to those letters you kept sending?'

Iolo was scarlet in the face by this time and his fists scrunched into balls. 'You, you mean she sold the business and the lease for the shop to you?'

'Lock, stock and barrel,' said Stanley.

Polly's heart was thumping hard against her chest. Prosser had never been a patient man, and, although thinner and less imposing looking, she reckoned he could cause a lot of damage.

'All right, what's going on here now?' said Sergeant Harries, stepping into the shop.

Behind him skulked Florrie. So that's where she'd run off to.

'I wondered when you'd poke your ugly mug in,' said Iolo. 'It's a runna my Eileen's done and cheated me out of my business.' He pointed at Harries. 'You'd better find her and bring her to justice. This business is mine.'

The sergeant rocked once on his heels, his hands clasped behind his back. 'I'm afraid it's you what did yourself out of a business when you started stealing goods and doing your racketeering.'

'You got the wrong man, Harries. This is your fault.'

'Caught red-handed you were,' said the sergeant.

Iolo turned back and stamped towards Gertie. 'Where has my wife gone? I demand to know! I'll give her one, selling the business and running off.'

In one swift action, Gertie grabbed a long knife from the counter behind, holding it in front of her. 'We don't bloody know, and even if we did, we wouldn't tell you.'

'Put that down now, Mrs Pritchard,' said Harries.

She narrowed her lips and glared at Prosser but did as the sergeant asked.

'Now, if I were you,' Harries said to Prosser, 'I'd be finding myself a new job and a new home, for you won't be coming back to this one. And don't you be tracing your wife or doing anything to her, for if I hear of her coming to any harm, I have several witnesses here what heard your threats. Now get yourself gone to wherever you came from.'

'Well, that's not far,' said Prosser, 'for I'm lodging with Mrs Williams, Edgar's missus.' He took a good look around the shop, at the customers there. 'Just making a note of the witnesses,' he said with a smirk.

He did an about turn, then marched out of the shop and across the road, to the pavement around the gardens. There was a communal sigh of relief.

'What on earth does that Esther Williams think she's doing, taking that villain in?' said Florrie.

'I'm not surprised,' said Enid Rhys. 'Thick as thieves he were, with Esther's husband. Appropriate, since they was all thieves together. Oh yes, I know my husband was involved too, but you'd never catch me taking that thug in.'

'I'd all be on your guard,' said Harries, 'and report anything untoward to me. Let as many people in the village as possible know. Something tells me this isn't the last we've heard from Iolo Prosser – or Reg Moss. Good day, all.' He tapped his helmet briefly and went on his way.

The customers quickly took their places in the queue once more, and Polly tried to recall the rest of her order. Chicken, that was it.

She was sure Sergeant Harries was right about the two men, and, working at the McKenzie Arms as she did, the menace added a new thread of anxiety to her life.

–

'That were very nice, Mrs Meredith,' said Gwen to her mother-in-law as she carefully placed her knife and fork together in the centre of her empty plate.

'One does one's best,' the reply came with a sigh as Margaret Meredith likewise placed her cutlery down. 'I thought the war ending would solve the servant shortage, but it seems it's not to be.'

Gwen said nothing, feeling guilty that she was the last in a long line of women who'd given up being Mrs Meredith's maid, even if it was to become her daughter-in-law. And Enid Rhys had given up being cook, to work in the sewing business she'd help start.

'Young women have had a taste of other jobs, some better paid,' said Tom. 'You can hardly blame them.'

'Even if some jobs have led to illness,' said Margaret, clearly referring to Gwen's stint at the munitions. She patted Gwen's hand. 'I dare say I'd have relished such a job, had they been available to me before I married.'

'By the way,' said Herbert, 'have either of you heard about Iolo Prosser and Reg Moss being back in the village?'

'Gwen knows something about that,' said Tom, regarding his wife with raised eyebrows.

Even though she got on well with her mother-in-law, Gwen always thought twice about speaking up too much.

'Um, yes. Henry was at the McKenzie Arms Hotel on Friday night, having a quiet drink with friends.' She felt the need to give the place its full title, so it sounded more respectable. 'Mr Moss apparently barged in, insisting he was still the boss. Henry said he knocked the barmaid off her feet, in his effort to get behind the bar.' She didn't mention it was Polly, given the state of affairs.

'What happened next?' Margaret asked, leaning forward with interest.

'One of Henry's friends challenged Mr Moss, as the girl he knocked over was his sister. Mrs Moss heard the noise and came out. After she'd told him what was what, half the men there surrounded him to show they supported her.'

'Good for them,' said Herbert, raising his glass of wine. 'By all accounts, she's been a better landlady than he was a landlord. And she did you proud for your wedding reception.'

'Really trying to get the hotel side going she is, Henry says. The place is certainly smarter than it was. And she's planning on developing a bigger restaurant.' Gwen was about to say more, but decided to finish there, afraid she'd be considered a chatterbox.

'Tell them about the butcher's and Mrs Williams,' said Tom.

'Oh, all right.' She'd heard this news from Enid Rhys. 'Mr Prosser turned up at the butcher's yesterday.' She told them all the details she knew. 'And then he revealed that he and Mr Moss were lodging with Esther Williams.'

'My word,' said Margaret. 'There always seems to be some trouble or other brewing in this village. I suppose we shouldn't be surprised that Mrs Williams is involved, for all her protestations of ignorance about her husband's theft and racketeering. Anyway, Tom, there's something your father and I wish to discuss with you.'

'It's to do with the money left from your university education,' said Herbert.

'I'm not returning to Surrey, if that's what you're thinking,' Tom said firmly.

'No, you misunderstand,' said Margaret. 'We earmarked that money from my father's estate for you, and we'd still like you to have what's left. You could set up a business or buy yourself into one. You don't want to be a colliery clerk for the rest of your life.'

Gwen experienced a tingle of delight. What a difference that might make to their lives. If they both developed successful businesses, they could obtain their own house, maybe even buy one. Or perhaps there was enough left in the inheritance for a deposit. She considered the dining room here, with its fancy furnishings: the mahogany table and matching sideboard, the porcelain figures on the bookshelves. Maybe one day they'd have such a room, instead of eating in the kitchen.

'Mm. Would you excuse me a moment?' Tom placed his napkin in a heap on the table, before rising and leaving the room.

'What is wrong with him?' said Margaret.

'Considering what he might do with the money perhaps?' said Herbert.

Gwen, however, had noticed the furrowed brow he always displayed when something bothered him.

'If you'd excuse me too,' said Gwen, who rose hesitantly to follow him.

She found him in the back garden, standing in the sunshine between the two patches of vegetables that Elizabeth still tended. He held out his hand as she approached, which she took.

'What's wrong Tom?'

'I've never thought it fair, you know, that Tadcu Powell's money was only used on me. I want to give half of what's left to Lizzie.'

Gwen's hope for the future dimmed.

'I can see by your face that you're disappointed. I could give half to you, for your business, I suppose.'

'No, that hadn't even occurred to me. It's like your mother says, you should start your own business. Taking the clerk's job was only temporary.'

'A business doing what? I'm educated, yes, but not practical. I don't know yet what I'll do with my half, maybe put it towards a house? But I am determined to give the other half to Lizzie. She does have a business she could put it towards.'

Gwen's disappointment turned to pride in her husband. He could have been selfish and kept the family inheritance for himself, but no, he was kind and cared for his sister, seeing her worth.

'Yes, it's the right thing to do,' she agreed, kissing his cheek.

Chapter Six

'Thank goodness we're here at last,' said Amelia as she alighted the train at Abergavenny station. 'I thought we'd never arrive.'

She walked past Henry, who was holding the door open for her, dusting down her burgundy velour coat, with wide sleeves and large cuffs. He'd never seen another in the village with such a splendid sense of style, not even Elizabeth, Mrs Meredith or his own sister.

'Yes, it's unfortunate we have to change twice,' said Henry, catching her up as she stood under the wooden canopy. 'But I think it will be well worth it once we get there. And at least with seeing the earlier evening performance, we won't be in a rush to get home.'

Henry looked at his wristwatch. 'Forty minutes to go, and it only takes about ten minutes to walk into town.'

Amelia's mouth opened in surprise. 'Are there no taxi cabs, or motorbuses from here?'

Henry thought about the money in his suit pocket. He'd planned to get good seats at the theatre, and maybe some tea afterwards, and had paid for the train tickets. He wasn't sure it could run to paying for more transport, despite the money he'd borrowed from his father, and the bits he'd saved up during the past weeks.

'It's a nice evening, and Abergavenny is a pleasant enough town. We could enjoy the sunset as we go.' He walked past the canopy and the station building, pointing to where the sun had sunk below the horizon, creating a swirl of azure and cerise. He'd noticed it on the train ride but hadn't wanted to interrupt

Amelia's account of her fractious day to point it out. The poor girl had obviously needed someone to talk to about it.

'Very well,' she sighed. 'I suppose it's not a bad evening for a walk.' She waited until he returned to her, before putting her arm through his so they could leave the station.

'*Peaches in Paris* has had some good reviews,' he said as they began the walk into town.

'I do like a musical comedy,' she said, cheering up a little. 'It's a while since I've been to the theatre, so I am looking forward to it.'

Henry felt a warm glow inside, hoping that her looking forward to it at least had a little to do with him.

Reaching the main road into Abergavenny, busy with a number of motorcars and a carriage or two, she started an account outlining all her visits to the theatre, and what she'd thought of the performances. Henry was content to listen, enjoying her light, trilling voice that reminded him of a flute.

By the time she'd finished they had reached the Angel Hotel, with its splendid, pillared doorway.

'I wonder if there'll be time to have some dinner in there afterwards,' she said, glancing up at the palatial Georgian building with admiration. 'I only had a little scone for afternoon tea, having had a more substantial lunch. But I'll be hungry by the time we come out.'

Henry felt slightly sick, wondering how he could explain that a miner's wage couldn't stretch to such things, not all at once. Yes, if he'd saved his money more diligently over the years, instead of having trips out to the public house, to the cinema and to sports events, maybe he'd have a bit put by. The much poorer pay of the army hadn't helped either. There'd been no opportunity to save there, sending most of it home to his parents as he had done.

'I suspect they only take reservations on a Saturday,' he said, thinking quickly, yet regretting he couldn't treat her. 'But I'm sure Beven's café, just up the street from the theatre, would be able to accommodate us.'

'You're probably right,' she said, not sounding wholly convinced.

'There's the town hall,' he said, indicating the brown stone building, hoping to distract her. 'That's where the Borough Theatre is. People are already queueing, so I think we should join them.'

'I hope the best seats don't go before we get to the front.'

He hadn't been planning on buying the three-shilling seats, just maybe the two-shilling ones. He couldn't disappoint her though. If necessary, he'd have to forego the trip to the Arms this week.

'I think we'll be close enough to the front not to worry,' he said, leading the way.

–

'Well that was a treat,' said Amelia as they came out of the theatre into the dark evening afterwards. 'Fancy them changing their whole repertoire of songs since the last performance. And it was so amusing. I loved Miss Daphne Jay's voice, and what a dancer! I wish I could dance so.' She had a faraway look in her eyes, as if picturing herself in the role.

'It was an excellent performance.' He had genuinely enjoyed it, but also knew it had been made all the better for her presence.

'And Dan Noel was so funny. I read that he performed for the troops in the war, including the Prince of Wales and the Belgian king. How brave he was to perform during the conflict.'

To *fight* during the conflict, like him and his battalion colleagues, would have been brave, thought Henry. But for all he knew, this Mr Noel had also fought, and maybe performed when he was in the back lines.

'I could certainly do with a cup of tea now,' she said, 'and something to eat. Where is this Beven's café you were telling me about?'

As he opened his mouth to reply, a car backfired, making him jump. His feet almost left the ground and he gasped loudly as the air was knocked out of him. His vision blurred for a second or two. With his sight clearing, he realised that people passing by were looking back at him with furrowed brows.

'Henry, whatever is wrong?' Amelia was glancing around, her expression one of embarrassment.

'Can we, can we just go down this side street for a bit?' He headed down it without waiting for a reply. It was a narrow road with fewer people. Reaching the back of the town hall he stopped. His worst fear had come true; his whole body was shaking, causing his teeth to rattle. This was the last thing he wanted Amelia to see.

She caught him up, her expression one of concern. 'What is wrong with you? Do you have a fever? You seemed perfectly well before.'

'N-n-no. It's, it's… I suffer from a little shell shock.' He suspected it was more than a little, but he didn't want to alarm Amelia and have her scuttling back to Dorcalon, giving up on him forever.

'Oh, Henry, how shocking for you!'

He doubted her pun was intended, though the absurdity of it made him want to laugh. But if he started that, it might turn to hysteria. It had happened once before, when he'd first returned home. Luckily, he'd been out walking on his own as the laughter had soon become helpless, sobbing tears. He hoped to God that didn't happen this time.

'It's, it's all right. If I just give it a moment, I'll be fine.'

She came closer, linking her arm through his, leaning her head on his shoulder. The sheer joy he felt as a result was the medicine he needed. He breathed in slowly, feeling the episode pass. It was going to be one of the short bouts, and all because of her. He wished he could kiss her, but it was too soon.

With the shaking at an end, Henry took a deep, cleansing breath. His head had cleared and he felt ready to carry on with the evening. 'Let's go to the café now, I could do with that tea you mentioned.'

'And something to eat,' she added. 'I'm really quite peckish now.'

'Anything you like,' he said, linking arms with her once more.

With a woman like Amelia by his side, he'd get through these dark times, he just knew he would.

Chapter Seven

It had been a busy Tuesday lunchtime at the McKenzie Arms, with men from the mine's nightshift taking refuge from the cold and wet November day in the public bar. Polly was relieved to depart when her shift finished at two thirty.

As she turned up past the Ainon Baptist Chapel on Gabriel Street, on her way to Islwyn Street, where her sister lived, she folded her worn coat around her chest and did up the buttons.

Her mind turned to the growing trade for meals at the hotel. Mrs Moss was attracting men from local establishments to the newly refurbished restaurant at the hotel for 'business lunches', as she referred to them. In addition, there had been more overnight guests requiring meals, travellers passing through on journeys to other parts of Wales. Polly had hoped to change jobs, to become a waitress instead, but Mrs Moss had re-employed two older women, who'd worked for her before the war, and before the hotel had gone to 'wrack and ruin', as she'd put it.

Reaching Islwyn Street, she crossed over and carried on down the alleyway to the back of the houses, to enter her sister Connie's house at the rear. She'd been looking after Herby today, while their mother visited a sister in Merthyr Tydfil, who was recovering from the influenza.

She knocked at Connie's back door, then opened it a crack to call, 'Hello, it's Polly!' She stepped into the scullery, relieved to be out of the rain, and gave a little shiver.

Connie's husband, Sioni Gower, stepped in from the kitchen, his shirt missing and his braces limp over his trousers.

The dark, wet hair, slightly too long, hung in ragged ringlets around his neck. His hairy chest and arms were well muscled. *Oh no, not again.* Polly looked away, towards the wash tub and wringer.

'Hello, Sioni. I've come to collect Herby.'

'Why else would you be here? Unless it's to see me.'

Out of the corner of her eye she could see he had lifted his arms, as if to display his partial nudity.

'You'll catch your death like that,' she said, repeating her mother's frequent words.

He laughed. 'Just had my bath, ain't I. Ruddy half cold it were. Your silly mare of a sister must have done it too early like, before she went out. And she's left my dinner cooking in the pot. Could've burnt the ruddy place down, she could.'

'Where is she and Herby?' She was staring at the larder door now, eager to get away.

'Left a note, she did. Said to tell you she's taken the kid to – Jenny's house – that were it.'

Jenny? Freddie's mother, Jenny? 'Do you mean Jenny Richards?'

'I dunno. She's got a kid what Connie's taken Herby to play with. Lives on Gabriel Street.'

So it was her. Connie wouldn't know about the possible connection. Nor did Polly really, but she'd long suspected that Freddie's real father might also be Herbert Meredith. It fitted. Jenny must have been pregnant before she married Joseph Richards. When he'd been killed in the mine accident, his family, who they'd lived with, had moved away – without her. It hadn't seemed right at the time.

There wasn't any real resemblance between the two boys she could put her finger on, but there was something. And Jenny had worked at McKenzie House when she'd fallen pregnant...

'You gonna stand there all day long, staring into space?'

Polly came to, realising Sioni had come a lot closer. He was sticking his chest out, a bit like a cockerel displaying his virility.

'I'd better get going.'

As she tried to step around Sioni and towards the door, he barred her way. 'Why the hurry? I'm sure Herby'll be enjoying hisself. You could pass a little time with me.'

'I'd rather get on.' She tried to get around him once more, but he stepped in the way again.

'That's not friendly now, is it? Reckon you should get what male company you can, not being prettied up like you used to be, and being saddled with a child.' He moved in closer, his torso almost touching her chest. His stale tobacco breath made her wince and turn her head away.

'Don't be like that now. You obviously like a bit of male attention, if you get my meaning. You must have dropped your drawers for whoever Herby's father was.'

'Gus was Herby's father.' At least, legally.

'Rubbish! The dates don't match at all. Whoever the father was, he clearly didn't think much of you.'

What could she say about that? Herbert Meredith hadn't loved her, nor she him. He'd been charming and thoughtful and *different*. Yet was he? He'd known he had nothing to offer ultimately, that she was simply a tumble in the hay – or the woods in their case. But she'd known that too.

Sioni brought his body even closer and started to undo her coat buttons. She wouldn't be able to get past him, and if she did, he'd probably grab her and she might never escape. There was only one thing to do.

As he brought his face in towards hers, intent, no doubt, on kissing her, she pushed him and made a dash for the door into the kitchen. Rushing through it to the hall, and ultimately the front door, she managed to get out as she heard him shout, 'Bitch, leading me on!'

She jumped onto the pavement and slammed the door shut, feeling safer now. Waiting there a moment to catch her breath, she spied Reg Moss coming up the street, sweeping the road. She remembered hearing he'd got the job as village scavenger, collecting the rubbish and keeping the place tidy.

'What you lookin' at?' he growled. 'I know you: you're one of those little cows working for my bitch of a wife what's done me out of a business.'

There was no point replying. She crossed the road, walking by the back gardens of the Gabriel Street houses, cursing her sister for taking Herby out and being the cause of all this. She should tell her when she picked up Herby. But what was the point? Connie was always defensive of Sioni, whenever anyone criticised him. She'd probably be blamed instead.

She couldn't really blame her sister for what had happened today. This was down to her vile brother-in-law and the old landlord.

Gus Smith, Sioni Gower, Reg Moss, Iolo Prosser. Not to mention Anwen's father, Madog Rhys, and Esther Williams's husband, Edgar. All rotten apples.

Yet there were good men: Anwen's, Violet's and Gwen's husbands, for instance. But good men didn't want her, and the rotten men wanted only to use her and taunt her.

No, she was better off without a man in her life, she decided as she headed off to collect Herby.

Chapter Eight

Violet and Anwen sat at Gwen's dining table, looking at the sketches Gwen had come up with to illustrate her outfit ideas for a possible client. Dresses and skirts had now become slimmer and straighter, sleeker and more elegant than the 'war crinolines' of a couple of years ago.

'Your design ideas are lovely,' said Anwen, 'but, well…'

'My pictures are terrible.' Gwen sighed, feeling the frustration of not being able to adequately illustrate her designs. 'Drawing never was my strong suit. I don't know how else we're going to show my ideas though.'

'I wonder…' said Anwen. 'Violet, you've done some lovely pictures for the kiddies in their drawing books. Gwen, do you remember those illustrations she did of Clarice's and Benjy's toy animals, Woof and Meow, and their adventures?'

'Oh yes, they was wonderful,' said Gwen, understanding what Anwen was getting at. 'You could illustrate my designs so much better.'

Violet shrank away. 'I couldn't do anything like that. I only do my drawings for the kiddies. That's all they're good enough for.'

'Nonsense,' said Anwen. 'You've got a talent, and it's one that could become very useful in our business.'

'Well, maybe I could have a go at re-drawing these,' she said, touching Gwen's sketches.

'Thank you,' said Anwen, smiling encouragement.

Gwen stood up. 'I'll fetch my pencils and some more paper.'

About to enter the front room, she was waylaid by Elizabeth, coming through the door from the hall. She was dressed in her working clothes of trousers and shirt. 'This letter was on the mat for you,' she said, laying it on the table. 'Looks like a hand delivery, as there's no stamp.'

'How curious.' Gwen came back to the table and saw it was addressed to 'Gwen Meredith'. She picked it up and opened it, then slid out the single sheet of paper. 'Oh no, how awful!'

'What is it?' Elizabeth asked as the three women gathered around her to read it.

> *You think yor so clever with yor fansy busnes and being marrid to a posh boi. But the Beibl says pride cams befor a fol.*

'Oh, that's not nice,' said Elizabeth.

'It's not even spelled right,' said Gwen, clucking her tongue.

'Not everyone can spell good,' said Violet. 'Do you think it could be Daniel Williams? The fact it mentions you marrying a posh boy. He was pretty put out when you rejected him for Tom.'

'I never *rejected* him, as you put it. He were only ever a friend,' said Gwen. 'And surely his English spelling would have to be better than that, working in a bank.'

'Unless he's pretending he can't spell so we think it's someone else,' said Anwen. 'Or it could be Esther. She were resentful at what she saw as Daniel's rejection too.'

'I dunno,' said Gwen, placing the offending piece of paper on the table.

'The best thing to do is be on the lookout in case any more letters are delivered,' said Elizabeth.

Gwen slumped onto the chair in front. 'Just when things seemed to be going well.'

'I wouldn't worry too much yet,' said Elizabeth. 'It'll be someone who's got nothing better to do with themselves. It's not like they're threatening to do anything.'

'Yet,' said Gwen. 'I'm going to report it to Sergeant Harries. Not that he's likely to do anything.'

'That's best,' said Elizabeth. 'I'm off to the allotment now. I'll see you later then. I'm making supper tonight, don't forget.' With that, she entered the scullery to go out the back way.

When the back door closed, Gwen said, 'I'll be glad when Tom and I can get a place of our own and have it all to ourselves.'

'Until the kiddies come along,' said Violet, looking at the pushchair stored in the corner, with a dozing Gethin.

'Mam's looking after my two for a while,' said Anwen. 'So I can't be too long.'

'Then I'd better fetch that drawing book and the pencils. Oh, and I've had an idea about sewing some Christmas decorations: stars, stockings, trees and whatnot, from scrap fabric. We might be able to sell some to our customers during the month.'

Violet looked heavenward. 'Christmas. Another thing to plan and worry about.'

Gwen entered the front room and located the book and pencils. Despite her words about forgetting the letter, she knew she'd be thinking about it for the rest of the day. Was it resentment from one person, or was it how a lot of people in the village felt, that she'd married above her station? She didn't act all hoity-toity to the villagers, did she? She hoped not. And she was still the same girl inside, wondering whether she was actually worthy of having married into the Meredith family.

'You all right in there?' Anwen called.

'Yes, just coming.' She picked up the pencils and notebook and went back to her friends.

Chapter Nine

'That was an excellent meal, Mother,' said Tom as he placed his cutlery in the middle of a bowl that had contained a homemade Christmas pudding and brandy butter.

Herbert, Elizabeth and Gwilym agreed, while Gwen nodded her head enthusiastically. Yet for all the sumptuous food and the lovely setting in the Merediths' dining room, with its expensive furniture, cloths and candles, Gwen longed to be sitting in her parents' house with them, Mamgu and Henry. And Tom of course. There she would have felt at home. At least they were spending Boxing Day there, while Elizabeth and Gwilym were going to his parents. She wondered if he was feeling the way she did.

'I'm so glad you all appreciate the effort I put in,' said Margaret. 'Now ladies, let us clear the table and take it to the scullery to wash up. Then we'll be able to enjoy the rest of the day.'

Gwen felt a twinge of resentment that the men weren't being asked to help. Her own mother would have had Henry up helping with such chores, declaring it would make him a better, more considerate husband.

As she was thinking this, Gwilym stood and said, 'I'll help too. We'll get it done quicker that way.'

Gwen smiled, wondering whether Mrs Owen had been the same with him and his younger brother, Evan.

'I wish I could help,' said Tom forlornly. 'But I fear this artificial arm would be more of a hindrance than a help on this task.'

Gwen squeezed his shoulder to reassure him.

With the washing up done, they congregated in the pale-yellow drawing room. There was a beautifully decorated tree in the corner, with glass baubles. The young couples took a chesterfield each, while Margaret and Herbert sat in the upholstered armchairs.

Herbert stood to pour them all a glass of port from the decanter that sat on the small occasional table. 'Have you received any more of those nasty letters, Gwen?'

'There was one pushed through the letterbox this morning,' she said. 'It must have been delivered pretty early, for I was up at half past six, and there it was.'

'And they had the temerity to put their unpleasant message on a Christmas card,' said Elizabeth.

'What did it say?' asked Margaret.

Gwen could have done without being reminded of it. 'It said, *You don't deserve a happy Christmas.* Badly spelled, as usual.'

'That was it?' said Margaret.

'At least there haven't been any actual threats,' said Elizabeth. 'Just spite.'

'It's still a serious matter,' said Herbert. 'Tom said you'd told Sergeant Harries.'

'I have, but he said that unless they're caught in the act, there's little he can do.'

'I suppose it's unrealistic to ask him to lie in wait, just in case.'

The group went silent for a while, until Margaret said, 'Your father and I have something to tell you.'

'The thing is,' said Herbert, 'I have a new job: manager of the Bargoed colliery. I start in February.'

'That's the largest pit in the area,' Gwilym piped up.

'That's right,' said Margaret proudly.

'Oh, but that means you'll be moving.' Elizabeth's eyebrows drew together.

'Of course. To a *bigger* house.' Margaret was clearly thrilled.

Gwen presumed it would be to a bigger wage too.

'That means more room when the family come to visit,' said Margaret. 'And I dare say those families will be growing in the not-too-distant future.' She displayed a broad smile.

Gwen felt herself colour as Tom said, 'We don't have any news on that front as yet.'

'Nor us,' said Elizabeth. 'And it won't be like having you only walking distance away.'

'If you and Tom get a telephone put in, we can keep in touch every day,' said Margaret.

'And we've decided you can keep the car,' said Herbert. 'For you both to use. And Gwilym and Gwen, of course.'

Gwilym sucked his breath in. 'Not sure I'm up to that.'

Gwen, on the other hand, became excited at the possibility. And the idea of owning a telephone.

'We're getting a new car,' said Margaret. 'A Wolseley Tourer. So you see, we'll be able to visit each other easily.'

'And I should think, having a motorcar at your disposal will help both the dressmaking and the market gardening business,' said Herbert.

He was right, and it made Gwen determined to learn to drive. Tom could teach her.

'Talking of which,' said Elizabeth, 'I've decided how I'm going to spend the money Tom gave me. Farmer Lloyd is selling a small field, which would be ideal for my market garden.'

'Does your husband have some say in this?' asked Margaret.

'I agree with her decision,' said Gwilym. 'And anyway, it's Elizabeth's money.'

'Exactly,' said Tom. 'You wouldn't find me interfering in Gwen's business. Not that I understand anything about dress-making or clothes.'

'You youngsters and your ideas,' said Margaret. 'The women looking after the financial affairs.' She shook her head.

'Quite so,' said Herbert, putting on a mock serious expression. 'I've always appreciated how you've left all the decisions on how our money is spent to me.' He couldn't keep it up and ended up grinning.

'Oh Herbert! I suppose I have had a bit of an input into our finances.'

'Are you going to give those ports out, Father, or are they going to sit on the table all day?' said Tom.

'Of course, I almost forgot,' he said, handing them around.

–

Polly had endured an adequate Christmas dinner at Connie's this year. Maurice was there with Mabel and little Lily, as were their parents, Jim and Delia.

Polly felt guilty about her ungenerous assessment as she did the drying in the scullery, while her mother tackled the washing up. Mabel was also there, emptying the scraps into a bucket.

Polly would rather have not been in Sioni's company all day, but what could she do? It was time for family.

'You'd think there'd have been a bit more meat and veg,' Delia grumbled as she rubbed the crushed eggshells over the pan to clean it. 'I did more last year, when meat was still rationed, and the veggies weren't as available.'

'Maybe they don't have the money, Mum?' Polly suggested, giving them the benefit of the doubt.

'Hm. Her Sioni earns no less than your father. And we've got you and Herby there.'

Polly felt guilty, until her mother added, 'Though you make your contribution, and appreciated it is too. And the year before last, Mabel did us proud, despite even more shortages.' She looked at her daughter-in-law.

'Aye,' said Mabel, 'though I was earning a good wage at the munitions then, so could afford things which were a bit more expensive like.'

'They've not even got any greenery in to decorate. How much would that have cost, to get a bit of holly or ivy from somewhere? I hate to say it of my own daughter, but Connie's always been on the mean side. Except when it comes to herself.'

Polly couldn't argue with that, but she didn't want to encourage her mother's unseasonal mood either.

'They bought Herby a nice teddy bear,' she pointed out. 'And Lily a nice doll.'

'I suppose,' her mother accepted. 'She does seem very fond of her nephew and niece. A pity they've not had any of their own yet.'

That was another thing Polly had felt guilty about when she'd fallen so easily pregnant with Herby. Poor Connie.

'Ain't you finished yet?' said her father, Jim, poking his head around the door. His London East End accent was as strong as when he'd moved here fifteen years ago, and even more obvious than Delia's, which had softened a fraction since they'd lived in Dorcalon. 'We're 'oping to play a game of Snakes and Ladders.'

'Well, if we'd had a bit of 'elp, we'd have been done by now,' said Delia.

'Let me put the fings away.' He removed the dried items from the table to take to the dresser in the kitchen.

When they'd finished, Polly went back to the kitchen to find Connie rocking Herby as if he were going to sleep, although he was clearly wide awake.

'Mummy!' he called, trying to pull himself up and out of his aunt's arms.

Polly bent down to take him, though Connie was reluctant to give him up at first. Eventually she gave up trying to keep the tot still and surrendered him to her sister.

'Well, if you must go to Mummy.'

He gave Polly a big cuddle, then said, 'I play wiv Lily, pease?' He looked to where his cousin was doing a puzzle at the end of the table.

'Of course, sweety.'

'Are we going to play this game or not?' said Maurice, who'd looked bored for most of their day there.

Connie got the board and pieces out. Sioni sat next to Polly, making her want to move, but then she'd have to explain why.

They played three games, Maurice winning two and Polly the other. Sioni's mood dipped with each loss, and he even grumbled that Maurice had cheated in the last game.

'How could I cheat?' he said, scowling. 'It's not like I can move without anyone seeing.'

Sioni gave a low rumble in reply.

'Aunty Polly,' Lily called in her wispy voice, 'Herby's fallen asleep.'

Sure enough, he was leaning his head on the table, his eyes closed.

'I knew he were tired,' said Connie, who started to rise.

Polly beat her to it. She pulled Herby's chair out and carefully lifted him off.

'He can sleep in the small room,' said Connie. 'There's a pile of blankets on the floor specially for him to lie on, and one to put over him.'

In the small bedroom, Polly knelt carefully and lay him on the prepared blankets. Her sister only had the one bed for her and Sioni, and the other two bedrooms were almost bare of furniture. Polly leaned down to give Herby a kiss, then covered him over.

Creeping backwards out of the bedroom, she gave a little gasp as she bumped into something. It was Sioni.

'Let's close the door so he's not disturbed,' he said, leaning around her, his hand gliding past her waist as he did so.

'But I want to leave it ajar, in case he cries.'

Sioni ignored her. 'Come and see Connie's new dressing table. Proud of it, she is.'

He shoved her through the partially opened door, one hand against her breast, then closed the door quietly.

'Is this more to your liking for a fumble than in the scullery, where you rejected me?'

'No,' she muttered, not wanting to alert anyone and spoil Christmas.

'Come on. You can protest all you want, but I know what a wanton piece you are. No time for me to show you all my tricks, I'm afraid, but a quick feel would be nice. Call it a Christmas present.'

She took several steps backwards, repulsed, bumping into the stool of the dressing table.

The door opened and in marched Connie. 'I wondered where you'd got to. What are you doing in here?'

Had she crept up the stairs, suspicious, Polly wondered, for she hadn't heard her coming up.

'I was showing Polly your dressing table, what I got you for Christmas.'

Now she got to look at it properly, she could see it was decent quality, a swirling walnut wood with two drawers either side and three mirrors, two of them set at a slight angle to the main one.

'It's lovely,' said Polly, wondering if the money spent was why the Christmas fare had been less than adequate.

'Second-hand,' said Connie, a little put out. 'Bought it cheap from the daughter of next door but one, eager to get rid of her mother's things when she died.' She gave Polly a pinch-mouthed glare. 'Well, you've seen it now, so let's get back downstairs.'

Connie led the way, tapping loudly on each step, despite Herby being asleep.

In the kitchen, they joined their family at the table once more, apart from Sioni who remained standing, his hands tight round the top of a dining chair. Jim was talking about the former butcher and erstwhile landlord.

'I hear Iolo's been hired as a scavenger in Pontlottyn now.'

'I bet Reg put a good word in for him,' said Maurice. 'Who knows who else in the community, or on the council, were in on their stealing and profiteering in the war?'

'Dunno about that, son,' said Jim. 'Though it does seem a little too coincidental. And that Reg has acquired 'imself an 'orse and cart for the job in Dorcalon now. Wonder where he got the money for that.'

'Maybe he still has some hidden away like, from before they was gaoled?' said Mabel. 'Or they have someone what didn't go to gaol, what's kept it safe.'

'They've done their time, the pair of them,' Sioni almost shouted. 'They should be allowed some kind of livelihood. A shame it is they couldn't get their businesses back. Iolo was a good butcher, and Reg a jolly good landlord, better than that harpy Nerys, with her ruddy rules.'

'Enough of the language,' said Maurice. 'Lily's here.'

'Well!'

'They was crooks, pure and simple,' said Delia.

'And what do you think?' said Sioni, looking at Polly. 'Not heard your opinion.'

They hadn't heard Connie's either, but she didn't often put forward one when he was there.

'I agree with Mum and Dad.'

Delia stood up. 'Enough of Reg and Iolo. I could do wiv a cuppa tea. And Lily's finished her puzzles, so let's play a game of Snap wiv 'er.'

'Yes please!' Lily beamed.

Sioni's mouth was down at the corners and his eyes narrowed. The whole day had thwarted him, she realised, with not winning a game, not getting what he wanted from her and having everyone disagree about Reg and Iolo.

When Herby woke up once more, she'd ask her dad to fetch him. She wasn't risking being left alone with Sioni again. Especially now he was in a real mood.

Chapter Ten

Henry had suffered enough of Maurice's moaning about the continual rain, what with Alun, Teilo and Douglas nodding solemnly, agreeing with him. What a night out at the McKenzie Arms this was turning out to be.

'You should see the poor sheep,' said Alun. 'Soggy and waterlogged, they are. Da's had to bring them all into the small field closest to the farmhouse, where at least it's not boggy. Not best pleased, he isn't.'

Henry could imagine that, having seen Farmer Lloyd get argumentative about plenty of things before.

'And trudging down to the pit each morning in the dark, in the pouring rain, ain't a bundle of fun,' Maurice complained. 'You get soaking before you get in the mine, and don't dry out all shift.' He took a noisy slurp of beer.

'What happened to being glad to get home?' said Henry. 'However bad the weather, it's a darn sight better than being in a trench. When it rained there, you was soaked for days. Look at all the cases of trench foot there was.'

'Aye, I was one of them,' said Teilo. 'Not been the same since, my feet haven't.'

'At least you won't get that here,' said Henry. 'I thank my lucky stars each morning I wake up, to be in a warm bed.'

'What have I got to be thankful for?' said Douglas. 'My Susan died of the influenza.'

'Aye, and sad that were, too,' said Henry. 'But at least you have your children, and a very helpful sister.'

'Hm.' Douglas wasn't impressed with his logic. 'Just as well, else they'd have gone to the workhouse. I couldn't have looked after them.'

Each of the men was sitting with an elbow on the table, their chins resting on a hand. Henry looked over to Idris and his group, Gwilym, Hywel and Twm Bach. They were chuckling about something. He'd been friends with them, before the war, and he longed to join them now.

'Look at that lot,' said Maurice, 'laughing and joking. All right for some what's got no memories from the war to bother them.'

And that was the crux of the problem, thought Henry. 'It's true I've got memories, enough for a lifetime. That's why I'd rather not keep on thinking about them.' This constant harking back to the war left him exhausted.

Maurice looked towards the bar, where Polly was doing a shift. 'And I'm still not happy about my sister working in a public house.' He tipped his head back to look at the bar's clock. 'I've got things to do now anyway.' He drank the last quarter of his pint down in one.

'Aye, me too,' said Teilo. 'The missus will have something to say if I stay out too long.'

The two other men also stood, mumbling about commitments.

'You coming?' said Maurice.

'Not yet. I've got a bit of beer to go.'

They exchanged farewells and the others were soon gone. Henry rose and made his way over to Idris's table.

'Hello there, mind if I join you?'

'Course not,' said Idris, pulling a chair over from another table for him. 'Nice to have your company. Gwilym were just telling us about John Bowen.'

'Only for our ears, mind,' Gwilym warned, 'as it's not public knowledge yet. Seems he applied for post of manager, Mr Meredith told me, but didn't get it. They was telling him this afternoon.'

'Thank heavens for that,' said Henry. 'He's bad enough as undermanager. Wouldn't want him getting any more power.'

'Hear, hear.' Twm Bach lifted his pint in agreement.

The conversation moved on to the bits and pieces of everyday life. Henry felt a cloak of relief settle over him at the normality of it. He could almost pretend the war hadn't happened.

Halfway through Twm Bach telling them about creating the Rover Scouts for the older lads of the village, there was a vibrating crash as the door was hurled open. Henry jumped, knocking the table with his knee, spilling everyone's beer. The chatter in the bar stalled.

'Sorry, sorry.' Henry could barely breathe.

'Don't worry, mun,' said Gwilym. 'I'll get a cloth off Polly to wipe it.'

'You all right?' said Hywel, clasping his arm.

'Aye, I will be.' He hid his trembling hands under the table, willing them to be still.

In through the door marched John Bowen. He was swaying slightly, as if already tipsy.

'Uh oh,' said Idris. 'I think he must have heard about the job.'

Bowen swaggered up to the bar, his mouth set hard.

Henry anticipated trouble. He clutched his hands tightly, imagining himself in the trench, having to put fear aside to get the job done. 'Think I'll join Gwilym,' he said, heading for the bar.

'Three pints of the 4d,' Bowen bellowed. 'And make it quick.'

Polly looked past him, probably wondering where the other two men were.

'No good looking for no one else,' said Bowen. 'They're for me. Drown my sorrows, like. The bloody injustice of it.'

He launched his top half over the bar as he said the last sentence, causing Polly to step back.

'Not in front of the lady, hey John?' said Henry. 'Whatever's wrong, it's not her fault.'

'Hmph!' was his only reply.

'Lucky Maurice has gone,' Gwilym whispered.

Bowen turned to the full bar, doing a sweep of them with his glare. 'I 'spose you lot have heard.' He seemed to be daring anyone to admit they had.

No one spoke. Most wouldn't even know yet what he was talking about.

'Should have been my turn as manager. Been undermanager here going on three-and-a-half year. But no, they've appointed someone what don't know our mine at all. That's not fair.' He thumped his fist on the bar.

Twm Bach's voice, low but still audible, was heard to say, 'Not surprised, you're not much good as undermanager.'

Bowen launched himself across the room. 'Was that your voice, Twm Bach? I'll give you what for.'

Henry saw Polly scuttle off through the door behind the bar.

All the men stood as one, those in front creating a barrier he couldn't get through. He started pushing men, who pushed back.

Nerys Moss soon returned with Polly, along with Steven, the live-in barman.

'That's enough now!' said Nerys, lifting the flap on the bar and coming out with Steven. Polly stayed put.

Bowen swayed as he regarded her.

'Go home now, Mr Bowen, or risk being banned from the McKenzie Arms Hotel for good.'

'Huh! Don't worry, I'll walk into Rhymney, to the Clarence Inn. I'll get a better reception there anyway.'

He lurched off, slamming into the door in his effort to open it. Steven followed, no doubt to make sure he did leave. Nerys marched back out of the bar.

Henry turned to the worried-looking barmaid. 'You all right, Polly?'

‘I am now,’ she said. ‘Don’t tell Maurice, will you? It’ll only give him another reason to have a go at me.’

‘I won’t, but I can’t guarantee he won’t hear it from someone.’ He indicated the busy bar. ‘Getting a bit of a habit here, disgruntled men charging in.’

She nodded, no doubt remembering Reg Moss’s visit.

The chatter slowly increased once more. Henry and Gwilym returned to their table.

‘Shall I get another round in?’ Henry asked.

‘Not for me, mun,’ said Gwilym. ‘Better get back for my supper.’

‘Aye, me too,’ said Idris. ‘And Twm here’s coming for supper with us tonight.’

‘And looking forward to it I am.’ He rubbed his hands together.

‘Suppose I’d better get back too,’ said Henry, sorry all the same to be leaving their company so soon.

As they passed the bar to leave, Polly called over, ‘Henry?’

He stepped towards the bar. ‘Yes?’

‘Thank you for speaking up, to Mr Bowen.’

‘You’re welcome. He shouldn’t have been so impolite.’

She smiled. ‘Thanks anyway.’

As they parted company outside, Henry contented himself with thoughts of seeing Amelia the next evening. He wouldn’t mention the incident with her uncle tonight. No point in getting even further on the wrong side of him.

-

Henry had longed all week to see Amelia, dreaming of her soft lips as he waited outside the Ainon Baptist Chapel, opposite the house she lived in with her aunt and uncle. So far she’d only allowed a peck on the cheek, but maybe tonight…

What would John Bowen do if he caught them? He’d have to make sure they kissed before reaching her home. He pulled his fob watch halfway out of his waistcoat pocket. She was a couple of minutes late so far.

Finally, she appeared, though she looked in a bad humour as she crossed the road to reach him. Perhaps she didn't fancy the walk to Rhymney on this chilly evening. He wished he had more money and could afford a motorcar. He envied Gwen's opportunity to learn to drive Tom's.

'*Noswaith dda*,' he said, leaning forward to kiss her cheek.

'Good evening, Henry,' she said stiffly, ignoring the gesture.

'Let's get going.' He offered his arm instead. 'We wouldn't want to miss the beginning of the film.'

She ignored the arm also, starting the walk along the wet pavement towards Rhymney. He caught her up.

'Been a hard week, has it?' He knew she wasn't enjoying teaching sewing as much as she thought she might.

'It's been tolerable.'

'Something seems to be bothering you.'

'I nearly didn't come tonight.'

'Oh.' His stomach sank as he wondered what he'd done. But he hadn't done anything. Something must have happened at home. Probably John Bowen's bad mood, if yesterday evening's performance at the Arms was anything to go by.

'Not after what Uncle John told me about how he was treated at the McKenzie Arms. Being thrown out by that Nerys Moss. And him the undermanager at the mine, too.'

Henry couldn't pretend her uncle had been wronged, and maybe hearing another side would help her see why he'd been asked to leave. He stuck his hands in his pockets and summoned up some courage.

'He did come in looking for trouble, if I'm honest, Amelia. He were upset about not getting the manager's job and was shouting quite a lot. Mrs Moss was understandably concerned.'

'That's not what Uncle John said! And furthermore, and even worse, someone on your table said he was no good as undermanager. It was him what's in charge of the Scouts, Twm Bach Breckon.'

'Yes, unfortunately Twm did say that.' No point saying he agreed with him. She'd likely turn around and go home if he did. 'That's what started the uproar what sent Polly Smith off to get Mrs Moss.'

'Polly Smith! I shouldn't be surprised that she'd do something against our family. Taking her dismissal from my mother's business out on my uncle like that!'

He shouldn't have mentioned Polly; he didn't want Bowen having some reason to get back at her. 'I don't think it were quite like that. She were probably afraid the other men would kick off too.'

'You didn't help though, did you?' Even in the streetlight he could see her pinching her lips in. 'You could have stuck up for him, given Twm Bach what for.'

'I didn't get the opportunity to give anyone what for.' Though if he had, it would have been Bowen.

She went quiet for a bit, her footsteps getting faster. At least she hadn't turned back. Gradually she slowed down, much to Henry's relief.

'I suppose it was a little unwise of him to go to the public house to complain about not getting the job. Not very dignified,' Amelia conceded. 'Aunt Matilda wasn't pleased he'd gone out, and he didn't get home till quite late.'

'He said he were going to Rhymney, to the Clarence Inn.'

'I shan't tell Aunt Matilda that. He said he'd been at a friend's house. I'd hate for them to fall out again.'

She did now take his arm. A small thrill ran through him. He could understand her being annoyed to begin with. At least now she understood.

'I hope I can trust you to keep that to yourself,' she said.

'Of course.' He didn't point out that everyone in the bar had heard him say it.

She snuggled in closer, and he was satisfied that the incident wasn't going to spoil the evening as he'd feared.

-

'What a lovely film that main feature was,' Amelia said as they filtered out of the Imperial Cinema in Rhymney. 'So romantic.' She let out a long sigh of pleasure.

He'd thought so too, appreciating *The Knave of Hearts* for encouraging her, at times of high tension, to move closer. He'd also imagined them each as the hero and heroine, building hope in his heart that they'd one day be that close.

'Shall we go to Perilli's for a drink?' she suggested, once they'd reached the street.

He did a quick calculation of the coins he had left in his pocket. After paying for the picture house tickets, along with the new shirt and tie he'd bought in the week to update his clothes a bit, he was a little short. He had a lot less than he had the night he took her to the theatre in Abergavenny. He couldn't keep borrowing from his father. But yes, he'd have enough for a couple of drinks, and maybe even some biscuits.

'Good idea,' he said.

They were seated quickly. She suggested a pot of coffee for two, which he readily agreed to.

'And, I will have a piece of the raspberry gateau.'

Henry went hot, then cold. She'd chosen the most expensive cake on the menu. He hadn't expected her to have something that filling this time of the evening.

'And you, sir?' said the waitress.

'Not for me, thank you.'

When the waitress left, Amelia linked her hands and placed them on the table. 'How very self-disciplined of you. I can't resist cake when it's available. I suppose it's not having it during the war. Or don't you like cake? You didn't have it in Abergavenny either.'

'I like it well enough,' he said in a light voice. 'I'm just not hungry.'

She treated him to an indulgent smile. 'I cannot believe I'll be twenty-six soon.'

Henry was confused at the change of subject, then panicked, hoping her birthday wasn't in the next week. How would he afford a present?

'Just under a month to go,' she added.

He sighed with relief. A bit of time to save up then. He wanted to get her something special. 'When exactly?'

'Fourteenth of February. St Valentine's Day! Appropriate, given how romantic I am.' She tipped her head to one side and emitted a little giggle.

He hadn't seen much evidence of it yet, but he guessed it was still early days for them. She was clearly a principled young woman, and right to be cautious.

'I hope you'll plan something extra special.' She regarded him with puppy dog eyes.

'You'll have to wait and see,' he said, winking.

She emitted another giggle. 'I'll look forward to it. When's your birthday, by the way?'

'September. I'll be twenty-nine.'

'A way off yet then.' She seemed to be pondering this.

Perhaps she was considering something special for him too. It was nine months away. By then, they might even be – no, he shouldn't get ahead of himself. But the idea excited him, nonetheless.

The bill arrived on a saucer shortly after they'd finished their coffee. One shilling and a penny. Yes, he should have enough money for that.

He dug into his trouser pocket and pulled out his coins. A dread gripped him as he counted them. Tuppence short? He checked again, twice.

'What's wrong?' Amelia asked.

'That's strange. I had more than enough earlier. Oh, I did take some out and put it on the drawers, as I was dressing.' At least that was true. 'I could have sworn I picked them up again.'

He didn't want her thinking he was someone who'd be short of money. How would that make him look as a provider?

Amelia pouted, looking sidelong at the nearest table, maybe hoping they hadn't overheard.

'It's easily done,' she finally conceded. 'I'm sure I can make up the difference.' She lifted her bag from her lap and dug inside, producing a purse. From it she extracted two pennies, adding them to the coins Henry had placed on the saucer.

What a relief. And she hadn't taken it too badly. There was no tip, but he could hardly ask her to contribute any more. 'Thank you, Amelia. I do appreciate it.'

'You can pay me back next time you see me,' she said.

He nodded. 'Of course.'

–

When they arrived back at Amelia's house that evening, they walked down the alleyway between her house and the school, so she could go in the back way. Halfway down, they stopped.

'Thank you for a nice evening,' said Amelia.

'You're welcome.' He bent forward to kiss her lips, but she shifted backwards.

'Better not,' she whispered. 'I wouldn't want to risk Uncle John seeing us and causing a fuss. He's very protective of me since my father died.'

'It's good you have a father figure to look out for you.' It was a shame it had to be Bowen.

'Good night, Henry.'

'*Nos da*,' he replied.

He waited there until she'd let herself in the side gate before heading off. So, not even a peck on the cheek tonight, let alone the lips. Give it time, he told himself.

Chapter Eleven

Polly could have done without such an early start this morning. It was six thirty and a frost had formed overnight. The pavement was crunchy as she plodded towards Gwen's house, the last one on Alexandra Street, and at the end of the village. And Elizabeth's and Tom's, she reminded herself, feeling apprehensive. The streetlamps were off now, so the only light was that coming from the hallways of the houses she passed. At least she didn't have to get out as early as the miners on the first shift, she supposed. Quarter to six her father left every day.

She didn't usually work at Gwen's, more often going to Anwen's. She preferred that, what with Herby's connection to Elizabeth and Tom. The early start was due to a commission they wanted to finish quickly, a wedding gown, made from scratch, along with two bridesmaids' dresses, for a bank manager's daughter in Tredegar. The reputation of the business was certainly spreading.

As she approached Gwen's house, she squinted into the darkness, seeing someone vaguely by the front door. She couldn't make out who it was, wondering if it could be Anwen or Violet. About to greet whoever it was, the figure bent down towards the letterbox. Curious.

Getting closer she was confused to see who it was, and then astonished when she realised what they were doing.

'Jenny Richards, what are you posting there?' she said in a loud whisper.

Jenny stood abruptly, her eyes and mouth wide with shock in the dim light of the hall.

'I – um, it's just a – oh, it doesn't matter now.'

She went to turn away, but Polly caught her arm before she had a chance to run off. She snatched the envelope from Jenny's hand, suspecting she knew what she'd find within. Jenny tried to grab it back, but Polly was too quick for her.

'Please, you've got no right. That's private, that is.' Jenny's low voice was croaky.

Polly ran her finger along the envelope and pulled out the paper within. Jenny tried once more to wrestle it off her. Polly twisted away, holding the paper up towards the light shining through the door. She managed to see the words, *Gwen, you don't deserve*… when a figure appeared in the hall. Before she could do anything with the letter, the front door opened, and there stood Gwen.

'What on earth is all this fuss?' Seeing the letter in Polly's hand, she snatched it away. 'I'll have that.' She perused it quickly.

Jenny started to run away, but Polly caught hold of her.

'Get inside, both of you!' Gwen hissed.

She pressed them towards the kitchen, where Elizabeth was sitting by the fire. She stood up.

'What's going on?'

'I found these two lurking on the doorstep, and this letter was in Polly's hand.'

Polly winced. Surely Gwen didn't think she had anything to do with it.

Gwen read it out. '*You don't deserve a rich husband and a successful – business. I'll tell people how rubbish your sewing is.* The spelling could certainly be better.'

'I've got nothing to do with it,' said Polly. 'I just found her on the doorstep. Don't suppose she were expecting someone to turn up so early.'

Jenny hesitated for a moment, in which time Polly felt the hand of doom descend. If she said they were in it together, who would Gwen believe?

'Polly's got nothing to do with it,' said Jenny, her hands going to her cheeks as she let out a brief sob. 'She caught me about to post it and snatched it off me.'

Polly sighed with relief. At least Jenny had the decency to tell the truth.

'It makes sense,' said Elizabeth. 'Polly's unlikely to post a letter like that and make herself the obvious culprit.'

Gwen narrowed her eyes, as if she didn't appreciate Elizabeth's input. 'Why didn't you bring it straight to me?'

'I was trying to, but Jenny kept trying to snatch it back.' Polly wasn't at all sure she would have passed it on, but she couldn't say that.

Jenny hung her head. 'It's true.'

'It's not Polly's fault,' said Elizabeth. 'She was trying to do the right thing.'

Gwen banged the letter on the table. 'Why did you do it, Jenny?'

She couldn't have suspected Jenny's connection with the Merediths, otherwise she'd surely have a clue. If that was anything to do with it. Polly wasn't sure herself.

'Just, just because I was jealous of your success,' said Jenny. 'I'm a bit down on my luck. I have to live with Aunty Myfanwy, and here you are, your own home, and a husband, whereas mine's dead. Didn't seem fair.'

'Polly here is in much the same position,' Elizabeth pointed out. 'But you don't see her posting nasty letters.'

'I've a mind to fetch Sergeant Harries,' said Gwen. 'The court should sort you out.'

'Oh please, no,' said Jenny, putting her hands up as if in prayer. 'If I went to gaol, who'd look after Freddie? And I can't afford a fine. I'm sorry, I really, really am. I don't know what got into me.' She started to sniff and the tears welled up.

'Don't know what got into you?' said Gwen. 'That might have been true if you'd done it the once. But this is the fifth letter.'

'I won't do it again, honest.'

'Well, it would be pretty stupid, since we'd know it were you,' said Gwen.

Elizabeth walked over to look at the letter. 'It's not like there have been any threats of harm. Providing it stops, I think it would be better to forget it.'

Gwen's jaw tightened, before she declared, 'I don't know.'

If Jenny's Freddie was Herbert Meredith's son, it might be foolish to get the police involved. Polly could hardly point that out though.

'All right. For now,' said Gwen. 'But I'm holding onto the letters, and if any more come, or I hear someone else has had similar, it will be used in evidence. And I have a witness what caught you in the act.'

Polly's breath hitched. If she got involved in this, would her dark secret come out too?

'Now get out of my house, Jenny.' Gwen pointed to the door.

Jenny scurried away, muttering profuse *thank yous* as she went.

After she'd gone, Gwen said, 'I'll go and fetch the bridesmaid's dress from the spare room, and you can carry on with it.'

Her face was still set with annoyance as she left the room.

'Oh dear, what a shock,' said Elizabeth. 'I thought it might have been Esther.'

'It's a shame Jenny felt so resentful.' Polly had learned to tuck that emotion away. It wouldn't have got her anywhere.

'Yes, it is.' Elizabeth looked thoughtful for a moment. 'Tell me, how is little Herby?'

Polly winced at Elizabeth using the name that had come from her own father.

'He's fine, thank you, Miss Elizabeth. He likes spending time with his mamgu while I'm working.'

‘It’s so good that you have your mother to help. Now, let me get you a cup of tea, then I must get on with my household chores.’ She went to the range, singing as she went.

Elizabeth enquiring about Herby had unnerved her a little, but she decided she was only being polite. She’d need to keep her head down from now on.

–

By two o’clock, Polly was glad to leave work. Gwen didn’t chat to her like Anwen and her family, nor was there ever much in the way of tea and biscuits on offer. At least she’d get a couple more hours’ money though.

Out of the door, she set about the mission she’d decided on while working. On Station Road, she knocked at number one. She hoped Jenny would answer, and not her aunt, so she wouldn’t have to make up a reason for seeing her.

Sure enough, Jenny opened the door, at first only a tiny bit as she peeped around. On seeing it was Polly, her face filled with concern.

‘Oh, did Gwen send you?’

‘No, she has no idea I’m here, so don’t worry.’

‘What is it then?’

‘Could I come in? I don’t want anyone overhearing.’

Jenny stood back and let her into the hall. ‘Come into the kitchen,’ she whispered. ‘Aunty Myfanwy is having a nap upstairs, as is Freddie.’

In the kitchen, Jenny didn’t invite her to sit down. ‘It isn’t money you want, is it, not to tell the police?’

Polly was shocked that Jenny would even think that of her. ‘Of course not! It’s only a simple question I want to ask, that’s all. I would appreciate a truthful answer though.’

Jenny’s brow creased and she looked away. ‘Go on then.’

‘Is Herbert Meredith Freddie’s father?’

Jenny wobbled, before clutching the back of the armchair to restore her balance. It was a few seconds before she said, 'Yes, yes he is.' She looked up now. 'Did Gwen tell you that?'

'No, and I've no idea if she knows. I just had a feeling. You see, Herby is his son too.'

Jenny looked agog. 'He is? I suspected he weren't Gus Smith's, but goodness. And you called him Herbert! That's the last name I would have picked.'

'I know. Looking back, I suppose it weren't the wisest choice, but then, I thought we'd stay in Surrey, or move back to London. Gus and his family came from Hackney, not far from where I was born in Whitechapel. I didn't anticipate Gus getting the idea he could avoid conscription if he moved to my old home, so he could become a miner. He'd managed to avoid conscription up till then, but the authorities were catching up with him.'

'That means Freddie and Herby are… half-brothers.'

'That's right.'

Jenny took a seat in the armchair now, looking somewhat dazed. 'Your Connie's brought Herby around to play with Freddie. That feels rather strange now. Does she know?'

Polly shook her head vehemently. 'She certainly does not, only that Gus isn't the father.'

'Take a seat.' She pointed at the other armchair. 'I can't say I've seen a particular likeness, but then, I haven't been looking.'

'They've different colouring, that's for sure. Your Freddie has your dark skin and Tom's dark auburn hair. Herby's fair, like me.'

'Neither of them have Mr Meredith's black hair.'

'No.' Though his was greyer now than it had been when they'd had their dalliance, what four-and-a-half years ago? It was strange that Jenny should refer to her son's father still as *Mr* Meredith.

'Do you think the family has any idea?'

'Herbert and Tom know about Herby, since they was both at the house the day I turned up to tell him. And to ask for money. I had to promise I'd tell no one and never ask for any more money. Not that the money went far once I married Gus.'

He'd considered her bit of money, put away to buy things for Herby, as his, and she'd no real idea what he'd spent it on.

'Whether they told Mrs Meredith and Elizabeth, I don't know,' Polly continued. 'I suspect not, otherwise surely Mrs Meredith would have made a big fuss. You know what she can be like.'

'Oh yes,' said Jenny. 'Having worked there, I can't imagine she'd have let you get away with it.'

'And Elizabeth is very nice to me when I go to their house to work.'

'I don't even know if Mr Meredith guessed about Freddie, or whether he just assumed he were Joseph's. Most people seem to have done.'

'How did you know he weren't Joseph's?'

Jenny looked offended. 'I didn't do – *that* – with both of them at the same time. But, but Joseph had pursued me a bit. I wasn't that interested as he were a bit… boring. When I missed my flow, I feared I must be pregnant. I started to encourage Joseph, and, well, did things with him, so I could say it were his. I told Joseph I was pregnant the month after, and we got a licence to marry quickly. His family weren't happy. When Freddie were born, it wasn't much past seven months after I, you know, with Joseph. Not knowing any better, he believed Freddie were early.'

Polly bit her bottom lip and placed her hands in her lap.

'I know it were bad of me,' said Jenny, 'but what else could I do? Did you tell Gus you was pregnant?'

She let out a brief laugh. 'It were already obvious when we met. But he took a shine to me and weren't put off. Or so I thought…'

'What?'

'I wonder whether he'd already had the idea of avoiding conscription. It wasn't long after we married that he suggested we moved. Once we was here, he didn't treat me nice no more. Soon after, a conscription official turned up, and Gus told him he'd had to leave his job in Surrey and move here as I was pining for my home and it was affecting my sanity.'

Jenny gasped. 'What a thing to say!'

'I was afraid he'd get me carted off to the asylum which is why I didn't fight back against him and his awful family. Anyway, he were sent to the conscription board, but they allowed him and his brother-in-law to keep their jobs at the pit.'

'At least you're well shot of him,' said Jenny.

'Until he gets out of gaol. I have no idea what he'll do then. It's a shame about Joseph though. He seemed nice enough.'

'Yes. I'd grown rather fond of him in the eight months we was married. Sad I was when he were killed. He were a good man.'

'You didn't want to move with his family to Porthcawl when they went? You were living with them.'

Jenny pressed her lips together. 'Joseph might have been clueless about what a full-term baby looks like compared to an early one, but his mother weren't. They already had me pegged as a fallen woman for being pregnant before we married. There were never any suggestion that I went with them, and they've never attempted to see Freddie since. I'm not sorry, really, but I do wish my parents hadn't already moved to North Wales.'

'What a pair we are,' said Polly.

Jenny stood up, looking more at ease now in Polly's presence. 'Would you like a cup of tea?'

'Thank you for the offer, but I'd better get back to relieve my mum of Herby. She'll be back on duty for me this evening, when I do my shift at the Arms.'

'Do you mind Connie bringing Herby over here?'

'I don't mind at all. In fact, I'd be happy to call around with him myself.'

Jenny looked pleasantly surprised. 'Yes, I'd like that too. You can't have too many friends.'

'You won't send Gwen any more letters though, will you?'

'Of course I won't.' Jenny looked down. 'I feel so bad about it now. But, well, I saw her swanning about with Tom, and with her new business, married into a wealthy family, when me and Freddie's got very little. Thought it was unfair, I did.'

'I don't think *wealthy* is the right word. Comfortable I suppose Mr and Mrs Meredith are. But Gwen and Anwen started the business from scratch as far as I can tell, not with any money from the Merediths. And Tom's got an ordinary job in an office.'

'Oh. I assumed Gwen must have got a bit to help her out.'

'I don't think so.' Polly rose. 'I'll leave you to it. And thank you, for being honest with me.'

'You know, it's a relief to be able to talk to someone about it.'

'We're in the same boat. You can come and talk to me anytime.'

Jenny smiled and nodded. 'You too.'

Chapter Twelve

Another Friday, another set of wages, thought Henry as the cage bringing the men from underground rattled upwards. After he'd given Mam her share, he'd put some away to save, but keep a bit back to take Amelia out. He also needed a haircut. He patted the too-long strands of his dark blond hair.

One side of him, Maurice was moaning about something his wife wanted to do that evening. He'd been in this mood all day and Henry was sick of it. Maurice was the worst butty he'd ever worked with, forever griping about something as they hewed the coal side by side.

'Always on at me is Mabel. Tonight, it's fixing the door. Dunno when she thinks I'm supposed to do this work towards the examiner's exam.'

'You're lucky you know, mun,' said Teilo Brice behind him, 'that your Mabel worked in the munitions in the war and was able to save up so much. Tidy sum it is, according to my missus.'

'She has her eye on renting one of them bigger houses on Mafeking Terrace or moving to a bigger town. Hm.'

Teilo was right, Maurice was lucky. At least he had a wife. He thought about Amelia, her dark copper hair, the stunning green eyes… He should be so fortunate.

'I don't care what she says,' Maurice continued, 'I'm going to spend a coupla hours in the Arms with the Pals this evening.'

They queued up to collect their wages. There were a few men there already.

Maurice rubbed his hands together. 'Should be a tidy sum today. We've filled a good few trucks between us this week.' He patted Henry on the back. 'If my missus thinks she's getting any of my extra, she's got another think coming. Got other things to spend it on.' His mouth went up on one side, in a half smile.

'I won't be joining you at the Arms this evening,' said Henry. 'I'm taking Amelia Bowen out.' He wondered if his pride had shown in his voice, as Maurice tutted and the smile disappeared.

'So you keep saying.'

'Leave the poor sod alone,' said Teilo. 'He's entitled to have a sweetheart. Just because you're fed up with marriage.'

'It's all right till they become your wife and all they're concerned about is the house and children.'

'Ooh, stop moaning, mun,' said Hywel, just ahead of them. 'A decent woman is Mabel.'

'Maybe I'd prefer an indecent one,' he quipped, laughing at his own joke, but no one else did. As they edged closer to the office window, where the wages were given out, he said, 'I wouldn't expect anything from Amelia Bowen, Henry. A woman like her, she needs a real man.'

'What, like you?' Teilo remarked. 'Look lively, we're moving.'

'I'd keep your voice down,' said Hywel, 'else John Bowen'll have something to say about that statement.'

He pointed ahead to where the undermanager was standing next to the clerk who was giving out the wages, his arms crossed over his chest. There seemed to be an argument going on with the man who'd just received his envelope.

'Wonder what that's about,' said Henry.

After Hywel collected his money, Henry went up to the window. He took the offered envelope and was about to walk away but stopped suddenly. Maurice almost bumped into him. He'd just noticed the amount written on the envelope.

'That's not right!' said Henry. 'With all the trams I've filled this week.' He felt awkward, with Bowen being Amelia's uncle, but he had no choice but to speak up. There'd obviously been a mistake that Bowen could put right.

'And I say it is.' Bowen glared at him, daring him to argue. 'You're earning a damn sight more than before the war.'

'And everything's gone up a darn sight more,' Henry retorted.

'Next!'

Henry stared at the envelope, wondering what to do next. Bowen handed Maurice his wage packet.

'Hey, I'm short too!'

'I'm going to speak to Mr Hopkins about this,' said Henry, his hand trembling.

Bowen threw back his head and laughed. 'Go ahead, boyo, you tell Hopkins. He's already informed me to get rid of any troublemakers. There's plenty of men what want jobs, like some of your mates from the Pal's battalion what weren't taken back on. So yes, please do complain. We'll have you out of here quicker than you can say, "unemployed", and have you replaced. Next!'

Henry stepped back. He couldn't risk losing this job, nor irritating Amelia's uncle again. Maurice hesitated, but did the same, swearing under his breath and adding, 'I'll get my own back on him, see if I don't.' He stormed off.

'That's a bit of a rum do,' said Hywel, who was waiting for Henry. 'I remember Williams trying that one on Idris when he were discharged from the army.'

'Were you short too?' said Henry.

'No, but being a fireman I'm not paid by the tram. It's the same every week for me, so they can't try that on.'

Up ahead, Tom left the office where he was a clerk to the manager. He looked equally crestfallen.

'Hello, Tom,' said Henry. 'You're not off home already, are you?'

'Yes. I've just been dismissed by Mr Hopkins. He reckons I'm not up to the job.'

'That can't be right,' said Hywel. 'You must be more than up to the job, with your education.'

'Not wishing to sound arrogant, but I think I am. I was getting on well with it. I don't think Mr Hopkins likes me, being the son of the old manager. I can't say it's been pleasant since he arrived, so in a way, I'm not sorry.'

'You're not the only one what's got a gripe with Hopkins,' said Henry. 'Me and Maurice Coombes have been short-changed in our wages. Can't imagine we're the only ones, neither.'

'That's not on,' said Tom. 'Word has it that Hopkins is good friends with the mine bosses, so it wouldn't surprise me if he was in on some scam.'

They started walking towards the gate. 'That can only spell doom for us all,' said Henry.

Perhaps, when he and Amelia married they could move to another village, and he could get work at a different mine.

When they got married? He was getting rather ahead of himself. *If*. But the thought gave him a glow that warmed him as he trudged through the cold air to his home.

-

'He did what?' said Gwen, thinking she must have misheard Tom.

'Sacked me, for not being up to the job.'

She came around the table in the kitchen to hug him, then considered his half-empty sleeve. 'Is this because of your arm? Because the government's said firms are to employ the disabled ex-soldiers. And that's only right given what you all sacrificed for your country.' She felt the anger rising.

'More likely it's because I'm the ex-manager's son. And there's more.' He told her about Henry and Maurice being short-changed.

'This is intolerable! Isn't there anything they can do?'

'Not really. Mr Bowen threatened to sack them, as there are plenty of men needing jobs. He said Mr Hopkins had told him to get rid of troublemakers. He seems to be thick with the bosses, so perhaps those instructions even came from them.'

'I'm all for giving that Aled Hopkins a piece of my mind I am.'

'Then he might dismiss Henry – and your father.'

She felt helpless. What could she, or any of them, do against the might of the colliery bosses? 'What are we going to do for money? The sewing business is picking up, but it's not enough to pay the bills yet.'

'We've still got the money from Tadcu Powell to see us through.'

'But you need that for when you decide what you'd like to do more permanently.'

'I'll get another office job, don't worry. I'll have a look in the newspapers I picked up from Mrs Davies.' He pointed to where he'd placed them on the table.

They heard the back door, then two voices called, 'Hello!' Gwilym and Elizabeth came into the kitchen.

'What are you doing back so early?' said Elizabeth. 'You don't normally finish until six.'

Tom groaned, and Gwen guessed he didn't want to go through it again.

'He's been sacked,' she said. 'And some of the men have been short-changed. Well Henry and Maurice at least.'

'Me too,' said Gwilym, looking glum.

'We'd better have a sit down and discuss our finances and the bills this week,' said Elizabeth, ever the sensible one.

'I'll serve the dinner first,' said Gwen, going to the range, 'And we can discuss it while we eat.'

–

Walking up Station Road from the mine after his shift a few days after the incident with John Bowen, Henry's head ached from mulling over his financial setback. Behind him, Teilo and Douglas chatted, but he took none of it in. He was relieved to have left Maurice behind, arguing with one of the other men about something.

After some consideration, he realised he had no choice: he'd have to ask his father if he could borrow a little money for Amelia's birthday. Da kept a bit back each week, for their 'old age', as he put it. If he said yes, he'd get washed quickly and go into Rhymney to find Amelia a present. Now he just needed enough for the meal and the theatre. He didn't want a repeat of their trip to Perilli's.

Approaching the turning for his street, he heard a cheery, 'Hello, Henry.'

His head went up and his heart did a little leap as he realised it was Amelia. Almost immediately he felt self-conscious about his scruffy clothes and the black dust that covered him. They both stopped outside the bookshop.

'Hello, Amelia. Fancy seeing you here.'

She gave a merry giggle. 'Not really, since I live here.'

'Yes, I mean… You're not at work?'

'No, I don't work Wednesday afternoons, because I take an evening class.'

'Of course. You did say.'

Several men stepped into the road to divert around them. A couple winked at Henry. Another displayed a more explicit gesture, making him glad that Amelia was facing the other way.

'I am *so* looking forward to my birthday,' she said, hands linked together in front of her chest, her smile so wide that her cheeks were plumped up like large cherries.

'Aye, it should be good.' His stomach's lurch belied his words, but he grinned back all the same.

'I've been wanting to see *Babes in the Wood* for so long. And I hear from a teacher at the school that the Central Hotel's restaurant is marvellous.'

So taken was he by Amelia's enthusiasm, he hadn't noticed that Maurice had caught up until he called, 'You don't want to bother with him, darling, you need a real man.'

He was about to ask Maurice to go away when Amelia said, 'Really?' She looked behind him hopefully, saying, 'Why, can you see one somewhere?'

Henry was inordinately pleased with her put down, though he did wonder if it would spark one of Maurice's moods. Instead, he put his head back and hooted with laughter. 'I like a woman with a sense of humour. You're wasted on serious Henry here. He'd be better off with my Mabel.'

He slapped Henry on the back several times. 'See you tomorrow, lover-boy.'

Maurice moved on, still laughing.

'Sorry about that,' said Henry. 'He can be very annoying.'

'Well, I put him in his place,' said Amelia, watching the retreating back. 'I know how to handle men like him. Anyway, I'd better let you get to your bath and dinner, and I will see you on Saturday.'

She entered the greengrocer's. Henry watched her until the door closed and she disappeared from sight, before carrying on home.

-

Henry took his wristwatch from the pocket of his jacket that was lying folded nearby with his shirt and vest. He lifted his lamp to look at the time. Eleven twenty. Another two hours and forty minutes of Maurice moaning, yet again. Currently he was on about his mother-in-law, Rhonwen Evans, and how she was always popping around uninvited.

His mind wandered to Amelia, to the treat he had planned for two days' time, on her twenty-sixth birthday. He'd already paid a guinea for a bottle of 4711 Eau de Cologne, on a trip into Rhymney the day before. More than a fifth of his five pounds wages! And he had to give his mam two pounds and ten shillings a week. He'd borrowed some money from his father and scraped together the little he'd saved. It would be worth it to see Amelia so happy.

He needed to look to the future, to save up more regularly, rather than spend glum nights out with the old Pals. Could he get another job, one that paid better? He shook his head; he didn't know anything else. Maybe do exams then and get a better job in the pit? Some of those weren't much better paid, as long as you could fill a decent number of trams of coal as a hewer. And being paid for those was a problem currently.

'You know, I think I was better off in the trenches,' said Maurice, before attacking a piece of coal with his pickaxe, joining the chorus of metal on rock.

'Of course you weren't,' said Henry, losing his patience. 'You hated it, being in France. You couldn't wait to get back.'

Maurice huffed out. 'You know what they say about being careful what you wish for. Should have taken more advantage of having leave in France, with some of the local ladies, if you know what I mean. I heard quite a few saucy accounts—'

'Give it a rest, Maurice,' a voice called from the gloom. It was Teilo Brice, barely visible in the light of his lamp. 'Have a bit of respect for our friends what didn't get the opportunity to return to their wives – and those what came back to deceased wives.'

'Meh!' Maurice flicked his hand in a dismissive gesture and wielded his pickaxe once more. 'I do wonder who was better—'

A crack and then a thudding bang boomed out from somewhere nearby. Henry barely had time to draw in a startled breath before there was a shower of splintered rock and the lamps all went out.

Chapter Thirteen

Everyone on the shift was above ground and accounted for, standing around the colliery yard. Henry was swamped with relief. He'd been in France when the last explosion in Dorcalon had killed twelve men, and by all accounts it had been horrific for everyone involved. He and the other three working nearby had been splattered with a few grains of rock and coal. Receiving a few cuts and bruises was as much as anyone was complaining about.

'You all right, Henry, mun?' Gwilym called from where he'd been chatting to Idris and Twm Bach.

'Just a few scratches,' Henry called back. 'And you?'

'Too far away even for scratches.'

Despite the lack of injury and Gwilym's light-hearted words, Henry could feel his hands shaking. He gripped them into fists, to still his cowardly body. He didn't want anyone seeing him in this state and mocking him.

Maurice elbowed him and knocked Teilo and his butty with the back of his hands. 'It were Sioni what were fireman in our area,' he said as the man in question came into view.

'Not like him to get it wrong,' said Teilo.

'I dunno, but I did smell alcohol on his breath a few days ago.'

Henry wondered if that was true, or whether he was after getting Sioni into trouble. Maurice had never been keen on his brother-in-law.

'I dunno what happened,' Sioni Gower was saying to Aled Hopkins as they came near. 'I laid it proper like, the explosive. Someone must have interfered with it or knocked it over.'

'You're a well-trained fireman by all accounts with years of experience,' Hopkins agreed, 'so I'd expect you to lay it right.'

'Aye, and I did, sir.'

'Well, I dare say there'll be an enquiry, and they'll probably find there was a slight rockfall or similar.'

The voices faded away.

'He's been declared innocent, even before they've had the ruddy enquiry,' said Maurice, narrowing his eyes.

'You can't say that just because you've got no time for the man,' said Teilo. 'I'm sure an enquiry will sort it out.'

'I wouldn't bank on it,' said Gwilym passing by.

Henry, about to add a comment to discourage any more moaning from Maurice, found his gripped hands had not done the trick. His arms and the tops of his legs were now shaking. It wasn't long before his head started too. His breathing became rapid.

'What the hell's wrong with you?' said Maurice.

Teilo was more concerned. 'Henry?'

'I – I – I—' He couldn't get the words out.

A murmur went round as Henry's trembling and his head jerking got worse. The more he tried to stop, the worse it got. Word must have got to Aled Hopkins, who soon loomed into sight once more.

'What's wrong with you, Austin?'

'I think he do suffer a bit from the shell shock,' said Teilo. 'Never seen him this bad though.'

'Get him 'ome, will you. I need to get some teams together to clear up, and he won't be no good. Bowen!' he called over on spotting the undermanager. 'Over here and get some men organised. I need to ring the company.'

Amelia's uncle was the last person Henry wanted to see him in this state. He tried to turn away, but Bowen eyed him suspiciously as he passed by.

‘Come on, mun,’ said Teilo, taking his arm. ‘Steady now. Maurice, take his other side and we’ll get him home.’

He’d have been better off sitting somewhere, until it passed, but he was drawing too much unwanted attention so tried to walk where Teilo was leading him.

‘Here’s his da. He’ll do it,’ said Maurice, waving and indicating for him to come over.

‘Henry! Were you hurt by the explosion?’ said Albert.

‘No, we reckon it’s the shell shock,’ Teilo repeated. ‘Gotta get him ’ome. Mr Hopkins’s orders.’

‘We’ve had a bit of trouble with this already.’ He looked pained. Henry only vaguely wondered what he meant as his hands trembled more.

‘Where are you goin’, mun?’ Teilo called to Maurice.

‘Got something to do.’ He disappeared into the crowd.

Henry had never been so pleased to get out of the colliery gate, away from curious eyes and more than a couple of sniggers. He guessed it looked funny, him twitching.

‘We’ll be home soon, son.’

He could only nod, not able to get the words past his throat.

–

The following morning, after a bad night of dreams and more shaking, Henry sat on the stairs in the dark, hands loose on his knees, his head flopped down.

His mother came into the hall, casting a light into it from the kitchen. She looked up. ‘You were having some more noisy dreams last night. Not the first we’ve heard.’

‘I’m sorry, Mam, if I woke you up.’

‘Don’t be daft. You can’t help it.’

His father, already dressed, joined Ruth in the hall. ‘I don’t think you should go in today, son. Have a rest. You need your wits about you, digging in that narrow passage you’re in.’

‘You’re right, Da. I’m too tired and feel a bit – disorientated.’

'I'll knock Dr Roberts up on my way to work,' said Albert. 'You need looking at.'

'No, I'll be fine,' said Henry, rallying, if only to show he wasn't bad enough to require a doctor.

'No, you're not,' Ruth insisted. 'It's not the first time you've ended up shaking. Don't think we haven't noticed. I've read about this in the newspaper. Shell shock they call it. Teilo said as much when he brought you back yesterday.'

There was no point arguing. He'd known for a while he had a problem, and that he'd seen similar when out on the war front. In their early days there, one of the men in his battalion with the shakes, a private, had run away. When they'd caught him he'd been deemed a traitor. After being tried and found guilty, he'd been shot. It had left a mark on Henry and the other soldiers. Later, another who'd suffered similar mental anguish had been sent to a psychiatric hospital, an officer in this case. The unequal treatment had not passed the men by.

But now, such men were increasingly being sent to asylums. He did not want to be one of them.

'Get Dr Roberts round then. I'm going back to bed.' He pulled himself up and dragged his body up the steps.

He'd simply have to play his symptoms down.

-

Dr Roberts put his stethoscope away and closed his bag. He had finally arrived at half past six in the evening, apologising because he'd had a lot of call outs, and had been on duty in the hospital.

He'd asked Henry many questions since he'd arrived, but had offered few comments to his replies, mostly nodding and adding, 'Mm mm.'

'Well, Henry, your physical condition doesn't seem compromised.'

'Meaning?'

The doctor sat on the seat opposite, near the range. 'I think you already know. Your friend suggested shell shock to your parents, and they'd already wondered about that themselves. Neurasthenia, we call it.'

He'd read the term in the newspapers, where there'd also been pieces about electric treatments. He shuddered, and it had nothing to do with his condition.

'I don't want to end up in an asylum,' said Henry.

'That's unlikely. You're coping with life most of the time. You only seem to get these episodes periodically. Is that right?'

'Yes. But it's still – embarrassing. The least noise, or something dropped, and I start off again.'

'We'll keep an eye on it. Hopefully, as your memories of the war fade, so will the shaking.'

Henry nodded, glad to be reassured of what he'd hoped would be the case, though at the same time not convinced the memories would ever diminish.

'If it gets worse, let me know. I wouldn't go back to the pit until at least Monday. Use the weekend to recover. Get lots of sleep.'

'Thank you, Dr Roberts.'

'I'll see myself out.'

Ruth came rushing out of the scullery to show the doctor out, suggesting she'd been listening at the door. Was nothing private?

About to put his head back and close his eyes, he became aware of another woman's voice in the hallway. He had hoped to sit by the warm fire for a while, but he might end up having to go back to his bedroom if his mother invited in whoever it was.

His spirits rose as the door opened and he spotted Amelia, but then sank again, wondering what she'd heard from her uncle.

'Henry, Miss Bowen has come to see how you are,' said his mother. 'Isn't that nice of her?'

He stood slowly. 'Amelia. I didn't expect this. But it's lovely to see you.'

'I'll leave you to it,' said Ruth, heading back to the scullery.

He rose and pulled the door shut, preventing any further eavesdropping.

'Oh Henry, I heard yesterday that you'd been taken unwell.' She sat in the seat recently vacated by the doctor, her face one of concern. She smoothed down her dark, plaid skirt and crossed her ankles.

'I suppose your uncle told you.'

'Of course. The explosion must have been terrifying. What a relief to hear no one was hurt. I can understand why you were so scared.'

Scared? It made him sound feeble, like he was a baby, startled by a noise.

'We all were. You never know what the consequences are going to be when there's an explosion.'

'No, I'm sure that's the case. But you were shaking.'

'It's just a—' How could he explain this? 'A consequence of all the explosions in the war. Get overwhelmed with them you do, in the trenches.'

'But Maurice Coombes and, and, Teilo Brice were in the war too. And others. Uncle John said those two were with you.'

'Well, we're all affected in different ways.' For Maurice, it seemed to have made him harder, constantly testy.

'So, you're having a rest today, your mother said.'

'That's right. Dr Roberts reckoned I should leave work until Monday.'

'That's convenient,' she said, clapping her hands lightly. 'Perhaps in that case we could get out a little earlier tomorrow, with not having to wait until you get back from work. I, of course, don't work on a Saturday. We could go to Merthyr early, maybe have a trip around the shops.'

Tomorrow. He'd quite forgotten about it. Henry panicked. For a start, he didn't think he'd be up to going anywhere just yet. Secondly, what did having a trip around the shops even mean? That he'd have to spend more money on her? Money he didn't have.

'I'm sorry, Amelia, but we're going to have to postpone our trip.'

'What!'

'Only for a few days, let's say a week, so it's next Saturday.'

'But will *Babes in the Wood* still be on at the Theatre Royal?'

He thought for a moment. 'I – I don't know. I'll have to check the newspaper.'

'But it's my birthday tomorrow.' She thumped her hands onto her lap. 'It's not like my mother will be here to do anything. In fact, would you believe it, she's gone away for a few days! I was *so* looking forward to our trip to Merthyr tomorrow too.' Her mouth fell into a severe frown.

Henry felt terrible. There he was, trying to impress her as much as he could, and all he'd done was disappoint her. All because of this dreadful weakness. He felt like punching himself for being such a fool.

'I'm so, so sorry, Amelia. Really, I am. I wouldn't want to hurt or upset you for the world. But we wouldn't have a good time if I'm feeling like this tomorrow.'

'Feeling like what? You're not shaking now, are you?'

'No, but I feel a little – anxious, I suppose.' It was the best way he could think to describe it without sounding utterly feeble. 'Like you do after a cold, or a fever, even though it's gone.'

'Really, Henry, the war has been over a year and a quarter. You can't let the fear of a bomb going off rule your life forever. It's time to pull yourself together. I am bitterly disappointed. I suppose I'll have to put up with it though.'

She sniffed a couple of times, then took a handkerchief from her handbag and dabbed at the corner of her eyes. This action completed Henry's shame. Look what his weakness had done to her.

He got up and knelt by her side. 'I'm so sorry, Amelia. I didn't want to upset you, quite the opposite. I'll tell you what, I'll get ready as quickly as I can next Saturday, and we can still have a walk around the shops.'

She rallied a little, pursing her lips into a circle. 'All right. I suppose that will have to do.'

He went to kiss her cheek, but she rose before he reached her. 'I have to go now. I promised Aunt Matilda I'd make supper tonight.'

'Oh, before you go, I must give you your present. You can at least open that tomorrow.' He'd be disappointed he wouldn't see her reaction, but it was better than her having nothing to look forward to from him on her birthday.

He fetched the present from the dresser, wrapped beautifully by the woman in the shop, and handed it to her proudly. She looked it over, top and bottom and side to side.

'How exciting. I'll look forward to opening it.'

He was about to ask if they could meet briefly in the week, but was pre-empted by her, 'Until next Saturday then.' She tucked the present beneath her arm, kissed her opposite hand and blew it towards Henry, before heading for the door. He went with her, but she was soon out of the front entrance ahead of him, waving as she walked down the street in the lamplight.

He leant against the door, watching her, until she turned the corner. He could only hope the expensive present would heal the disappointment.

–

Henry poked his head around Gwen's back door the following Thursday, dreading what he was about to do. He'd cleaned himself up first, and had some dinner, hoping that anyone who might have been at home might be out again by the time he got around here.

'Hello?' he called, before stepping into the scullery and pulling his cap off.

'In the kitchen,' called Gwen.

He went in to see her sitting at the table, sewing.

'Hello, Henry. How are you now?'

'Perfectly fine now, thanks. On your own?' he asked.

'I am. Tom's at an interview in Bargoed, Elizabeth's not long gone back to her field, and Gwilym's gone with her to help. I had that daft Polly here earlier, doing some work, but her shift is over, thank goodness.'

'Why do you always refer to her as "daft" Polly? She seems perfectly fine to me.'

'Yes, I'm sure she does to you men.' She raised her eyebrows. 'To what do I owe this visit? I'm going out when I've finished this hem, to take this lot to Violet's to be ironed. I've just completed a couple of orders for men missing limbs.'

'So word's getting round. That's good.' He took a deep breath, as if inhaling courage. 'I'm in a bit of a tight spot, just for a couple of days, like. We're being short-changed by the colliery at the moment, see, and with missing a day's money because of my – condition – I was wondering if I could borrow a bob or two off you, and pay it back in the next few weeks.'

'Henry, Tom is out of a job and the sewing business is in its early days. I can't afford to lend you money.'

'But you've got savings, haven't you, from an inheritance?'

'*Tom* has savings. And if he doesn't get a job soon, we'll be dipping more and more into them. Couldn't you ask Da?'

He rolled his cap in his fingers. 'I've, um, already borrowed a bit from him.'

'Why do you need it? You're living at home. It's not like you have many expenses.'

'I'm taking Amelia out on Saturday, for her birthday, and want to make it extra special like, after having to postpone it from last week.'

Gwen lifted her head, her eyebrows raised once more and her mouth screwed up to one side. 'What on earth are you planning for this birthday?'

'Just a nice meal and a theatre trip. But I've already bought a present, and, thought, well, I might treat her to something else while we're out.'

Gwen thumped down the jacket she was working on. 'She sounds mighty expensive, does Miss Amelia Bowen. Why does she need so much spending on her? I certainly don't expect that from Tom, even with his bit of inheritance, and I'm sure Elizabeth, Violet and Anwen never had such expensive treats from their husbands when they was courting.'

'She doesn't expect it…' even as he said this, he wondered, from her reaction, whether she did. 'You know I've long admired her, and I want to show her she means a lot to me.'

'It seems to me, Henry, that if she needs that amount of pampering to keep her interested, that she's not worth having in the first place.'

How could he explain that having displayed such weakness, he had to prove himself a worthy mate to her? Not being able to humiliate himself like that, not even to his sister, he resorted to, 'You just don't understand!'

'No, I don't. I don't understand why, if she's really interested in you, she needs such fripperies.'

'I'll leave you to it,' he said, slamming his cap back on and leaving the way he came.

He was running out of options of where to go to borrow money. He'd have to think of something quick.

-

By the end of work on Friday, Henry realised he had one option left, and even that was a long shot.

He managed to avoid walking back with Maurice, who in any case was in a hurry to get home and out somewhere. He ended up instead with Teilo Brice and Douglas Ramsay.

'I was wondering, lads,' he opened cautiously, as they started up Station Road, 'whether any of you would have any idea where to get a loan.' He didn't want to go into the whole birthday thing again, and have them criticising his judgement, or Amelia, so he said, 'I could do with getting myself smartened up, like.'

'Don't believe in borrowing money,' said Teilo. 'It can get you into all sorts of bother. *Neither a borrower nor a lender be.* That's my motto.'

'I had to borrow a bit of money to bury my Susan,' Douglas said in a quiet voice, staring ahead. 'Didn't want her ending up in an unmarked grave.'

'Where did you go?' Henry asked.

'Sioni Gower, him on Islwyn Street.'

'Maurice's brother-in-law?' said Henry.

'Aye, that's him. Had to be paid back with interest, of course. But the quicker you pay it back, the less interest you suffer.'

'Where does he get the money from to lend it?' said Teilo. 'No wonder Maurice hasn't any time for him. Sounds a bit dodgy to me.'

'I've no idea where he gets it,' said Douglas. 'But I suppose the more he lends, the more interest he gets, so the more he can lend. That's how it works, isn't it?'

'Don't think it's quite that simple,' said Henry. 'He must keep some for hisself, else there'd be no point, but anyway, thanks for telling me.'

'He doesn't like his missus knowing about it, so make sure you approach him away from his house.'

'There you go,' said Teilo. 'Told you it were dodgy.'

No time like the present, thought Henry. 'Look lads, I've got something to do, so I'll see you tomorrow. I'd appreciate it if you kept this to yourselves.'

They both agreed and he walked back towards the pit. They'd been among the first out and he hadn't noticed Sioni along the road, so he might be able to catch him.

He scoured the faces of the men but had no success. He was approaching the gate when he saw Sioni talking to John Bowen. He didn't want the undermanager knowing his business. He lingered a few yards away, lifting his hand in greeting to those he knew well.

'Coming to the Arms tonight?' asked James Floyd, one of the ex-Pals.

'Not tonight, James,' he said, keeping an eye on Sioni at the same time. He didn't want to lose the opportunity.

'Aw, go on, mun. A few of us Pals are going.'

'Got something else on, sorry.' He was eager for his friend to pass on.

'See you next time then.'

'Aye.' Henry was relieved when he walked away. He shook his head at James's reference to them as the Pals. There was no point thinking of themselves as that for evermore.

Sioni at last moved away from Bowen and headed off up the street, alone. Henry hurried to catch him up.

'Could I have a word, Sioni?'

'Better make it quick. Got places to go and people to see, after I gets my wash.'

'I'm told you do a bit of lending on the side.'

Sioni kept walking but twisted his head to look at him sharply. 'And who's been shooting their mouth off?'

'Is it true? Cos I could do with a bit of a loan like.'

'Could you now? Well, I'm always up for a bit of business. How much was you looking for?'

At last, thought Henry, this would surely solve his problem.

'Five pounds should do it.'

'Almost a week's wage, eh?' said Sioni. 'That'll be twenty per cent interest, paid back at six shillings a week.'

'Fair enough.'

Not that it was, but what choice did he have?

Chapter Fourteen

Henry stood by the table while the waiter pulled out a chair for Amelia. When she had sat down and made herself comfortable, he took his own seat.

He looked around at the fancy décor of Merthyr Tydfil's Central Hotel's restaurant. 'I hope this was worth waiting for. It is very elegant.'

'It is. I'm so glad I chose this dress to wear,' she said. 'The women here are so sophisticated.' She looked down at her attire, a high-waisted brown dress. The fabric was velveteen and satin, she'd told him when he'd admired it earlier.

'You always look sophisticated, Amelia. Some of these women couldn't hold a candle to you.'

She lifted one shoulder and giggled. 'Oh Henry, you say the nicest things.'

'And the perfume I bought smells wonderful on you.'

'Oh yes. The eau de cologne. Very nice.'

The waiter laid the menus on the table and left them for a while. Henry's breath caught when he noticed the prices. But at least this time he had enough money to cover it. Even if it meant heavy payments to Sioni Gower every week. With any luck, he'd have something left and he could pay back part of the loan quickly.

'My, there are some delicious sounding meals on here. I'm going to have a hard time picking something,' she said.

'Pick anything you want. For delaying your birthday treat it's the least I can do.'

She lowered the menu a little. 'Henry, I do apologise for getting cross when I came to your house. To be honest, I was a little under the weather myself.'

'Amelia, you should have said.' He put his hand briefly on hers. 'Are you better now?'

'Mostly. It was only a bit of a cold.'

Now she'd mentioned it, she did look a little paler than normal.

'Such a pity *Babes in the Wood* is no longer on though,' she said. 'I suppose this comedy thing will be entertaining though. Now, what shall I have for my hors d'oeuvres?'

Hors d'oeuvres. That would add to the bill. No point going without himself though, otherwise she'd be eating on her own and it would be awkward. No doubt she'd have dessert too. As the stress started to build, he brought his whirring mind to a halt. He had the money. He wasn't going to be embarrassed like last time. They'd bought the theatre tickets before they'd come to the restaurant – circle seats, at one shilling and five pence each – so he didn't need to worry about them. They hadn't had much time to peruse the shops, so no opportunity had arisen for him to buy her any extra presents. That was something at least.

'I think I've chosen,' she said. 'I'm going to have the smoked salmon hors d'oeuvres and then the roast saddle of mutton and red currant jelly, with some French beans.'

He looked at the menu. They were the two most expensive items on the appetisers and the main course lists. He was tempted to pick the two cheapest, since everything here was bound to be good, but what would that look like? Instead, he chose the third cheapest appetiser, the sardines, and the cheapest main course, the fish pie. Not that any of them were cheap.

It was then the waiter returned, and they ordered. Hopefully she wouldn't notice that he'd chosen the less expensive items.

'And what wine would sir and madam like to order?'

Henry felt the beads of sweat form around his fringe.

'Do you have a bottle of the Rioja?' she asked.

'Of course, madam. With two glasses?'

'Oh yes. I wouldn't be drinking it all on my own.' She chuckled.

'Very well, sir, madam,' said the waiter, making a note of it. With that, he lifted the menus and retreated.

'Have you ever tried Rioja, Henry?'

'No, I've never had wine at all.' He hoped it was wine she was referring to.

'You must simply try it! My stepfather had a bottle when I went to dinner with him and my mother. Wonderful!'

Henry patted his pocket, feeling the wallet in which sat the unfamiliar ten-shilling notes. There'd be enough, he was sure. He'd just have to face the fact that he wouldn't be paying off as much in his first instalment as he'd hoped.

–

Amelia had been quiet as they'd left the theatre that evening. He'd chatted about how he'd enjoyed *Three Bites*, hoping to illicit some enthusiasm from her.

Eventually, as they reached the foyer, she said, 'That was entertaining enough, I suppose. But it wasn't *Babes in the Wood*.'

Her brow creased and she looked rather peeved, adding to the guilt he already felt.

'Henry!' said a voice from across the foyer. Soon Elizabeth was walking purposefully towards them, Gwilym by her side. 'Hello, Amelia. We wondered whether we'd bump into you here. It was Gwen mentioning that you two were coming that informed us it was on. We do both like a comedy.'

Henry could only imagine the reason Gwen had mentioned it: to moan about him taking Amelia out.

'I wasn't sure about it, to be honest,' said Gwilym. 'But I enjoyed it. What about you two?'

'Yes, me too,' said Henry.

Amelia simply nodded and smiled.

'Are you off home now?' said Elizabeth. 'Or are you going on somewhere for refreshments?'

'We had dinner earlier,' said Amelia. 'At the Central Hotel on the Market Square. And lovely it was too.'

And expensive, thought Henry, but at least she was more enthusiastic about it than the show.

'We're heading for the train station now,' said Henry. 'We'd better get going as we have to change a coupla times. Are you heading that way?'

'No, we've brought the motorcar, so why don't we give you a lift home? Seems silly not to.'

'It's kind of you to offer,' Henry started, about to turn the offer down in his longing to have Amelia to himself for a while.

'Oh, that would be lovely,' said Amelia. 'It would be so much more convenient than catching three trains this time of night, especially as it's rather cold now.'

He could hardly contradict her, so Henry simply said, 'It is. Thank you, Elizabeth.'

'We're parked just over there.'

In the motorcar, Amelia stared out of the side window for most of the journey, turned away from him. He didn't want to go fumbling for her hand and risk touching her inappropriately. Or worse, risk her rejection. He felt a little woozy from the wine, of which he'd only managed a glass and a half. He'd not enjoyed the burning sensation on his tongue and in his stomach. Amelia had managed two glasses, resulting in half the bottle going to waste. But she'd enjoyed it, so that was the main thing.

Despite what Gwilym had said, the journey took a little longer than the train would have done, even with the two changes. Since they had to drive down Gabriel Street to get into the village, they stopped directly outside the Bowens's house.

Gwilym got out to open Amelia's door for her. Before she alighted, she said, 'Thank you for the lift home. It was so much better than going on the train.'

Henry said, 'Thank you, Elizabeth,' adding nothing about the convenience. Under any other circumstances, he'd have been grateful for the lift, but on this occasion he felt robbed of part of the pleasure of his evening out.

They both watched as the motorcar drove away.

'Thank you for a splendid birthday treat,' said Amelia, wrapping one end of the shawled collar of her coat around her neck.

He went towards her, in the hope of a kiss. She turned her head and allowed him to peck her cheek.

'When shall we go out next?' said Henry. 'Is there anything you'd particularly like to do?'

'I'll have to think about it. I'll let you know. Good night, Henry.'

'*Nos da*, Amelia.' He was about to turn away when he remembered something. 'The first of March, St David's Day.'

'I dare say I'll be around for some of the events,' she said.

'In the evening, there's a talk at the Workmen's Institute. "Captain Scott and the South Pole." I'm going along. Would you like to come to that? There'll be lantern slides too. It starts at eight o'clock.'

'Yes, why not. It might be interesting. I'll meet you outside then, at a quarter to eight. Good night.'

She went through the gate, then hurried down the path to the front door.

He would have liked to have seen her in between now and then. 'You should have suggested it then,' he scolded himself, shoving his hands in his coat pockets and heading home.

Chapter Fifteen

'Thank goodness for that!' said Tom, scanning the letter Gwen had passed him after she'd picked it up off the hall mat.

'Good news?' she asked, laying out the second-hand dress she was currently working on.

'I got the clerk's job, at *Y Newyddion* newspaper, in Bargoed.'

'Well done! Didn't you mention that the editor had made a point of saying he were keen to employ a disabled ex-soldier?'

He frowned. 'He did, though I hope that's not the only reason he picked me.'

'Of course not. You've got lots of skills to bring to the job.'

'It's a start, anyway, until I decide what I want to do long-term. And it gives us some money. Being without my wage for nearly a month is quite long enough. I don't want to dip too far into my inheritance. I'll write a letter now, to confirm I'll be there on Monday the eighth of March as requested. It'll be handy my parents being up the road too, in case I want to pop in and see them.'

He disappeared to the front room and fetched back a writing pad and fountain pen, then sat opposite her at the table. He opened the pad, then held it steady with his artificial hand while he wrote. He no longer fidgeted with the false hand when he did this, making her hopeful that he was at last getting used to it.

They worked in silence together like this, until the back door opened and closed, and Elizabeth called, '*Prynhawn da!*'

She looked into the kitchen. 'My, you are both busy little bees.'

'I got the job at *Y Newyddion* and am just replying.'

'That's wonderful, Tom! And such a relief for you. I've come to make the lunch, so the beef sausages will have to do for a celebration, along with my own potatoes, leeks and carrots, of course.'

'Sounds delicious,' said Tom.

–

When Gwilym had returned, had his bath and dressed, they sat down for lunch together, or dinner, as Gwilym still insisted on calling it.

'Well done again, Tom,' said Gwilym, lifting a forkful of sausage as a toast.

'Perhaps I could get hold of a bottle of red wine so we could have a proper celebration tonight,' said Tom. 'Now Mrs Brace has an off-licence to sell wine and beer.'

'We're out to that talk tonight,' Elizabeth reminded him. 'The one on "Captain Scott and the South Pole", at the Workmen's Institute.'

'Henry is apparently taking Amelia Bowen,' said Gwen, raising her eyes heavenward. 'I can't imagine it being her cup of tea.'

'You don't like her much, do you?' said Tom.

'Especially not since Henry seemed to think he had to spend so much on her birthday. And they went to the Central Hotel in Merthyr, for dinner. And Mam told me she overheard her making quite a fuss when she came to the house and found out Henry didn't feel well enough to take her out on her actual birthday. She seems quite spoiled to me.'

'I guess it's Henry's business,' said Tom. 'We didn't like anyone interfering in our relationships, now, did we?'

'I'm not interfering,' said Gwen. 'Just concerned.'

'I can understand your worry,' said Elizabeth. 'I suppose we can only hope things are better than they seem.'

Gwen nodded and smiled. What else could she say? If Henry was determined Amelia was the one, she could only hope things worked out better than she had an inkling they would.

–

'This should be good,' said Henry as he and Amelia took their seats in the sixth row of the stalls in the Workmen's Institute lecture theatre. He'd been inordinately pleased to have found some so near the front.

Next to him he found Idris and Anwen.

'Well hello, Henry,' said Idris. 'So you fancied finding out about Captain Scott too. I especially liked the idea of the lantern slides.'

'We're looking forward to it, aren't we, Amelia?'

She turned from where she'd been looking, across to the left, where people were coming in. 'Hm? Sorry? Oh yes, of course. Fascinating.'

He realised then that Esther Williams was in the seat in front of him. He wondered if she still harboured resentment against his sister, for marrying Tom, not her Daniel. Gwen seemed to think she might.

'Look, there's your sister,' said Amelia, indicating behind them.

She was with Tom, Elizabeth and Gwilym. They'd had to take seats much further back on the stalls, which made him feel a little smug after his argument with his sister.

Amelia put her hand up to her mouth, stifling a yawn. 'I'm so sorry, do excuse me. It's been a busy day.'

'The talk should wake you up. More than eight years ago now it happened, Scott and the Antarctic. I can't imagine going somewhere so – hostile, so alien. The South Pole must be amazing to see though, don't you think?'

She gave a little shiver. 'Freezing cold, more like. No thank you. Give me a day out at Swansea any day.'

Was that a hint? 'When the weather's a little warmer, maybe we could take a trip there.'

'Maybe we could,' she said, treating Henry to an indulgent grin.

Only a couple of months until the weather got summery. It would give him time to save up a bit. And maybe he'd have finished paying off Sioni Gower by then.

He noticed a couple from the battalion up ahead: Teilo Brice with his wife and Alun Lloyd from the farm, with his sister, Nora. It was good they were out and about. And there was Maurice Coombes, on his own by the looks of it.

Five minutes later, someone came onto stage and announced, 'Ladies and gentlemen, we are pleased to introduce you to Dr Rupert Price, clergyman and naturalist, and an expert on the subject of Captain Scott and the South Pole.'

There was a hearty round of applause while onto the stage came a balding middle-aged man with silvery hair, dressed in black with a dog collar. He waited for the applause to stop before he started on his subject. Henry sat up a bit straighter, leaning forward to take it all in.

He glanced at Amelia every now and again, whose eyes were fixed on the stage. A bit later, he took another peek at her, but this time she seemed to be looking to one side of the stage, or maybe to the seats in front. Was she bored already?

A few minutes after, he noticed her yawn, then glance at her wristwatch. A gloom settled on him. What could he do? Maybe engage her attention, so she'd see he was more interested in being here with her than in the actual talk.

He slid his left hand over to where her right one was settled on her lap, attempting to take it in his. Immediately she shifted it, putting that arm around her waist. She didn't look at him, but at least she was concentrating on the talk once more. How very clumsy of him, to grope for her hand in public like that. He always seemed to do the wrong thing.

Dr Price wound up the first half of the talk, telling the audience what he'd be covering in the second half, during which one of the doors opened with a clatter. A figure stormed in. It was hard to see who it was in the semi-darkness. Although the speaker hadn't finished, the lights on stage revealed John Bowen taking the steps up, much to the surprise of Dr Price.

'Sorry to interrupt your little gathering,' said John, marching to the middle of the stage, 'but this does give me the opportunity to address a whole lot of you.'

'Excuse me, sir,' said the man who'd introduced Dr Price, entering the stage from the back, 'but we're in the middle of a lecture, if you don't mind.'

'I just heard this fellow here say it were break time, so I'm not interrupting nothing. Now look here, you lot.' He pointed a menacing finger at the audience. 'Had a robbery, I have, at my house. Money's been taken, see, and I'm telling you that if anyone here knows anything about the thieving swine, or swines, you'd better tell the police, see. Or even better, tell me. I'll sort the buggers out.'

Beside him, Amelia sighed dramatically. Henry guessed she was finding this embarrassing.

Sergeant Harries, who'd been sitting in the front row in a suit, stood up. 'Mr Bowen, that's enough of that now. You should have come to me before flying off the handle and spoiling the talk.'

'I did,' said Bowen. 'Knocked on your door, I did, but your neighbour said you was here, so I've come here to tell you.'

'You're still making a nuisance of yourself,' said the sergeant. 'And if you don't get off that stage now, and get home, I'll be arresting *you* for disturbance of the peace, never mind these so-called thieves.'

Bowen wasn't taking the hint. 'No sign of a break-in there weren't, so it's someone handy with picking locks I reckon. But there'd been a few bits of furniture thrown round, as if they was looking for the money. Must have happened when we was out of the house earlier.'

'Did you know about this?' Henry whispered to Amelia.

'Yes. We arrived home around the same time, and found some disarray, before discovering that money was missing. Aunt Matilda was visiting her mother in Bute Town, luckily. I don't know why he has to make such a public fuss.'

'You didn't say anything about the break-in when we met this evening.'

'I just wanted to forget it.'

'Go home now, Mr Bowen,' said the sergeant. 'I'll come round after the performance has finished and have a look, for there's nothing I can do any different if I come immediate like.'

'Make sure you do,' said Bowen. With that, he marched back off the stage and towards the exit.

Already there was murmured chatter. Amelia stood and whispered, 'I'd better go. I don't want to leave poor Aunt Matilda on her own to deal with that.'

'I'll see you back then,' he said, although disappointed to miss the second half of the lecture.

'No, you won't. I'm not spoiling this for you. I'll see you soon.' She made her way along the row, apologising as people moved their knees or stood for her. At the aisle she rushed down. A couple of other people left the hall, whether from not enjoying the talk or leaving early for the break.

He was tempted to get up and follow her, but what would be the point if she was catching Bowen up?

'Excuse me, ladies and gentlemen,' said Dr Price, 'I'm so sorry about the interruption. We'll take our break for fifteen minutes now, and I'll tell you what's coming up when we return. Thank you.' He took a slight bow and left the stage at the back.

'Well, that were unnecessary of Bowen,' said Idris. 'Sorry, Miss Bowen, I know he's your uncle—' He looked around Henry. 'Oh, where has she gone?'

'A bit worried about her Aunt Matilda, she were, with him in a mood.'

'Why, would he do something to her?' Anwen's eyes widened in alarm.

'No, no, just because it's difficult coping with someone in a temper, I suppose.' He'd thought the same but didn't want it going around that he'd said Bowen might abuse his wife. Especially with a gossip like Esther Williams in earshot. He wished now he'd kept his trap shut.

'You don't think it could have been Reg or Iolo, do you, what stole the money?' said Idris pointedly, staring at Esther's back. 'There's been a couple of incidences since they returned. And what with Reg doing the rounds of the village.'

Esther turned around from her seat in front. 'I know that were said loud for my benefit, Idris Hughes, but Reg and Iolo are staying in a guesthouse in Usk overnight. They left this morning. They're visiting…' She glanced at Anwen.

'My father in gaol?' she said.

'And my husband, Edgar. That's what they said at breakfast. All trying to get their lives in order now, so I dunno why you have to keep picking on them.' She turned back, her nose in the air.

'That sounds like it could lead to a whole heap of trouble,' Idris murmured.

Henry could only agree. And Sioni seemed to be quite pally with them. Probably had nothing to do with anything. Perhaps he'd lent them money too, so they could buy the equipment for their jobs? That reminded him: come Friday, he'd have to pay off a bit more of his loan, not only to Sioni, but to his da. He should have enough to take Amelia out somewhere not too expensive. A walk on the hills would cost nothing. And maybe tea somewhere cheap, but nice. He'd have to give it some thought.

–

Polly wasn't sorry to be leaving her work at the public house that evening, even though it had been less busy, what with the Institute having a talk on. It made it rather boring, standing around, waiting for orders to be given.

She'd have liked to have gone to the talk herself, to see the lantern slides of the South Pole, but even if she hadn't been working this evening, she'd still have had to rely on her parents to look after Herby.

Coming out of a door that brought her out almost opposite the gate of the gardens on Jubilee Green, she noticed three figures hanging around there, under the light of the streetlamp. Smoke rose up from them, as they each held a cigarette. It was Reg and Iolo, along with Sioni. Luckily there wasn't a streetlamp directly above her here. If she crept along quietly, they might not notice her. Once she got to the road and crossed over, she could get to her own side of the street and run down to her house.

She'd only gone a few steps when Sioni called over, 'Hey, what's wrong with saying hello then?'

He started to cross the street, throwing the spent cigarette onto the ground. Her heart thumped as she considered what to do. It was too far to her home. She turned back quickly and rushed back into the door of the public house.

As she shut the door behind her, making sure it was locked, Nerys came out of the door to the saloon bar.

'What on earth's wrong with you, Polly? You look like you've seen a ghost.'

She didn't want to admit she was frightened of her brother-in-law. 'Reg and Iolo are outside, hanging around by the gardens.'

'They do that quite a lot. Just trying to frighten me, they are. Well, it won't work. I'll get Steven to walk you home. They won't dare try nothing, the size of him.'

She went through the door she'd just come out of and brought Steven back from the bar. He was tall and broad-shouldered, so Nerys had a point.

'I'll get my jacket,' said Steven, looking cross.

'I'm sorry to put you out,' said Polly.

'Oh it's not you what's putting me out, *fach*, it's them two maniacs, always trying to intimidate us all. Come on now.'

As the door opened, and Polly stepped out once again, Sioni straightened himself and went to cross the road once more. He was halted by Steven coming out behind her, quickly returning to his position.

As Polly and Steven set off, Reg called over, 'A bit young for you, isn't she?'

Steven ignored him and they kept on walking.

After they'd put a little distance between them, Polly said, 'I'm sorry about that, Steven.'

'Not your fault, *fach*. And I'm used to Reg's tongue. I'm not afraid of him. I do wonder why your Sioni is hanging around with them though.'

This was awkward. 'I've heard him say he's sympathetic with them and reckons they should be given a chance.'

'Oh aye,' Steven laughed. 'That'd be fair enough if they'd reformed at all, but they clearly haven't. If anything, they're worse than ever. I'd advise Sioni to keep away from them if I were you. He wouldn't have let them hurt you, would he?'

He'd have been the one doing the hurting. 'I've no idea, Steven. And I wouldn't assume to tell Sioni nothing.'

'He does come over a bit cocky like, when he's in the Arms.'

They reached Polly's front door, and she thanked him. 'Will you be all right, going back on your own?'

'Don't worry about me. If they try it on, I'll give 'em what for. See you tomorrow evening.'

'Yes, bye, Steven, and thanks.'

She watched as he walked away, still worried that Reg and the others might try something. As she stared down the road, she noticed a few people walking past the end of the street. The Institute talk must have finished. Good. There'd be other people around when Steven got back to the Arms. She let herself into her front door, satisfied he'd be all right.

–

It was over a week before Henry was able to arrange anything with Amelia again. Always she had other things to do of an evening, seeing a friend, preparing some work or helping Aunt Matilda. By the time Saturday came, the day they'd settled on, he was desperate to see her.

In his bedroom, he straightened his tie once again and re-combed his hair. He'd made sure to wash himself properly after finishing his shift; he didn't want to miss a smudge of coal. He wished he could afford some of the men's cologne he'd seen advertised in the newspapers. Perhaps when he'd paid off the loans.

He shoved his hand in his pocket and pulled out the coins. Yes, definitely enough for afternoon tea, whatever Amelia might choose. It would be another week of evenings in for him though.

Downstairs he finished off his cup of cold tea from earlier.

'Where are you taking Amelia today?' said Albert.

'To the Perilli Brothers Refreshment House.'

'Very nice,' said Ruth, though she had a slight air of disapproval. 'She'd be welcome to come to tea here one day, you know. She's only been the once, and it were a short visit. I can make decent scones and cake, and I've homemade apple and bramble jelly.'

'A very good baker you are, Mam. I will bring her soon, I promise.'

It would save him a bit of money, though it was nice to have her to himself.

'You look very smart, son.'

'Thank you, Mam.' He checked the carriage clock on the dresser. 'I'd better get going.'

'Good luck,' said Albert.

Amelia was waiting for him when he reached her house on Gabriel Street. Would she allow a peck on the cheek today, as she sometimes did? He bent forward to test the waters, and she turned her cheek to allow him to kiss her. That was a good start.

'Shall we get going on our walk to Rhymney then?' he asked. 'We're lucky with the sunshine.'

'Walk to Rhymney? No, we'd better catch the bus at five past three, otherwise we'll get to Perilli's far too late and won't have time to enjoy ourselves.'

'You're right. Come on, then.' He bent his arm, hoping she'd accept the invitation to link hers through it. She did. The day was getting better and better.

They walked to the end of Mafeking Terrace, where a new motorbus stop had been placed recently. It wasn't long before the single decker motorbus came trundling along the road, on its route from Tredegar to Rhymney and beyond. When it ground to a halt, Henry helped her up the two steps before following on. They sat at the back, Amelia next to the window.

Henry hadn't factored in the bus fare, but he was sure he had more than he required, so wasn't worried when the conductor came to collect the money.

In Rhymney, they got off in the high street, just outside the Imperial Cinema. Amelia went immediately to look at the posters for the films they were showing. Could he afford the picture house later as well?

'Aunt Matilda wants to go to the pictures next week and I said I'd go with her,' she said, 'So I wondered what was on.'

She took his arm once more. She did seem to be warming to him romantically today. The thought excited him, putting a smile on his face.

'You look happy,' she said.

'I always am in your company, Amelia.'

She gave a little chuckle. 'How sweet of you.'

'Has your uncle had any luck finding out who stole his money?'

'No, and Sergeant Harries hasn't been much help either. Said he couldn't find any evidence in the house to help discover the guilty party.'

'It does seem strange that they was able to get in without breaking the locks. Did they break anything, looking around.'

'No, just messed it up a bit. I'd like to know who it was: I'd give them a piece of my mind. Yet at the same time…' She held onto his arm more tightly. He waited for her to go on. 'I do feel vulnerable in the house now, in case someone breaks in again when I'm alone.'

'If they've had all the money, I doubt they'll come back. I wish I could be there to protect you, all the same.'

'Thank you for that thought, Henry.'

His mind raced ahead to a time when he might be in a position to protect her, should they be in the same house… married. If she kept up this affection, he might be able to propose soon. But how would he afford it? He'd pay off his debts first. She was earning as well, so there'd be two incomes to pay for a home. They could even live with his parents for a while. *Or you could live at her uncle's.* He shuddered. No, not that.

'What's wrong now,' said Amelia, slipping her arm out of his and stopping. The smile had disappeared. 'Are you starting that shaking again?'

'No, just a bit of a cold breeze going through me, I think.'

'I didn't feel it. I thought it was mild for March.'

'Maybe it were one of those feelings like someone's walking over your grave then, as they say.'

'Oh dear.' They carried on walking, but she didn't place her arm back through his.

Never mind; whatever he'd said wrong, he had the rest of the afternoon to make it up to her.

Chapter Sixteen

Gwen had been up late the night before, after getting home from the theatre, cutting out the pieces for Anabel Thomas's dress on the kitchen table. Getting a commission from the pastor's wife had been a huge lift for their business. With any luck, she'd like the dress enough to tell other people about it and get them more work.

The downside of staying up so late was that she'd almost fallen asleep in Pastor Thomas's sermon and had yawned behind her hands a few times. The service had now finished, and people were starting to rise and move around.

Anwen and Violet came over to speak to her.

'No Tom again?' asked Violet, looking around.

'No. He's adamant that he can't believe in a God what would allow such a terrible war.'

'He should have a conversation with Pastor Thomas,' said Anwen. 'He's clearly put together a few thoughts on that.'

'It might turn into an argument though.' Gwen was sad that Tom had turned away from his faith, but nothing she'd said had persuaded him to come with her.

'I've finished that laundry and ironing you gave me,' said Violet. 'It's hanging on the rail in my front room.'

'We'll have a look at it tomorrow,' said Gwen. 'Shall we go to the other room? Elizabeth's already gone, and I want to see if Mrs Thomas has baked any of her lovely biscuits again.'

They walked in a line through the diminished congregation. In the side room, they spotted Elizabeth chatting to Anabel, who was pouring tea into a second cup.

'We've come to see if there are any homemade biscuits,' said Gwen.

'At the other end,' said Anabel, pointing her petite hand towards them. 'It's so nice to be able to provide such treats now.'

'Huh,' said Florrie Harris, approaching the table. 'Just encouraging gluttony, that is. And *that's* one of them Seven Deadly Sins in the Bible.'

'Actually, they're not mentioned in the Bible, Mrs Harris,' said Elizabeth. 'They're originally of pre-Christian Greek origin.'

'Pride's another one of the seven,' said Florrie. 'And showing off your education comes under that.'

Elizabeth turned away, shaking her head slightly.

'While Mrs Owen is correct in what she says,' said Anabel, 'gluttony is, of course, frowned upon in the church. However, I do not think our Lord would object to us enjoying a few biscuits, Mrs Harris. Did he not provide wine from water, which is surely a treat and not a necessity?'

'Hm! Perhaps these young women should concentrate on turning out a nice bit of sewing, instead of lazing around eating biscuits.'

'What *do* you mean?' said Anwen.

'I've heard tell that the needlework from your business is somewhat shoddy.'

'I can assure you it isn't!' said Gwen, rather loudly, engaging the curiosity of those around them. 'Who on earth has told you that?'

'It's not my place to say.' She folded her hands under her bust and pursed her lips.

'Then you'd have done well not to say anything at all,' said Gwen. 'If someone has a problem with work we've done for them, they should come and see us.'

'One of the ten commandments states that one shouldn't bear false witness,' said Anabel. 'And even if it's true, the good Lord does not hold with tittle-tattle. Have you even seen the garments in question, to know whether they are, as you say, shoddy?'

'Well, no. But I have no reason to believe the person would lie.' Florrie's stance suggested she refused to be swayed by Anabel's words.

'I've had some alterations done to William's clothes to accommodate his missing leg,' said Joan Griffin, coming forward, 'and there were nothing shoddy about them. Lovely bits of work they was.'

'And I bought a nice second-hand blouse off them, what was updated to the latest fashion,' said another woman. 'Nothing wrong with that whatsoever.'

Gwen was touched that people had jumped to their defence. But there would still be plenty willing to believe the gossip.

'Well, that's what I've heard,' said Florrie, not about to withdraw her allegations.

'I have every confidence they will deliver me an excellent garment,' said Anabel.

'I hope you're right,' was Florrie's only concession before she walked away.

'Here, have some tea to calm you down.' Anabel passed cups to Gwen and the others. 'Don't worry about Mrs Harris; she's a well-known gossip so no one will believe her.'

They collected a biscuit each and moved away from the table to drink their tea.

'I'd like to know who the devil has been saying such things,' said Gwen.

'Someone what's jealous of our success?' said Anwen.

'Amelia Bowen, maybe?'

'She could have carried on the business, surely,' said Anwen. 'If she'd wanted to, despite what her mother said. She doesn't do any private sewing now, only the schoolwork.'

'It's probably not worth guessing, for that makes us as bad as—' Elizabeth started.

'What about Jenny Roberts?' Gwen interrupted, spotting her looking over at them. She was standing with Mabel

Coombes, but also Polly. Now why would Polly be keeping her company?

'Because of the letters?' asked Violet. 'Surely she wouldn't be so daft, as she'd be an obvious culprit.'

'Exactly! She's the most obvious suspect I can see.' Gwen marched off towards her.

'Gwen, wait a minute,' Anwen called, but she wasn't in the mood to comply.

Marching up to Jenny, she didn't hesitate before saying, 'Is it you again, causing trouble?'

'Wh-what?' said Jenny, taking a step back. 'No, course not. I wouldn't tell people your work was shoddy. I've never even had anything made by you.'

'That wouldn't stop you.'

Anwen's, 'Gwen, don't you think—' clashed with Ruth's, 'What's all this about?' as she marched over to the group.

Now they had everyone's attention in the room.

Ruth continued with, 'I've just heard about the accusation that Florrie Harris did make.'

'It's all right, Mam, I can handle it.' Gwen didn't want her mother sticking her nose in like she was a little girl who couldn't handle her own affairs. 'Anwen, what I think is that it's too much of a coincidence, what with those letters, and now this gossip.'

'Jenny Richards were sending the letters?' said Ruth, surprised.

'Gwen, that doesn't mean she has anything to do with this,' said Elizabeth. She added in an undertone, 'And it's maybe better to keep that to ourselves.'

Gwen realised she meant in case people somehow linked Jenny's child to the letters, but she thought that highly unlikely. She turned her attention to Polly. 'And what are you doing with Jenny? Have you hatched this together so you can start your own sewing business?'

'Now wait one moment,' said Mabel, crossing her arms, her expression screwed up in annoyance. It was unusual for her, who normally kept out of arguments and had the mildest of tempers. Gwen had worked with her at the munitions, and she'd never known even a slightly cross word pass her lips. 'Jenny is a friend and Polly is my sister-in-law, so why shouldn't they be seen together?'

'Well, your *friend*,' said Gwen, moving her finger to point at Jenny, 'sent me some very nasty letters, and now with these libellous rumours…'

'Slanderous,' Elizabeth corrected.

'What? I don't care what they're called!' She'd had enough of this. Why weren't her friends supporting her? 'I said I'd let them go and not report it to the police, but now the nasty little gossip—'

'It weren't me!' Jenny shouted, before running off towards the chapel.

'That proves her guilt,' said Gwen.

'No it doesn't,' said Elizabeth.

'I'm afraid I agree,' said Anwen. 'There's plenty what would start nasty rumours.'

'Or who would send letters,' Elizabeth added pointedly.

'Like Florrie herself,' said Mabel.

What did Elizabeth mean? They already knew Jenny had sent the letters. Gwen was about to tackle her on this but was interrupted.

'If you don't mind me saying,' said Mabel, 'you're not going to encourage people to come to you for sewing if you go around accusing folks of all sorts.'

Gwen ignored Mabel, turning to Polly. 'And what do you know about it?'

'Nothing. The first I knew of it were hearing Mrs Harris's accusation.'

'I've a good mind to—' she started, wagging her finger. It was tempting to give Polly her marching orders. That would solve another problem too.

'What's all this I've been hearing?' said Myfanwy Priddy as she shuffled her ample body into the side room. 'My niece has just gone running off in tears, and now I'm told you've been accusing her of all sorts. Where's your proof of these letters, and of her running your business down?'

'I'm sorry, Mrs Priddy, it was all a misunderstanding,' said Elizabeth, standing in front of Gwen. 'Things are getting mixed up. Someone said Jenny might know something, but clearly she doesn't.'

Gwen felt the fury rising. Why did Elizabeth feel she had the right to take over? It wasn't even her business! And where was Sergeant Harries when you needed him?

'Then there should be an apology given to Jenny for upsetting her,' said Myfanwy. 'Not nice, that's not.' She pointed at Gwen. 'You're as bad as that Esther Williams used to be.' With this, she trundled off.

'Come on, let's get out of here,' said Anwen, almost pushing Gwen through a side door. It brought them out on the small road that went up between Gabriel Street and Islwyn Street.

'Stop shoving, will you?'

Elizabeth and Violet followed them out into the weak sunshine.

'It's a good job Tom's not here,' Gwen snapped. 'With you all interrupting me and pushing me around.'

'If he were,' said Elizabeth, 'I hope he'd make you see sense.'

'See sense! What do you mean?' She came to a halt on the pavement.

'You're not helping the situation,' said Anwen. 'All you've done is make Florrie's accusation more obvious and people will be wondering why you're bullying Jenny.'

'We can't be sure she had anything to do with the rumour,' said Violet.

'And also,' said Elizabeth, hesitating as she looked around, 'you know she has something on our family, and if we push her too far, she might just tell people. Which is a point, because if she wanted to make trouble, all she'd have to do is reveal her little secret.'

'That would make *her* look bad too,' said Gwen.

'Would it? The poor young maid taken advantage of by the master, then married off to someone else. And my father is no longer here to take the brunt of that revelation, so it would be the rest of the family who'd no doubt suffer. And maybe your business too.'

Gwen tried to calm herself, taking several slow breaths. Things had got out of hand rather quickly. She'd maybe gone too far, annoyed as she was at the slur on their skills. 'If it isn't Jenny, someone's got it in for us. Maybe Polly were taking advantage of the assumption we'd blame Jenny and being friends with her is just to cover her tracks.'

'I think you've been reading too many Sherlock Holmes novels,' said Elizabeth. 'We're not dealing with criminal masterminds here. There are others who sew for a living who might have wanted to take advantage of Mrs Bowen's departure to build their businesses.'

'Polly needs her job with us, so it doesn't make sense that she'd try to ruin us,' said Anwen. 'Esther Williams would be a better candidate. And she worked a bit for Mrs Bowen but didn't get any work from us.'

'It certainly needs looking into more deeply,' said Violet.

'Let's find Gwilym and get home,' said Elizabeth.

Gwen nodded slowly.

'And we'd better get back to our husbands and children,' said Violet, taking Anwen's arm.

When they'd gone, Elizabeth said to Gwen, 'I'll fetch Gwilym if you want to wait here. We want to go across to the field first, to pick some carrots.'

'You do that,' said Gwen, in the mood to be alone for a while, 'I'll see you back home.'

She set off even before she'd finished the sentence.

-

'I wonder what all that noise from the side room is,' said Amelia, placing her cup on its saucer and leaning up to see over someone's head into the room where they served tea. 'Looks like your sister is having a row with someone.' She tutted.

'Excuse me a moment.'

Henry went to have a look through the door but was soon back. He gathered Gwen had a problem with Jenny Richards, or maybe Polly Coombes, something about letters and rumours, but he'd no idea beyond that.

'Just a lively discussion, I think,' he said when he returned, playing it down. He didn't want her to think his family was one for public brawls. What on earth was wrong with Gwen these days? He'd have thought she'd have been content, having married the man she loved, after the trouble they went through to be together.

'Didn't sound like a lively discussion to me.'

'I'm sure whatever it is they'll sort it out. I was thinking, we're lucky it's a sunny day, even a bit warm, considering it's only the middle of March. Where shall we have that walk today?'

Seeing Amelia two days in a row was a rare treat. The tea at Perilli's had been lovely, but at least with going for a walk today they'd have an opportunity to be on their own. Perhaps, just perhaps, she'd let him kiss her properly?

'How about going along the stream, and up into the hills. I haven't walked there in a while.'

Could it be she relished the idea of being alone with him too? 'Yes, let's do that,' he eagerly agreed.

A group of the Pals were huddled in the corner, keeping their own company as usual. Only Maurice looked out from their small club, peering at him and Amelia. Henry hoped he didn't come over and make one of his smart remarks again.

Amelia drained her cup and handed it to Henry. 'Do you mind returning this to the tea table for me? I told Aunt Matilda I wouldn't be late for luncheon.'

'Of course.' He balanced her cup and saucer on his.

'And the quicker I get home, the more likely I'll meet you on time. I'll see you at three thirty, by the bridge.'

'I'll look forward to it. I'd better get Mam and Da home now.'

Amelia put her hand to her mouth and emitted a slight cough. 'I'm so sorry, how rude of me.' She unclipped her handbag and took out a handkerchief, before producing another small cough.

'Are you all right, Amelia?'

She cleared her throat delicately. 'Yes. Just the end of a winter cold, I think. I'll see you later.' She gave him a broad smile, then looked over to the huddle of old Pals and raised her eyebrows as she walked away. It wasn't only him that thought it strange then.

About to take the cups to the other room, he was called over by Maurice. Henry wasn't in the mood for hiding himself away with them, so buoyant was his mood at the thought of having Amelia to himself later. He'd greet them quickly and move on.

'You haven't bothered speaking to us today,' said Maurice. 'Not good enough for you now, are we?'

'I wanted to spend time with Amelia,' said Henry.

'You're seeing her this afternoon for a walk, so you could have spared a little time for us.'

He considered them there, the ones who came to chapel. A gloomy looking lot. Like the rest of them that weren't here because they went to another place of worship. Or to no place of worship at all.

'Now listen, lads, I do need to get rid of these cups and find my parents.'

'Aye, you do that,' said Maurice. 'Excuse me, I've got to be somewhere else now.' He rushed towards the doors and left.

Teilo scratched his head. 'He's a card, isn't he? Says you should talk to us, then runs off somewhere hisself. He's been a lot like that recently, distracted like. And there's Mabel. Wonder if she's looking for him.'

She was squinting around the crowd as if trying to locate someone.

Henry couldn't be bothered with this. 'I've gotta go. I'll see you another time, lads.'

He didn't want to be late this afternoon. Maurice had a cheek, listening in on his conversation with Amelia, for how else had he known about their walk out?

How much had he heard? Where they were heading? He'd better not turn up and spoil it, otherwise he'd have a few words to say.

–

All through Sunday dinner, Polly had fretted about Jenny, hoping she hadn't taken Gwen's words too much to heart. She didn't like to put on her parents too much, particularly her mother, who bore the brunt of Herby's care while she worked, but perhaps if she explained a little, they wouldn't mind.

As she cleared the plates after the main course, Polly said, 'I need to go out for a bit. Would you mind looking after Herby for an hour or so?'

'Course not, love,' said Jim. 'What's so urgent though?'

'A friend of mine got upset at chapel this morning, and I want to make sure she's all right.'

'Who's that then?' Delia asked.

'Jenny Richards, what was married to the old pastor's son.'

'Oh yes. Poor girl, to be left wiv a baby,' said Delia. 'I didn't know you was friends.'

'Herby and her Freddie are only five months apart in age, so it's nice to have them play together.'

'That's kind of you, to make sure she's all right,' said Jim. 'And it's good you're makin' friends again, after Gus.'

'Yes,' she said, while considering how many in the village still ignored her.

'Don't you want your bread and butter puddin' first?' Delia asked.

'No, I'm stuffed. I'll have it when I get back.'

She kissed Herby's head. He was still eating his vegetables. 'Mummy's going out for a while. I'll play Snap with you when I get back.'

'Awright Mummy,' he said, his mouth half full.

–

Reaching the end of James Street, about to turn onto Station Road, Polly spotted her brother on his own, crossing from the bookshop to the pavement running past the bottom of the gardens on Jubilee Green.

'Where are you off to, Maurice?' she called.

He swung around, his expression like that of someone caught doing something they shouldn't be.

'Can't a man have a walk? It's good to be on your own sometimes.' It was said in a disgruntled tone. 'Mabel's always yapping about stuff I couldn't care less about, and Lily chatters on about that nonsense world of hers. I need a bitta peace. Are you following me?' He stuck his head out towards her.

'Don't be daft. I'm going to see a friend. Oh Lord, what's he doing now? And on a Sunday.'

Up Gabriel Road ahead, Reg drew up in his horse and cart and stopped outside the school.

'Probably picking up some rubbish,' said Maurice. 'He is allowed to do that.'

'As long as that *is* what he's doing. There's been talk of Reg and Iolo being responsible for that robbery at the Bowens'.' She pointed in the direction of Amelia's house just past the school.

Maurice reached the opposite pavement. 'That's what 'appens when you're stupid enough to keep savings in an obvious place. Mabel was doin' that, silly mare, in a biscuit tin on the dresser. I've stowed it away much more safely.'

'You're right, it's not sensible to leave a lot of cash around.' Not that she ever had enough to worry about.

'You get on with your visit now, I'm heading up 'ere.'

He carried on towards Gabriel Street, without a farewell. Polly tutted and shook her head. He'd never been the politest of men, but he had been an optimistic one. The war had changed him. Hopefully, in time, he'd settle down once more.

–

When Jenny answered her door at number one Station Road, Polly said, 'I'm so sorry about what happened earlier. I've come to make sure you're all right.'

'Thank you, that's most kind. Come in.' She led her to the kitchen and invited her to sit by the range. 'Aunty Myfanwy's in the garden, showing Freddie how to plant seeds. He loves helping her.'

'It's good they get on so well.'

'I told Aunty about the letters earlier. I thought, better coming from me than someone what overheard it at chapel and got the wrong idea – or the right one. Aunty was disappointed but put it down to young mother's melancholia, as she called it. Reckoned my mother suffered from it too. Maybe she's right, though it's been a while since I had Freddie. I told her I'd apologised. She said at least I'd learned my lesson and I was usually a good girl and that we all make mistakes. If only she knew! I think she still sees me as little Jenny in a pinafore, skipping in the garden.'

'She doesn't know who Freddie's real father is then?'

'Goodness, no.'

'At least she didn't throw you out, as you feared,' said Polly.

'No. I think she's rather fond of me and Freddie, not having children herself. Her fiancé died of typhoid in 1889.'

'How awful for her.'

'I only hope what Gwen said doesn't get me the sack from the grocer's.'

'Miss Elizabeth seemed to be trying to play the letters down, saying it was a mix-up, so hopefully that's what people will think.'

'If we keep our ears open, we might find out who's spreading the malicious gossip,' said Jenny. 'It's not good for you neither, what she said. You don't want them sacking you.'

'Anwen seems to be on my side, and Violet, so I'm hoping it won't come to that. I'll leave you to your Sunday rest, now I know you're all right.'

They both rose.

'Thank you again, Polly. I feel blessed to have a friend what cares.'

'I'll see myself out.'

On the street once more, Polly was relieved to see that Reg had moved further along and that her brother was nowhere to be seen.

-

Henry glanced at his wristwatch for the fourth time since he'd arrived. Quarter to four. Amelia was fifteen minutes late when normally punctual. He'd wait another five minutes before deciding what to do.

Only two minutes had gone by before he decided to go to her house. He only hoped John Bowen hadn't taken it upon himself to ban her from seeing him, especially after Twm Bach's comment about him being a useless undermanager. Damn him. If that had in any way ruined his chances with Amelia…

He arrived at her gate, swinging it open before he could think better of it. He promptly knocked on the door. It was a while before he heard it being unlocked, like someone was pulling back a bolt on the front door. Really? Most houses in the village had their front and back doors unlocked in the daytime, especially on a Sunday, and they certainly didn't bother with bolts. It must have been installed after the robbery.

When the door opened, Matilda Bowen stood there, looking grim. Was she about to send him away with a flea in his ear?

'Can I help you?' she said.

This was awkward – and a rather strange way to address your niece's suitor. It was almost as if she didn't know about him.

'I was supposed to be meeting Amelia at three thirty, by the bridge, but she hasn't turned up. I was wondering, is she still at home?'

Matilda closed the door a little, hiding slightly behind it. 'Amelia is not well.'

'She were only at church a couple of hours ago. Is it the cough?'

'Yes, yes, that's right. She won't be going out with you today.'

'It must have got worse then. I do hope there's not another round of influenza on its way…'

'It's a cold, and I'm sure she'll get better quicker if she's not bothered.'

She made it sound like he was pestering her. 'Of course. Would you tell her I called, please? And ask her to contact me when she's—'

Matilda closed the door, not allowing Henry to finish.

How rude. He walked away, towards the school, his body limp with disappointment. He'd longed to have her to himself once more and had held such hope for today. What would he do now? He'd go for a walk to the stream, as they'd planned. The rippling water might help to soothe his anxiety. He didn't want to go home and admit what had happened, not yet.

It was strange though, that Amelia hadn't constructed some words of apology to pass onto him. She must have known he'd call if she didn't turn up. Maybe she had, and Mrs Bowen hadn't wanted to pass them on. Mean old mare.

That cough, it bothered him. It had been like she was trying to hide it this morning.

At that moment, Sara Rhys, Anwen's sister who'd died of the consumption at fifteen, came to mind. The sweet little girl who Anwen had named her half-sister after when she'd adopted her. Such a tragedy. The terror of this threw him off balance. He grabbed the railings at the front of the school to steady himself.

Consumption had taken three women from the village in the last year, that he knew of, and an eleven-year-old boy. One of the women had just given birth, and the baby had died too. What if Amelia had the consumption, and that was why Mrs Bowen had been so distant, not wanting to let on?

He felt sick. He couldn't go home and let his parents see him in that state.

A family, laughing and chatting, left a house opposite and began to walk to the village. He doubled back towards the Bowens's house and turned down the alleyway next to it. If he kept to the paths and avoided the streets, he'd encounter fewer people. He'd make his way to the stream and walk off this surely ridiculous conclusion he'd jumped to. She wouldn't have been in chapel this morning if she'd been that ill.

Whatever the reality, he needed to be alone.

Chapter Seventeen

Gwen left the house the next afternoon on the way to see her mother. She'd promised to pop around to see her yesterday about a couple of her skirts she wanted shortened and updated. But after all the arguments at chapel, and the less than amiable atmosphere at home afterwards, she hadn't been in the mood.

Henry was fixing a hook onto the picture rail when she arrived. Her father was sitting at the table, reading his newspaper, as he always did after his dinner.

'Hello, Gwen,' said Henry, stepping off the chair, hammer in hand. 'You haven't heard anything about Amelia being ill, have you?'

'Ill? No. Mrs Bowen was in James the Veg's when I went earlier and she didn't say nothing. Seemed quite cheerful too. Why'd you ask?'

He explained about her not turning up the day before, and his visit to her house.

'Not this again,' said Ruth, coming in from the hall with a metal bucket and a scrubbing brush. 'I told you, it were probably a cold like she said. People cough all the time, it don't mean they've got the consumption. No doubt she wanted to get better for work.'

'Consumption?' said Gwen, almost laughing.

'It's not funny,' said Henry.

'It is when you're being ridiculous. She were at chapel yesterday and looked perfectly healthy.'

'But what about Mrs Bowen's attitude, as if she were hiding something.'

'What, snooty Matilda,' said Ruth. 'You know what she's like.'

'She's not the only one,' said Gwen. 'Amelia is as big a snob as her aunt. I wouldn't be at all surprised if it were her way of putting you off, by getting her aunt to do the dirty work.'

'She wouldn't do that!' Henry hollered.

'That's enough of that shouting, *bach*,' said his father, looking up from his newspaper.

'That's not very fair, Gwen,' said Ruth. 'She seems very pleasant, doesn't she, Albert?'

'Oh aye, pleasant enough.'

'She'd make a fine addition to the family.' Ruth smiled at Henry.

'Good heavens, I do hope not,' said Gwen.

'Tell me, Gwen, do you approve of anyone?' said Henry. 'You seem to have something against Jenny Richards and you're rude about Polly Smith. Since you married Tom, you've turned into a snob. And it's not like Tom is one. If you're not careful, you'll turn out like your mother-in-law.'

'Henry!' his mother admonished.

'Well, that shows how much attention you've been paying,' said Gwen, severely tempted to punch her brother's arm, as she used to when they were children and he'd been annoying. 'Mrs Meredith is a reformed character, has been since, since, she had a change of heart about Elizabeth and Gwilym, after her accident.'

'Then I can only assume that *you've* taken her place with your judgemental comments and mistrust of everyone.'

'Henry, stop that now,' said Albert.

'Someone needs to tell her. A bloke at work today told me that his wife were going to have a look at your second-hand clothes but didn't like you shouting at Jenny at the chapel. It's custom you'll be losing at this rate.'

'You do seem to have something against the girl,' said Ruth, 'which I don't understand. Quiet thing she's always been, and a good little worker as a maid at the Big House, by all accounts. And her with no husband now. Poor girl. As for Polly, if I'm honest, I've heard the way you've bossed her around when I've been to yours and she's been working there. I know people harbour a grudge because of her bringing that Gus Smith and his family to the village, but she were as much a victim of his badness as others were.'

She'd had enough of being blamed for things others didn't understand.

'The thing is, you have no idea about the situation with Polly and Jenny.'

'Why do I have a feeling there's something you're not telling us?' said Ruth.

Henry huffed. 'Or just being overdramatic – again.'

'You think I'm being overdramatic? What if I told you that those letters we were getting *did* come from Jenny?'

'That wasn't just an idle accusation?' said Albert.

'No. I caught her red-handed. Well, Polly did, when she arrived early one morning.'

Henry sat down slowly, looking puzzled. 'Why would you hold that against Polly?'

'I'm not entirely sure that Polly's innocent. Though she did seem to have grabbed the letter off her, and Jenny swore she weren't involved.'

'And you didn't report it to the police?' said Albert.

'No. Elizabeth and Anwen persuaded me it wouldn't be in anyone's interest.' She experienced the resentment all over again.

'I don't understand,' said Henry.

Should she tell them about Mr Meredith being the father of their children? At least then they'd understand.

About to open her mouth, a voice came from the scullery.

'Helloo, just me.' It was Rhonwen Evans, Mabel's mother.

'I'll call back later to measure you, Mam. You seem rather busy now,' said Gwen. She left immediately by the front door.

Walking back to her house, she realised that Mrs Evans had done her a favour. It would be too risky letting yet someone else know about the situation with Mr Meredith.

'Oh, now you're just being stupid,' she murmured to herself, tugging her handkerchief from her skirt pocket as the tears began to fall. Henry's accusations had stung. Perhaps he was right. She was becoming a cross between the old snooty Mrs Meredith and the gossipy Esther Williams.

But Henry didn't understand the situation. Tom and Elizabeth still didn't seem to appreciate just how much damage might be done to the family if Jenny's and Polly's secrets became known. It was having a sheltered upbringing, in a big house outside of the reality of the village, that was to blame. It was up to her to protect them against any consequences by making sure there were no revelations.

But she also needed to take a step back, to be sensible, and not be overdramatic. She'd do her utmost to forget the letters, and the rumours about her business, and put her efforts into making it the best it could possibly be.

–

Henry folded the newspaper and slammed it against the kitchen table. Not seeing Amelia for so long was driving him nuts. She hadn't been in chapel again this morning, the second week running. He'd asked a couple of people who lived on her street if they'd heard anything about her being ill, but nobody seemed to know anything about it. One of the Pals even thought he'd seen Amelia at the motorbus stop, going to work. He could have asked John Bowen about it at the pit but didn't have the courage.

'If you're that worried about her, go and knock on her door, *bach*,' said Ruth, who must have guessed what he was fretting about.

'I wasn't exactly welcome last time, Mam. I don't want Bowen banning me from seeing her altogether.'

'Why would he do that? She's a grown woman. I should think he'd be happy for her to find a nice young man to court her.'

'After that to-do over the wages, I doubt that's how he considers me. And they might have someone better in mind for her than a miner.'

'Get away with you. What's Bowen, but a jumped-up miner? I remember when he were a hewer, back in the day. And if Gwilym Owen is good enough for the Merediths…'

'Maybe. But I am worried, Mam. I think Amelia might be ill, despite what Teilo said about seeing her at the motorbus stop.'

'Why don't you go for a walk, instead of sitting there, stewing? It's a pleasant enough day. It'll be April in four days. The year's going by quickly.'

It felt like it had gone quite slowly to him, with the recent gaps between seeing Amelia. 'You know, I think I will.' He fetched his jacket and cap from the hall, then returned to the kitchen door to call, 'I'll see you later, Mam. And if Amelia does call round, tell her I'm in Jubilee Gardens.'

'Right you are.'

All the way down James Street, the colliery loomed over him. It felt like a prison, hemming him in on one side, whilst the long terrace of houses did the same on the other. A life of servitude to the mine stretched ahead. Would Amelia be more enthusiastic about their relationship if there was a promise of an escape from it? Perhaps he could be a clerk, like Tom. He'd been smart enough at school. Or maybe start his own business. There must be something he was good at.

At least the grinding wheels were quiet today. They no longer turned on a Sunday, with the coal company not needing the same volume of coal for the navy anymore.

He was mulling this over as he crossed the road from the bookshop to the gardens. At first, he thought he was hallucinating, with Amelia having been on his mind constantly the last fortnight. But no, there she was standing halfway down the path in the gardens, by a bed of pansies, talking to Maurice, of all people. They were the only ones in the gardens.

Then he realised it was more like she was telling him off. The little blighter must be bothering her. He broke into a run and bolted through the gate. The sound of it clonking back in place alerted them to his presence, as their heads shot around.

Amelia turned back to Maurice to say, 'Stop bothering me. I'm in no mood for your cheek.'

Henry caught them up. 'What do you think you're doing, harassing the young lady?'

'Harassing her? Huh!'

'I think you should leave. And don't let me hear you've been bothering her again.'

'Bothering, harassing? It's just a bit of conversation. Some pal you are.'

'We're not fighting in a field in France now, Maurice. And yes, you're bothering my – my—'

'Your *what*?' Maurice let out another, 'Huh!' much louder this time. 'You don't even know.'

'My young lady then!' said Henry, hoping he wasn't crossing a line.

'Maurice, just go please,' said Amelia, quiet but determined.

'Oh aye, I'll go.' He marched off down the path, turning with a stamp of his feet after he'd walked out of the gate, like he was on guard duty.

Once he'd disappeared, Henry said, 'I'm so sorry about that. He can be difficult. Why on earth was he pestering you?'

'To be honest, Henry, I think he's doing it to annoy you.'

There might be something in that. 'He hasn't been, you know, trying to compromise you, has he? I'll give him what for if he is. And him a married man.'

'He just thinks he's funny, running you down. Saying how scared you were in the war.'

What the hell was his game? 'He said that? We all were.'

'But you're the one with the shakes.'

Henry found it hard to swallow. He didn't want to go into that, afraid he might start trembling simply at the thought.

'Where have you been, Amelia? I called round that Sunday we were supposed to meet, to see why you hadn't turned up, but your aunt were a little sharp with me.'

'I'm sorry. She didn't tell me you'd called round until later.'

'I was worried sick.' He went to take her hand. At first she moved it a little away, but then let him hold it. 'I thought you might have the influenza, or maybe even consumption, with that cough of yours. Especially when you didn't come to chapel the last two Sundays.'

She gave a small chuckle, putting her free hand to her mouth. 'Oh Henry, what an imagination. Goodness, it was just a chesty cough. I needed to get better for work, especially as I've had an extra couple of classes to do in the evenings. I'm sorry, I should have called around to explain earlier. I was on my way around just now – after I'd had a look at the blooms in the garden.' She indicated the lingering daffodils and the tulips, along with the primulas.

'Two weeks has been a long time not to see you. It feels like a lifetime.'

Amelia tipped her head to one side and looked up at him through her long eyelashes. 'You know what they say about absence making the heart grow fonder.'

That coy look of hers always melted his heart. Was she afraid that if he saw too much of her, he'd tire of her?

'It would grow fonder however much I saw you, Amelia.' He caressed her hand.

'How sweet.' She grinned widely.

'Now you're out, could we go somewhere together?' The prospect had his heart racing.

'Not today, I'm afraid. I'm meeting a friend in Rhymney.'

'Oh, all right.' The disappointment was overwhelming after such hope. 'But you said you were calling round.'

'Just to say sorry for not seeing you for so long.'

'I hope you have a lovely time with your friend.' There was no point being resentful. He didn't want her to think he was the kind of man to stop her having friends and going out. 'Shall we arrange a day out – or evening – while we're here?'

'Next week is Easter Sunday,' she said. 'We'll go for a walk somewhere. I'll see you in chapel and we'll make the final arrangements then.'

'I'll look forward to it.'

She was the first to walk away, blowing him a kiss as she went. He watched her until she'd left the gardens and disappeared beyond the hedges.

He let out a deep sigh. He'd go home now, content that she was well and that he would see her next week.

–

'It's good to get out of the house sometimes,' said Gwen as she closed the front door behind her. 'Even if it is only to go to the grocery shop.'

'I do miss working on the allotments,' said Anwen. 'It's not like we can take the sewing outside.'

Gwen checked her wristwatch. 'We need to get back for ten o'clock, as Anabel is coming for her fitting. I can't believe it's the first of April today. And the sun's actually shining! Let's hope we don't get too many of them April showers.'

They chatted about the work that needed doing.

'I have to admit that Polly is a good all-rounder,' said Anwen. 'I'm glad we agreed to take her on. She could be a good asset in the future.'

'Mm.' Gwen pursed her lips, then remembered her resolution not to let the problem of Polly cloud her judgement. 'Yes, I suppose she is.'

'We still haven't got to the bottom of those rumours though. Hopefully they'll just go away and we won't have to bother.'

'Hopefully,' Gwen agreed, curtailing any further comments.

The queue in Mrs Brace's shop wasn't long, only two people ahead of them.

'I still can't get over how full the shop is of everything, after the shortages of the war,' said Anwen.

'Yes, it took a while, but there's at least as much as there was before. I dare say it won't be long before we forget there ever were shortages.'

The door opened once more, and Mary Jones came in, an empty sack bag over her arm.

'Hello, Mary,' said Anwen. 'I hear you're going to be working part time in Elizabeth's market garden.'

She grinned broadly. 'That's right. Starting Monday. Looking forward to it, I am.' The smile slipped. 'I was 'oping to see at least one of you. I don't want to talk out of turn, and my Percy did say not to get involved, but—'

What was coming now? Gwen dreaded the answer. Not a complaint about the dress they'd made for Mary's daughter, she hoped.

'Go on.' Anwen sounded equally hesitant.

'Well—' She waited as the person at the front left the shop and the next in line got served. She lowered her voice to continue. 'I did hear that Esther Williams a few days ago, telling someone that you had done some sloppy work. Don't think they knew I was there, as I was behind a hedge in the gardens, and they was out on the streets. I stayed to listen, to see if she'd say where she got that from, but unfortunately she didn't say.'

'So it might have been her what started the rumour?' said Anwen.

Mary nodded. 'That's what I was thinking.'

Gwen patted Mary's arm. 'Thank you for telling us. Don't worry, we won't let on you said anything. You know she thinks I jilted her Daniel and has disliked me ever since.'

'Now that's another thing,' said Mary. 'I heard in the butcher's just now that Daniel and Christopher left the house, day before yesterday, to lodge with Gwilym's parents.'

'That's only two doors from my mam,' said Anwen. 'How strange.'

'Is it though?' said Gwen. 'Daniel said all along he only came back to the house for Christopher's sake. Maybe now they can afford to lodge elsewhere.'

'I think we should pay Esther a visit after getting our bits. If we have time.'

Gwen checked her watch. 'Yes, there's time.'

–

After fetching their shopping, they lugged their wicker baskets to Esther's house on Jubilee Green, on the other side of the gardens. Anwen knocked stridently on the door.

Gwen was relieved to see Esther answer, not either of her lodgers.

'What do you want now?' Esther snapped, folding her hands over a grubby grey apron. Her hair had come loose from her bun, and Gwen noticed her skirt hem had come down on one side.

'It's come to our attention,' said Gwen, 'that you've been spreading rumours about our sewing work being shoddy.'

Esther's face, more lined than it had once been, puckered with irritation. 'Whoever's been telling you that is a liar! Who was it? I'll get them sorted out.'

Get them sorted out? She and Anwen glanced at each other.

'Several people,' said Gwen. 'It don't matter who.'

'They're all liars! As if I haven't got enough on my plate, with Daniel and Christopher moving in with them Owens.' Her mouth puckered, emphasising the age lines above her lips.

'I'm sorry about that,' said Anwen. 'But don't go spreading malicious gossip about us.'

The door banged shut, causing the two women to step back.

'Did she do that or did someone else push it from behind?' said Gwen.

'I dunno, but I'm not sure how much good us confronting her did.'

'Me neither. Come on, let's get back for that appointment.'

-

After their appointment with Anabel Thomas, Gwen and Anwen went to Enid's house for a meeting at eleven o'clock. Violet was already there with nineteen-month-old Gethin. He was being shown a picture book by Sara Fach as they sat on the chaise longue, with ten-month-old Hope sitting on her other side, looking on in wonder. Enid stood at the range, waiting for the kettle to boil, ready with a teapot warming on a hotplate. Cadi was putting out teacups and saucers from the dresser.

Polly was also there. Gwen didn't need her to be party to the conversation. 'You'd be better off sewing in the front room now. It's getting a bit crowded here.'

Polly picked up the blouse she was altering and went into the other room, where the normally folded-down table was up permanently for them to use for cutting out and sewing on.

'I'll bring you a cuppa in,' Cadi called.

'Thank you, Mrs Rhys,' Polly called back.

The three younger women sat around the kitchen table.

'First of all, we should tell you what happened this morning,' said Anwen.

'Hold on,' said Gwen. She got up and shut the ajar door to the front room. 'Go on now.'

Anwen went through the conversations with Mary and Esther, with Gwen contributing here and there.

'I think you should report it to the police,' said Violet. 'Whether they can prove it or not, at least if something else happens they'll already know about it.'

'Excuse me,' said Cadi, taking a cup through to Polly. When she returned, she left the door ajar once more.

Gwen was tempted to get up and shut it again but didn't want to risk looking petty. 'We did consider before whether

Esther started the rumours, and whether Reg and Iolo had put pressure on her to cause trouble. But could it have been Daniel told her to cause trouble, because he thought I'd jilted him? And, I'm sorry to say it, but could that be why he's lodged with the Owens next door but one, to be a spy when I'm working here and—'

'I don't think it's any such thing,' said Cadi, cutting her off. 'Meg did tell us yesterday that Daniel's mother told him you'd been pining for him, Gwen, and that his annoyance was aimed more at her than at you. Daniel told Meg that himself.' She unpicked the tacking from a hem as she talked. 'And besides, Meg reckons there's a young lady he's walking out with, as he was out yesterday afternoon, smelling of that cologne stuff.'

'Daniel's a decent young man,' said Enid. 'As is Christopher now, after his wobbly start, so no more talk of him being responsible.'

That had told her, thought Gwen. 'All right. That brings us back to Esther then. I'll report her to Sergeant Harries when we leave here. That's the best we can do.'

They all agreed.

'Now we need to look to the future, as we've two more brides what want to discuss dresses,' said Enid. 'And we've got to sort out the second-hand clothes we have in our various houses.'

'And I was thinking,' said Gwen, 'maybe it's time to think about hiring a couple of sewing machines? It would speed things up a bit.'

'You can sew on your fancy machine,' said Cadi, 'but I'll stick to doing it by hand, if you don't mind.'

'There's no one does a hem like you, Mamgu,' said Anwen.

'Except Polly,' said Cadi. 'She's a good little stitcher. It's a shame we can't give her more work at the moment.'

Now Cadi was sticking up for Polly. Gwen had to agree she was talented, the neatest needlewoman she'd ever come across. But she was an ongoing problem which would surely get worse.

Tom and Elizabeth might not think so now, but what would happen when little Herby was older, and the family likeness was maybe stronger?

The open front room door was still annoying her. She rose to shut it before they carried on with their plans.

Chapter Eighteen

Polly found her parents in the third pew back, after she'd dropped Herby off at the Sunday School in the next room.

Delia shifted up on the seat. 'Was he all right this time?'

'Once he saw that Jenny's Freddie was there, yes. Luckily Mrs Thomas is very kind to them when they're shy.'

'I saw Mabel come in wiv Lily while you was droppin' off Herby. No sign of our Maurice though.'

Jim leant forward. 'Probably havin' a lie-in. Seems to have done that a coupla times recently on a Sunday.'

'Here's our Connie,' said Delia.

'And Sioni's actually wiv 'er today.'

Polly didn't look up, not wanting to acknowledge her brother-in-law. She'd managed to avoid being alone with him since that incident in the bedroom at Christmas, but he never missed a chance to give her a lecherous once-over when he thought no one was looking.

The pair must have spotted them, as they came over and settled in the next pew, Sioni sitting at the end directly behind her. Polly's stomach squirmed at the thought of him so close.

All through the service, she was aware of Sioni's proximity. When they rose to sing the hymns, his voice drowned out all the others around her. He had a good voice, but to her there was an edge of threat to it.

At the end of the service, she breathed a sigh of relief, looking forward to finding Jenny and having a few words. But Sioni wasn't finished with her yet.

As Connie was leaning forward, speaking to their parents, he came out of the pew into the aisle as a group of people went by. He feigned being pushed into her, his hand gliding over her behind.

She went to protest, but it was all over almost as soon as it had started. He swaggered off up the aisle. Polly looked at her sister, deep in conversation about the new curtains Sioni had bought for the front room and kitchen. She'd had a few new bits for the home recently. How could they afford it?

No point in telling them what Sioni had just done. He'd only say it was an accident, and she wouldn't be able to prove otherwise.

–

Henry had arrived at chapel earlier than his parents, hoping to see Amelia come in. He hadn't noticed her so far, and now the service had finished, he couldn't see her in the congregation as they stood around chatting. He went into the side room, but there was no sign of her there either.

'Are you looking for Amelia, *bach*?' said his father, Albert, as he passed him.

'Yes, Da. We were supposed to be finalising our trip out today.'

'Perhaps she's unwell.'

He didn't have time to consider this before one of the double doors crashed open and John Bowen strode inside.

'There you are!' he hollered, spotting Henry and marching over.

'Oh, what the blazes now?' a man close by grumbled. The voices in the chapel ceased.

'What have you done?' muttered Albert.

'Nothing.'

Bowen stopped, hands on hips, a couple of yards from Henry. 'What do you know about Amelia leaving with Maurice Coombes?'

'What's he done to her?' Henry shouted, remembering the times Maurice had hassled her.

'Calm down, son,' said Albert.

Ruth appeared from behind. 'What's he going on about, Henry?'

'You must know about it,' said Bowen. 'You was always pestering her.'

From the quietened crowd, someone tutted loudly.

Henry was awash with shock. 'I – I never pestered her. We was walking out together.'

'Yes, they was,' said Ruth.

'That's not what she said. You kept bothering her, is what she said. Why do you think she pretended to be ill that Sunday? To avoid you.' Bowen stuck his face forward as he said the last words.

'That's terrible, to be bothering a young woman like that,' said a voice.

'But I didn't bother her. She let me take her to tea and to the theatre and what not. She never said she didn't want to go.' Henry was having difficulty taking this in. Maybe Bowen was mistaking him for Maurice.

'Aye, that's right,' said Albert, tapping his son on the shoulder. 'Spent money on her, he did, especially for her birthday. And she did come to tea one time. Didn't look like no one had forced her. And what would any of this have to do with Maurice?'

'Henry here likely set up their meetings, and pretended he was walking out with her himself, to help Maurice abduct her.'

'You should get Sergeant Harries,' Florrie Harris called over.

'I don't understand,' said Albert. 'How'd you know she's gone with Maurice?'

'Cos she left a note to say so. And a lot of her clothes have gone.'

'Then she can't have been abducted, as you put it, can she?' Ruth said stridently.

'Um, excuse me,' said Twm Bach, holding up his hand and coming forward. 'I was out on my early walk this morning, just as it were getting light, and I saw Miss Bowen leave with Mr Coombes. They was on Reg Prosser's cart, going out of the village towards Rhymney. She didn't look like she were being forced.'

Henry felt sick. Why would she go off with Maurice, who she seemed to detest? 'I don't understand,' he said slowly, willing it to be a mistake.

'Oh, I do,' said John Bowen. 'You couldn't have been up to much if she ended up running away with a married man.'

When had she got together with Maurice? It can't have been since he'd last gone out with her; it wasn't long enough for a relationship to form. He recalled them in the gardens. Had they been planning it? Henry's head ached with the betrayal; it was all he could do not to cry. He hadn't done that since half his mates from the battalion had been killed at Mametz Wood. No, he couldn't let anyone see him do that.

–

Polly was standing with Jenny, listening to John Bowen as he tried to blame Henry for Amelia running off. Was he seriously saying she'd gone with her brother Maurice?

'Where is Mabel?' Jenny whispered.

'Went to get a biscuit.'

'She obviously doesn't know about this.'

'Someone should get her.' As Polly said this, she saw Connie and Sioni creeping out of the still open door. Her sister wasn't going to hang around and find out what had happened to her own brother?

Polly's mother, Delia, walked into the chapel from the side room. 'What's all this someone's been telling us about Maurice going—'

'Yes, your Maurice,' said John, coming towards them. 'He's got a lot to answer for, and him married.'

'Don't know why we should be surprised: it were Amelia what tempted him,' said Delia. 'Always batting 'er eyelids at the men she were, married or not.'

'Don't you talk about my niece like that!'

As they argued Polly considered poor Henry. His eyes were cast down and she could tell he was broken by the news.

'Where's Maurice, where is he?' screamed Mabel, running into the chapel area, followed by her mother, Rhonwen. 'Someone just said he's run away.'

'Off with John Bowen's hussy of a niece,' someone called out.

'You shut your gob,' Bowen shouted. 'And you can't be up to much, Mabel Coombes, if your husband had to look elsewhere. No wonder really. Look at you. Not elegant like our Amelia, or my Matilda, and your hair's all over the place.'

Mabel stood in front of the centre pews and screamed, long and loud. Two babies started to cry.

'Shut up, you stupid mare,' Bowen hollered.

'Don't you talk to my daughter like that,' said Rhonwen, running up to him, shaking her fist.

This was awful. Polly went to her sister-in-law's side, taking her to a pew to sit down. She started sobbing.

'What's the point of being elegant, if you're a little floozy?' said Rhonwen. 'She always was a spoilt brat. Her mother did her no favours there.'

'Don't you say that,' Bowen hissed. 'Blame the parents of him what lured her away.' He pointed at Delia and Jim. 'It's them what brought up a dishonourable scoundrel for a son.'

'Maurice told me he were doing an extra shift this morning, and that I needn't bother to get up,' Mabel whined.

'There are no Sunday shifts any more, you dozy mare,' said Bowen.

Polly had heard enough. She was sick of his words. She stomped over to where Bowen was now facing her parents, who were standing in front of Henry's parents. They, in turn, were standing in front of the limp Henry.

'I've heard enough of your insults, Mr Bowen,' she said. 'And I've had enough of that word, "mare". It's no better than calling a woman a bitch or a cow.' There, she'd said it, even if it had meant swearing.

'Hear, hear,' called Ruth from behind Polly's parents.

'Your niece has always been a snobby piece,' said Polly, 'what thinks she can use and abuse people. And I should know, I worked with her long enough. Her mother, Mrs Bowen, was a nice lady, always kind to me, so I've no idea why Amelia turned out the way she did. More like her father's side of the family, I'm guessing.'

'Yes, that'll be it,' said Rhonwen.

Now she'd got going, Polly couldn't stop. 'I've long thought her a nasty piece of work, what put on the airs and graces and pretty smiles, then sneered behind everyone's back.'

She felt exhausted after that, though it had been liberating too. It had been a long while since she'd spoken her mind in public, put down and silenced by Gus and his family as she had been. She noticed Gwen standing by the chancel with Elizabeth. She didn't suppose her being outspoken would go down well with them.

'Giving me lip, are you?' said Bowen. 'You'll be sorry.'

Through the still open front door, Matilda Bowen came running. 'John, have you found out anything? Someone's just told me they were on Reg Prosser's—'

'Yes, I know that already,' Bowen said sharply.

Matilda came to a standstill, out of breath. 'You two!' She pointed at Jim and Delia. 'I suppose I shouldn't be surprised to hear our niece has been led astray by one of the Coombes family.'

'We've been through all this,' said Delia, 'so you can just—'

'*I* haven't been through it.'

Polly had said her piece. She was going back to Mabel to make sure she was all right, then fetch Herby and go home.

She turned to go as Matilda continued with, 'Them and their disgusting London ways. Look at that Gus and his family that Polly brought to this village.'

She came to a standstill. Not this again. People had stopped giving her those *looks* recently, and some had even started talking to her, maybe because she'd been so quiet and contrite. This was the last thing she needed.

'You can't go on blaming my Polly for evermore for Gus and his awful clan,' said Delia.

'Nah,' said Jim. 'She was bullied and mistreated by 'im. As for our "disgusting London ways", we've been an 'ardworking fam'ly, never got into no trouble. Never bin wiv'out jobs. Never stolen from no one, not like some from 'ere what's been banged up in gaol. Yeah, my son's done wrong, leaving 'is wife and kiddie, but you should look at yourself before you point the finger. You're just an 'oity-toity what's no better than she oughta be, puttin' on the hairs and graces.'

Polly saw Gwen marching over, no doubt going to put her two penn'orth in as well.

Coming to a standstill, Gwen said, 'You seem to forget, Matilda, that Amelia led my brother on, whatever you say. She clearly acted as if they was courting, so is a right deceitful piece. I can't say I'm sorry she's gone, though I'm sad for Mabel and Lily. But I never thought Amelia good enough for Henry.'

'Not good enough for Henry?' Matilda forced out a laugh.

'No, because I wouldn't mind betting that the money what was stolen from you, with no sign of a break-in, was taken by Amelia for this little adventure.'

Matilda opened her mouth to argue, but then it seemed like a light had dawned. She and John looked at each other.

Mabel stood abruptly, screaming, 'My savings!' and ran from the chapel.

Rhonwen started to follow her but stopped next to Delia on the way. 'Would you look after Lily for a bit while I go with Mabel? She's in the side room with Mrs Thomas.'

'Of course.'

Delia and Rhonwen headed off in opposite directions.

Matilda surveyed the rest of them involved in the argument. 'You are all – you're all beneath my contempt!' She rotated on one shoe and walked out, muttering, 'Ruffians and criminals, the lot of you!' This last comment was clearly aimed at everyone in the chapel, the way her hand swung round to encompass them all.

John Bowen, adding nothing, followed her out.

–

Henry watched as Mr and Mrs Bowen left, wishing he could turn back the clock to before this debacle, back to when he was still hopeful of a happy ending with Amelia. But it had all been an illusion.

The next best thing would be to get away from everyone here, but the pain and distress of losing Amelia was pinning him to the spot. His friends from the Pal's battalion gathered around him ever more tightly, as if feeling his suffering.

'Don't worry, mun, we're here for you,' said Douglas Ramsay. 'I know what it's like to lose someone dear to you.'

'Aye,' said Alun Lloyd. 'But she weren't good enough for you, Henry, that's clear now. That should help you get over her at least.'

The rowing had distressed him, but the cosseting of him by his Pals made him feel hemmed in, like his chest was being crushed.

If only he could escape.

'Come on, son, we should get home,' said Albert, lifting him from the pew he'd sunk into.

'Good idea, Mr Austin,' said Douglas.

His mother linked her arm through his, and, with Albert on the other side, they led him home.

With the Bowens and Henry gone, Polly went back towards the side room to collect Herby. She heard singing as she approached. Inside, the children had been taken to the other end of the room. Anwen and Anabel were among the women keeping the children occupied, singing, 'I'll Be a Sunbeam'.

None of them arguing in the chapel this morning had been sunbeams, for Jesus or anyone else, she thought, shouting at each other as they had been. Possibly she should have kept quiet, not drawn attention to herself.

Elizabeth came in behind her. 'Polly.'

Oh dear, was she in trouble already?

'That was very brave, challenging Mr Bowen's language. He deserved it.'

'Well, I'm sick of men what think they can say or do what they like to us because we're women.'

Elizabeth patted her arm. 'Quite right.'

'It's Henry I feel sorry for though. I saw him out walking with Amelia, a couple of times. She didn't look at all put out. Quite the opposite. So I'd say that business about Henry pestering her is rubbish. He's always seemed a decent man.'

'Yes, he is. Of course, he's sort of my brother-in-law, but that's not why I'm saying it.'

'Just because someone's your brother-in-law, don't mean you'd always stick up for them.'

Elizabeth regarded her curiously.

'Forget I said that. Please.' Polly didn't want anything getting around about Sioni that might have come from her.

The song came to an end.

'Has it finished out there?' Anabel called over.

'Yes,' Elizabeth replied. 'The Bowens have left.'

'All right, children, off you go and find your mothers and fathers.'

Herby ran to Polly and hugged her legs. 'That were lovely singing, Herby.' She bent down to hug him.

Anwen came over, holding Sara Fach's hand. 'It might be best if you came to mine to work on Wednesday, Polly.'

'All right.'

'You can make a start on the bridal dress.'

'Which one?' Polly asked.

'The one for the woman in Rhymney. I'm afraid the other one's been cancelled.'

'Oh.'

'That's the second order cancelled since the rumours of our so-called shoddy work began. I'm hoping people see the clothes we've made for theirselves and realise it's all lies.'

The pastor's wife made her way over to them.

'Goodness,' said Anabel. 'Lewis would choose this time to visit a sick parishioner. But we'd had word he was nearing the end. I trust the argument came to an end amiably.'

'I wouldn't say amiably,' Elizabeth commented, 'but it ended without blows, which, given the threats from Mr Bowen, was about as much as one could hope for. What a shame my father isn't still manager here. I'd have made sure he got a dressing-down for his behaviour.'

'I don't know if Mr Hopkins would do anything,' said Anwen.

Polly wanted to agree with her, but she felt too overwhelmed by the company now to say anything.

'I'll have a word with Lewis about it,' said Anabel. 'He won't be happy that Mr Bowen's been here causing trouble. And on Easter Day too! He might have a word with Mr Hopkins.'

'Are you ready to go?' Delia called by the door.

Polly was relieved to hear her mother calling her. 'Yes, we're coming.'

She followed her out but was still thinking about the cancellations. If this carried on, she might be laid off.

She'd have to make sure her sewing was as good as it possibly could be, and that she kept quiet when Gwen was around.

‘Let go of my arm, Mam,’ said Henry as they walked slowly down Gabriel Street. ‘You’re making me look like a weakling.’

‘You didn’t seem very steady on your feet when you stood up,’ said Ruth.

‘I’m all right now.’ It wasn’t true, and already he could feel his hands trembling. He was determined not to let it get the better of him.

Henry, concentrating on the pavement until now, raised his head to cross the road at the bottom of the gardens on Jubilee Green. It was then he noticed Sioni Gower standing by the bottom entrance of the gardens. He had a roll-up between his thumb and forefinger, sucking on it and lifting his head to blow the smoke upwards.

Sioni threw the stub on the floor and crushed it with his foot. ‘Could I have a word, Henry?’

‘Not now,’ said Ruth, ‘he’s not feeling well.’

‘It won’t take a moment.’ His tone took on a more insistent level.

‘It’s all right, Mam. I won’t be long.’

Despite his subtle dismissal, Ruth and Albert stood only a yard or so away.

‘It’s private, like,’ said Sioni.

Ruth crossed her arms tight against her chest. ‘We don’t have no secrets.’

‘Maybe I do, though.’ Sioni fixed her with a frown.

‘You two go on,’ said Henry. ‘I’ll be along shortly.’

The pair hesitated, before heading off down the road. However, they stopped by the bookshop to watch them.

‘What’s this about, Sioni? I’ve paid my due this week.’

‘That’s just it, you haven’t quite. Realised when I got home that it were a shilling short like.’

‘No, it was the same amount as usual.’

‘Ah, yes, but you’ve had the debt more than six weeks see, so the interest has gone up to forty per cent. I don’t lend out money from the goodness of my heart, you know. It's a business. Try getting a loan from a bank. Now, I'll expect the missing money in next week's payment.'

'Right.'

'Have a good week,' was Sioni's parting shot as he walked away, before he laughed.

The mixture of anger, anxiety and Amelia's loss propelled him along the pavement. His hands had started trembling once more and by the time he reached his parents, his arms were shaking too.

Albert took hold of him, trying to keep him still. 'What on earth has he said to cause this?'

'Nothing. It's nothing to do with him. He were just telling me something about Amelia he knew.'

Ruth kept apace with him as he steamed along the road. 'As if you didn't know enough about her to see she were a wrong'un.'

'I don't want to talk about it. I just want to get home.'

Before the shaking became so bad that he couldn't walk.

Chapter Nineteen

Henry woke with a start. His head ached and he was sweating copiously. It was still dark. He threw back the sheets. Lying on his back he tried to still his racing heart by taking in slow breaths. No, not again, not that suffocating feeling of panic he got so regularly now. He felt like he couldn't breathe, but he was actually breathing too quickly.

'It's all right,' he told himself. 'Calm, be calm.' But he couldn't swallow, and it felt like he was choking.

He flung himself out of bed. Walk, he needed a walk. Once again, he attempted to slow down his breathing, but it would always catch as he tried to take a long breath out and he'd be forcing in air again. He crept onto the landing, down the stairs and into the kitchen, where he flicked the electric light on. He kept walking, barefoot, from the front room, through the kitchen and into the scullery, then back again. The clock on the wall of the kitchen told him it was coming up to quarter past six. In the front room, he lifted the net curtain to see out, peering left. There was a little light in the sky over the forested hill.

Had his breathing got better? No, and now his hands had started to quiver, and soon, his arms. He started walking again. What had awoken him? It felt like something terrible had happened. That was it: he'd been on a battlefield, explosions all around, fallen comrades lying on the ground. Up ahead his lieutenant had called to him. He'd tried to catch up but had found it difficult to move. Then the lieutenant had become

Amelia. There'd been another explosion… and Amelia had disappeared, blown into a thousand pieces.

'Amelia,' he groaned as he sank into one of the armchairs by the now cold range. His lieutenant *had* been blown up, though Amelia was very much alive. But, she'd gone, out of the village, out of his life.

It was then he realised his whole body was shaking and his teeth were chattering. It wasn't quite like the jerky movements he suffered with his shell shock, more trembling than shaking, but it was equally frightening. He was still gasping for breath.

He got up, determined to take another walk, but in his clumsiness knocked over the fireplace tools on their metal stand, causing them to clatter against the range.

'Stop it, stop it, stop it,' he hissed, banging on the plate of the range.

Soon the tears were falling as they had done for so much of yesterday as he'd lain huddled on his bed.

'What on earth's going on?' said his father, coming through the door.

Henry jumped. In his self-absorption, he hadn't heard him coming down the stairs.

'I'm sorry, I'm sorry, I didn't mean to wake you. I felt – panicky.'

'Come on now, sit down.' He was half dressed, trousers on his lower half and pyjama top above. 'Why you're trembling like a leaf, *bach*. Come to bed with you.'

'Is he all right?' said Ruth. She was in her dressing gown and her hair was in a long, greying plait.

'Another one of his shakes,' said Albert.

'Come on, let's get you to bed.'

He was about to protest, but realised his breathing had calmed down, along with his heart. He was still shivering and felt dead on his feet. Yes, he needed to get to bed.

When Henry awoke once more, the sun was streaming through the gap in his curtains. He was on his back and his brain felt fuzzy, the remnants of a headache still present. Something was wrong and he couldn't quite put his finger on it. As his mind cleared, a picture of him facing John Bowen came to mind.

Amelia. She was gone.

He groaned and turned on his side, covering his head with his sheet and blankets. Amelia.

Absence makes the heart grow stronger. That's what she'd said. But it had been Maurice her heart had grown stronger for. Is that who she'd been seeing all those times she'd claimed to be seeing a friend, or doing extra work? What an idiot he'd been, not realising that her putting him off so many times, the bigger gaps between seeing him, the chaste kisses and sometimes the refusal to kiss at all, had all been a sign. He thought she was being cautious, proper, ladylike.

Henry peeped above the blankets at the small carriage clock on his bedside table. Just after nine o'clock. It wasn't like him to sleep in so late, despite it being a holiday. Years of getting up at five fifteen, to get to his shift by six o'clock, meant he'd now got out of the habit of the lie-ins he'd enjoyed as a schoolboy. He was lucky it was Easter Monday, so he didn't have to go into work, after the humiliation of what had taken place in the chapel.

Checking his hands, he was relieved to see he wasn't trembling anymore. He got up and went to the washstand, removing his pyjama top before pouring some of the water into the bowl. He didn't care that it was cold. He gave his face a quick wash, then dried it with the towel folded on the shelf beneath.

He'd get dressed, go downstairs and try to concentrate on one of the novels he'd borrowed from the Workmen's Institute library.

In the kitchen, his mother greeted him with a solemn face, rushing to him as he came through the door from the hall.

'Oh Henry, you didn't have to get up. Come and sit down.' She took his arm and attempted to lead him along.

Henry shook her off. 'Mam, please. I'm not an invalid, and I'm not a little boy. Can we just act like it's any other day?'

'The kettle's on the boil and I've got some bacon and eggs to cook.'

He realised, with surprise, that he was starving. He'd eaten nothing the day before after chapel, having gone to his bedroom and stayed there. 'Yes, please. And some fried bread would be nice.'

'You sit yourself down. Your da's gone down to the Institute with his euphonium for another practice with the band for the carnival this afternoon.'

The carnival. And various other activities. He'd been looking forward to them before. He was glad they lived near the end of the village so he wouldn't have to suffer too much of the merry cheering and joyful noises.

'Saturday's paper is on the table, if you want a read.'

'Thanks, Mam.'

He sat down and picked it up to scan the front page: French troops occupying major cities in Germany and riots in Jerusalem… Henry wondered whether the war had ever really ended but had simply carried on in lots of different ways. The aroma of bacon reached his nose as he heard it start to sizzle. He folded the newspaper back up and placed it on the chair next to him, getting up instead to fetch his book from the dresser. *The League of the Scarlet Pimpernel* should afford him some escape to a very different place and time.

'Would you like to come along to the festivities later? They start at two,' said Ruth as she placed a cup of tea in front of him. 'It might be a good distraction. And your da will be playing.'

'Sorry, but no thank you.'

'Well, I'd like to pop along for a bit to have a listen and see the kiddies in their costumes, if you don't mind.'

'Please, go to the whole event. I don't need a nanny.'

'I might watch a bit of the races too then.'

Henry opened the book. The longer she stayed out the better, giving him some peace and quiet, not constant questions and suggestions.

-

'What a shame I couldn't persuade my brother to come to the festivities,' said Gwen, clutching Tom's good arm as they walked past the bookshop, taking a trip around the shops in the village to see how they'd decorated them for the event.

She knew this wasn't really Tom's idea of entertainment, but at least he was looking forward to the performance of *Yeoman of the Guard* at the Institute later.

Tom looked sideways at her. 'I can't say I blame him. I'd have felt the same. It took me long enough to face the villagers when I lost my arm.'

'This isn't anything like losing your arm!'

'No, but it's demeaning, none the less. And think how upset he'd be to be losing the woman it looks like he was pretty serious about.'

'Amelia Bowen's no loss. Henry will realise that one day.'

'Hopefully, but we need to allow him time to get over her.'

Coming down Jubilee Green they spotted several women judging the decorated shops. They included Anabel Thomas and the wife of the rector of St Peter's, Agnes Banes. It also included Matilda Bowen. They each held a clipboard and a pencil.

'I'm surprised she's feeling up to doing this, as if nothing's happened,' said Gwen, indicating Matilda.

'Strange to think my mother would have been among them, had they not moved. Aled Hopkins's wife doesn't even appear to be there.'

'She doesn't get involved in the way your mother did.'

It was a shame the Merediths had moved, Gwen considered. Margaret had wielded some influence on committees in the area and might have brought their dressmaking business some new custom.

They reached Mr James's greengrocery at the top of Jubilee Green.

'So, which shop do you think is decorated the best?' said Gwen.

'Mr Schenck's bookshop without a doubt. I bet Mrs Schenck spent a lot of time cutting out paper flowers, and they have an attractive arrangement of spring-related books in the window.'

'It would get my vote too.'

They took the route around the narrow top of the gardens, past the Workmen's Institute and down the other side of Jubilee Green.

Sergeant Harries strolled by. 'Mr and Mrs Meredith, good afternoon sir, madam.' He performed a small salute.

'Good day to you, Sergeant,' said Tom.

When he'd passed them, Gwen said, 'I do rather enjoy the respect he pays us. All because of you, of course.'

'I wish he'd just treat me the same as everyone else. It's not like my father's the manager here anymore.'

A crowd was gathering for the carnival due to start at two thirty. There were a lot of children in fancy dress, and quite a few adults too. Several girls were dressed in variations of the Welsh national costume with its tall, tapered hat, cap, cape, shawl and skirt, mainly in red, white and black.

'I'm guessing that Charlie Chaplin is one of the categories in the fancy dress,' said Tom as they spotted a couple of men dressed as the comic actor.

'Oh look, there's Idris's brother!' said Gwen. 'Anwen said she was helping him put together a costume.'

Jenkin came ambling up the street in his baggy black suit and old bowler hat, imitating Chaplin's walk. He had a little false moustache fixed under his nose and was carrying a long, straight twig as a cane.

'You really look the part,' Gwen called to him as he passed.

Jenkin lifted his hat and bowed his head, saying nothing before shuffling on.

Arriving at the bottom of Jubilee Green once more, Gwen and Tom looked up and down the length of the road there.

'There's quite a throng here now.' He pointed across the road. 'Look, there's Lizzie and Gwilym talking to your mother. Let's join them.'

About to cross, she halted Tom. 'Hold on. What's that going on up there? It's Amelia Bowen! What on *earth* is she doing back here? And she's having a row with Rhonwen Evans.'

The pair of them were standing on the pavement outside the school. Six-year-old Lily was pulling on her grandmother's arm. Delia ran up to them and hurried the little girl away.

'Come on,' said Gwen.

Tom held on to her. 'Let's leave them to it.'

'No.' She untangled herself from him. 'That little madam is not getting away with what she did to my brother.'

Ruth looked over the road and waved. Gwen pointed to Amelia up the road, which had her mother running off in the opposite direction. Strange. Coming back along the pavement at the bottom of the gardens was Sergeant Harries.

Gwen lifted her hand and flapped it around, calling, 'Sergeant! There's Amelia Bowen. You need to question her about Mr Bowen's money.'

He hurried over to them. 'I don't know about that, but this quarrel needs dealing with. Ah, Constable, there you are. Come on, lad.' Harries took PC Davies's arm and turned him back round.

'It might be best if we let the police deal with her,' said Tom.

'Absolutely,' said Gwen, edging forward. 'But let's get closer to see what she's got to say for herself.'

-

Henry was enjoying the peace of the house without his parents there. He'd be sorry not to see Da play with the Silver Band, but if he kept the doors to the front room and the hall open, he'd hear them coming along sure enough, then he could go to an upstairs window and watch their progress.

He'd only got a couple of sentences into his book when the front door clattered open. His mother came flying through the kitchen door, out of breath.

'Henry, Amelia's come back. Brazen as anything, she is.'

He stood up, dropping the book on the chair. 'What? You mean, she's left Maurice?' A smidgeon of hope stirred. 'She's decided she's made a mistake. Or he had abducted her after all?'

'I don't know. She were having an argument with Rhonwen when I saw her, outside the school.'

'Right. I'm going to get this sorted out.'

'Do you think that's wise, *bach*?'

'I don't care. I want the truth, not speculations.'

He went to the hall to fetch his jacket and cap and headed straight out. Whatever had happened, he was going to talk some sense into her.

Chapter Twenty

Henry ran along James Street determined to get to Amelia before she moved on. His mother, struggling to keep up, got further behind.

He came up short when he realised she was now outside the McKenzie Arms. Rhonwen was still there, shouting at her, but with her now was Matilda. Sergeant Harries was swaying up and down on his heels, clearly trying to get a word in edgeways. Constable Davies was standing in the road, scratching the side of his face, looking at a loss to know what to do.

Rhonwen pushed Amelia, who tried to push her back but was shoved away by Mabel instead. The sergeant threw out his arms to separate them and was evidently giving them a telling off.

As he came into earshot, Henry heard Mabel shout, 'I want my money back! I worked hard for that in the munitions, and a tidy sum it were. Now you give it back right now you thieving, *floozy*.'

Amelia gave a dainty little giggle. 'I'm sure you worked very hard for it, Mabel, but I haven't a clue what you're talking about.'

'You liar! You've stolen my husband and my money!'

Henry blanched hearing this. It didn't sound like she'd given Maurice up at all.

'Are you all right, Henry?' said Ruth, catching up.

'Of course I'm not! Stop asking.'

'Sergeant Harries!' Rhonwen yelled. 'Get her to give the money back.'

He took a breath in and shook his head. 'Unfortunately, there's not a lot I can do, if Maurice took money from his own house.'

Rhonwen turned and landed Amelia a sharp slap across the face, throwing her against the wall. She clutched her cheek.

'Now that I can arrest you for,' the sergeant said to Rhonwen, taking hold of her arm.

'Give over,' a man in the large crowd who'd gathered round called, 'Amelia ruddy deserved it. Arrest the right person at least.'

There were several calls of agreement. The sergeant let her go and looked troubled as he took in the unsettled gathering.

Henry was making his way through to the affray, when his sister shouted, 'Yes, and what about that money she stole from her uncle? That weren't hers.'

'Gwen!' he hissed as he approached. 'What are you doing? You don't know she stole that.'

'Open your eyes, Henry, she's a hussy and a thief.'

'It is rather looking that way,' Tom agreed.

'I'll have to see if her uncle wants to press charges,' said Harries. 'He's not said as much to me so far.'

One of the doors in the public house opened next to them, and out stepped Polly.

'Mrs Moss wants to know what's going on,' she asked. 'Oh, it's *her*.'

'Yes, your brother's floozy's just turned up,' came the rather sharp answer from Gwen.

Polly took a few steps towards Amelia. 'All this noise is disturbing the patrons still eating lunch. If I wasn't working, I'd give you a piece of my own mind.'

Amelia pulled herself together, standing tall. 'I'd like to see you try, Polly.'

Henry went forward now, stopping a yard or so away.

'I don't understand why you ran away with Maurice,' said Henry. 'You made out we were a couple.'

Opening her mouth to reply, Amelia was stalled by Esther Williams who pushed through to whisper something to her.

'You're pathetic,' said Amelia, nudging her away. 'I've paid you enough for passing around the rumours about Gwen's awful dressmaking business.' She emphasised the last four words.

There was a mutter of disgust from the crowd. Several people booed. Esther sloped away, her lips pursed.

'You nasty little madam,' said Gwen, coming forward once again. Henry tried to stall her, but she barged past him. 'Get out of the way! How dare you, Amelia. At least now the villagers can hear who it was tried to destroy our reputation.' She turned to the crowd. 'Did you hear that, everyone? Spread it around, please. It were Esther what spread the rumour around, started by Amelia Bowen.'

People near the front of the crowd passed the information back to those who hadn't heard.

Amelia composed herself, her green eyes were cold with malice. 'Well, Henry, you were a useful distraction. I was never interested in you, not really. You're a weakling, made pathetic by the war, whereas Maurice is made of stronger stuff, not jumping at every little noise and shaking like a leaf. But, because I was walking out with you, people never suspected I was really seeing a married man.'

Henry stumbled back. It was worse than he'd imagined. It wasn't even that she'd liked him at first but had grown to prefer Maurice. She'd used him to play her own selfish game. And all that money he'd spent, and was still spending, because of the loan.

'Why you—' this time it was Ruth who ran forward and pushed Amelia, making her stumble.

'Get out of my way!' cried another voice. It was Matilda Bowen. 'So you've returned, have you? I came over to see why no one was coming to hear the results of the decorated shop competition, and I see you all ganging up on my niece.' She leant down to Amelia. 'Come on now. Let's get you home. I knew you'd see sense.'

Amelia allowed her aunt to help her up, then said in no uncertain terms, 'I'm not coming home, I've only come to collect the rest of my things. Mr Moss is waiting with his cart to help me.'

'Don't be daft. What on earth would your mother say? You've caused enough trouble already. Now get home!'

Matilda tried to grab her arm to pull her along, but Amelia resisted. 'You wait until Maurice hears you've shouted at me. He'll give you what for. He'll give all of you what for.'

Henry watched the whole thing mindlessly, unable to move after the damning revelation. It was like he was reading the scene in a book. It couldn't really be happening.

'Look, John's chasing Maurice,' Idris Hughes called, his height allowing him to see further up the road.

Everyone leaned up or changed position to get a better look. Sure enough, Maurice was running towards them. Bowen, a good twenty years older, was a little behind.

Maurice caught Amelia up. 'Did someone slap you? Your face is all red. Which one of you was it?'

'Maurice!' shouted Mabel. 'What on earth do you think—'

'Oh shut up, Mabel,' Maurice barked.

As Bowen caught up, shaking his fist, Harries and Constable Davies stood in the way, not allowing him to get to Maurice.

'That's enough of that now, sir.'

'You ungrateful little madam,' yelled John.

Mabel and Rhonwen took the opportunity, while the police were concentrating on Bowen, to lunge towards Maurice, both pummelling him with their firsts as he cowered. Amelia, trying to stop them, only succeeded in getting knocked over once again.

Harries and Davies, realising what was happening, came to Maurice's rescue, hauling the women off him.

When things had calmed down once more, Harries asked Bowen, 'If you wish to press charges for the missing money—'

'What would that do?' said Bowen. 'Except bring a court case and shame to the family, and my late brother's wife. And would I get it back?' He walked away, muttering, 'No. There's more than one way to skin a cat.'

'Come on, Maurice, let's collect the rest of my things,' said Amelia.

'Oh no you don't,' said Matilda, brandishing her clipboard in a threatening manner. 'You're not taking anything. Those dresses and knickknacks you've left will help pay for the money you stole.'

'But you can't have my sewing things, I need them for the classes!'

'Then buy some more with the money you both took.'

For the first time, Amelia looked unsure of herself.

'It's about time you folks left.' Sergeant Harries indicated Reg Moss's cart up ahead. He and the constable stayed two steps behind them as they walked away, to the jeers and comments of the gathering.

While everyone, including his family, was concentrating on their departure, Henry slipped away, through the throng. He couldn't even see himself being bothered about his book now. He was going to go to bed and catch up on that sleep he didn't get the night before.

If he could get to sleep. He looked down at his hands. They were trembling once more. He'd better hurry before one of his family, or one of the Pals, tried to catch up with him.

-

'Why don't you go and see *The Yeoman of the Guard* this evening?' said Delia as she buttered the end of the loaf before slicing it off. 'Your dad and me'll look after Herby for you.'

Polly could see that going down well after the day's events, especially if she went on her own, and who was there to go with? Mabel certainly wouldn't be feeling up to it, and it was too short notice to ask Jenny.

'I don't think so, Mum. I'm rather tired after my shift at the Arms, and then going down to the field to watch the races. And there were, you know, a few comments about Maurice.'

'I noticed. As if it's our fault 'e's gone off with a—' Delia looked at her grandson, where he was watching his mum take the top off his boiled egg. 'With someone no better than she oughta be.' She cut the slice of bread into five fingers and leant over to put them on her grandson's plate.

'No, but we'll still be blamed.' Polly stroked Herby's soft blond hair.

'Uh oh. Your dad's in a mood,' said Delia as the back door slammed shut.

The scullery door was pushed open to reveal Maurice, not Jim.

'Hello Uncle Maury,' said Herby as he dipped one of the pieces of bread into the top of the egg.

'What on earth are you doing back 'ere?' said Delia. 'I thought you'd gone off in Reg Moss's cart with that *woman*.'

Polly was tempted to pick Herby up and remove him from the room, but she didn't want to leave her mother on her own with Maurice.

'Reg brought me back,' he said, 'after a job he had to do. Went to my house to get some of my things, but Rhonwen was there with a coupla male cousins, so I couldn't get past the scullery.'

'Are you surprised? You oughta give her that money back.'

'That's my money. I'm the one what fought in the war. And if we men hadn't been fighting, the women'd never have had a chance to earn such money.'

'That is a really selfish thing to say,' Polly hissed, standing away from Herby.

'I agree with your sister,' said Delia. 'Who on earth do you think you are? Now, I dunno why you've turned up 'ere, but you're not welcome.'

'I've come here to find out if it's true, what Amelia told me about Polly.'

'Amelia knows nothing about me that you don't already know, so I've no interest in what *she's* got to say,' said Polly.

'Hello, I'm back,' called Jim's voice from the scullery. He came in swiftly, his face neutral, until he spotted Maurice standing next to the dresser. 'What on earth are you doing 'ere? You were told by Sergeant Harries to leave, and I thought you had.'

'I've come for a word with Polly.'

'Mum, would you keep an eye on Herby? I'll talk with Maurice in the scullery, out of the way.'

'Good idea. Come on, Herby, eat up. There's a nice bakestone for you when you've finished.'

Jim led the way into the scullery. He took the space by the sink, Polly by the pantry door and Maurice by the wash tub.

'Now what's all this got to do with Polly, son? It's you what's got some answering to do, leaving poor Mabel like that. Decent sort, she is.'

'Unlike Polly here,' said Maurice, 'with her flyblow.'

'You've got a nerve,' she said.

'She's right,' said Jim. 'And our Polly's officially married, so Herby's not considered no flyblow. What do you think your children'll be if you have any with Amelia?'

'It was Amelia told me she thinks she knows who Herby's father is.'

Polly's face heated up. Could Amelia possibly know that, and if she did, why hadn't she said anything before?

'I doubt she knows when the rest of us 'aven't a clue,' said Jim. 'And I for one don't care anymore. Herby's part of our family, and that's that.'

'But what if I told you Tom Meredith is the father? Amelia said she saw them walking out together a coupla times.'

Polly heaved a sigh of relief, making it sound like irritation. At least she wouldn't have to lie. 'I can guarantee you, absolutely, that Tom Meredith is *not* Herby's father. And if Amelia saw us out walking, it's because that's exactly what we were doing. I do remember coming across him a few times, and we chatted, just like anybody else would.'

'And what about Herby's name? Tom's father is called Herbert. You've used a family name.'

'I've used a *common* name. Gus was involved in naming him too.' Though she'd suggested it to him, still having a streak of rebellion in her at the time.

'Well, someone was the father, and I still reckon Tom Meredith's at the top of the list, though I'm sure there could have been plenty of other contenders.'

'That's enough!' Jim bellowed. 'You've disgraced yourself and you've disgraced our family. You've dishonoured Mabel. And what about li'l Lily?'

'What about her? I never wanted to be a father in the first place.'

Polly felt herself welling up. 'That's a terrible thing to say. Poor little mite doesn't deserve a rogue like you as a father. You'd better be paying Mabel some money for Lily.'

Without answering, Maurice reached the door in three long strides and flung it open. He marched out, not bothering to close it.

When he'd gone, Polly said, 'Tom Meredith is not Herby's father, Dad.'

'Polly love, I've no interest in knowing who the father is. The moment when it would 'ave done any good has gone. We need to just get on wiv our lives.'

'Oh, I'm all for that,' she said, heading back to the kitchen.

-

'Good heavens, who on earth is charging into the scullery?' said Elizabeth as she sat at the table flicking through a book on horticulture. 'I could do with a rest before we go to the performance this evening.'

'Me too,' Tom admitted, yawning as he sat by the fire.

'Probably my mother with yet something else to say about what happened earlier,' said Gwen, blowing out a huff of air as she stirred a pot on the range. That was the trouble with having her nearby, she thought, where it was too easy to pop by all the time. 'In here, Mam,' she called, wearily, readjusting her pinny.

The door from the scullery was thrown open, but it wasn't Ruth Austin who came through, it was Maurice Coombes. 'I wanna word with you, lover-boy.' He brandished a fist in Tom's direction.

Gwen went to Tom's side and watched Elizabeth run to the hall. 'Gwilym!' She hollered up the stairs, where he was fixing the leg on the dressing table Elizabeth had brought from McKenzie House.

'I've heard you're the father of my sister's Herby.'

'I most certainly am not!' said Tom. 'The most I ever did was talk to her in the gardens, and once walked along with her into the village when she passed by McKenzie House.'

'You're a bloody liar,' he said, almost poking his forefinger into Tom's face.

Gwilym followed his wife through the door. 'For God's sake, Maurice, don't be such an idiot. If Polly told you that, she's lying.'

'And you'd know who the father is, would you?'

'I know it's not Tom.'

Maurice leapt across the room. 'Why, is it you?'

Elizabeth jumped in front of Gwilym and flung her hands out. As Maurice lunged into them, he was thrown back a little. 'Don't you lay a hand on him, otherwise I shall fetch Sergeant Harries,' she said.

'Fetch the old buzzard, you posh cow. I don't care. For all the use he is.' Maurice turned back to Tom. 'Polly's son is called Herbert, after your father. I should have realised before.'

'Herbert is a *very* common name,' said Elizabeth.

'Oh, I shall give Polly what for, telling you such a lie,' said Gwen. 'She won't be employed by us anymore.'

'Yeah, well it weren't Polly what told me. She's never let on about the father. She said the same about Herbert being a common name. It's almost like you've all rehearsed it. It were Amelia what said she'd seen Tom and her together.'

'Like I said—' Tom started.

'But you're a ruddy liar. All your class are.'

'Says the man what deceived his wife,' said Gwilym, going ahead of Elizabeth now.

Maurice stepped towards Gwilym, raising his fists. 'You want to stick up for the despoiler of young women.'

Tom stood and took a few steps towards them, so he was on the other side of Maurice. 'I can swear to you, quite categorically, that I am not the father of Polly's child.'

'Pff. Really. On the Bible would that be?'

'If you want.'

Gwen knew he didn't believe in it, but it might still be enough to persuade Maurice.

'Go on then, big mouth. Let's see you do it then,' he hollered. 'Huh! At least you won't be much use at forcing a woman to do your bidding anymore, with that creepy limb.' He pointed to Tom's artificial arm, more obvious now with his shirt sleeves rolled up.

'Do shut up, Maurice,' said Elizabeth, being unusually rude.

Gwen was about to fetch one of the Bibles off the bookshelves in the front room, when the door from the scullery opened.

'What's all this noise?' said Anwen, stepping in. 'Oh.'

Gwen was relieved to see Idris just behind her. Three men against this lout. Would he be so sure of himself now? And Idris was formidable on his own, being tall.

'I suppose you two know how the Merediths have made a fool of my family,' Maurice snarled. 'Should have guessed, that stupid cow of a sister, calling him Herbert.'

'You can't pick on Tom because of something his father did,' Anwen said. 'I suppose because he's got one arm you think he's an easy target.'

Gwen took in a sharp intake of breath. The whole room went silent and still, apart from Idris, who said, 'She's right, though.'

'Sorry,' Anwen said, looking around. 'I'm not suggesting Tom is any less of a man for having lost an arm.'

Gwen had no idea what to do next. Maurice's mouth hung open, plainly shocked by this revelation. There was no point in anyone denying it because Maurice simply wouldn't have believed it.

'Your *father* is Herby's father?' he said with disgust in his voice, his face red with rage.

'I – I thought you knew that,' said Anwen, her eyes wide.

Maurice ignored her, carrying on with, 'That's even worse. Well, he's not here...'

Through the scullery door Henry flew. 'A neighbour said they saw you come in here,' he yelled.

'...but I can still teach him a bloody lesson,' Maurice finished, thrusting his fist towards Tom, who ducked.

Gwilym and Idris went to grab Maurice, but Henry reached him first, landing him a punch in the face that had him staggering backwards. He ended up bumping into the front room door before he steadied himself. He was dazed, looking ahead as if he didn't know where he was. His left eye was already red underneath.

Gwen clasped her hand to her mouth. She didn't know Henry had that in him. He'd always been more the sort to walk away from trouble or try to sort things out. Nobody else said anything, maybe surprised by Henry's uncharacteristic action too.

Maurice waggled his head and appeared to become aware of his surroundings.

'So that's what you do to someone you fought side by side with, is it, and who's your butty in the pit.'

'I can't believe the hypocrisy I'm hearing,' said Tom. 'You take Henry's girl away, not to mention leaving your wife and daughter, and you've the nerve to criticise Henry's response? Talk about double standards. And you seem to forget, Maurice, that although we weren't in the same battalion, we were both in the 114th Brigade. Yet you were happy to hit me. It seems to me that you make up your morals as you go along.'

'I'll go to Sergeant Harries I will. Tell him Henry assaulted me. God, it hurts.' He pulled a face and touched his eye, causing himself to wince.

'There are several witnesses here who'll tell him he were defending my husband,' said Gwen. 'Who do you think Harries will side with, given the trouble you've already caused today?'

'You lot, I hope you all get what you deserve, especially when everyone finds out who the father of Polly's son is.'

Gwen opened her mouth to say something, but what could she say? Nothing to persuade him not to tell. What people's reaction to them would be because of her father-in-law's mistake, she couldn't begin to foresee.

'Unless, of course, you'd like to give me a tidy sum of money to keep me quiet,' Maurice sneered, which made his face look all the more peculiar because of the slowly swelling eye.

Oh no, thought Gwen. That could be Tom's inheritance gone.

To her surprise, her husband laughed. 'Not a chance,' he said. 'You're not going to blackmail us with that. It was my father's mistake, and I took the blame for that mistake once, and it nearly cost me my future.' He looked over at Gwen.

She recalled how she'd refused his attentions at first, believing him to be the father of both Polly's and Jenny's babies and that she'd just be another conquest.

'It's your decision,' said Maurice. 'You'll have to live with it.'

He stormed out, slamming both the door to the scullery and the back door.

'What are you going to do?' said Gwilym.

'Nothing,' said Tom. 'What can I do? My father caused this problem. At least he and mother aren't in the village anymore, which makes things a little easier. For them at least.'

'I'm so sorry,' said Anwen, in some distress. 'I really thought he'd found out it was your father. I would never have… oh dear.'

'You really should have found out what was going on before you jumped in,' said Gwen, as angry with the feeling of powerlessness as she was with Anwen. 'What a stupid thing to say.'

'Sorry, I'm confused,' said Henry his eyebrows scrunched. 'You're the father of Polly's child or not, Tom?'

'No!' said Gwen. 'Weren't you listening? Herbert is the father, not Tom! And now everybody in the village will know, after we've managed to keep it a secret this long!'

'I think we'd better leave them in peace,' said Idris.

'Yes,' said Anwen, stifling a sob as she hurried out, Idris in tow.

'That was unnecessary, Gwen,' said Tom. 'And you know what? Maybe it's better that people know it was my father, not me, because me denying I had anything to do with it wasn't going to stop Maurice telling people it was me.'

'What a mess,' said Elizabeth. 'I don't think we should blame Anwen though. She didn't cause the problem. That honour goes to my father, and he's not here to take the consequences. And this revelation isn't going to be good for Polly either.'

'Damn Polly!' said Gwen. 'She's only got herself to blame.' She undid the pinny and threw it on the table.

-

Polly had just come down from putting Herby to bed and was looking forward to carrying on sewing the shorts and sailor top she was making for him. But as she came down the stairs, there was a knock on the front door, and she could see two figures through the glass. Now what? They didn't look like Amelia or Maurice, at least.

Opening the door, she was surprised to see Anwen, with Idris behind her.

'Oh Polly,' said Anwen, 'I'm so sorry.'

'What, what on earth's happened now?'

'I've come around to apologise. Please, could we step in? We don't want other people hearing.'

Polly didn't like the sound of this. She could tell them to go away, but Anwen had been good to her since Gus had been arrested. She must have a genuine reason for turning up.

'Come into the kitchen.' She was glad Herby was already in bed and that her parents had gone into the garden to discuss what vegetables to plant up for summer. She led them through, taking her place on the range side of the table, while Anwen and Idris stood, looking awkward, at the other end.

'I'm so sorry, Polly,' Anwen repeated. 'I really thought Maurice had gone to Tom and Gwen's because he knew.'

'He went to Tom's?'

'Yes, to accuse him of being Herby's father.'

'He *isn't* Herby's father, I told Maurice that.'

'I know he isn't, but because I came in partway through the conversation, when Maurice was about to hit Tom—'

'Hit him? Oh Lord, is he all right?' Polly rubbed her forehead with her fingers and closed her eyes.

'He's fine,' said Idris. 'Maurice isn't so good though, as Henry punched him one.'

'Henry was there too? Oh Lord,' Polly repeated.

'But the thing is, when I came in Maurice was about to hit Tom because of who Herby's father was, and I assumed that, well, he really knew, so I said he couldn't hit Tom for something his father had done, not realising he thought Tom was the father. So, the cat's out of the bag.'

Polly placed her hands flat on the table and leant her head forward onto them. It was a wonder Maurice hadn't been straight back with that bit of information to rub her face in it.

'I'm sorry, Polly. I just thought he—'

Polly straightened herself. 'Hold on. You knew?'

'Yes. I've known for a while, as do Gwen and Violet. Though I did originally think it were Tom and told Gwen, to make her wary of him when he first took an interest in her.'

'So, you all knew, but you still took me on to work?'

'Mrs Bowen asked us to do so. It was a condition of her giving us the rails and bits and pieces. It seemed reasonable, with your situation and with you having a babby to raise. And you're a good seamstress.'

All this time she'd thought she'd been harbouring a deep secret and they knew?

'Does that mean lots of people know?'

'Not that I'm aware of. Only us. And Gwilym.'

'I don't understand. Only Tom and Mr Meredith knew, and they said they'd keep it to theirselves.'

'Elizabeth knew too.' The next words came tumbling out. 'Then I saw you at McKenzie House when I worked there, and saw you was pregnant, and thought it must be Tom's. Apparently, he'd agreed to say it were him if anyone guessed it had something to do with the family, like I did. So when Elizabeth found I'd been in the hall when you left and had overheard and assumed it was Tom's, she didn't contradict it. I'm afraid I told Gwen and Violet.'

Polly thought she had the gist of that. 'How do you know it was Mr Meredith now then?'

Anwen sighed. Idris all the while stood behind her, head bowed.

'Because Gwen confronted Tom when he tried to court her, when she were maid at the Big House, and he told her the truth. And about Jenny's baby, because Gwen had seen the likeness between Freddie and Tom's childhood photograph.'

'Oh. Jenny never told Mr Meredith though. So does he know now?'

'Yes, he does.'

'Jenny doesn't know that. I suppose I'd better tell her. Maurice doesn't know about her, does he?'

'No. Jenny's name didn't come up.'

'That's something. My parents don't know. I suppose they'll find out, so I'd better tell them.'

They'd be disappointed anew, despite what her father had said.

–

Henry's fist hurt, but that's not what he was worried about. Inevitably, he was shaking, but this time it had started in his shoulders, not his hands, so was more obvious.

Elizabeth was saying, 'Oh dear, I wonder how long it will take for that to go around,' when Henry felt a hand on his shoulder. It was Tom's.

'Are you all right, old chap? You're trembling.'

Gwen went towards her brother. 'Good heavens, you're shaking quite badly. Sit down.'

'I don't want to sit down. I'm fine. Just angry. That's what it is. And frustrated.' He wanted to persuade them of this, and maybe himself, but he feared it wasn't the case. If he kept still, he might get worse and make a fool of himself. If he moved, he wasn't sure whether he'd even make it to the door before his legs collapsed.

'Henry, I think it's a bit more than that, isn't it?' said Tom. 'I've noticed it before. Believe me, I know what it's like, having suffered in a small way myself. Have a seat, please.'

Henry sat in one of the wooden armchairs by the range as instructed.

'Mam said you'd been shouting in your sleep, and that you'd been shaking quite a bit,' said Gwen, 'but she also thought it was getting better.'

'Me too,' he admitted. 'At least, until I thought Amelia might be seriously ill. Then yesterday, when she left… I had a very bad night. It was only hearing that she'd come back that got me out of the house earlier. Then, when I thought Maurice might be causing trouble for you…' Now he'd started, he couldn't stop. 'It was quite bad, the shaking, when I first came home, remembering all those deaths, the noise, the explosions, but walking out with Amelia somehow… gave me hope, and, and—' he broke down, leaning forward, head in hands. 'But it never went away, not really, and now I'm afraid I'll get worse, and shake all the time. Or start jerking and having fits like a couple of the men in the battalion. Ended up in the loony bin, they did. That's where I'll end up too. I've got shell shock but I've been trying to pretend I haven't.'

Tom hunkered down next to him. 'I don't think you'll be sent anywhere, Henry. You just need a bit of help dealing with it. Those who end up in the psychiatric hospitals are far worse and can't live normally at all. Some can't see or hear or think they can't. They can't hold a job down like you can.'

'It's hard sometimes, being in the dark, underground. Like my nightmares of having the trench blow up around me and being buried alive. But at least working hard with a pickaxe keeps me going. It helps me avoid that smothering feeling.'

'Oh Henry!' Gwen knelt down next to her brother and took his hands. 'I hadn't realised you was going through so much.'

'Amelia said I was weak.'

'Amelia is a nasty piece of work.'

'But I wonder if she'd have stayed if I'd been stronger. She wouldn't have picked Maurice.'

'Maurice isn't strong,' said Tom. 'A strong man doesn't abandon his wife and child. And the fact that Amelia would abandon you so readily shows she wouldn't have been a good wife to you. A good spouse would stick with you through thick and thin.'

Henry noticed him glance at Gwen. She had chosen Tom, despite his disability. He knew in his heart they were right about Amelia, but his heart wouldn't let her go.

'I know someone who can help you,' said Tom. 'It's the psychiatrist in Cardiff who I used to see once a week. I was reluctant at first, but it did help me.'

'I can't afford that,' said Henry. He was in enough debt as it was. 'And I've heard terrible things, about how it's more like a punishment, making men do things they hate and depriving them of things they enjoy. And there's the electric shock treatment.'

'My psychiatrist is a bit more up to date than that, thank heavens. He used something called psychotherapy. It helps you work through the problems. And you don't have to pay. I'll sort out the paperwork for you, as I know what to do, then the government will pay, as you're an ex-soldier.'

'I appreciate your help, Tom.' Henry looked up and realised Elizabeth and Gwilym were no longer there.

'Your shaking seems to have subsided a little,' said Tom. 'Why don't I walk you home the back way, and we can tell your parents about it.'

Henry nodded. If this psychiatrist could help Tom, it was worth a try. He stood slowly and found he was steady enough to walk.

'I'll fetch my coat.' Tom went to the hall and Gwen followed him.

Henry took the opportunity to walk up and down the kitchen to test his legs out and steady his breathing. Yes, he could make it home.

-

In the hall, Gwen took a jacket down off the hatstand as Tom put his coat on and did it up. He was adept at it now, even with the artificial arm.

'Are you coming too? You don't have to,' he said.

'Actually, I have another errand I need to run.'

She wanted to get it over and done with while she was still angry enough to do it. It was something she probably ought to ask the others in their sewing business about first. But no, she was sure they'd agree, now, that it was the right thing to do.

'I didn't know the government paid for your treatment with the psychiatrist,' she said.

Tom moved in close to her, whispering, 'It didn't. But I can afford to use a little of my inheritance to help your brother. It's the least I can do for a fellow soldier.'

'Oh Tom.' She welled up as she threw her arms around him. 'What did I do to deserve you?'

'Everything. It's me who doesn't deserve you.'

'Nonsense.' She let him go, smiling tearfully. 'Will you be back in time to go to *Yeoman of the Guard*?'

'Yes, of course. It doesn't start till eight o'clock and it's only...' He looked at his wristwatch. 'Five fifty. But do you still want to go after all that's happened?'

'Yes, I really do. I need a little escape from it all. We all do.'

He nodded. 'Yes. Where are you going, by the way?'

'I'll tell you when I get back. You take Henry home now.'

He held her arm lightly. 'Don't do anything rash, will you?'

Had he read her mind? 'It's for the best.'

His brow creased but he didn't question her.

'I'll see you later.' She stretched up to kiss his lips, before leaving by the front door.

-

The scullery door opened and Polly twisted around, wondering who it was now. Only her mother, thank goodness.

'Hello Anwen, Idris,' said Delia. 'Didn't realise anyone had called round. We was in the garden, talkin' about plantin' some veg. Oh dear, you're all lookin' a bit serious.'

'Mum I have something I'm going to have to tell you and Dad.' Polly bit the side of her bottom lip, dreading the conversation. At least it wouldn't be as bad as when she had to tell them she was pregnant.

Jim's voice was heard from the scullery saying, 'What's this about now? We've 'ad enough trouble for today.' He came through, followed by Gwen, whose arms were folded tightly across her middle.

Now Polly really did feel like she was in trouble.

'I've already told her, Gwen,' Anwen said. 'And apologised. So we might as well leave them in peace.' She started to move towards the hall door.

Gwen came further into the kitchen, looking stern. 'That's not why I'm here. Well not entirely.'

'Maurice hasn't been back causing more trouble, has he?' said Polly.

'Been back where?' said Jim.

'To my house!' replied Gwen, none to delicately. 'The cheek of the man, accusing my husband of being the father of Herby, when of course it were Mr Meredith.'

'*Mr* Meredith, the father?' Delia's eyes were wide.

'Gwen, Polly hadn't told her parents yet!'

'That's not my fault!'

'Herbert. Ah, now it makes sense,' said Jim. 'He could afford to give you a bit of money for Herby.'

'He already gave her a sum of money to keep her quiet,' said Gwen. 'And look what happened.'

Polly wasn't going to take that. 'I did keep quiet. Seems it's everyone else, whose business it isn't, what's been spreading it around.'

'It was our fault it came out,' Anwen said to Gwen. 'Yours and mine mostly. But mine that Maurice found out.' She looked forlorn.

'Maurice knows?' said Delia. 'Oh Lord, that's not good news, given 'is current mood.'

'We'd better go.' Anwen was more insistent now.

'In a moment,' said Gwen. 'I hope you've told Polly her services are no longer required.'

A wave of nausea passed through Polly. She shouldn't have been surprised, but it still seemed unfair since they'd already known.

'No, I haven't!' said Anwen. 'Because they *are* required. It wasn't a secret to us when we took Polly on that Herby was your father-in-law's.'

'You all knew, and we didn't?' said Delia.

'I'll explain later, Mum.'

'What difference does it make that we already knew?' Gwen held her hands up and out.

Anwen's voice went up a few tones as she said, 'Because nothing has changed.'

Gwen pinched her lips into a narrow band. 'Of course it has. We all know that we know now, so can't pretend otherwise. And everyone else will know if Maurice has his way.'

'Oh Lord.' Delia threw her head back and groaned.

'And people will think it mighty strange,' Gwen continued, 'if we keep Polly on knowing that.'

'And I say she's staying,' Anwen insisted. 'If you don't want her working at your house, that's fine, she can work at mine. My stupidity is not going to put her out of a job.'

Polly, contributing nothing now, had the feeling she was an onlooker to a drama taking place on a stage.

'And I say she's dismissed!' said Gwen.

'No, she is not! And I'm the one what came up with the idea of the business.'

'Pulling rank, is it? Think you're the manager or something? We'll see what the others have to say.' With that, Gwen turned on her heel and left the way she'd come.

After she'd gone, Anwen said, more quietly now, 'I'll see you Wednesday morning, Polly.'

'Are you sure?' Although desperate for the work, Polly didn't want to turn up only to feel uncomfortable all day.

'Yes, I'm sure.' She looked back at Idris. 'We'd better get going. We'll see ourselves out.'

After they'd gone, Jim said, 'I think you'd better tell us your side of the story before anyone else supposes to tell us their version.'

'All right.'

Though there were certain details she'd be leaving out.

Chapter Twenty-One

Polly had been dreading going to work at Anwen's that morning, convinced she would have changed her mind about wanting her to work for them, and in fear of Enid and Cadi being short with her. But if anything, they'd been even nicer to her.

'We're so sorry about all the rumours going around,' Enid said not long after she arrived, settled at the front room table with a children's dress she was altering as Polly worked on the bridal gown. 'We know what it's like when people can't keep their noses out of other people's business.'

Violet dropped by not long after, to collect some second-hand clothes they'd bought from a market, to take home to launder. She'd been cheerful in her greeting to Polly.

Polly was now on her own, working on a blouse. The bridal gown was on a hanger, hooked over the picture rail. It was peaceful sitting here, away from everyone, doing something she was good at. If only she could do this full-time. Her lunchtime shift at the McKenzie Arms yesterday had been away from the bar. One of the waitresses at the public house had been ill, and Nerys had asked Polly to take over instead. The guests that lunchtime had been from outside the village, so nobody had known about the trouble. Her stomach did a little jerk as she thought about that evening's shift. Hopefully the men would only be interested in their beer and a gossip and would leave her to be as invisible as she normally was.

The clock on the mantlepiece in the front room struck two. She'd finish off the hem of the sleeve she was sewing before she left.

'You still working?' said Anwen as she came into the room five minutes later.

'Just completing this. There.' She cut the extraneous thread off and hung the blouse back up.

As she lifted her shawl from the chair, she felt immensely thankful to the point of being tearful. She sniffed it back, not wanting Anwen to fuss over her.

Polly stepped through the front door warily. She was meeting her mother in the village so they could stock up on some food to avoid being in the village too much. Not that it helped when it came to buying meat, especially now it was getting warmer.

As she passed the bookshop, she noticed her mother and Herby waiting outside the shop on the opposite side of James Street, where the grocery store was the only building.

'I'm sorry to have kept you waiting,' said Polly, noticing her mother's long face.

''S all right,' she said in a monotone.

Something was up, but Polly didn't want to go into what it might be with Herby there.

As soon as they entered, Florrie Harris was at the end of a queue of three. She turned round to glare at them.

'Huh, I was just saying to your mother, I'm surprised you've the nerve to show your faces.'

So that's why Mum had looked so put out. Maurice had been true to his word, no doubt, and spread his discovery around.

'And I told you to mind your own business,' said Delia. 'None of what's 'appened has affected you.'

'Poor Henry, being made a fool of by *your* Maurice.'

'Come and look at the biscuits,' said Polly, wanting to take her son away from this conversation. She could still hear it though, even as she spoke to Herby about the different types in the barrels.

'My Maurice, as you put it, is an adult and what he does is certainly not my doing. We've disowned him. I think he's a stinker for what he's done to Henry, but even more so to poor Mabel. You don't seem to have considered her in your criticism though. Got something against her too, have you?'

Florrie ignored that and said instead, 'Well, knowing what we know now about Meredith's flyblow, it's clear to see Maurice is just like his sister. The holy estate of matrimony means nothing to neither.'

Delia turned away from Florrie and didn't reply. It was probably the best way to deal with it. A disappointing sense of inevitability gnawed at Polly's insides. Far from eventually forgetting this, she realised that people would remember it and shun her forever.

The doorbell pinged and Polly felt her stress rise as Esther Williams entered. Now the two worst gossips were in the shop.

'I don't suppose the apple has fallen far from the tree,' Florrie persisted, perhaps hoping to rile her mother into a reply.

Polly expected Esther to catch on and add her own two penn'orth, but she kept resolutely silent, looking around at the merchandise instead. Having run out of things to say about the biscuits, Polly went back to stand next to her mother.

'And it's not decent sorts what work in public houses as barmaids neither,' Florrie said.

'I'm sure Elsie Thomas would be happy to hear your opinion of her. As would Nerys Moss,' said Delia.

Florrie didn't reply. Hopefully her mother would leave it there, having had the last word. But it wasn't to be.

'And another thing: don't be havin' a go at me when the person what started the nasty rumours about Anwen and Gwen's sewing business has just come into the shop. Perhaps you'd like to have a go at Esther for causing trouble. And for taking money from Amelia Bowen as payment! Probably some of that she stole from her uncle.'

Esther turned around and went back out of the shop, without a word.

'That's enough of that now,' Mrs Brace called over from behind the counter.

'You didn't say that when Florrie's mouth was flapping,' said Delia.

'I'm saying it now. And I'm talking to all of you.'

'Suits me for people to keep their traps shut,' said Delia.

Polly just hoped there wasn't someone ready to pass judgement when they got to the butcher's.

–

The McKenzie Arms was busy that evening, for a Wednesday. As she'd hoped, the men were more interested in getting their orders of beer filled than they were concerned about what Polly – or her brother – had done. She was nevertheless happy to have Steven there, serving at the other end of the counter from her.

There was a lull in trade and Polly took the opportunity to wash a few glasses.

'I'll just go and sort out a few more bottles of gin and rum from the cellar whilst it's quiet,' said Steven. 'I won't be long.'

'All right. I'll get these done.'

As she dried the glasses, she looked out at the public bar, three-quarters full this evening. There was a hum of chatter, with a chorus of laughs from the table closest, with Noah Schenck and half-a-dozen men from the Silver Band on it.

In one corner, on two tables, sat eight of the men who'd been in the same Pal's brigade in the war. As usual, they were the quietest of the groups. Whenever she'd passed them, to collect glasses, they'd always talked in muted tones. Henry Austin was at one end of a table, his head resting on his hand, the men either side clapping him on the shoulder every now and then. She'd been surprised to see him come in earlier, maybe cajoled into it by his friends.

As she finished drying the last glass, the door into the bar opened, and in came three men. Her heart sank when she saw that one of them was Connie's husband. He said something to the other two, who went off to find a table. Sioni came to the bar to order.

'Fancy seeing you here,' he said, looking down towards her chest, even though she had a high neckline.

'Two pints of the 4d and one of the GHB.'

'Coming up,' she said cheerfully, as if he were any other customer. She didn't want him to see she was afraid of him.

He leant on the counter as she turned the tap to fill the first two glasses. 'I hear you were Meredith's bit on the side for a while,' he whispered.

She told herself to ignore it.

'I'm guessing it's the bit of money he could afford what encouraged you to lower your drawers, is it? I'm sure we could come to a similar arrangement, like. What d'ya say?'

'How is Connie?' she said, to change the subject and to remind him he had a wife.

'Not nearly as pleasing on the eye as you are. Bet you've got a few tricks up your sleeve too. Or up your petticoat, in your case.' He put his head back and laughed, as if he'd just told her a very funny joke.

'And a pint of the GHB, wasn't it?'

'I could meet you on the way home tonight. We could go under the bridge. I'd make it worth your while.'

'That'll be one and sixpence, please.'

He took some coins from his pocket and counted out the appropriate ones. He put them on the counter but placed his hand over hers as she tried to scoop them up.

'Not good enough for you, am I?'

'I'm not that kind of girl,' she muttered.

'What about Meredith?'

'That was a mistake. And not one I intend to repeat.'

She shifted her hand from under his, causing the coins to drop onto the floor.

'Clumsy!' he called good-naturedly. He managed to pick up the three glasses between his fingers and conveyed them to a table in the middle.

She bent to retrieve the coins, taking a moment to squeeze her eyes shut. What if he was hanging around again after work, and tried to act on his suggestion?

Steven came back through the door clutching gin bottles in one hand and rum in the other.

'You all right, *fach*?' he said.

She stood, holding the coins. 'Yes, just dropped the money that's all. Steven, would it be possible to walk me back home after stop-tap again tonight? It's just—' she glanced at her brother-in-law. 'It's just I heard Sioni saying he was meeting Reg and Iolo when he's finished here, so I know they'll be around.'

She knew no such thing, but once again it seemed wrong to implicate a member of her family in something shady like this.

'Of course, it won't be a problem. Only a coupla minutes, isn't it.'

'Thank you, Steven. I think I might ask my dad to meet me in future.'

'Any time you want me to oblige, I'll be more than happy. I know Nerys has always worried about her women staff going home late at night. Never had an incident so far, but you can't be too careful. Especially the way people have reacted to these revelations. Like it's their business… What can I get you, sir?' He turned to serve a customer.

She wondered how many other men might think they could take their chances with her now. The thought depressed her. Perhaps she should move to somewhere nobody knew her. But how would she afford the rent, even on one room? And her mother wouldn't be there to help with Herby. And he wouldn't have his own room, and maybe not a garden to play in…

'Eight half pints of the GHB, please, miss.'

'Mm? Oh sorry, I was miles away.'

It was Douglas Ramsay. 'You looked it,' he said with a smile that still looked sad.

'Eight half pints coming up.'

Unless her father moved to another mine, and her parents moved house – a lot to ask of them – she was stuck in Dorcalon.

–

It was the end of the working week, with a day off to look forward to tomorrow. Henry considered this as he made his way from the lamp room to the gate promising him freedom. But before that, he had his first appointment with the psychiatrist in Cardiff to get through. It had been organised by Tom after a couple of phone calls and scheduled swiftly, only five days after, due to a cancellation.

With Maurice gone who knew where to work, Teilo had become Henry's butty. He'd been suffocated by the constant enquiries of his well-being all week. Now he'd probably have the doctor delving into his feelings too if what Tom had said was anything to go by.

Nearing the gate his spirit sank a little lower when he heard his name called by a familiar voice.

'Henry Austin!' John Bowen bellowed, marching towards him from his office.

He turned around slowly, by which time Bowen had caught him up.

'Been yapping to the bosses about me you have, telling them I was violent in the chapel.'

Henry shook his head, squeezing his lips together. 'I never said no such thing. I haven't even seen Mr Hopkins this week.' The new manager had never been as hands-on as Herbert Meredith, who'd always kept an eye on what was going on all over the colliery.

'You bloody liar. How come I got a telling off then? And Hopkins said one of the coal board bosses had phoned him up too, having heard about it.'

'Like I have any contact with the bosses,' said Henry.

'But your sister is the daughter-in-law of Herbert Meredith. I bet you told him and he has some contacts in the company.'

'I haven't even seen Mr Meredith since she married Tom.'

'But your sister could have passed it on.'

It wasn't beyond the bounds of possibility. Then Henry remembered something. 'The Bargoed colliery, where Meredith is manager now, doesn't even belong to the Tredegar Coal Company, so it's different bosses, isn't it?'

'Beh! They're all thick as thieves, the lot of them.'

Idris came up behind him. 'There are people with higher status in the village what would be in a better position than Henry to pass on what happened.'

'But there's no one what's got no better motive than him here.' He pointed a finger at Henry. 'I've had to explain that it's all a lie, and that I was just a concerned uncle looking out for my niece.'

'There's somewhere I've got to be, so if you don't mind.' Henry walked away, Idris following on.

'Don't think you'll get away with this,' Bowen shouted. 'Taking Amelia's departure out on me.'

Out of the gate he speeded up. Idris kept apace.

'Where have you got to be, mun?'

Henry didn't want to talk to Idris about it, not yet, even though he knew he could trust him.

'Gotta get a train for an appointment. I'll tell you another time. Keep that to yourself.'

'Of course. Anwen told me that Pastor Thomas's wife was going to ask him to have a word with Hopkins, so that might be how he knew about Bowen's outburst.'

'Wouldn't make any difference to Bowen even if he knew. He just wants a reason to take it out on me.'

Reaching the corner of James Street, Henry said, 'Right, this is me. See you at chapel Sunday.'

'Don't suppose you want to have a pint with us in the Arms later? If you can draw yourself away from the old Pals.'

'Not tonight. Can't afford it at the moment.'

With that, he swung onto his street and marched down it, not wanting to miss his train.

–

Henry was staring out of the window when the new greenery of spring disappeared and the houses of Bargoed loomed into view once more. The train started to slow for its stop at the station there. The one other inhabitant in the carriage, a middle-aged woman, looked up from her book briefly, but satisfied it wasn't her stop went back to reading.

The first session with the psychiatrist in Cardiff today had not been as terrifying as he'd feared. The doctor had talked of remembering the horror, rather than reliving it, and had allowed Henry to tell him dispassionately what had happened to him in the war, and since. He'd been hesitant to begin with, admitting he felt like a weak fool. But with the doctor's assurance that he was no such thing, and that the condition was nothing to do with weakness, he'd encouraged him on. Henry had found that the more he'd talked of it, the more he wanted to, getting out all those experiences and emotions he'd bottled up, not sharing with anyone. The fact the doctor was a stranger, and non-judgemental, had helped. At the end, the doctor had said it had been a good start, and that many patients took a lot longer to say as much as Henry had.

Despite this, it had been a relief to get it over with. Henry wasn't sure yet how much use it would be ultimately, but if the government were paying, he might as well give it a go.

A quarter of an hour later, as the train drew into Dorcalon, he wondered what he'd do with his Saturday evening. It was light until around eight o'clock now, so he might go out for a short walk on Twyn Gobaith. Perhaps afterwards he'd sit with his parents in the kitchen and read a book, rather than hide in his bedroom, as he had been doing since Amelia had left.

Amelia.

What would he have done had she come back this very day, begging forgiveness, to be with him once more? He knew what he should do, but he also knew that his feelings for her still ran deep. What a fool he was.

Through the windows, he was embarrassed to spot a small reception awaiting him, consisting of his parents and Gwen. It was like coming back from the war once more. He waited until the brakes of the train squealed to a halt before getting up.

'Good evening,' he said to his silent companion as he left.

She replied in kind, with a smile and a nod.

Out in the corridor a mad idea occurred to him, to stay on the train and go onto Rhymney, to go to the picture house and lose himself in the darkness, not have to face his family with their questions. No: running away was never the answer. The psychiatrist had said as much.

Almost immediately he stepped off the train, his family ran up the platform and surrounded him.

'How'd it go?' said his mother.

'It was… all right.'

'What did he do, this psychiatrist fella?' said his father.

'Did it help?' said Gwen.

'I really don't want to go into it now. I have a lot to think about.'

'Of course, son, of course,' said Albert.

'But it was worth it?' Ruth persisted.

'We'll see, we'll see. I hope there's some supper ready, I'm starving.'

'Of course. I've got a nice cut of lamb and some lovely veggies from the garden,' said Ruth. 'And Mamgu's made a nice roly-poly pudding for dessert, for a special treat. Gwen and Tom are coming for their supper too, see.'

So much for his walk out. And reading his book. Never mind; there'd be plenty of time for a walk tomorrow. If it was a nice day, he'd take his book with him, to sit and read with a view.

'That's good,' he said, not wanting to show his disappointment about the evening. 'As long as we don't talk about my trip to Cardiff today.'

'Righty ho, *bach*,' said Albert. 'I'll take care we don't.'

–

'Are you sure this is a good idea, Mum?' said Polly on the walk to chapel that Sunday.

'It's our place of worship too. Why, I could tell you a few fings about the people what turn up there each Sunday, holier than thou. What about Esther? People used to pick on 'er when she first went back. Now they've moved on to the next target, which is us. No doubt, someone else'll do somefing soon and they'll move on to them.'

'I fink she's right, you know, love,' said Jim. 'We've just gotta stick it out.'

The chapel was only beginning to fill up when they got there.

'You take those seats near the door,' said Polly, 'and I'll take Herby to Sunday School.' She wasn't certain of the wisdom of this, but Anabel Thomas was one of the women who ran it so it should be all right.

Walking her son through to the side room, she met Jenny.

'*Bore da*, Polly.'

'Um, *bore da*, Jenny.' Even after sixteen years of being in Wales, she always panicked initially when someone spoke to her in what was, for her, a shaky second language.

'How have you been?'

She looked around to make sure no one was listening, then whispered, 'Not so good, if I'm honest.'

'There still doesn't seem to have been anything said about Freddie, you know.'

'I haven't heard anything. I'm sure if people had found out, you'd already know about it, if my experience is anything to go by.'

'Oh Polly, I'm that sorry for you.' She pulled a face of genuine sympathy, but she must also be thinking, thank goodness it wasn't her. She'd certainly have thought that if the situation had been reversed, so she couldn't blame her.

'I'll drop Herby off now and go back to my parents.'

'Freddie's just over there.' She pointed to where her son was sitting, crossed legged, near the wall.

Coming up to the little boy, she was about to say, *Here's your friend, I'll see you later*, when old Mrs Morton, a Sunday School teacher when Polly first came here, stepped out of the other room. Was she helping at Sunday School again? That didn't bode well.

'Excuse *me*,' said Mrs Morton, standing stiffly in a long black dress. Her hair was pulled back into a high bun, 'but would you kindly remove yourself and the child from these premises. You're not welcome here.'

Polly didn't know what to do, to go meekly and not cause a fuss, or to stick to her right to be here. 'I don't think we should take this out on the children, should we?'

'Born in sin, he is a *sinner*.'

The children looked round in alarm; no doubt some of the older ones would be aware of the accusations and rumours. Maybe they'd pick on Herby – and even Freddie, just because he was his friend.

'I will take my son now, but only because I don't want him taught by a mean-spirited shrew like you. Come on, Herby.'

'But I want stay wiv Freddie.'

'We've got to go.'

'But I not want go.' He started crying, resisting her as she tried to lift him up.

Anabel Thomas came out of the other room with a stack of paper.

'What's going on?'

Polly got her side in before Mrs Morton had a chance. 'I've been asked to leave, as I and my son are apparently not welcome.'

'Why would you think that?' said Anabel.

'Ask Mrs Morton. Apparently Herby is a sinner, as she put it.'

Anabel placed the paper on a table and turned sharply to the Sunday School helper. 'Mrs Morton, we are not here to judge people. Only the Lord can do that. And to pick on a child!' Polly had never seen her look so cross.

'No one wants her here,' Mrs Morton persisted.

'That is not for you to decide. I'm sorry about this, Mrs Smith. Please, do leave your son where he is.'

'Don't expect me to teach today then,' said Mrs Morton.

'That is entirely your choice,' said Anabel.

She didn't know what to do. The damage had been done; it wouldn't be a good idea to leave her son here. As Polly picked up a grizzling Herby, her mother came into the room.

'Polly, we're leaving. I don't come to God's house to be insulted.'

'Oh Mrs Coombes, I'm so sorry,' said Anabel. 'I will fetch Lewis, so he can have a stern word.'

'Thank you, Mrs Thomas, but I'm not in the mood for staying now.'

'Good riddance,' Mrs Morton announced, over loudly.

When they were halfway across the chapel, Rhonwen called, 'Where are you going in such a hurry?'

'Back home where we'll be more welcome,' said Delia, catching Jim up by the door.

Polly tried to keep up, juggling her son to her other hip.

About to leave, Pastor Thomas's voice called, 'Hold on, Mr and Mrs Coombes.' He ran across the chapel. 'Please, don't feel you have to leave.' He had everyone's attention now.

'They should go,' Florrie Harris called. 'No better than they should be, any of them. I told them, I did.'

Polly and her family lingered by the door, even though all she wanted to do was leave. Anabel came out next, running to her husband's side as he appealed to them to stay.

Mrs Morton came out behind her and was soon standing next to Florrie. 'We don't need no strumpet here, tempting our men to give her money for favours.'

Strumpet? Paid for her favours? It was true that Mr Meredith had given her a little extra spending money, but she'd never thought of it as being paid for her services, not at the time. Now it filled her with a hot shame.

'My daughter's no strumpet,' said Delia.

'Yes she is,' Florrie countered. 'And an adulteress.'

'Well I knows me Bible,' said Delia, 'and I know that when the Pharisees asked Jesus to condemn the adulteress, Jesus told them, "Let the one among you what is wiv'out sin, cast the first stone." He knew they was 'ypocrites, just like you lot! She's married and a decent woman now and has atoned for any sin she might have committed. But gossip and meanness are sins too, and you lot have both in plenty.'

'And there is your first sermon for today,' Pastor Thomas told them.

'Thank you, Pastor,' said Jim, 'but I think we'd better go, all the same.'

Lewis Thomas nodded sagely. 'I understand. I will come to visit you.'

They went down the steps as Elizabeth, Gwen and Gwilym rushed up.

'Are you going?' said Elizabeth.

'Sorry, I can't talk now,' said Polly, looking back as she hurried after her parents.

'Probably been thrown out,' she heard Gwen say, and wondered what they'd hear about the incident when they went inside.

She was thankful to the Thomases for sticking up for them, but she doubted it would do much to change the opinion of those determined to bully them. Gus and his family, Maurice's misconduct and now finding out who Herby's father was: she was unlikely ever to be forgiven.

Chapter Twenty-Two

It was time to leave Anwen's for the day, and Polly couldn't say she was sorry. Gwen had come over for a meeting earlier and had once again sent Polly to the front room and closed the door. It was disheartening, making her feel even more of an outcast than she already felt.

Gwen mostly gave instructions to her via Anwen, but when she did speak to Polly, it was in the manner of a teacher, all haughty and critical, not in the kind, chatty way Anwen or Enid would talk.

Polly shut Anwen's front door behind her, deciding she'd go and see her sister-in-law, Mabel, after school had finished. That way Herby could play with his cousin, Lily, while Polly found out how Mabel was faring. Mabel had cried each time she'd been to see her, even if it had now become a stifled sniffle.

Turning onto Bryn Road, the shortcut to James Street, in a world of her own, she was shaken back to reality by something barked in her direction. She didn't hear what it was at first, only noticing the snarling face of Gertie Pritchard from the butcher's, as she came closer.

'You little whore. Stanley might have stopped me from banning you from the shop, but he can't do anything when I'm on the street and he can't hear me. You should be ashamed of yourself, not walking round the village, bold as brass, like. No one wants to see your ugly face. That's it, walk away without a word of defence. I'm surprised any man would look at you, let alone two, and who knows how many others what have paid for your services. Though I don't suppose they have to look at your face.'

Whatever she said next drifted away in the distance as Polly's steps speeded up. Soon she was taking the back lane towards her garden gate, hurrying even faster.

She held in the tears until she pushed open the back door and fell into the scullery, when they flowed down her cheeks, accompanying the long whine.

'Is that you love?' said Delia, coming into the room. 'Oh my Lord, what on earth's 'appened now?'

Polly ran to her mother, throwing her arms around her. 'Oh Mum, it's been a month and a half now, and still people are being horrible. I can't take it anymore.'

'Who was it this time?'

'Gertie Pritchard. She said she could say what she liked because Mr Pritchard wasn't there to stop her.'

'She's got a bleedin' cheek when her daughter is in prison now for perjury when she tried to get Mrs Meredith locked up for manslaughter.'

Polly felt the shame anew each time Margaret Meredith's name was mentioned. Especially now Polly knew that she'd known about the dalliance for a long while.

'It's all my fault, and now it's coming back to haunt me.'

'Now now.' Delia stroked her back as she sobbed once more. 'What you did wasn't right, but you've more than paid for your mistake, whereas Herbert Meredith got away almost scot-free. And this has only come out now because of Maurice's stupid behaviour.'

'I'm sorry, Mum. It's all being blamed on you and Dad too. Where's Herby?'

'In the kitchen doin' an old jigsaw puzzle of Lily's, what Mabel brought round for him. Now don't you worry about us bein' blamed. We can 'andle it.' She pulled Polly upright, took out a clean handkerchief from her skirt pocket and passed it to her. 'I reckon you could do wiv a break though, love, and I've had an idea.'

Polly wiped her eyes and then blew her nose. 'What's that, Mum?'

'We've saved a little bit a money for you to spend on a day out, Cardiff probably, as we know ya like it. You can look round, get yourself a little treat and 'ave some tea somewhere. You've still got a coupla tidy dresses in the cupboard upstairs. Stick on some of that face paint you used to use – a bitta rouge and some lip stain, and 'ave a nice time. Maybe this coming Saturday. You're not workin' till the evening, and I'll look after little Herby.'

'Oh, I don't know. I've not done nothing like that since, well, since before I left for Surrey.'

'Well, there you are then, it's long overdue.'

'Well… Yes, all right. Thank you, that would be nice.'

'Mummy!' came a voice from the kitchen door as Herby spotted her and ran to her legs to hug them.

'Hello, my lovely boy.' She scooped him up and hugged him. Though she regretted the hurt her affair with Herbert Meredith might have caused, she couldn't regret having had him.

–

What a lovely afternoon in Cardiff that had been, visiting the arcades, the market and the department stores. She went over it in her head as she stood on the platform, waiting for the train back to Dorcalon. There had been so much she'd have loved to have bought – a stylish green cloche hat, some fabric and a pattern to make a wide-necked blouse and some blue Mary Jane shoes. But with the little spare money, she'd only had enough for tea at The Dutch Café and a colouring book for Herby.

The platform wasn't as busy as she'd feared, so that when she got on the train she managed to get a carriage to herself.

She'd only just sat by the window, when another passenger slid back the door and stepped in, out of breath as if they'd been running. She looked up to smile at the newcomer, but her face stalled in the gesture halfway when she realised it was Henry Austin.

Expecting him to leave once he'd spotted her, she was surprised when he said, 'Oh, hello, Polly. Do you mind if I sit in here?'

He didn't seem put out by her being there, which encouraged her to say, 'No, of course not.'

He sat down opposite, a little closer to the middle.

Polly was relieved when a couple more people got into their carriage, one sitting on the same side as her, next to the sliding door, the other opposite. This would make the need for any awkward conversation between her and Henry unnecessary.

She'd always enjoyed train rides, looking out at the countryside in between the various familiar towns and looming collieries as the engine chugged along. The person on her side got off at Caerphilly. Nobody else got on, so that when the other passenger alighted at Bargoed, it left only her and Henry in the carriage. By this time, Henry was reading a slim volume she'd noticed him get out of his pocket not long after the train had left Cardiff.

Settling back to watch the racing landscape once more, she was surprised when Henry said, 'I'm sorry for all the abuse you've been getting from the villagers. It probably wouldn't have happened if Amelia hadn't shared her suspicions with Maurice.' He put the book open, upside down, on his lap.

'You've nothing to be sorry about, Henry. It's them what can't keep their thoughts to theirselves what need to be sorry.'

'I heard about Florrie Harris in chapel. Quite unforgiveable, especially from someone what claims to be such an ardent Christian. Your mother put her straight, from what I heard. I think Pastor Thomas might have altered his sermon, as he mentioned the Pharisees being invited to cast the first stone again.'

'I didn't know that. We're really sorry, my parents and me, about Maurice stealing Amelia away. He's dead to us, is

Maurice, after what he did to Mabel and Lily. He's always acted the hard man, since he were a youth, but he used to adore Mabel and Lily. I dunno what happened. I suppose I could blame the war, but the rest of you don't seem to have turned hard and uncaring.'

'If anything, most of us have become too much the other way,' said Henry. 'But we've all been changed. Just in different ways.'

'How could anyone not be changed by what you went through?'

He nodded but didn't reply.

'And things are so different for everybody.' She hadn't meant to keep talking, suspecting Henry wanted to get back to his book, but he was such an easy person to speak to, she couldn't help it. 'Some of it's good, like some women getting the vote. Not me, of course; I'm too young. And the fashions are so different. I can't imagine what our mothers would have said if we'd worn clothes like this before the war started.' She looked at her loose jacket, over an equally loose dress, no shape, no pinched-in waist. One petticoat instead of several. And a liberty bodice under that, rather than a pinching corset.

'I bet they're a lot more comfortable,' he said, laughing.

She couldn't help but laugh too. 'Oh yes, very much so.'

He closed his book and slipped it back into his jacket pocket. 'I remember you being very colourful before we went off to war. Quite a picture really.'

'You mean gawdy and a show-off,' she amended. When he was about to protest, she added, 'Oh, I know what I was like. Wanted attention, I did, back then. Now it's the last thing I want.' She let out a long sigh. 'I recall you being a bit of a heartbreaker in your younger days, with your light blond hair, always fashionably cut.' She hoped he wouldn't take offence at that, as if he were somehow substandard now.

He threw his head back and laughed. 'Ah, yes. I think I fancied myself as a bit popular with the girls back then. My hair's not as light as it used to be.' He patted his hair subconsciously.

'Mine were nearly white-blonde as a kiddie. I guess there's none of us how we used to be.'

'The war sobered me up all right, and most others too.'

'I wonder what the 1920s will bring? Hopefully peace and some prosperity, surely, after all we've been through.'

'Let's hope,' he said, though his face didn't reflect his words.

She guessed he was thinking about his own situation, though she'd been thinking about the wider world. Her own situation she couldn't see changing any time soon.

'We're slowing down,' he said. 'We'll be at Dorcalon soon. It's been nice having a conversation with you. I never get the opportunity normally, as you're usually working in the Arms.'

'It's been nice talking to you too,' she said. 'And I'm relieved to learn you don't blame my family for the things what have happened.'

'Here we are.'

The train ground to a screeching halt, after which Henry stood up and held open the sliding door for Polly, followed by the outer door.

'Thank you,' she said as she stepped down.

He lifted his cap. 'Take care.' With that, he marched off ahead, out of the station.

That had been a pleasant end to an enjoyable day. What a shame she couldn't make a friend of him. She lifted the shopping bag from her wrist to the crook of her elbow, looking forward to seeing little Herby's face when she gave him his present.

–

All week Henry had been thinking about his trip home on the train with Polly. Walking up Twyn Gobaïth, behind the Workmen's Institute the following Friday, he was still pondering it.

He hadn't mentioned the chance meeting to his parents in case they said something to Gwen. She would not have been pleased after the outburst she'd had at their parents on Easter Monday evening, about how no one had agreed with her at the meeting they'd had about dismissing Polly. Why had she such a bee in her bonnet about her, since neither Tom nor Elizabeth seemed concerned about her working there?

He'd been tempted out on the walk after his bath today by the warm, bright sun, feeling particularly disheartened by the darkness of the pit today. He'd just tramped over the peak of the hill, to look down on the valley on the other side, towards Tredegar at one end and Rhymney on the other. He'd been imagining Polly there with him as he'd climbed upwards, his thoughts communicated in his mind as if to her. He'd enjoyed their conversation on the train, a little livelier as it was than the ones he had with the old Pals who still gathered him in as one of their own.

And that was all there was to it. Amelia hadn't even been gone two months, so what else would it be? Yet, as each day went by, his indignation with her grew, slowly drowning the tenderness he'd felt, as he recalled small details of their trips out, reinterpreting them in light of what he now knew.

He took a deep breath of the warm air and turned around to head back down. Better not wander too far in case he had another attack of the shakes. The psychiatrist's visits did seem to be helping. He hadn't had an incident for over a week, and then it hadn't lasted as long, as he'd tried out the doctor's suggestions for simply going with it, not fighting it. He seemed to think they were closer to panic attacks than shell shock.

He neared the bottom of the hill, by the fire station and Workmen's Institute.

A sweet scent wafted over from a honeysuckle shrub that was heavily in blossom in the gardens, encouraging him to go and have a look at the flowers there. The beautiful displays of nature had long been a salve to him in troubled times, so he was glad of spring's abundance after a long winter. He imagined it as a crutch for him as he limped through his current life.

He could see that the garden was indeed in full bloom, but an even nicer surprise awaited him as he spotted Polly sitting on the bench near the bottom gate. Herby was nearby, pushing a toy dog on wheels that looked like a terrier. He went through the gate and walked down towards her. It wasn't until he was halfway down that she noticed him and at first her face was filled with alarm, while her stance suggested she was about to get up. Would she rather not have seen him here? He was disappointed at this idea. But as he came closer, she sat back and smiled.

'Hello again,' he said, stopping at the opposite end of the seat from where she was sitting.

'Hello, Henry. I'm glad it's you what come in. I was so pleased to find the gardens empty when I arrived and was afraid…'

'That someone unsympathetic was coming in?'

'Yes,' she sighed.

'May I sit here?'

'Of course.' She stretched out her open palm as an invitation.

'So, I'm guessing you're in between your sewing shift and your one at the Arms?'

'That's right. I was going to help my mum with cleaning upstairs, but she said it was such a nice day that I should take Herby for a walk. I think she wanted the pair of us out from under her feet, if I'm honest.' She laughed, not the silly giggle she'd had at school, but a jolly, yet wary one. 'I still wasn't keen on the idea.'

'You can't hide away forever.' He laughed too. 'Sorry. Says he what hid away the best part of a month after Amelia left.'

'Look, Mummy,' Herby called, running at a good pace down the slope with the dog. 'Barney's racing, like the whippets Grandpa took me to see.'

'So he is,' said Polly. 'Be careful you don't fall, lovey.'

'He speaks good English for a what, three-year-old?'

'Three-and-a-half. And English is more or less the only language he speaks. He has a few Welsh words. Gus and his family obviously didn't speak it. My mum and dad have learned enough to understand the service at the chapel, and a few common phrases, though they struggle with the sermon, so they're grateful for Pastor Thomas's bits of English thrown in.'

'What about you?'

'My Welsh is patchy, which is why I don't speak it much. I guess I learned enough to get by, and people here speak English to you if you speak it to them. I understand more than I can say. And people can still hear I'm English, even though my English relatives think I sound Welsh!'

'Usually, the children here don't learn English properly till they go to school. I can remember getting my knuckles rapped a good deal for speaking Welsh in class.'

'Whereas I was praised for my good English,' she said, amused. 'Which wasn't the case in London! But it's terrible really, isn't it, when you think about it, to have your knuckles rapped for speaking your own language? I did struggle in the playground, with most of you speaking Welsh, especially already being eleven and not being able to join in properly. I think that's why I liked drawing attention to myself with pretty bows and suchlike and being a little madam.'

They were silent for a while. The question Henry was thinking, he was sure he wasn't going to ask, but it suddenly popped out.

'Do you ever get out, of an evening like?' He had a vague idea of where this question was going and warned himself against it.

'Not really. Who is there to go with? Mabel's still in a kind of mourning, even though Rhonwen has urged her to get out while she looks after Lily. My friend Jenny has a child too, and her aunt looks after him while she works, so she doesn't like to take too much advantage.'

'Would your mother look after Herby if you came out to the picture house one evening? Just as friends, like, as we've both been let down. It'd make a change to sitting in the Arms with the Pals, that's for certain.'

She seemed to think about it for a moment, before replying, 'It's very kind of you to suggest it, Henry, but even if it's just as friends, people would assume otherwise. They'd probably say I'd charmed you for money, or something.'

'Don't take any notice of them. They're just unpleasant people.'

'And there's also the fact that I'm still married, so it wouldn't be seemly.'

'You can hardly call it that. I'm sorry, but you know what I mean.'

'Oh, I do,' she said. 'It was barely a marriage from the beginning, or, at least, once he'd got his own way about moving here.'

'It were just an idea, to give us both a bit of social life.'

'Thank you, Henry, that's kind of you. Uh oh.'

She looked up at the top gate, causing him to do the same. Florrie Harris had just entered the garden.

'I'd better get going,' she said.

'I'll see you this evening then.' When she looked confused, he added, 'Friday evening trip to the Arms with the Pals, as usual.'

'Of course. I'll have your usual brew ready,' she chuckled. 'Eight, or six, or however many half pints of the GHB.'

'Maybe I'll have a rum or two to confuse the matter,' he quipped, only half joking. More likely to numb the despair he felt sitting with them.

'See you later, then.' She caught up with Herby, where he was playing near the bottom gate, and they left the gardens.

By this time Florrie Harris had caught up with him. She was wearing a buttoned-up coat and gloves, despite the warm day.

'Wouldn't talk to her unless you want to get yourself a reputation,' she said. 'We all know what she is.'

'Yes, a very kind person,' he said, standing. 'Unlike you, what is a nasty gossip and should look at yourself before criticising others.'

'Well!' She pursed her lips, forming lines like a concertina above her mouth. 'Dunno why I'm surprised. You fight for your country and think it gives you the right to say what you like. Or do what you like, as it did her brother Maurice.' She marched off to the bottom gate and let herself out.

He sat back down. He should have known Polly wouldn't agree to a trip out. And maybe she was right in her reasoning. Still, it was a shame.

He sat there for a while, regarding the explosion of blooms he'd come in to see. If only he'd brought a book to read.

After a while, bored with his own company, he got up and left by the bottom gate, on his way back home.

-

'Hello, loveys,' said Delia, pulling herself upright from weeding as Polly and Herby walked through the back gate. 'Did you two enjoy your trip out?'

'I took Barney for walk and he race like whippet,' said Herby.

'That's lovely,' said Delia. 'He looks worn out.'

'He want rest now.' Herby wheeled him to the open scullery door and over the step, announcing, 'Grandpa!' as he went in.

Once Herby had disappeared, Polly said, 'Something quite funny happened in the gardens.' She still felt uplifted by the recent presence of a friendly face.

'What was that, lovey?'

'I came across Henry Austin. He stopped for a chat again.'

'That was kind of him. He's obviously decided you're all right after talking to you on the train. He shows up a lot of the villagers here, and no mistake. After all, if anyone has reason to resent our family, he does. But what was funny about him being there?'

She wished now she hadn't mentioned it, but she couldn't think of a way of getting out of it.

'You see, he did ask me, just as a friend like, to go to the picture house. You know, because he's lonely and I don't get out much. He was being kind, but I said no. Even if we see it as just friends, no one else will. You don't get men and women being friends.'

'Mmm,' said Delia, clutching her chin. 'Seems to be more common now though, young men and women, going out in groups. You see it in the films.'

'The rich and middle class, maybe. They go to those jazz clubs and dance places and whatnot. They're not like the dances around here, with the men on one side and the women on the other. Either way, it don't seem right, having a trip out with a young man as a friend, does it? And me still married.'

'Hopefully not for much longer. You need to see a solicitor.'

'We've been through this. I can't afford it.'

'What if he comes back here when he gets out? He's due out in, what, November 1922? That's only two-and-a-half years away.'

'I suppose I'll cross that bridge when I get to it.'

'Nobody could blame you for finding company with another man. And it's not like Henry Austin doesn't know you're married. You wouldn't be committing adultery if you just kept him company at a picture house. Life's too short, my gal, and goodness knows, with losing my mother at thirty and a sister at sixteen to the consumption, and my bruvver to the cholera at twenty, I'd say there's no point in 'anging around. What's done is done. You gotta take opportunities when they come. If, by chance, or otherwise, you got rid of Gus, well, Henry would be a nice young man to be involved wiv.'

'Mum, you're forgetting that there's also the fact he's related to the Merediths.'

'Only through his sister. No, if I were you, I'd go back and tell him you've changed your mind and you'd like to go to the picture house wiv 'im.'

Could she? 'But what would people say?'

'It couldn't be any more than they're saying already. And even if you was just friends, he'd be a nice friend to have.'

'I'm gasping for a cuppa tea,' said Polly.

'You put the kettle on, and I'll wash my hands and fetch them Garibaldi biscuits from the pantry.'

Polly went back to the kitchen to collect the kettle and greet her father, who was already playing Snap with Herby. She'd appreciated her mother's words of encouragement, but she'd need to give it serious thought. Nevertheless, she was sure she'd end up deciding against it.

-

Polly had seen Henry on Friday evening in the Arms but would never have said anything to him about going out with so many people nearby. She'd then pictured herself several times over the weekend, approaching Henry to accept his invitation, and she was doing the same thing on Monday, going along James Street on the way to the grocery store, staring at the pavement. Imagining was all she was ever likely to do, and where would she have seen him to tell him in any case, unless she'd purposefully gone to the colliery at two o'clock, and waited for him to come out? She could imagine what people would have to say about that. He only lived up the street from her, but she didn't often come across him.

Reaching the end of the street, her head full of fantasy, she was surprised to hear it come to life, with the words, 'Hello again, Polly.'

She jumped, looking up with her eyes stretched wide.

'Sorry to startle you,' said Henry, washed and spruced up after his shift. His hair, combed to one side, was still a little wet.

'No, I was just miles away. As usual,' she quipped.

'A good way to escape the place when there's no other option,' he replied. There was a sadness in his eyes as he said it.

Could she do this? It was now or never. Now then! 'I've been thinking about what you said, about a trip to the picture house together. And I think it would be a nice idea after all.' It would be just her luck if he'd changed his mind in the meantime.

But his expression didn't suggest that, just the opposite. 'Well, there's a nice surprise for a change,' he said, beaming.

'I talked it over with my mum, and she's more than happy to look after Herby.' This would remind him she had a child and give him a chance to back out of the offer. 'She seems to think I need to get out more.'

'She's right. How about a trip to the cinema in Rhymney, or the one in Bargoed? I'll have a look-see in the newspaper, to find out what's on, and what we fancy the sound of most. Shall we say Wednesday?'

'Wednesday it is,' she said.

'I'll knock on your door on Tuesday, just to make final arrangements.'

'Come round the back,' she said, not wanting too many villagers nosing into her business. He'd only have to go down the alley at the rear, so not many would spot him there.

'Righty ho. Good idea.' His wry smile suggested he understood why. 'Just been to the bookshop,' he said, 'to sell a Sherlock Holmes back to Mr Schenck. I was lucky enough to find another second-hand one so I'm off for a walk and a read.'

'It's a lovely day for it.' She looked up at the clear May sky.

She crossed the road to the grocery store, and he headed back down James Street. Excitement was mingled with apprehension. Someone would be bound to spot them heading off to the railway station, or the motorbus stop, it being light in the evenings. Oh, let them. She'd had enough of their judgements on her. She entered Mrs Brace's shop in a better frame of mind than when she'd left her house.

-

Polly and Henry had agreed to meet at the station, to reduce the chance of people seeing them and gossiping around the village. She'd arrived first, a little early, hoping she didn't look too eager.

She bought her ticket, since she'd insisted on paying her way, and walked onto the single platform. Closing her eyes, she leant her head back, enjoying the late afternoon sun. Worrying on Monday evening about what she'd wear, it had been Anwen who had come unwittingly to her rescue the following day, with one of her jumble sale finds of a straight-cut blue chemise dress with a square neck. Polly had bought it there and then, altering and washing it that evening.

'*Prynhawn da*,' Henry called over as he entered the station, which was devoid of anyone apart from the station master, who didn't live in the village so was unlikely to know anything of their problems.

'And another lovely one it is too,' she said, hoping they'd be able to find something to talk about apart from the weather.

'I'm looking forward to seeing *Bleak House*,' said Henry. 'I've read the book, so it'll be interesting to see what the film makes of it.'

'So you know the end,' she said. 'I've never read it, so please don't tell me.'

'What do you like reading?' he asked.

She was embarrassed that he might find her choice a little on the frivolous side, but she wasn't going to make anything up. 'I'm afraid I like something a little lighter than Mr Dickens,' she said. 'Like the Wizard of Oz books, or the Anne of Green Gables ones. I know they're for children really, but I find them a nice escape from, well, life.'

She'd often read library books in the kitchen after Gus and his family had fallen into bed drunk, or at least tipsy, most nights.

'Nothing wrong with those. I'm a bit partial to the Oz books myself.' Henry peered into the distance. 'Ah, looks like our train's on its way.'

Polly peered down the line, seeing the smoke from the train's funnel in the distance. The excitement in her grew; it had been so long since she'd been to the picture house. Gus had been one for going to the public house for his entertainment; he'd never considered she might need a diversion too.

The train journey took only fifteen minutes, in which time they chatted about their week, discussing only mundane matters about their jobs, along with little snippets of news others had told them. Soon they were leaving the station and taking the route through the high street to reach their destination. She'd only been to Bargoed a couple of times in her life, and never to the picture house here. For someone who'd spent her early life in London and had lived a short while in Surrey, her life had been limited.

They reached the Hanbury Electric Theatre, where there was a small queue. She looked up at the wide triangular roof as they got into line. It was then she became nervous. What if Henry tried to hold her hand? Or tried to kiss her on the way home, or worse? But hadn't he stated that they should go together simply for company? Was he just spinning words, like so many men, or could she really trust him? She had no evidence he might act like a cad. She'd known him since she was eleven in a way, though not well. Could she trust his word? Only one way to find out.

–

When Henry and Polly emerged from the picture house, it was still light outside. Had they been in Rhymney, Henry might have suggested refreshments at Perilli's, but he didn't know what the cafés here might be like. Then again, he might not have taken her to Perilli's either, with its recent memories of Amelia. His heart sank once more as her name flitted into his mind.

'That was an intriguing tale,' she said as they wandered back towards the high street. 'I enjoy a good mystery.'

'Mm.'

'You don't seem so sure.'

'It was all right. It only included one thread of many in the book though.'

'I'm glad then that I haven't read the book.' She laughed. 'Maybe I wouldn't have enjoyed it as much.'

Oh dear, had he said the wrong thing? 'I'm sorry, I didn't mean to spoil it for you. I'm glad you enjoyed it. It's just, in my experience, films are never as good as the books.'

'I agree. I've seen a couple of films based on the Oz books. They was fun to watch though. I do enjoy the picture house.'

'Me too.' She'd been good company, not finding fault in everything like Amelia had often done. 'Would you like to go again?' he asked before he lost the nerve. 'Or maybe to the theatre?'

Her mouth made a little 'O' in surprise. Or it could have been awkwardness because she'd decided not to do any more trips with him.

'That would be nice. I've only ever been to the theatre once, a very long time ago. The Theatre Royal, in Merthyr, about ten years ago.'

'Ah yes, the Theatre Royal,' he said, recalling his trip there with Amelia. 'What play was it?'

She hesitated, looking down before saying, '*Her Road to Ruin*. Some might find that appropriate.'

'Not me. And I've not seen that one.'

He spotted a café up ahead, causing him to change his original thoughts. He was warmed a little by the idea of her extended company. And he'd pay, even though it would make him short for the rest of the week.

'How about a cup of tea or coffee in there. My treat?' He pointed up the road, at the sign that stuck out from the wall.

She seemed to consider for a moment. 'Thank you, but not this evening. I've got an earlier start tomorrow, as we've had another wedding order, short notice, which includes two bridesmaids' dresses.'

'That's good news for Gwen and the others.'

'There are more orders coming in since it was revealed, well, that Esther was passing around the rumours.' She mumbled the last words and linked her hands in front of her awkwardly.

Paid for by Amelia Bowen was left unsaid. He appreciated her tact.

'So we'll just head for the station then, shall we?'

'Yes, please.'

'Perhaps we'll have refreshments another time?'

'Yes, maybe we will.'

She gave him a smile at this point, which encouraged him to believe she had enjoyed their evening out and wasn't leaving early because she couldn't wait to escape him.

He checked his wristwatch. 'There's a train in seven minutes, so if we hurry, we won't have to wait half an hour for the next.'

They broke into a brisk walk, discussing favourite films as they went.

–

'Only me,' Polly called as she let herself into the scullery.

Her mother rushed into the room, saying, 'How did it go? Was he as nice as he seems? Are you seeing him again?'

'Goodness, let me get my jacket off and get a sit down first.' She walked into the kitchen, her mother following.

'Sorry love, I'm just so pleased you've got to walk out with a decent man.'

'How'd it go then?' her father repeated.

'Not you too, Dad. Hold on a moment.' She took the jacket off and placed it and her bag on the table, before turning one of the chairs there around towards her parents' armchairs and sitting down. 'First of all, how was Herby? Did he wake up at all?'

'No, been fast asleep the whole time, bless 'im,' said Delia. 'So, how did it go?'

'For a start, I'm *not* walking out with him, as you put it, Mum. It were just company, like. Friends.'

'Huh, can't imagine going out with a gal as a friend in my young days,' said Jim. 'You sure Henry sees it like that?'

'It's what he said. Remember, he's not long ago had his heart broken by Amelia Bowen.' She stood up. 'Anyway, I'm exhausted and going to Anwen's early tomorrow.'

'But you ain't told us nuffink,' said Jim.

'Right. We went to see *Bleak House* in Bargoed. We both enjoyed it. Henry suggested a cup of tea after, but I pointed out I had to get up early. We agreed to have another trip out. Happy?'

'He didn't try to kiss—'

'No, Mum, he didn't.'

'Like she'd tell you if he had.' Jim laughed.

'Night Mum, night Dad.'

'Night night, love,' they said in chorus.

She was relieved to get up the stairs and undressed quickly for bed. After using some of the water in her jug to brush her teeth with the tooth powder, she got into bed and lay on her back. Closing her eyes, she thought about the evening in detail, what they'd said to each other.

If she allowed herself to develop feelings for Henry, could he possibly ever feel the same? Especially if more elegant women, like Amelia, were what he was attracted to.

She was forgetting the ever-present problem of being married to Gus. So, she and Henry could only ever be friends. She felt a smidgeon of disappointment at that conclusion. Her mind wandered purposefully to the work she had to do tomorrow, and during this, she fell asleep.

Chapter Twenty-Three

Henry was leafing through the *Monmouth Guardian* he'd bought on his way home that afternoon, looking to see what films were being shown at the Hanbury cinema next week. He'd have a little to spare after paying Sioni on Sunday. Would Polly see him as being a bit forward? They'd only gone to the pictures three days ago. It might be better to wait a couple of weeks. Yet he was eager for her cheerful company again. Better that than paying out for beer to sit with his humourless old Pals from the battalion.

'What's the deep sigh for, *bach*?' said Albert, bringing in the coal bucket that he'd filled up from the bunker in the back yard.

'I was just thinking, I wish Teilo and the others would cheer up a bit and mix with other people. It's been fifteen months since we returned from the war. It's like we're all still sitting in a gloomy trench when we go out together.'

'Aye. You seem to be the only one what mixes with others.'

'And they're always resentful when I do.'

'Well, that's their problem, *bach*. Can't imagine what it must be like for their wives, them what's married. And the others aren't making any effort to settle down, now they're home. At least you're doing that. Or you were. Sorry, you probably don't want to be reminded.'

Henry shrugged. He hadn't told his parents about the trip out with Polly in case they got the wrong idea. He'd only said he was going to the picture house. 'To be honest, Da, I realise I had a lucky escape. Amelia clearly used me to throw people off the scent of her affair with Maurice.'

They heard the back door close. It was probably Mam arriving back from the grocer's.

'That's the spirit, *bach*. Not good enough for you, she weren't.'

The door from the scullery was pushed further open and Gwen walked through. 'Talking about that Polly, I shouldn't wonder,' she grumbled.

'Polly?' said Henry, wondering why Gwen would jump to that conclusion.

'You mean Amelia,' said Albert. 'And yes, we were.'

'No, I meant Polly, for I heard from someone what saw Henry coming out of the railway station with her. That's the place to go now for trysts, is it? Nice and quiet, sneaking away in a dark corner.'

'We most certainly were not,' said Henry, standing quickly and causing the seat to scrape backwards on the stone floor. 'We went together to the Electric Theatre in Bargoed to see a film. It was nothing like you're imagining.'

Who had told her they'd been together though, for they'd seen no one? Must have been some nosy parker looking through a window.

'You went with Maurice's sister?' said Albert. He seemed surprised, but not offended.

'Who went where with Maurice's sister?' said Ruth, back from her errand and clutching a brown paper bag.

'Henry, very stupidly, has been walking out with Polly Coombes,' Gwen said with disapproval.

'I have not! We only went to see a film, as friends.'

'You can't be friends with that woman,' yelled his sister. 'She's a – a – tart!'

'That's a bit strong, lovey,' said Ruth. 'You know what Pastor Thomas said about casting the first stone when you're *without* sin.'

'I haven't done anything like she's done! Coming between a man and his wife.'

'Which is most unfortunate,' said Henry calmly, not wanting to lower himself to shouting. 'But it's in the past, and she didn't break the marriage up, like Amelia did. And don't you think Mr Meredith had a good deal of the responsibility here? He was supposed to be a decent and respected manager. Have you shouted at him?'

'That is not the point!' said Gwen. 'And now everyone knows, they'll think us most strange. We might lose work again. And what about Elizabeth and Tom? How do you think they'll feel, my brother walking out with their illegitimate brother's fallen woman of a mother.' She wedged her fists onto her waist and puckered her mouth.

Henry crossed his arms and stood in front of Gwen. 'It's like Tom said: it's Mr Meredith's mistake, not his, and he can't be expected to pay for it. Well, it weren't my mistake neither, so why should I pay for it?'

'But she has an obviously illegitimate child and is married to a criminal.'

'Who treated her appallingly by all accounts. She didn't deserve that. And you employ her, so how is that any different to me being friends with her?'

Her voice rose half an octave. 'Because I'm not in a relationship with her. And if I had my way, I'd dismiss her.' She drooped and huffed out. More quietly now she added, 'I might have to persuade the others that we'll need to let her go if you carry on like this.'

Ruth put the bag down on the table, where it spilled out a couple of chocolate digestives. 'You tried that before, but none of them agreed. And I think they was right.'

'But it'll be different if Henry is walking out with her!' Gwen's voice got louder once more.

'For the last time, I am *not* walking out with her. But I don't see why I can't be her friend. And if you ask me, you're acting no better than Mrs Meredith did when she found out about Gwilym and Elizabeth. I've heard the story from Gwilym since, about how she threatened to get him dismissed if they carried on their relationship. But she realised she was being foolish in the end. Do you really think you're better than Polly?'

'He's talking a lot of sense, *cariad*,' said Albert.

Gwen pressed her lips together, thumped her fists downwards and let out a sound akin to the snort of an angry bull. With that, she turned abruptly and flounced out of the kitchen. A few moments later they heard the back door slam.

'Oh dear,' said Albert. 'She's got a bee in her bonnet, and no mistake.'

'She's going to have to get over that,' said Ruth. 'She can't be acting lady of the manor just because she's married to a manager's son.'

Henry had a nasty feeling she was unlikely to 'get over that', as his mother had put it.

Chapter Twenty-Four

There'd been some comments in the last month, about Henry and Polly being seen out together, but not enough to worry him. Whether they'd said worse behind their backs he didn't know, nor did he much care. The former soldiers from the brigade had said little, maybe appreciating Polly's welcome smile and kind words when she served them in the McKenzie Arms. Not that he'd been there with them much. The weekly trips to the cinema, and once, for refreshments on a Saturday afternoon, had rendered him short of cash.

He was waiting now at the very end of Station Road, near the colliery gate, having gone on ahead after chapel, expecting Sioni Gower to turn up for his next payment. Five months it had been now, with the interest going up twenty per cent every six weeks or so, extending the loan further than he'd anticipated. He was now paying back nine shillings a week, and had paid eight pounds, fourteen shillings back so far, after only borrowing five pounds. As long as Sioni didn't put up the interest again, he should be free of the loan in the next four weeks.

Sioni, five minutes late, swaggered down the street, lifting his head to regard Henry as he got close. Henry offered the nine shillings straight away, eager to escape Sioni's menacing presence as soon as possible. How he regretted borrowing anything off him now, especially considering the reason he'd done so.

'There you go. It's all there.' Henry held out the money.

Sioni checked anyway. 'No it's not. The interest has gone up again.'

'It can't have done! I've only been paying eighty per cent interest the last two weeks.'

'If you will mingle with nasty little tarts like Polly, what do you expect?'

'What's that got to do with it? I borrowed the money to take Amelia Bowen out. Polly don't expect nothing expensive.'

'No? She's my sister-in-law, remember, so I know what she's like. Are you telling me she's never asked for money for a little, how shall I put it? Favour?'

'No she hasn't! What would Connie say, if she heard you talking about her sister like that?'

'Huh! She'd agree, mun. She knows what she's like.'

Connie always went around with a face that suggested she didn't approve of anyone, so it wouldn't surprise him if she said untrue things about her own sister.

'Anyway, it's no skin off my nose, mun, as long as you pays your debt. I'll give you until next Sunday to pay the extra shilling for this week, plus next week's, of course.'

'But I've paid more now than I borrowed.'

'That's how it works.'

Henry thought for a while. It might be better to finish paying this week's money so he didn't have to stump up more next week. 'Here, I'll pay the extra now.'

Sioni shoved the coins in his pocket. 'Thanks, mun, you're a right gentleman.' He sniggered as he said it, then gave a half-hearted salute as he sauntered off.

Henry had been thinking of taking Polly and Herby for afternoon tea later. He shouldn't have bought the new shirt during the week. He could borrow a few shillings from his mother, with the promise of paying it back Friday. She kept some savings in a tin under the floorboards in the bedroom.

He could hardly ask his father again. Not only had he just managed to pay him back for the last loan, but he'd bought his father presents for his birthday yesterday: a music book for his euphonium and a couple of novels. It would make it look like he hadn't been able to afford them if he asked for money.

He'd wait until after Sunday dinner to ask his mother, when his father would be heading off to the allotment he'd recently started renting.

–

Polly had been thrilled when Henry had asked her to bring Herby along for their walk today, by the small Nantygalon stream. He wanted to get to know him, he'd said. It was the fact that he'd taken an interest in her son, not that she had any hopes of the relationship getting serious. Despite Gus's name being on her son's birth certificate, he'd not taken any notice of him at all, either forgetting he had to be considered, or moaning when he cried or made a noise.

How many times had she imagined what the experience might have been like with a loving husband?

Wanting him to look particularly smart today, she'd dressed her son in the summery sailor suit with shorts she'd made him. Not that he was ever shabby; she made sure of that. Henry was currently walking ahead with Herby, crouched over, holding his hand, pointing at the stream.

'Mummy, Mummy, look,' he said, pointing his pudgy little hand towards the water. 'Fishies, Mummy.'

Polly went over to have a look. 'So there are. Only little ones. I wonder if they're babies, or just small grown-up ones.'

'They're baby grayling,' said Henry. 'I used to fish here with Idris and Gwilym… I was wondering, if you and Herby would fancy a trip to Perilli's in Rhymney, for some tea and cake.'

'Cake?' said Herby, eyes wide with delight. 'I like cake.'

'I think that's your answer,' said Polly, grinning. She was pleased for herself too, for she'd never been to Perilli's, though had heard good things about the café from others.

'Not that you're not partial to a piece of cake yourself?' Henry joked, his eyebrows raised.

'Me?' She pointed to herself. 'Of course not. Can't stand the stuff.' She laughed.

'Just what I thought. Rather like me then.'

They both laughed, and Herby looked confused. 'But you do like cake, Mummy.'

'I know, lovey. I was joking.'

'Oh.' He only vaguely got the idea of a joke as yet.

'If we walk back to the village now, we can catch a bus at five past three.'

'Lovely. Come on, Herby, shall we have a little race?'

He nodded enthusiastically and she ran next to him, keeping just behind. Henry joined in, blowing as if out of breath.

'You're winning, Herby,' he said.

'I good runner.'

'You are. When you're a bit older, you should go in for the children's races.'

When they reached the little bridge that linked James Street with McKenzie Cottages, Herby came to a stop.

'That enough now,' he said. 'I out of breff.'

'Come on, Herby, *bach*,' said Henry, 'I'll give you a piggy-back to the motorbus stop.'

He picked up an eager Herby and swung him onto his back. Soon the boy was giggling with the joy of being jiggled up and down.

'Go, horsey, go!' he said as Henry trotted along.

They waited for the motorbus by the stop outside the McKenzie Arms. Polly looked up and down the road several times, half expecting Sioni to pop out from somewhere. But no, by the time the motorbus came trundling along, he'd not made an appearance, and nor had anyone else.

Herby scrambled onto a seat and sat peering with wonder out of the window, his trips on the motorbus being few. Polly sat next to him and Henry behind. As they passed the last house of Mafeking Terrace at the end of the village, Herby spotted Farmer Lloyd's horses in a field. The short trip into Rhymney High Street was full of delight for Herby, as he pointed to the various landmarks along the way.

'Here we are,' said Henry as the motorbus stopped just past the Imperial Cinema. He waited for Polly to get up, then scooted her son up to get him off the vehicle quickly.

'Where we going?' said Herby, once he'd been put on the pavement.

'It's a café down here a bit. You'll like it, I'm sure.'

When they reached Perilli Bros Refreshment House, Herby gazed, open-mouthed, at the shop window, jammed with chocolate bars and boxes, jars of sweets, cigars and cigarettes.

'It's a bit fuller now than it was during the war, so I'm told,' said Henry. 'It got quite empty apparently.'

'So did all the shops,' said Polly. 'It's certainly something to behold now.' She felt the same kind of awe that Herby had on his face.

'Come on then.' Henry opened the door and they entered to the scent of tobacco.

Herby wrinkled his nose. 'It smell like Miss Davies's shop.'

'It does,' Polly agreed. 'But there's a lot more of everything here.' She was mesmerised, wondering if she had enough in her purse to take a little something home to her parents.

'*Signore, Signora*, good afternoon to you, and to the *bambino*.' A small, tanned gentleman in a white apron approached them; he bent down and shook Herby's hand, which made the boy chuckle. 'Are you looking to buy from our extensive counter, or would you like a table in the café?' He indicated both in turn.

'We'd like a table, please,' said Henry.

'*Certo*.' Spotting one of the waitresses in their smart black and white outfits, he called, 'Loretta, you show our guests to a table, please.'

'Of course, Papa. Good afternoon. Come this way, please.'

Polly noticed the waitress give Henry a curious look, as if she were maybe trying to recall him from somewhere. She showed them to a table to one side of the room, near the cake displays, and brought them menus.

'I'll be back in a while to take your order.'

'Look, Herby, they have lemon squash,' said Polly. 'Would you like some?'

'Yes, pease, Mummy. The cakes look nice,' he said hopefully.

'We'll see what they've got that's a bit smaller. Or you can share with me.'

'Can I look?'

'Go on then, quickly.'

He shuffled off the seat and went to have a look through the glass of the display case.

'Our waitress, Loretta,' Henry started as Polly perused the menu, 'she were here when I came with Amelia, and they knew each other. Mrs Bowen apparently used to make the uniforms. I wonder what they do now?'

'Yes, I wonder,' said Polly.

'Anyway, Amelia told me that Loretta's brother was killed in the war, in Italy. And the chap what greeted us, it must have been his son. He weren't here last time; it was his brother what greeted us.'

'How terrible for them.' So he'd brought Amelia here. She felt slightly offended at first. But why should she? They were only friends. And the fact he'd been able to bring her somewhere he'd taken Amelia must mean he was getting over her, which was good for him.

'Mummy, look at this,' said Herby.

Polly stood and joined her son where he was pointing at a vast Victoria sponge. 'I think that's definitely one for sharing,' she laughed. 'It does look delicious though.'

She led him back to their table and sat him down once more. 'That's me and Herby decided,' she said. 'And I think I'll try some coffee for a change.'

'Me too,' said Henry. 'Here's the waitress.'

When she'd taken the order, she said, 'Am I right in thinking you're a friend of Amelia's?'

'Yes, you served us when we came in, nearly a year ago now. I suppose you heard she left?' he said.

'No, I didn't. I know her mother married and moved, as my mother's been looking for a new dressmaker for the uniforms but hasn't had any luck.'

'She ran off with my brother,' said Polly, not wanting to pussyfoot around the matter. 'What's married with a child.'

Loretta clapped her hand against her mouth. 'Oh my goodness. What a terrible thing to do. I am sorry. I can't say I knew her terribly well, only because of her mother really.'

'So you're looking for someone to make new uniforms?' Polly asked.

'Yes, that's right. Mama hasn't been satisfied with quotes and examples of work so far.'

'Well, I work for the business that took over from Mrs Bowen's. She sold her equipment to them. Henry here, his sister is one of the women what runs it. Have you tried them for a quote?'

'Oh, no, we haven't. Didn't even think to go looking again in Dorcalon. Do you have any details?'

'If you have a pencil and paper, I could write them down.'

Loretta tore off one of the back pages of her order pad, and handed it and a pencil to Polly, who wrote down Gwen's details. She'd have preferred to put Anwen's, but Gwen's house was the one with the telephone.

'Thank you,' said Loretta. 'We'll have to look into this. Needing some uniforms quite soon, we are. I'll get your order sorted out now.' She tucked the piece of paper into her pocket and walked away.

'That was generous of you, considering…' Henry began.

'Considering your sister doesn't like me? I do know that. But it's also my livelihood, and the more work they have, the more likely they'll keep me on.'

'Well, it was good of you. And I'll make sure Gwen knows about it.'

'That's not why I did it, but thank you, Henry.'

She had a feeling it wouldn't make any difference.

–

Henry had a fancy for some sweets after his bath on Monday, walking down to Mrs Davies the confectioner, to see if she had any. While he was there, he'd see about getting a little chocolate treat for Herby, maybe a Five Boys bar, if they had one. He was seeing Polly for a walk tomorrow, so he'd give it to her then.

Reaching the shop, he pushed the door open to the sugary aroma of confectionary, mingled with the fragrant scent of tobacco, not unlike Perilli's, but more heavily on the sweet side. Douglas Ramsay was in there, buying his usual Waverley cigarettes, ones he seemed to smoke constantly since Susan's death.

'Hello there, Henry,' he said. 'You started smoking, have you?'

'No *bach*, it's too expensive. And I don't reckon it's good for the lungs neither, what with breathing in the coal dust too.'

'Get away with you,' said Douglas, 'they reckon it's good for you. Read it I did. Clears the lungs out, see.'

'I dunno about that.'

'You trying to lose me trade, Mr Austin?' said Mrs Davies. 'Encouraging my customers not to buy my cigarettes? There's your change, Mr Ramsay.'

Douglas took the coins and turned to Henry. 'Some of us are meeting in the Arms tonight. You coming?'

Henry reckoned a selection of the Pals met there almost every night, and Douglas was invariably among them.

'Not tonight, mun. I'll probably be there Friday. Bit expensive for me to go out every night.'

'Right you are,' said Douglas, nevertheless looking down about it. 'See you Friday then.'

As he left, Henry turned back to the counter, saying, 'Now let's see what I might fancy,' but it wasn't long before the door opened once more.

'I'm glad I've seen you,' said the shrill voice of Matilda Bowen, trying to sound posh, but not quite managing it.

Not her now! 'Good afternoon, Mrs Bowen. What did you want to see me about?' he said, being polite.

'It's come to my attention that you've been walking out with that Polly, and after her brother abducted your sweetheart too. How could you?'

'I don't want no trouble in here, Mrs Bowen,' said Mrs Davies.

'It's not me who's the cause of it,' she said haughtily.

'You've changed your tune,' said Henry. 'Before, you said Amelia had never been interested in me, that she'd claimed I'd been harassing her. I've come to realise what a cruel piece of work she is—'

'How dare you!'

'And she were hardly kidnapped. That were clear when she came back to collect some of her things. And she stole your savings and didn't care that Maurice had stolen Mabel's.'

'Well, exactly! Maurice was a thief, and his sister's from the same mould.'

'Oh no, you've got that wrong. Amelia and Maurice are the wrongdoers here. Amelia made fools of us all. Polly is a far better person than her brother or your niece.'

'My niece isn't a slattern, like Polly Smith.'

'I don't see what else your niece is, going off with a married man!' said Mrs Davies.

'Do you want to lose my trade?' said Matilda.

'Huh, like I get much of it, anyway. Especially since you bought that motorcar. I wouldn't normally speak out like, but I think what your niece and Maurice Coombes did was terrible. Poor Mabel, and poor little Lily, bless her. You certainly have no claim to the higher ground, Mrs Bowen.'

'Well! I *was* going to buy some sweets and a newspaper, but I certainly won't now.' She pulled the door open and stomped into the street, not bothering to close it.

'Yes, of course you were,' said Mrs Davies, even though Matilda wouldn't have heard her.

'Thank you,' said Henry. 'For speaking up.'

'Well, who does she think she is? Amelia Bowen always thought far too much of herself. I've heard her mother refused to see her when she went to visit her in Tredegar recently, said she were a disgrace to the family, so I'm surprised Matilda Bowen would still stick up for her.'

'Think it was more a case of picking on Polly Smith,' said Henry.

'Aye, quite likely. Well, Mrs Smith has never been rude or disrespectful to me, so I've no complaints about her. Now, have you chosen yet?'

'I'll have some of the toffee humbugs, a *Monmouth Guardian* and a bar of Five Boys, please.'

–

'What a cheek that woman has,' said Polly as they reached the summit of Twyn Gobaith and looked down the slopes towards Tredegar and Rhymney. The warm breeze blew at the loose tresses of her hair, bringing with it a kind of serenity she never had walking through the village.

Henry had just related the conversation in the sweetshop the day before, saying he didn't want to keep anything from her, which she appreciated.

'It was nice of Mrs Davies to say what she did, though. Especially after the comments I had in the Arms today,' said Polly.

'The Arms? I thought you never had any trouble in there.'

It had been the men she'd seen Sioni hanging out with from time to time, who were on the evening shift and able to get to the public house at lunchtimes. She didn't have to mention Sioni though.

'I haven't until now. It was some comment about me, well, asking me if I wanted to earn a bob or two on the side, as they'd heard I like to… do favours for married men.'

'What a damn cheek! Sorry, but I'm angry that they'd be so disrespectful. Who was it?'

'Oh, I dunno their names.' It wasn't true, as she'd been good at learning customers' names. She didn't want Henry tackling them and getting into any trouble.

'I hope you told Nerys Moss about it; she wouldn't stand any nonsense.'

'I haven't yet, I didn't get a chance today.'

'You can do it tomorrow evening.'

'Thank you for sticking up for me in the sweetshop,' said Polly. 'I do appreciate it.'

'Of course I would.' He looked a little embarrassed, which is maybe why he changed the subject and said, 'Where did you say your mother was taking Herby?'

'To buy him some new shoes in Rhymney.'

'I was wondering if you fancied walking a bit further, while the sun's shining brightly.'

'I would, though it's getting a bit dark over there.' She looked towards the north, where grey clouds were gathering on the horizon.

'I'm sure it'll be a while before they get here. There's still a lot of blue sky.'

'Come on then. We could walk down to the woods between Dorcalon and Rhymney. There might be some nice wildflowers out.'

'Then we could walk back along the Rhymney River,' said Henry.

'I need to be back by five thirty though, to start supper.'

'I'm sure we'll be back way before then.'

They set off, discussing walks in the area they enjoyed. She should really be home getting on with the ironing, it being one of her afternoons off, but she'd have to do it this evening. Then there was the kitchen to scrub. It was her turn to do it this week. She didn't want to leave her mother with the burden of the housework, along with looking after Herby, but then, it had been Mum who'd insisted she should come for the walk today, when she'd shown some misgivings. Was her mother trying to pair her up with Henry? The thought was surely absurd, but at the back of her mind she considered how delightful it might have been, given different circumstances.

Halfway down the hill towards the woods they were heading to, she realised the clouds that had been on the horizon were creeping slowly across the sky, like billowing monsters. They were slate coloured now.

'Oh dear,' said Polly, 'I think maybe we should hurry along a bit.'

'No, *fach*, they won't be a problem. It's still sunny.'

But as they were three-quarters across the remaining distance, the rain whooshed down from the sky in a sudden shower. The sun was still shining over the hills and valley to the south, creating a strange, washed-out light. They started running, Polly gripping her small handbag to her chest. They reached the woods at the same time, both soaked, laughing at their drenched state.

Henry thumped his back against a tree trunk. 'Phew. I'm glad to be out of that. I really should have brought my jacket.'

Polly's hair was half hanging down now, the grips dislodged by the rain and the effort of running. 'Oh no, I must look a mess.'

'I'm sure I do too,' said Henry, leaning his head to the side to look at her. His shirt was stuck to his body, showing the outline of his chest.

'At least you have short hair.' She put her hand up to her head and groaned. She had a small brush in her bag, but how would she pin her hair back up neatly without a mirror? There was nothing else for it. She pulled the pins out and let her dark blonde hair fall down her back.

'It looks better like that anyway,' he said, coming towards her. He was opening his mouth to add something when a look of surprise appeared on his face and he tripped, before flying towards the ground. His arm knocked her, and she went down too, her handbag sailing off who knew where.

She was confused for a while but soon realised that she'd landed right next to him.

'I'm so sorry.' He started to push himself up, but halted part way.

Her heart was beating hard against her chest. She should move, and quickly, but she was not inclined to. Nor was he, apparently, as he looked down on her, eyes wide, taking her in. She looked back up into his face, matured by a brutal war, but still attractive.

Right, she decided, this time she was going to take charge. She hauled herself into a kneeling position, took hold of his surprised face and kissed his lips. He responded in kind. Pulling away after some seconds, she said, 'That's all I'm giving away, Henry. I like you more than just as a friend, I realise that now, but I'm not going to end up like before.' She stood up.

He stood too. 'I like you more than just as a friend too, but I would never expect anything of you, you didn't want to give.'

'Good, then we agree on that.'

'So it would seem.'

They looked at each other, unspeaking, until she couldn't bear it any longer. She went forward, leant up a little on her tiptoes and kissed him once more. This time he placed his arms around her waist. She lifted her arms up and around his neck. While they were still kissing, he shuffled her to the closest tree, and they leant against it. The embrace lasted a lot longer this time.

When they broke away once more, Henry said, 'I didn't expect that when we set off today.'

'Neither did I,' she said. 'Let me find my handbag and we'll take that walk by the river now.' She didn't want to tempt fate by staying too long in the dark, brooding woods.

'Good idea.'

They headed through the woods and out, taking the last of the hill down onto the road that went from Dorcalon to Rhymney. They crossed over and walked over the field, to meet the river, which was parallel with the road. They walked along its bank, towards the village, following the flow of the bubbling water.

'What are we going to do, Henry? We're in an impossible position.'

'Now, maybe. But who knows, things may change. People will forget Amelia and Maurice, and our part in the whole debacle.'

'They won't forget that I'm married. And to be honest, I don't think I can afford a solicitor to do anything about it.'

'You'd have a strong case if you did. But in the meantime, we should stick to doing things in Rhymney, or Tredegar, or Bargoed, like we have been. You won't have any of the same time off as me until Sunday now, will you?'

'I'm afraid not. So, you want to keep on seeing me, after kissing me?' She felt uncomfortable mentioning it but felt it necessary.

'Yes, even more so now.' He took her hand. 'So, let's meet next Sunday afternoon again. With Herby, of course. I don't want to leave him out when we can include him.'

She felt a little disappointed, wondering how they'd kiss with her son there, but she was equally grateful for Henry's consideration.

'All right. Maybe we could meet Monday or Tuesday evening then, to have some time to ourselves.'

'Yes. Definitely.'

Polly was happier than she'd been for a long time. But still there was a frame of gloom around her blissful state. It was an impossible situation, but she'd enjoy it while she could.

Chapter Twenty-Five

Polly was putting the finishing touches to her outfit to meet Henry today, looking in the hall mirror. She'd found a blue cloche hat with a black band in a sale in Rhymney the week before, a nice straw one for the summer, so had treated herself. But that wasn't all: having bought the modern hat, she'd realised that her old-fashioned, pinned-up hair wouldn't suit it at all. Consequently, she'd made an appointment with a hairdresser and she'd had it all cut off, into a bob.

Henry hadn't seen it yet, and she was afraid of what he'd make of it. It was her hair though, wasn't it? She wouldn't presume to tell him how to have his cut. But still, she hoped he liked it. Anwen's family had all admired it, when she'd gone there to work, as had Nerys and the staff at the Arms. The customers had barely noticed. Only her mother hadn't been too sure about the transformation.

Satisfied the hat was on straight, she went back to the kitchen, where Herby was kneeling up at the table in his sailor suit, drawing a picture in a sketch book with wax crayons.

'Come on, lovey, let's get your hat on.'

He got down obediently, looking up at her as she tied the strings of the sailor hat around his chin. Normally he'd resist leaving something he was enjoying, but he knew where they were off to today.

'I 'cited to go to Prelli's again,' he said, mispronouncing the café's name.

'So am I, lovey. We're going to meet Henry in the gardens and we don't want to be late, so let's get going.'

Her mother came through the door from the scullery, giving them both the once-over. 'Oh, don't you both look very smart,' she said. 'You'll turn heads for sure.'

Polly's dress, a dark blue drop-waisted dress she'd made herself, also had something of the navy about it, with its sailor collar, white band around the short sleeves and another around the drop waist.

'Thank you, Mum. We'd better go now.'

Outside the sun was shining as she walked down James Street to the gardens. She started humming 'I'm Forever Blowing Bubbles'.

When they reached the gardens, she pushed open the gate and Herby rushed in, running to where Henry was seated on the bench in the middle.

'Hello, *boi bach*. You're looking dapper today.'

'You're looking very dapper too,' said Polly, catching her son up. Henry was wearing his suit and had foregone his cap today.

'Why thank you. Oh! Have you had your hair cut into one of them bobs?'

She lifted the hat off and neatened her hair down, hoping desperately he wouldn't be disappointed.

He gave it the once-over, smiling. 'It really suits you.'

'Thank you, Henry. It's a lot easier than putting long hair up all the time.'

'Yes, I can imagine.' He laughed. 'We've got a few minutes before we need to get to the motorbus stop, so you might as well sit down.'

Herby scrambled up next to Henry, giving him a toothy grin. Polly sat on the other side of him.

'I wasn't sure of the wisdom of meeting here, in public,' Polly whispered. 'Perhaps we should have walked up to the next stop.'

'If people want to talk, they'll talk. Let them. I'm fed up with it.'

'Yes, you're quite right, of course. It's about time they minded their own business.'

Polly looked down when she heard the bottom gate squeak. She smiled when she saw Elizabeth opening it, though it soon turned to a frown when she noticed Gwen emerge from behind the bushes by the railings.

'Oh dear,' she said.

Henry looked up. 'Don't worry about her. I'll give as good as I get if she starts.'

But it wasn't only the two of them. Chatting to Gwen was Margaret Meredith, who must have come to visit. Both she and Gwen were looking down as they talked and hadn't noticed who was in the gardens. Elizabeth did spot them, performing a small wave, but her smile was thin.

They were several steps in before both Gwen and Margaret looked up, spotting Polly and Henry on the seat.

Margaret's eyes darted from Polly to Herby and back again, her lips tight. Then she turned on her heel and headed back out the way she'd come.

'Mama,' Elizabeth called. 'Where are you going? Please, let's just walk…' Whatever else she said was unheard.

Gwen marched up to them, arms on hips, as had become a habit of hers when she was in a bad humour.

'I knew you walking out with, with – *her* – would cause trouble for me. What on earth is my mother-in-law going to think of me now?'

It was said so sharply that Herby burst into tears, maybe thinking he was being told off.

'It's unnecessary to shout,' said Henry. 'And this has nothing to do with you, and particularly not with Mrs Meredith.'

'Of course it has! Now I'll be in her bad books.'

'And you're in my bad books for shouting at us and making Herby cry. You seem to forget that it were Polly what got you the business with Perilli's.'

'No, she didn't, she only mentioned us. *I* got the business by showing Mrs Perilli how good our sewing is. She had *nothing* to do with it.'

Polly stood and picked Herby up, even though it was a struggle these days.

'I'm taking him home,' she said. 'I can't expose him to this any longer.'

'I'm sorry, Polly,' said Henry. 'Could you wait a moment?'

'No, I'd better get him back.'

She rushed past Gwen, resisting the temptation to knock her arm as she went, so angry was she with her.

'Polly?' Henry called, but she didn't stop. The tears were pricking at her eyes and she didn't want Gwen seeing that.

She'd so been looking forward to today, what with her and Henry having turned a corner in their relationship, and it hurt to walk away like this.

'But I want go Prelli's and have cake,' Herby whined.

'You can have a couple of Nanny's bakestones instead, lovey.'

'It not same.'

It wouldn't be, but the day had been spoilt by the inevitability of the situation. Their romance had been short-lived, but hadn't she always known it would be? It had just been a little shorter than she'd imagined.

'I'll make you a nice cup of cocoa too,' she said, to soothe her still sobbing child. She felt like sobbing herself.

But he continued to bawl, all the way home.

–

'Now look what you've done!' said Henry, standing stiffly in Jubilee Gardens with his hands jammed against his waist. 'Can't you see you've no right to criticise and poke your nose in?'

'I'm doing you a favour and saving you from trouble.'

'Like you did with Amelia, I suppose.'

She tilted her head at a haughty level as she said, 'Well I was right there!'

'But you're *not* right in this case. You've ruined the day for me and Polly, not to mention poor little Herby. What on earth has happened to you? Ever since you married Tom, you seem to think you're something special.'

'I do not, I'm just trying—'

'Just go away and leave me alone!'

'Don't worry, I will. I need to catch up with my mother-in-law and smooth things over, all because *you* are being ridiculous.'

'*I'm* being ridiculous?'

Gwen plodded down to the gate in an unladylike fashion, considering she was dressed elegantly today, no doubt to impress Mrs Meredith. He, likewise, tramped up to the top gate, and exited the gardens there, angry as hell with his sister. He only hoped he could mend things with Polly. Why, when finally he'd found a good woman, one he could see a future with, did there have to be all these problems?

He marched twice around the outside of the garden, trying to walk off the anger, but it didn't work. He was going to have to go to Gwen's house and have it out with her again. He didn't care if Mrs Meredith was there. If she had just passed through the gardens and ignored them, it would have been fine.

-

He went the back way into their house on Alexandra Street, opening the scullery door and calling, 'It's me, Henry!'

The door from the kitchen opened and Tom entered, holding a book. 'Hello, Henry. If you're looking for Gwen, she's out with Lizzie and my mother. And if it's Gwilym, he's doing some work on Lizzie's field.'

'Gwen and the others didn't come back here then?'

'No. They haven't long gone out. I think they were having a walk up to Jubilee Gardens. What's up, Henry? You look out of sorts.'

'I've just met them in the gardens, unfortunately.'

'Ah, I hear a tale of woe in your voice. Come into the kitchen and have a seat.'

'I don't want to disturb your reading.'

'Don't worry about that. Come on.'

Henry followed him in, wondering if he was the best person to tell this to. After all, Gwen was his wife. The pair of them sat in two of the four armchairs packed in either side of the range.

'What's happened?'

'I'm afraid I've had a blazing row with Gwen. I was in the gardens with Polly and Herby, where we met to start our journey to Rhymney and afternoon tea, and Elizabeth walked in with Gwen and your mother. Your mother took one look at Polly and went straight back out. Gwen stayed behind and shouted at me for being with Polly, and then Herby cried and Polly took him home, which was the end of our afternoon out. I told Gwen she should mind her own business, but she kept on and on about how I shouldn't be seeing Polly and it was for my own good.'

'Oh dear,' said Tom, closing his eyes and pinching the top of his nose. 'I'm so sorry, Henry. You're quite right, of course. It's not our business. After all we went through, and particularly Lizzie and Gwilym, I'd have thought she'd have realised that. I know it's awkward, and it's unfortunate that the cat was let out of the bag when Maurice barged in here and Anwen read the situation wrong, but it's still not our place to interfere. I really think my mother should have had a little more decorum, since she's so keen on it. I'll have a word with Gwen. After all, if Lizzie and I are prepared to overlook what happened, then I don't see why she's so concerned about it.'

'Thank you for being so understanding,' said Henry. He stood up. 'I think I need to go for a long hike now, out of the way, by the stream, to walk off my annoyance.'

'That's a good idea. Always works for me. Would you like any company?'

'You're all right. I don't want to disturb your quiet afternoon of reading.'

Tom laughed. 'It is nice to have the place to oneself sometimes, with the four of us living here.'

'I'll see myself out.'

Henry felt a little better after that, for knowing that Tom, and Elizabeth too, had some sympathy for his situation. Whether either could persuade headstrong Gwen to stop her ongoing campaign against Polly was another matter.

The best place for a walk, to keep away from others, would be along the Nantygalon stream. He'd go around the edge of the village, past the allotments, to the bridge, and begin his walk there. There'd be fewer people on that route.

-

As he was on the path that skirted the end houses of Lloyd Street and James Street, he had a feeling someone was behind him. He turned round a few times, but there was only an old chap bending down near the top, digging a patch of ground. Perhaps it was the light breeze rustling the trees on the other side of him making him think otherwise.

At the end of James Street, he tramped down the path that led to the stream, humming the sad tune of 'David of the White Rock' that fitted his mood. Soon he was under the shade of the trees, enjoying the coolness and anonymity. The snapping of a twig brought him to a halt. He looked around once more. Nothing. It could have been a fox, or a rabbit, moving in the undergrowth. And if there was someone else walking here, they were as entitled as he was.

He strayed off the path, down to the stream and hunkered down to watch it as it flowed past, on its journey to join the Rhymney River. Conscious of not wanting to get his suit dirty, he started to pull himself upright, only to find himself sprawled on the ground, face down. He was aware of a pain in his back.

Before he had a chance to pull himself up properly, there was another sharp pain in his leg. This time he knew it had come from a kick.

'That's what you get, boyo, when you don't pay your debt in time,' said a voice he recognised as Iolo Prosser.

What had he got to do with anything? But even as he had the thought, the answer became obvious. Was it wise to try and get up, only to be knocked over again? He stayed where he was, but soon was having to comply with the barked command.

'Get up, ya blighter,' said Iolo.

Henry turned onto his stomach so he could use his knees to heave himself up. He stumbled a little as he got to his feet. It was then he saw that Sioni was there also, arms folded and legs apart.

'But I have paid. I paid this morning, didn't I, Sioni?'

'You paid some. But interest has gone up again, see, will do every week from now on.'

'But it already went up this—'

'Shut your mouth,' said Iolo. 'Sioni here reckons he overheard you tell your sister you were supposed to be going to Perilli's in Rhymney. Bit fancy when you're short of cash, if you ask me.'

Henry felt like saying, *but I didn't ask you*. He thought better of it.

'And I'm thinking, like, since you haven't gone, that you'll have the money you was going to spend there. Am I right, boyo?'

Henry said nothing, fearful of what was on Iolo's mind.

'Reckon his silence says it all, don't you?' said Iolo.

'Oh aye.'

Sioni leapt forward and landed a kick in Henry's stomach. It sent him reeling as a throbbing agony set into his gut. He landed in a bush, doubled over. Sioni came forward once more, grabbing his arm to pull him up, then pushed Henry up the bank, where he stumbled and landed on his knees.

Iolo pushed him down, his feet resting on his stomach as Sioni searched his pockets.

'Here we go,' said Sioni, pulling the purse from Henry's inside jacket pocket. 'Ooh, very nice. We'll call it a bit extra for good will, shall we?'

'And no opening your mouth to anyone, look you,' said Iolo. 'Specially not the police, else you'll suffer worse next time. And we can get enough people to swear we was nowhere near here, see. And you wouldn't want pretty Polly finding out you're up to your eyeballs in debt, would you? Or your parents.'

Sioni gave Henry one more kick in the legs before Iolo removed his foot from his stomach and they headed off.

-

'Oh my goodness, what on earth's happened to you?' said Ruth as Henry stumbled through the door.

'I tripped and fell down the bank of the stream. I landed on a rock and banged my leg.'

'You look in a bad way. Sit down.' She pulled out a chair from the scullery table. 'Al – bert!'

Henry's father came scuttling into the scullery. 'What's wrong – goodness me, *bach*, what the devil's happened to you?'

He repeated the story he'd concocted on his way home, grateful for living so close to the stream.

Ruth helped him off with his jacket. 'Oh, your poor suit. Now, let's see what damage there is.' She went to lift his shirt.

'No, Mam, I'll be fine.'

'Don't be daft; you're obviously in a lot of pain.' She had the shirt up before he could argue further.

'Good heavens, lad, that's a bruise and a half. We'd better get Dr Roberts up here.'

'No, Da, I don't need him.'

'And I say you do, and you're under my roof!' He turned to go out of the back door but stalled. 'Hang on a minute, what happened to Polly? I thought you were taking her to Rhymney.'

'Gwen saw us and interfered and Polly ran off home with Herby. I went for a walk instead.'

'Our Gwen is going to have to learn to keep her nose out of it,' said Ruth. 'Don't know what's happened to the girl. If she hadn't interfered, you'd never have had this accident.'

That hadn't occurred to Henry. It was certainly true, though not for the reason his mother thought.

'Right, I'm going to get the doctor.' Albert left the house.

'Can you make it upstairs with my help?' said Ruth.

'I'll try,' said Henry, not looking forward to the steep, narrow steps.

–

'Luckily it all seems superficial, if painful,' said Dr Roberts, who'd examined Henry's stomach as he lay in bed and was now looking at his legs. 'The bruises will hurt for a while. I wouldn't go to work for at least a couple of days.' He stood upright, clutching his chin, considering the leg bruises once more, and then the stomach ones. 'Are you sure these were caused by a fall?'

Henry attempted a chuckle, as if the doctor's words were absurd. 'I should know where I got them.'

'Mm. They almost look like you've been kicked, though I suppose if the rocks were pointed enough, it would give the same impression. Where exactly did you fall?'

'I think I'd been walking along the stream for about five minutes when I tripped.'

'I take a walk along there from time to time. I'm not aware of any rocks that you could fall onto. Still, maybe you walked further than you thought.'

'Yes, maybe.'

'I'll get your mother to organise some cold compresses for you. Then you'll need some Zam-buk balm, if you have some in the house.'

'We've always got Zam-buk in the house.'

'Good. Now, I'll leave you to rest.' The doctor closed his bag up and walked to the door. 'Remember, at least two days off work.'

'All right.'

As soon as the door closed behind Dr Roberts, Henry groaned. Two days off work. Maybe longer if he didn't feel better by Wednesday. And all that money lost. How would he pay Sioni off this week? And what was he going to do about Polly? Should he come clean, and tell his parents?

No, this was his problem, and he'd need to sort it out himself.

-

Polly had been half awake for a while, her eyes blinking in the light of another sunny morning, but it was only now that she was fully conscious. What a night of dreams that had been, and none of them good. She'd thought a few hours of sleep might have made everything clear, but no inspiration had come to her about her situation. The options were as they had been.

Even if she'd had the money to divorce Gus, there was still the stumbling block of Herby's real father. It was irritating to think that the person standing in the way wasn't Elizabeth or Tom, but Gwen. Did Henry's sister really think that her brother's relationship with her would make it awkward for her in the Meredith family?

She considered the future, what they'd tell Herby about his father if she did get together with Henry, or even if she didn't. Surely, with Gus's name on the birth certificate that would be enough. Why would they need to tell him about Mr Meredith? *Perhaps because Gus is not the kind of father any boy would want to be part of*, a little voice told her.

Overlaying all of this, was the fact that her job relied on her not annoying Gwen too much. So far, the others in the business had disagreed with sacking her, but what if they decided her relationship with Henry was too close to home?

She flung the covers back and propelled herself out of bed. Whichever way she looked at it, she and Henry being together was not a good idea.

It was just before five o'clock, according to the bedside clock, though the sun was already peeping through the curtains.

There was a muffled sound coming from downstairs, suggesting her mother was up, getting her dad's breakfast ready. She took her dressing gown from the back of the door and slipped it on as she tiptoed down the stairs. The kitchen was empty, but she could hear her mother in the scullery. It gave her an opportunity to creep into the front room and shut the door. That way she wouldn't have to explain what she was doing until after she'd finished.

She switched the light on and went to the drawers, pulling the top one out carefully to retrieve the writing paper and fountain pen they kept there. She took them to the small oak table that was folded down on one side. Sitting on the chair at one end, she chewed the inside of her mouth as she considered what to write. There was no point stalling; she just needed to get down what she'd been thinking that morning.

It was slightly rambling, going around in a couple of circles, but she couldn't think of how else to explain it. Her shaking hand made it hard to write. It reminded her that Henry's shaking had got better recently. That was something positive for him at least. It wasn't as if he would be unfamiliar with the reasons she was giving, and he'd surely see the situation for them was impossible.

When she'd finished, she signed it and waited for the ink to dry before placing it in the envelope and addressing it. It was at this point that the door opened.

'Oh!' her mother yelped, jumping. 'I didn't know you were in here. What are you doing?'

'I've just written a letter to Henry to tell him we can no longer meet.'

'That's a shame, lovey. Are you sure about that?'

'I don't see I have any choice. It's just too complicated. I'm going to get dressed now, and I'll drop it round later.'

She rose and made a hasty retreat, taking the letter with her to her bedroom. She placed it on the bed as she got dressed.

Having managed to keep her feelings at bay as she'd written the letter, it wasn't until she was placing her chemise over her head that she felt her chin wobble and her eyes sting. By the time she had the garment in place she was sobbing so much she had to sit on the bed.

Could she really go through with this? Her feelings for Henry had grown slowly and were maybe the stronger for it. Yes, she had to do it. Better now than after they'd got even more involved. And when Herby had got used to Henry.

She blew her nose with the handkerchief on the bedside table and carried on dressing, her chin set firm, determined to see this through.

Chapter Twenty-Six

'There's a letter for you, Henry,' said Ruth as she brought his dinner up for him on a tray. 'Hand delivered I think, as there's no stamp.'

He pulled himself into a sitting position with difficulty, groaning with the pain.

'Hold on, *bach*, I'll give you a hand.' She put the tray down on top of the chest of drawers and went over to help him, plumping his pillows up afterwards as he sat forward.

She handed him the letter first, then waited. Not having any idea how private it might be, he put it down beside him. 'I'll have something to eat first, then read it after.'

'If you're sure,' she said. She lifted the tray down and placed it next to him, since his legs hurt too much to carry the weight of it.

'Would you like some help with the cawl?'

'No thanks, I'll be able to manage this with the spoon you've brought.'

'Righty ho. I've put it in a mug so that should make it easier. Bang the floor with the stick when you're done, or if you want anything.' She pointed to the old broom handle she'd found in the shed.

When she'd gone, he picked up the envelope and ran his finger along the top of it. He'd feared it might be more threats from Sioni, or Iolo, but decided the writing was too neat for the likes of them. It wasn't Gwen's writing, so it wasn't an apology from her – or more nagging. He hooked out the letter and glanced at the end first. Polly. That was more like it. He went back to the beginning and started it. He hadn't got down far when he was wishing it was from anybody but her.

She was ending the relationship, and it had hardly started. Yes, they'd been having trips out as friends for a while, but as a couple… He could see the sense in everything she'd written – about his sister, about Herby's father, about being married – but it didn't make it any easier to read.

When he'd finished it, he held it against his heart, eyes shut tight. He'd thought he was heartbroken when Amelia left, but it was nothing to how he felt now. Maybe because he'd known, deep down, that Amelia was a selfish woman who'd cared for no one's welfare but her own. She'd complained about anything that caused the least little inconvenience to her, always putting her feelings before his, even when it was clear he was suffering some sort of mental problem. To her it had been an annoyance, an embarrassment. Polly, on the other hand, had been kind and considerate any time he'd started shaking.

And then it occurred to him: his symptoms had diminished in proportion to the growth of his relationship with Polly. He was only going once a month to see the psychiatrist now. Although that doctor had been helpful with the treatment he'd given, Henry believed much of the credit had to go to Polly, who'd made him see he could lead a normal life again. What would he do without her?

He pulled the paper away from his chest, realising something was wrong. His hands were shaking again, and his breathing was rapid. Another panic attack. It was the thought of the void ahead, without Polly in his life. He prayed it would pass quickly, and that he'd be able to eat the food before his mother came up to see if he'd finished.

Damn his sister, damn Herbert Meredith and damn Sioni and Iolo. He flung his arms out in a sudden anger at the world. He'd forgotten the tray was next to him. It went flying, the crockery crashing to the floor with the food, the tray landing on top. As he heard his mother come running up the stairs, calling his name, he hid the letter under his bedcovers.

'Henry, what happened? Oh my goodness, look at this mess.'

'I'm sorry, I had a spasm, with the pain like, and I knocked it over.'

'Oh dear, oh dear. There's a plate and mug gone. Not to mention the wasted food. Never mind. I'll get you some more and help you with it.'

He could hardly argue, though he had lost his appetite and longed to be alone. His own fault for getting so angry. He'd have to hold in the emotional pain for now and postpone his mourning until later.

–

'All I'm saying is, you had two days' wages, so you must have had a bit more than one pound to give me on Friday,' said Ruth as she served up an egg to join the bacon at breakfast on the following Monday. She placed it in front of Henry with a bit of a clatter.

'Leave the lad alone,' said Albert. 'He deserves a little spending money after what he went through with the fall. We can manage well enough for a week.'

'If he'd been married, with his own household to keep, it would have been a poor show if he'd only given his wife that,' Ruth countered.

'Aye, but he hasn't. Yet.'

Henry sat mutely as his parents discussed him and his lack of contribution to the household bills, the aroma of bacon not lending him that feeling of eager anticipation that it normally did.

Sioni had come looking for him straight after work on the Friday, not even waiting until the Sunday, to get his share of the money, ten shillings now. With the pound he'd given his mother, he had five shillings left.

'Are you going to watch the rugby matches later, on the West Street field?' Albert asked. 'And there are some races and games for the kiddies. I bet little Herby would enjoy that.'

'I'm sure he would.'

'Cheer up, *bach*, it's a bank holiday. There's an eisteddfod this afternoon at the Workmen's Institute too. And a dance this evening. All the money collected is going towards the war memorial they're hoping to build. Are you going to anything with Polly?'

'I must say, I think she could have popped by in the week to see how you were,' said Ruth.

'She doesn't know about the accident.'

'But I told Idris, Gwilym and Teilo, and a few people got to know and asked how you were, so she must have got to hear,' said Albert.

'I wish you hadn't.' Henry was losing the little appetite he had. 'Only management needed to know.'

'Teilo's your butty, so he'd have wondered where you were, as would the others. What on earth's wrong with them knowing? And I agree with your mother, you'd think Polly would have—'

'For goodness' sake!' Henry scraped his chair back as he stood. 'Polly and me, well, we're not, not, walking out. That letter, it were from her, saying it were best we didn't see each other.'

Henry, feeling exhausted after the confession, slumped back down into the seat.

'Oh.' Ruth stalled midway through placing an egg on her own plate. 'Why didn't you say, *bach*? That sorry I am. You seemed keen on her.'

Albert patted his son's arm. 'That must be a blow, after Amelia too.'

'It is, but that's an end to it, so can we stop talking about it?'

His parents went silent.

Another August bank holiday alone. He had no one to go with, and no money to spend if he had. Perhaps it would be better if he hid away for these occasions from now on. The thought set a blanket of despair over him. He looked ahead and saw only years of loneliness. He started on his breakfast, barely tasting it. What had he gained in coming home after the war? Nothing. He might as well have been lying in a field in France, like so many of his army Pals.

-

It had been a busy shift at the McKenzie Arms today, being a bank holiday. Polly yawned now as she picked up her shawl from the pegs in the hallway. Despite breaking off her relationship with Henry, deep in her heart she had hoped he would come to the public house, just so she could see for herself that he was all right now.

She'd heard about his fall down the riverbank from Anwen. It had been tempting to head around to his house there and then but, hearing he was recovering, she'd decided it would do neither of them any good. They needed a clean break.

The thought still tugged uncomfortably at her insides. She took a moment as the emotion rose inside her.

'You all right, love,' said Nerys, coming out of the door of the bar.

'Yes, just having a bit of a yawn.' She affected another to demonstrate.

'Aye, busy today it was. You get off now and I'll see you tomorrow.'

Polly opened the door onto Gabriel Street, busy with people chatting and laughing.

She shouldn't resent her parents a day at the seaside at Barry Island, by themselves for a change, but it had meant them leaving Herby with Connie once more. She wondered what snide comment her sister would come up with this time, as she had increasingly since the revelation about Herbert Meredith. She hoped Sioni had gone to the rugby, so she wasn't treated to one of his leering grins.

People mainly ignored Polly now, not even bothering to insult her. A few still greeted her, like Enid and Cadi, who'd just passed by. People were starting to forget her indiscretion and moving on to gossip about the next person, like her mother had predicted. Maybe, eventually, the whole incident would be lost in the mists of time.

She took the back route into Connie's house, to enter the scullery, calling a greeting as she opened the door. She'd make this visit as short as possible.

Polly felt slightly sick when she entered the kitchen to find Sioni there, smoking a roll-up, sitting by the range.

'Ah, here she is, the woman what thinks she's good enough to walk out with a relation of the Merediths.'

'I'm not walking out with no one. Where are Herby and Connie?'

'No, not walking out with him now, since he's found out what you are.'

'Where are Herby and Connie?'

'Herby's upstairs, having a nap, so Connie's popped out to catch a bit of the eisteddfod.'

The last thing Polly wanted was Sioni in charge of her son, but how could she tell her sister this without causing more offence? 'I'll fetch Herby and take him home; I'm in a bit of a—'

He stood up and barred her way. 'Not so fast now. The boy's still asleep, so what's wrong with keeping me company for a bit?'

'I don't want Herby to miss the kiddies' games.' She tried getting around him, but he stepped back, filling the space between the table and the armchairs.

'Ten more minutes won't hurt.'

He put his hand out to take her arm, so she moved backwards. If she could scoot around the other side of the table, past the chaise longue, she'd be able to get out of the door into the hall. Her attempt was blocked by Sioni once again, who put out his hand to push her back. As her shawl fell from her shoulders, she lost her balance, plonking down awkwardly onto the chaise, half falling over. She attempted to pull herself up but found herself sprawled once more, as Sioni shoved her back and placed half his weight on her. She winced at the stench of cigarettes, beer and sweat.

'Don't you pull that face at me. Not good enough for you, aren't I? You had a chance to make a bitta money by satisfying me; now I'll get what I need for free.'

What could she do? If she shouted, only Herby was likely to hear. She didn't want to alert him to anything, or risk him coming down the stairs to find her in this position.

Sioni's hand went to her blouse, tugging carelessly at the buttons, causing one to snap off. When she hit out at his arms, he grabbed her slender wrists and gripped them firmly in one of his substantial hands, pinning them above her head. She whined at the pain as he grasped them more tightly.

'Glad I am of these liberty bodices,' he growled. 'So much easier to deal with than those old corsets.' With one tug, the bodice was ripped to the waist. He scooped out one of her breasts and started to fondle it.

'Stop it – Sioni, please. What – about Connie? How – would she – feel?' The last sentence came out on several sobs.

'She don't need to know, unless you're stupid enough to tell her. But go on, admit it, you're enjoying it.'

'No, no I'm not. I hate you; you're disgusting.'

When he removed his hand, she assumed that knowing how much he sickened her had put him off. However, his hand went lower, lifting up her skirt and tugging at her bloomers. She broke out in a sweat and wriggled, but her legs were secured by the weight of his.

'Disgusting, am I? I'll show you just how disgusting I can be. You're not the first whore I've been with.'

Did he mean since marrying Connie? She had no time to ponder this as his hand succeeded in yanking the bloomers down to her knees. With one foot, he pushed them down the rest of the way, past her feet and off. The more she struggled, the tighter he held her wrists and the further he pushed his other leg against one of hers.

His hand grabbed her knee, then slowly travelled up her inner thigh, higher, higher. She wanted to scream but knew she couldn't, then the urge to be sick overwhelmed her, but that didn't happen either. What if she relaxed, gave him a false sense of hope, so he let his grip go a little? She could maybe throw him off and make a run for it. But she'd have to get Herby first, and that meant going upstairs, which might be even worse. She had to try something though.

'That's better,' he said as she stopped struggling and the tension left her body. 'I knew you wanted it really.'

His hand stopped short of its supposed destination, and he lifted his hips to undo his flies. The longer she left it, the less he'd realise her plan. She waited until he'd undone his bottom button, then with one almighty effort she attempted to shove him off. But as she did this, she heard the back door slam. Connie must be back.

'Help! Help me!' she screamed, only to be treated to a resounding slap across the face by Sioni.

'You little bitch!' he hissed, jumping off her and backing away past the table.

'What the hell!' Connie shrieked as she rushed through the door.

'Oh, thank God!' Polly sobbed, getting up from the chaise.

'The shameless little piece ripped her clothes off to entice me to ravish her,' Sioni yelled, doing up the buttons of his flies.

'Of course I didn't! How could I? You're much stronger than me. He tried to rape me, Connie,' she wailed.

'I wouldn't lower myself with a hussy like you, you liar.'

'And he said he'd been with prostitutes before.' Polly grabbed at the bloomers, slumped by the chaise leg, and pulled them on hastily but awkwardly, trying to protect her modesty by staying behind the table.

Connie's horrified gaze shifted from one to the other as each spoke.

'Course I blinkin' well haven't,' he said. 'Trying to cover up for your wanton ways you are.'

'Why would I rip my own clothes? Oh Connie.' She ran to her sister with her arms out.

'Stay away from me.' Connie stepped back, her hands up as if defending herself. 'You're a nasty piece of work. Always have been. First you seduced Mr Meredith, and now my husband. You're a shameless hussy.'

'No, Connie, please, it was Sioni what tried to rape me.'

'Rubbish. My Sioni wouldn't do that.'

She should have known that Connie would never take her side, yet the evidence was there in front of her eyes.

'He pulled off my bloomers and was undoing his flies.'

'No, you did that.' Sioni's distorted features gave him the look of a gargoyle as he poked a finger in her direction.

'How could I undo them all unless you'd let me? I'm telling you, Connie, it was him what started it. And it's not the first time he's tried it. Last Christmas, he followed me upstairs and pushed me into your bedroom. You remember, when he told you he was showing me the dressing table? Then he made suggestions to me in the scullery, when I came to pick Herby up. Another time he started following me home one night from the Arms, and I had to ask Steven to accompany me home.'

'Lies, all blinkin' lies!' He shook his fist at her.

'More likely you tempted him into the bedroom and made improper suggestions to him,' said Connie, her teeth gritted. She stormed into the hall before they heard her clomp up the stairs.

'You bloody bitch,' said Sioni. 'You go spreading this around and I'll do for you, you see if I don't.'

As she did up her remaining blouse buttons, she said, 'It couldn't be any worse than your foul body on mine. You're, you're – revolting! I wouldn't go anywhere near you, even if you were single.' She retrieved the shawl from the floor, wrapping it around her shoulders and doing it up in a knot in front.

Soon there was a stomping back down the stairs and Connie re-entered the room, carrying a bleary-eyed Herby. 'I've a good mind to keep my nephew,' she said. 'You're an unfit mother.'

'You give him to me now!' said Polly, afraid she'd really try to keep him, especially with Sioni there to back her up.

'Why should I? I'll tell the authorities I will, what a wanton piece you are, and they'll give him to me instead.'

Polly wanted to grab Herby off her but was afraid she'd hold on tighter and hurt him.

'You give him to me now, or I'll get Sergeant Harries here,' said Polly.

'You do that and I'll tell him what you did,' Connie threatened.

'Better give her the boy,' said Sioni. 'We don't want no trouble here, people talkin' about us.'

Connie hesitated, pressing her lips together. She stared at Sioni for some seconds, her eyes wrinkled, as if she were weighing up the options.

Finally, she put Herby down on the ground. He rubbed his eyes and yawned. Polly stepped forward and picked him up, cuddling him to her. 'I don't want you looking after him no more, especially not with *him* here. You have no idea what your husband is capable of, and now he's cavorting with that Reg and Iolo, who knows what they're up to.'

'Rubbish! I'm not up to nothing with them. I just give them the time of day, that's all, not like some of the snooty pieces around here what don't give them a chance to make amends.'

Polly didn't stay to reply, instead heading into the hall and straight to the front door.

'Why you and Aunty Connie shoutin'?' Herby asked as she marched along Islwyn Street.

'We weren't shouting, just having a moan about something, lovey.'

'You said I not goin' there again.'

'It's only that Aunty Connie can't look after you anymore cos she's got other stuff to do.'

'I 'fer Nanna lookin' after me.'

'So do I.'

At this, his head slumped onto her shoulder and he snoozed.

She kept on walking, down the side street past the chapel, onto Gabriel Street. Her heart sank when she realised it was still busy with people. She marched on, trying to steady her breathing, pushing down the rising emotions, ignoring those around her. She prayed she wouldn't see any of the Merediths, or, even worse, Henry. At last, she reached her house on James Street. She opened the front door and carried her son into the kitchen. She placed him on one of the armchairs, then slumped onto another, unable to hold the tears back any longer.

Herby shuffled off the chair and went to her, placing his hands on her knees. 'What wrong, Mummy?'

'I – I don't feel well, lovey.' The last word came out on a long wail.

'Poor Mummy.' Herby's chin wobbled and he started crying too. Polly slipped off the seat and hugged the little boy, and they sobbed together.

–

It was gone eight that evening when Delia and Jim returned from their trip to Barry Island. Polly had already put Herby to bed and was at the range, stirring the stew she'd prepared for their supper.

'Hello, love,' said her father, coming through the scullery door. 'That smells good.'

She smiled wanly as she said, 'Hello, Dad. Did you have a good time?'

'Wonderful,' said her mother as she followed on. 'Such a shame you were working.'

'You deserved to get away on your own after all the help you've given me and Herby,' said Polly, going to the cutlery drawer in the table to pull out some knives and forks.

'You look tired, lovey,' said Delia. 'Did you and Herby manage to get to the games after you picked him up?'

Polly stiffened, not knowing what to say next. She'd rehearsed this over and over in her head during the afternoon, but it had made it no easier.

'What's up?' said Jim. 'You've gone a bit pale.'

She breathed out a long, laboured sigh and clattered the cutlery onto the table. 'I've got something to tell you, and I dunno how, but it's horrible and it's hard to say and I feel terrible but it really wasn't my fault.'

'Oh gawd, what's 'appened now?' said Jim. 'No one hurt, I 'ope.'

'Would you sit down, please,' said Polly.

'Now you're worryin' me,' said Delia.

'Please, Mum.'

Her parents did as she asked, each looking sidelong at the other.

'When I went to pick Herby up at Connie's, she'd gone out and left Sioni in charge.'

'Oh, is that it?' said Delia. 'I agree, I don't think he's good with kiddies. I'll 'ave a word, make sure she doesn't—'

'No, that isn't it. And I don't ever want Herby going there again.'

'Did Sioni slap him or somefing?' said Jim. 'I'll give him a piece of my mind—'

'No, Dad! Please, let me finish.'

'Sorry, love.'

'When I went in, Sioni obviously thought Connie was going to be a while at the eisteddfod, and, well, he tried it on.'

There was a chorus of, 'What!'

'Worse than that, he actually tried to, he tried to—' She dropped into the nearest seat, unable to finish the sentence.

Jim left his chair to stand beside her. 'Ah you saying he tried to molest you?'

'Yes. And it's not the first time he's tried, but this time he actually, he, well, he ripped my blouse and chemise, and, and, got my bloomers off.' Her head went down and she couldn't stop the tears from flowing.

She felt her father's hand on her shoulder. 'How dare he, the bastard! Is Herby all right?'

'Yes. He were asleep when it took place.'

'Are you sure that's what happened?' Her mother sounded unsure.

Polly looked up. 'Oh yes, I'm absolutely sure. He pushed me onto the chaise longue, tore my clothes and, well, what I just said. I can show you the torn clothes, if you don't believe me.'

'We believe you,' said Jim decisively.

'Did you do something that might have encouraged him?' said Delia. 'Maybe unintentionally?'

'No, Mum, I didn't!'

'No need to get upset, love,' said Jim. 'We do believe you.'

But Polly wasn't sure her mother did.

'It's just, you don't always have the best judgement with men,' her mother persisted.

Polly kept her voice level, though she felt like shouting. 'Mum, I knew what I was doing when it came to Mr Meredith. And Gus. No, I had terrible judgement when it came to them, but I have not encouraged Sioni in the least. It's not the first time he's tried it on.' She briefly explained about the other occasions. 'And he implied to me he'd been with other women, you know, women of the night.'

'The cheating blighter,' said her father. 'I think me and a few of me mates need to have a quiet word. Connie don't need to know.'

'But she already does,' said Polly, trying not to cry again. She told them what happened next. 'How she could have believed him, with my liberty bodice ripped and his buttons undone, I don't know.' Even now, the thought of it made her nauseous.

'None so blind as them what won't see,' said Jim.

'Dad, please don't confront Sioni, alone or with friends. I've more than a feeling he's up to something with Reg and Iolo, and I don't want them having any reason to do something to you.'

Jim stood and came over. 'You fink 'e's in with them two?'

'Definitely. I've no idea what they're up to, but you can bet it's nothing good.'

'I never did take to Sioni,' said Delia. 'Always seemed to be a bit – sly – to my mind.' She tutted. 'It's a rum do, and no mistake. Well, I suppose I'll be left with all the childcare now.'

'I'm 'ere in the evening to 'elp put 'im to bed, ain't I? And I don't fink that's the main problem 'ere,' said Jim, sounding peeved. 'We gotta keep an eye out and protect our own. Dunno what we can do about Connie though.'

'She's made 'er bed,' said Delia. 'No point telling 'er nuffing. You know how 'eadstrong she is.'

'Even so, I doubt she knows what Sioni's up to,' said Jim.

'We should report 'im to Sergeant Harries.'

'Maybe. But what would that do to our Connie?'

Delia shrugged. There was a thoughtful pause before she added, 'The supper smells good. Let's 'ave it now and we can 'ave a fink about what to do.'

'Sit down and I'll serve,' said Polly, though she still had no appetite.

Chapter Twenty-Seven

It had been a quiet lunchtime session at the Arms on the Tuesday, with a few of the evening shift workers taking up three tables, and a couple propping up the bar. It was always the same the day after a bank holiday. Polly would have appreciated the opportunity to keep busy, after being awake half the night, with thoughts of the previous day going around her mind in a constant circle.

At two thirty, with the room already empty of customers, and Polly absent-mindedly wiping a pint glass, Nerys came through to the bar.

'You might as well get off now,' she said. 'Looks like you've already washed and wiped everything. Hardly seems worth opening the bars lunchtime after a holiday, though no doubt we'd get complaints if we didn't.'

'Probably,' said Polly, feigning interest.

'See you tomorrow evening.'

Polly fetched her shawl and sack bag from the hallway and made her way out onto Gabriel Street. She had a couple of shops to visit on her way home.

Arriving at the grocer's, she came across a couple of stragglers dawdling up from the pit, but luckily not Sioni. Pushing the door open, she noticed a queue of four women ahead. The last three turned briefly to look at her. None greeted her, but at least nothing else was said. Florrie Harris, at the front of the queue, was rabbiting on to Mrs Brace about the state of Alexandra Street, and how 'that Reg' clearly wasn't keeping it as clean as he was supposed to.

Florrie took her change from Mrs Brace, placing it in her pocket as she turned to leave. Polly didn't look towards her, but noticed, out of the corner of her eye, that she was halfway across the shop when she stopped.

'I'm surprised you'd have the nerve to be seen in public, you dirty little hussy.'

'Oh, do give it a rest, Mrs Harris,' Mrs Brace called from the counter. 'It's about time people left Mrs Smith alone now, don't you think? You've all had your say. And I don't appreciate you making my customers feel uncomfortable.'

Florrie turned back to the counter and set her beady eyes on the grocer. 'You obviously haven't heard the latest then. Tried to seduce her sister's husband, of all people. I know cos Connie told me herself, this morning. Disgusting behaviour it is. She's just proved one more time what a terrible woman she is.'

It was tempting to run away, right now, but why should she? 'That's where you're wrong, Mrs Harris, for it were Sioni what attacked me, see. He tried to, well, he tried to… rape me.'

There was a gasp from the other three women in the queue.

'Nonsense,' said Florrie. 'If that were the case, why hasn't Sergeant Harries been around?'

'Because we haven't told him since it's only my word against my brother-in-law's. And Connie's, for she did see the state I was in, with torn clothes, which only he could have done. She won't hear nothing bad about him, but I'll tell you, he's a scoundrel.'

'Pff! You would say that! It wasn't the first time you've tried it on with him, by all accounts, it's just it's the only time you've been caught. You're a fallen woman and you'll never be nothing else.'

The other three women, though hesitant, looked at each other and tutted.

'That's not nice, that's not,' said the nearest. 'I know what I'd do if some woman tried that on with my husband.'

'That's enough now,' said Mrs Brace. 'It's one person's word against another, and I'll take no sides in this shop unless anyone can prove otherwise.'

'You shouldn't serve the likes of her,' said Florrie. 'You don't know where she's been, filthy little hussy. Ah, there's Sergeant Harries now, on his rounds.' She hurried to the door and pulled it open, calling the sergeant's name.

Harries walked languidly towards the shop. 'What is it now, Mrs Harris?' His voice was weary.

'Connie Gower did tell me this morning that Polly Coombes here did try to seduce her husband. There must be a law against that, surely. Arrest her!'

'No, *he* tried to rape *me*,' Polly countered, feeling jaded with the mess of her life. 'Honestly, Sergeant, that is what happened.'

'No, you're a nasty piece of work, we all know it!'

The policeman stepped into the shop and closed the door. 'Calm down now, Mrs Harris. There's no law against a woman seducing a man, as you put it, so even if it was true, I couldn't arrest no one. But the accusation of rape is serious. Do you have any proof, Mrs Smith?'

Polly would rather not have gone down this road, but it was too late now. 'A torn liberty bodice and a button ripped off my blouse.'

'Huh! As if she couldn't have done that herself,' said Florrie.

'Do be quiet, Mrs Harris,' said the sergeant. 'I wasn't talking to you.'

Florrie tucked her hands under her armpits, the bag over her elbow hanging limply as her mouth plunged down at the corners.

'Now, Mrs Smith, do you want to bring charges? It is the case that your evidence isn't much to go on. And if Mrs Gower is speaking up on her husband's side…' His face suggested it was unfortunate.

Did she want to go to court, risk more ridicule, and from people she didn't even know? Would it even get that far if there wasn't enough evidence? And there was the ever-present threat of Iolo Prosser and Reginald Moss in the background.

'I – I don't know,' she said.

'See, she is lying, like we all knew she were,' said Florrie.

'No, I'm not, but what's the point? People can do what they like to me, accost me and abuse me, and nobody ever believes me or comes to my rescue.' The urge to scream sat at the base of her throat. She needed to escape before she let it go and convinced everyone she was mad.

She ran out of the door, heading first in the direction of her house. But after half-a-dozen steps, she realised Sioni was coming down James Street towards her. She looked wildly in several directions, finally deciding to run back in the direction of the public house. Goodness knows where she was heading. Only home felt like a safe haven. Where was Sioni even coming from? Her house? Had he persuaded her parents she'd tried to seduce him?

Crossing the road, over to the corner where the McKenzie Arms sat, she saw Reg Moss driving down in his cart, the horse trotting obediently in front.

'I've 'eard about what you did to Sioni, you little floozy you,' he shouted over, pulling on the reins to bring the horse to a halt. 'Maybe I should try my luck too, missing a wife for my needs like I am.'

He gave her the once-over as she slowed down and kept close to the public house wall, his lewd grin making her shudder.

'Come on then, climb on, we'll find a quiet corner of the woods and I'll give you a bitta spending money for your attentions.'

Polly heard a creak as a door further ahead opened and Nerys stepped out carrying a couple of bags, singing. She looked up, spotting her estranged husband on the cart, and Polly cowering against the wall.

'What the hell are you doing, Reginald Moss? You harassing my staff again?' She lifted a fist and shook it. 'Get out of my sight before I get Sergeant Harries on you. Look, there he is.' She pointed to where he was leaving the grocery store. 'I'll have him on you, I will.'

'Pah, you silly old cow,' he yelled, before lifting the driving whip and encouraging the horse on once more.

'What did he want?' said Nerys, regarding Polly. 'Why, love, you're shivering. Come in here a moment and tell me what the old sod's done.'

Polly stepped into the hallway. Nerys had barely closed the door when the last two days poured out of Polly. Towards the end of her tale of woe, the tears started falling. She closed her eyes and leant against the wall.

'Well, love, for what it's worth, I believe you,' said Nerys. 'I've had to put up with some nasty old sods in my time, including my old man, what'll soon be my ex old man, if I have anything to do with it.'

'Thank you, Nerys. I'm so glad someone believes me,' Polly said between sobs.

'Here, have my handkerchief.' She pulled a clean one from her pocket and handed it to Polly. 'I've seen that Sioni sneaking around with Reg and Iolo, spying on me, trying to frighten me. Well, just let them try anything. I'll have the police on them before you can say GHB beer. I'm gathering evidence, see.'

Polly was wondering what kind of evidence Nerys was collecting as the landlady called, 'Steven?'

He soon popped his head around the door of the lounge bar, which they'd recently redecorated.

'What's up, Nerys?'

'Would you walk Polly to her house? Those scoundrels Reg and Sioni are pestering her.'

He grunted his annoyance. 'Not again. We should ban Sioni from here.'

'I dunno,' said Nerys. 'It's better if we keep an eye on him.'

'You're probably right. Come on, lovey, let's get you home safe.'

Polly appreciated their concern and help, but, as they left the building, she pondered how much longer this would go on before something serious took place. Back in the spring, she'd wondered about moving, but had dismissed the idea. She needed to think it over again. A fresh start somewhere might be her only choice.

-

Polly was relieved to get back from her sewing work on Friday, even though she'd worked the last three days at Anwen's house. Herby was playing with a hoop in the back yard, giving her a chance to collapse into a chair and lean her head on her hands.

'Hard morning, was it?' Delia asked.

'Gwen called around for their weekly meeting, and, as usual, I was shoved off to the front room. I don't mind working in there, but it were the whispering. I'm sure Gwen's heard about my latest so-called disgraceful behaviour and is trying again to persuade them to sack me. But Anwen's already told me she's heard it and doesn't believe it, cos she's never liked Sioni. He apparently tried it on with her once, when she were eighteen. And she were betrothed to Idris at the time.'

Delia put a plate with a small lamb chop and some vegetables in front of her daughter. 'See, there are people what know what 'e's like. Others'll soon realise who the guilty party is. If only we could persuade Connie of it and get 'er out of that house. But I went to see 'er yesterday evenin' and she were 'aving none of it. Sioni was out, the Lord knows where.'

'Oh Mum, you didn't tell me you'd gone.'

'Well, you was tired when you got in from your shift at the Arms. Was Sioni there?'

'No, thank goodness. He doesn't come in so much now, probably because he gets a cold reception from Nerys and Steven. Where's Dad? He should be back by now.'

'Come and gone. He's walking into Rhymney to buy some new trousers.'

There was a loud rap at the door.

'Oh, who is that now?' said Delia. 'You eat up and I'll 'ave a look.'

Polly picked at the plate of food, cutting a small piece off the chop. There were voices which soon became raised. She wanted to put her head on the table and cry. She'd had enough trouble. Instead, she put her cutlery down and stood; her mother might need a bit of support.

Delia came back into the room, yelling, 'I can assure you it's all lies.' She was being followed by a tall man and a red-haired woman, both looking serious. He was in a dark brown suit and tie, and she had on a plain matching skirt and long jacket, with a small hat perched on her head. He was carrying a briefcase and she had a couple of sheets of foolscap in her hands, with both typed and handwritten words.

'This is my daughter, Polly,' said Delia. 'My other daughter what's complained, Constance, is a liar what's sticking up for her scoundrel of an 'usband. Right bad'n, he is.'

'Where is the child?'

'Who are you?' Polly asked, her hands trembling.

The man handed her a card, on which was written 'The National Society for the Prevention of Cruelty to Children'. Underneath it said 'Colin Brownlow'. She felt the air leave her lungs in one rapid breath, and she had to hold on to the table. Polly had thought Connie's assertion about reporting her had been an idle threat.

'He's playin' in the yard,' said Delia.

'Unsupervised?' the woman asked, aghast.

'He's right in front of the open scullery door, playin' with an 'oop,' said Delia.

'May we see him, please?' Although worded as a question, the woman made it clear it was a demand.

'Course you can,' said Polly's mother. 'He ain't invisible.'

The woman pinched her mouth in, clearly unimpressed with Delia's flippant reply. She followed the older woman out. Polly went next, with Mr Brownlow behind her.

'Mummy!' Herby called, running to clutch at her legs.

'He makes it sound like he hasn't seen you in a while,' the woman said pointedly.

'I was at work until two thirty,' said Polly. 'My mother looks after him while I'm out.'

'And very well I look after him too,' said Delia.

'Where do you work?'

Polly was relieved she'd been to Anwen's that morning, not at the Arms. 'I do sewing for a local business. Mrs Hughes on Edward Street.'

'And she works for the local 'otel too. A good little wage earner she is.'

Why had her mother mentioned that? At least she'd said *hotel.*

'Hotel?' Mr Brownlow questioned.

'The McKenzie Arms.'

'Oh, the public house,' said the woman, screwing up her nose.

'It's a respectable place,' said Delia, 'with its guests and lunches and dinners.'

'And where in this establishment do you work?' Mr Brownlow asked.

'In the public bar.' There was no point in lying about it; they'd probably check.

'I see,' was all he said.

'Herby, have a look and see how many peapods you can count on Grandpa's plants,' said Delia. When he'd skipped off, she said, 'You should know that Constance's husband, Sioni, tried to molest Polly 'ere, so we're not leavin' 'im with 'er anymore. So, if anyone's unacceptable to look after a child, it's 'er, not Polly. Just as well she's never 'ad none of 'er own.'

'That is a serious accusation,' said the woman, watching the boy as he pointed to each pod in turn. 'Have you reported it to the police?'

'I have,' said Polly. 'I saw Sergeant Harries in the grocer's two days ago, but he said it was my word against theirs, and there are two of them and only one of me.'

'Why would she support her husband if he's been assaulting you?' said the woman, clearly sceptical.

'Constance knows where 'er bread's buttered,' said Delia. When the woman tried to interrupt, she ploughed on with, 'Sioni brings in the money, and seems to 'ave extra from who knows where. Not honest money, I'll be bound.'

'I was asking Mrs Smith,' said the woman.

'I agree with my mother. And furthermore, Connie's always been jealous of me having a child. She said when I last saw her that she should be looking after him. I think she'd like to take him away from me.'

'Right. And am I right in thinking that your husband…' she checked the paperwork, 'a Mister Augustus Smith, is in gaol at this moment, for stealing and arson?'

'That's right. And glad I was when they took him away, for he were a mean husband what frittered away the little savings I had.' It wouldn't do to mention that the money had come from Herbert Meredith.

'And your son, Herbert, is actually the product of an adulterous affair?'

She should have guessed that Connie wouldn't spare them the details.

'A youthful error, made by many a young woman,' said Delia.

'It's usual to take away babies from unmarried mothers,' said the woman, 'as they are invariably unfit.'

'She weren't unmarried when she 'ad Herby. She were married to Gus. Or *Augustus*, as you called 'im. And she's still married now.'

Herby came running down the garden path, back to where they were standing. 'I count twenty-four pods,' he said proudly.

'See, he's great at counting for 'is age,' said Delia. 'That's cos my daughter's a good mother, see.'

'Well done, Herby,' said Polly, bending down to give him a hug. 'We'll pick some later for our supper.'

'I help too?'

'Of course.'

The visitors looked at each other, the man with raised eyebrows.

'We will have to go away and consider this matter,' said Mr Brownlow. 'We'll probably need to speak to other people, your employers, for instance.'

Polly hoped Gwen didn't get involved, who'd no doubt love an excuse to get her into trouble. At least Nerys was on her side.

'Fair enough,' said Delia. 'I'm sure you'll find out she's a decent woman and mother, despite what *some* bigoted people would say. And you could talk to Pastor Thomas and his wife, Anabel, too. They'll tell you what she's like. Now you're here, you might as well leave the back way. Turn left out of here onto Lloyd Street, and you'll come out on Bryn Road.'

'Very well,' said Mr Brownlow. 'We'll be in touch.'

Polly stood, placing her hands on Herby's shoulders. She and her mother watched as the pair exited the garden.

'Right, you go and finish your dinner.'

'I'll warm it up later. I don't feel like it now.'

'Fair enough. I've got some washing I need to hang out.' Delia went back into the scullery.

'Let's go in and do a jigsaw puzzle, Herby,' said Polly.

'Aw right, Mummy. I like doin' that.'

His cute, beaming smile had her bending down to give him a hug. 'I know you do, my lovely boy.'

-

Henry blinked repeatedly as he left the cage that had brought him up from the depths of the mine. The sunshine was blinding, hurting his eyes as he stepped from it and walked across the courtyard. It was still only Monday, with another six days to go until the Sabbath and another day off. Each day seemed to get harder. The effort he'd once put into this job, for the reward of money, seemed pointless when most of it went to Sioni and his mother. Not that he resented the latter, only the fact he was left with little to save. And Sioni had continued collecting his share promptly on the Friday, as soon as they left work. But then, what did he have to spend it on these days? The ache of Polly's absence seemed to increase each day.

By the gate, as usual, was Esther Williams, waiting to talk to her son, Christopher. But he never wanted to talk to her, always ignoring her as she tried to speak to him. She seemed thinner and more bowed as each week went by.

About to exit the gate, Sioni caught him up. Henry groaned quietly to himself. What now? More interest?

'Suppose you've heard about that trollop of yours, claiming I tried to molest her. As if I'd touch that dirty cow.'

'What?' said Henry, twisting around to face Sioni. 'If you've touched—'

'Like I said, as if I'd touch her. No, she tried to seduce me. The missus caught her, and Polly told her I'd tried to rape her. Bloody little liar. You're well shot of her.'

Henry grabbed Sioni by the shirt, pulling him to a stop. 'If Polly says you tried that, I'd believe her over you, any day. You leave her alone, you dirty sod.'

Sioni grabbed Henry's hand and wrenched it away, then put his coal-blackened face right up close to Henry's. 'Don't you be assaulting me, mun, else you'll find yourself in an even worse condition than last time. Maybe even dead in a ditch.'

'What's going on here, lads?' Idris caught them up, Gwilym by his side.

'Just letting this fool know what his erstwhile lady love is really like. Lady! That's a joke.' Sioni stepped away. 'After anything in trousers, that one. I can't believe you didn't get her attentions, if you know what I mean. Never mind, the NSPCC will sort her out. Connie made sure to report her. Not a fit mother she's not.'

'What the hell have you done?'

'Gotta get home to my good lady wife now,' said Sioni. 'See ya.' He went off up the hill, laughing.

'What's been going on?' said Henry, turning to the other two.

'You really haven't heard?' said Idris.

'I've not been very sociable recently. A bit under the weather I've been.' More like he didn't want to mix with anyone, he thought, feeling that mantle of gloom tighten around him as each day went by.

'I'm sure your parents must have heard,' said Gwilym. 'Mine certainly have.'

They probably had heard but had spared him the details. They'd been particularly protective of him recently, and he hadn't had the energy to fight against it.

'Connie *apparently* found Polly seducing Sioni in their kitchen when she came back from the eisteddfod,' said Idris. 'But Polly insists he tried to molest her, and he tore her blouse and um, liberty bodice.' He whispered the last word, embarrassed by it.

'And then Connie reported her to the child cruelty organisation, and they came round to find out if she were a fit mother,' Gwilym added.

'I bet it's all lies!' Henry insisted.

'Oh, I agree with you,' said Idris. 'But there's plenty in the village prepared to believe it.'

'Including Gwen.' Gwilym shook his head. 'They're going to look into Connie's report further.'

'That's terrible.' While Henry paused to take it all in, Christopher passed Esther by as she tried to talk to him, ignoring her completely as usual.

'Please boy, come and talk to your old mam. Please.' But her pleading was to no avail.

'Dunno why she don't give up,' said Gwilym. 'She's been doing this for months.'

Henry couldn't muster an opinion on Esther either way, so concerned was he about Polly. 'If I hear Sioni's tried that again, I'll personally sort him out myself.' Even as he said it, he knew it would only make things worse for him and for Polly. And Sioni's threat that he'd end up dead in a ditch filled him with a cold fear.

'I wouldn't, *bach*,' said Idris. 'There's something going on with him and Prosser and Moss. They always seem to be skulking around at night-time. I mentioned it to Sergeant Harries, off the record like, but he just said he'd look into it, like he always does.' He tutted and raised his eyes.

Albert appeared out of the gate at this point. 'I hear Sioni Gower's been bothering you,' he called. 'Come on, let's get home.'

He caught them up and took Henry's arm, steering him up Station Road. Henry tried to shake him off, to no avail.

'Da, why didn't you tell me about the accusations between Sioni and Polly?'

'You don't need to get involved with that. I'd say you've enough on your plate, wouldn't you?'

'What d'ya mean?'

'Someone saw you, last Friday, giving money to Sioni. What the hell's going on, son?'

'Nothing, Da.'

'Don't give me that, *boi bach*. Now you'd better tell me before we get home, and before I go round and ask Sioni Gower myself.'

The game was up. As they walked home, Henry told him about the loan, the ever-growing interest and finally, the beating he'd taken from Sioni and Iolo.

'You bloody fool,' said his father when he'd completed the sorry tale. 'You bloody fool.'

Chapter Twenty-Eight

Polly looked at the large wooden clock on the bar wall, with its Roman numerals, to find it was twenty-two minutes past two. She wiped yet another glass and placed it on the shelf. It had been a week of skulking to work and back for her, hoping those around would at least ignore her, but even when there weren't comments, there were enough challenging looks to make the short journey from her home to either the public house or to Anwen's uncomfortable.

'Time gentlemen, please,' Steven called from his place near the bar hatch.

'Already?' a voice called from a table next to one of the windows overlooking Station Road.

'You want to be fit for your shift this evening,' Steven replied.

'Aye, suppose.'

Steven wiped down the bar while Polly's mind wandered. She'd had a letter from the NSPCC that morning, saying they'd be sending somebody shortly to do a more detailed investigation into her circumstances. Whatever that meant. She'd tried to tell herself that they wouldn't find anything that would justify them taking Herby away from her, but she knew, from other people's stories, that they weren't beyond removing children on the flimsiest of pretexts. She felt perpetually queasy thinking of the possibility of Herby's absence from her life.

Afraid of giving in to her melancholy, she pulled herself upright and straightened her shoulders. The men in the bar slowly removed themselves, in pairs and groups, until the room was empty.

'I'll clear the tables,' she said, heading for the hatch.

'No, you get off, lovey,' said Steven. 'I can manage fine. I'll get the washup to do the glasses in the big sink in the scullery.'

'Thank you, Steven.'

She collected her handbag from under the bar and let herself out of the hall door onto a sunnier day than it had been when she'd arrived.

The tiny bit of pleasure this created for her was washed away when she saw who was leaning against the wall a few yards down.

'There she is, the lying little bitch.' Sioni, still sooty from the mine, looked her up and down with a sneer.

'Go away, Sioni. You're not doing yourself any favours. People will see that you're harassing me.'

'I'll just tell them that I'm asking you to leave us alone because you keep bothering us.'

'What are you doing?' said Henry, appearing around the corner, flanked by Idris, Gwilym and the diminutive but tough Twm Bach. 'I thought I saw you come round here.'

Polly's heart leapt at the sight of Henry, as it always did, before sinking into the inevitable sadness that their hopeless situation always brought.

'Just telling Polly to leave my wife alone,' said Sioni. 'For she do keep trying to tell her that I did something I didn't, see.'

'I haven't even seen Connie since you attacked me,' said Polly, wondering why she was bothering.

'We thought you might try something,' said Idris. 'We're keeping an eye on you.'

Sioni pushed himself away from the wall, looking sullen like a naughty child. 'I'm only trying to protect my reputation from her lies.'

'What, by bothering Polly?' said Henry.

'Ah, away with the lot of you.' Sioni kicked a screwed-up paper bag, left on the side of the pavement, into the road. 'Like I care what you lot think. I'm telling you, she'll get her comeuppance, you see if she don't. And you lot too, if you don't keep your noses out.'

Polly had endured enough. 'I'll get my comeuppance?' she hollered. 'There's not a lot more anyone could do to ruin my life. Now get out of my way. All of you!'

With that she ran down the road as fast as she could, picturing herself punching Sioni. She hated him, hated him with a passion. Even if Gwen hadn't made a fuss about her association with Henry, he'd have ruined the relationship with his dirty actions and his lies.

Reaching home, she pushed the front door open with a clatter and ran into the kitchen.

'What on earth!' said her father, standing in front of the tin bath, full of hot water, about to undo his shirt.

'It's Sioni, he were outside the Arms, waiting for me. Luckily some other men stuck up for me. But I'm sick of it, Dad, sick of it!'

'I know, lovey. Your mum and I 'ave been talkin' about it. I'm lookin' into changing mines so we can rent an 'ouse somewhere else. Mabel will be all right with her family here.'

'But what about my jobs?'

'You'll get work elsewhere, a clever seamstress like you. I fink it's for the best.'

She pressed both hands against the table and hung her head for a moment. She'd never see Henry again. The reality of that made her feel sick. But it was over, so what difference did it make?

When she looked up she said, 'You're probably right.'

Chapter Twenty-Nine

The McKenzie Arms was the last place Henry had wanted to go this Saturday evening, but his father had given him two shillings and insisted he go out with Teilo when he'd called by after supper. He'd already been out earlier, to his monthly session in Cardiff with the psychiatrist. It seemed he was getting better, and it was true that the shaking had become only an occasional inconvenience now. But the overriding sense that his life was going nowhere had got worse.

Arriving at the Arms, he and Teilo had inevitably sat with their old brigade Pals and currently Alun Lloyd was telling them in a whisper about how another lamb had gone missing from his family's farm. Henry was only half listening, staring at the still light sky through a window, aware of Polly at the bar in his periphery vision.

'And they're a fair size now,' said Alun. 'It'd take more than one person to steal it.'

'Maybe it just ran away,' said Teilo.

'No, mun. We checked the fencing and there weren't no gaps. Henry might know something about it.'

He swivelled around. 'What d'ya mean? I've not stolen no lamb.'

'Keep your voice down, mun!' Alun glanced across the room, and they all looked to where Sioni Gower was sitting with John Bowen, an infrequent visitor to the public house. 'No, mun, I didn't say you had. It's just, my da is convinced it's got something to do with Reg and Iolo, and that Sioni Gower might be involved. I know you've had a run-in with him, over Polly. I overheard Idris telling Hywel Llewellyn.'

They all moved their attention to where Idris and Hywel were sitting with Gwilym and Twm Bach, three tables away from them.

Polly was leaning her arm on the bar, staring into space. Behind her, Nerys Moss was talking to Steven, looking rather serious.

Cyril Davies, the butcher's boy, approached the bar. 'Cheer up, love, and get me a pint of the GHB.'

Nerys bristled and marched to the bar in three steps.

'Uh oh,' said Teilo. 'Young Cyril's for it.'

'If people stopped their nasty gossip about Polly, maybe she could cheer up,' Nerys announced. 'And I'd appreciate it if you displayed some manners, young man. You've always been a cheeky young devil. And what happened to "please"?'

Cyril looked crestfallen. 'Sorry, Mrs Moss... Please may I have a pint of the GHB, Polly?'

'That's better.' She indicated to Polly that she could fulfil the order, then turned her attention to the customers. 'And I'd better not hear no nasty gossip about any of my staff here, for I had Florrie Harris giving me an earful of it earlier, at James the Veg's, and I told her what for.' She looked pointedly to the left of the room, where Sioni was sitting.

'I'm surprised she allows Sioni in here at all, if she's so protective of Polly,' said Teilo.

Henry had wondered about that too and could come to only one conclusion. 'Sometimes you've got to keep an eye on what your enemies are up to.'

'Better to have them where we can see them all right,' Alun agreed. 'Talking of which, they seem to be leaving. Wonder what Bowen's got to do with anything.'

'Probably nothing,' said Henry. Yet he felt there was more to it. Bowen was normally reluctant to mingle with any of the workforce, who he seemed to consider below him in his capacity as undermanager.

'Same again, lads?' Henry asked the four other men at his table, disobeying his self-inflicted restriction not to have more than one with them. Polly was serving a couple of other men, so now was a good time to go up.

There were various versions of acceptance and Henry rose, scooping up the glasses with his fingers. When he got to the bar, Mrs Moss and Steven were in conversation with Idris.

'Haven't seen her the last three days,' said Idris.

'Who's that?' Henry hoped he wasn't interrupting a private conversation.

'Esther Williams,' said Steven. 'Same again?'

'Yes, please. She's not been at the colliery gate as usual.'

'Exactly,' said Idris. 'She's maybe given up on Christopher, at last.'

Steven chuckled. 'Or Iolo and Reg have got fed up with her gossiping and have tied her up and gagged her, like her husband did young Christopher when he tried to run away to enlist. She can't half go on when she gets started.'

'Yes, she can,' Nerys agreed. 'But I wouldn't wish that on anyone, not even Esther Williams. She hasn't been seen skulking around the shops neither, from what I've heard. But who knows? Maybe she's been going to Rhymney, to avoid people.'

'I'm sure she's fine, either way,' said Steven. 'Looks after number one always, that one.'

Having paid, Henry took the first two glasses over to his table, then went back to the bar for the others. Idris was doing likewise, arriving back at the bar at the same time.

'You're always welcome to join us in here again, you know,' said Idris. 'Used to be good friends, we did.'

'Aye, I know. It's hard with this lot though when they still don't want to mix. They feel no one understands what they've been through, and I, well, I don't want them to think I'm abandoning them.'

'It's been nigh on eighteen month since you all returned. They're surely not going to keep this up forever.'

'I have tried to speak to them about it, but it's not done no good so far.'

'Well, you know where we are.'

'Aye.'

He picked up two more glasses as Teilo came to fetch the last one. As they sat down, Henry wondered if he should tackle them about mixing with the others again. He knew some of their own old mates had tried to take up their friendships again, but they'd all resisted. Or did they all feel like him, that they were staying in this tight-knit group so they didn't let the others down? He'd only know if he asked.

'I was thinking, lads, I know we've discussed this before but, well, isn't it about time we let our old friends into our lives again?'

'I don't have nothing in common with them anymore,' said Alun. 'Bryn were always the more outgoing one. His friends tended to be mine. Now...' He shrugged, his face forlorn at the thought of his late brother, killed at the battle of Mametz Wood.

'Susan were my best friend,' said Douglas Ramsay, his voice quiet. 'I didn't really go out much when she were alive.'

They were all living in the past, thought Henry. But then, wasn't he?

'Well look now—'

But he didn't get a chance to finish before Idris stopped by their table, the rest of his party passing him and heading for the backroom. 'Any of you fancy a dominoes tournament?'

This might be the chance to move them forward to being more sociable, but before Henry could say anything, Teilo replied, 'No, we're all right, thanks.'

'Right you are.'

'Maybe next time,' Henry called over, feeling the frustration grow within him.

He was tempted to get up and say that he fancied a game and leave them all to it, but, seeing them all slumped and gloomy, he couldn't bring himself to do it.

Sporadic conversation and occasional sips at beer glasses were Henry's entertainment for the next half hour, until a couple of chairs scraped across the tiled floor. Henry looked up to see Sioni polishing off his pint while John Bowen waited for him by the exit door. Having finished it, he smacked his lips and plonked the glass down on the table, before joining Bowen. He took a long, last look around the room before leaving.

'Thank the heavens Bowen's gone,' said Teilo. 'It felt like he was watching us, sitting there, eyeing everyone up.'

'Aye, it's a shame Mrs Moss allowed him back after banning him,' said Alun.

Another tedious half hour passed by, with Henry glancing at the clock every few minutes, longing for stop-tap. Mrs Moss and Polly disappeared from the bar just after serving the last orders. Finally, Steven called, 'Time, gentlemen please!'

Henry tried not to make his sigh of relief too obvious. All the men took various amounts of time to drain their glasses, in which time, Idris and his group came back through the door from the backroom.

Out on the street, there was a crowd of men a little ahead, and a large group behind, with the old Pals in the middle, silent, while the others around them chatted and laughed.

Henry felt the loss of his pre-war friends keenly in this moment. Yet it was his own fault, feeling responsible for this band of ex-soldiers. If only he could—

But Henry didn't get to finish the thought before he found himself hurled to the ground, along with those around him, as a terrific blast was heard nearby. There was a clatter as fragments of wood, glass and rubble hit the ground.

He wasn't sure how long he'd lain there, dazed, when he looked up, probably only a matter of seconds by the look of everyone. He peered up towards the public house, bewildered, unable to focus properly, but aware of smoke rising up from it, lit by the nearby streetlamp. He was aware of pain in his hands and cheek, where they'd been scraped along the road.

There were shouts and screeches, then somebody hollered, 'What the bloody hell happened!'

Henry's grogginess cleared a little, and one name came screaming into his mind.

'POLLY!'

Chapter Thirty

'What the hell was that?' shrieked Tom as he propelled himself out of his armchair and grabbed Gwen, taking them both to the floor, face down.

'Tom!' Gwen yelled, hitting her elbow on a stone flag. A pain shot up it, to her shoulder.

Elizabeth was already on her feet, heading to the hall, as Tom, struggling to get his breath, gasped as he said, 'Sorry, I'm so sorry. I thought I was back in the trenches.' He struggled to get up, then pulled her up next to him. 'Was that from the mine?'

'It must have been.'

They followed Elizabeth into the hall. She had the front door open and was standing outside. Gwen and Tom joined her. Almost every door was open, with people looking across at the colliery, though darkness had settled now.

Slowly a peal of shouted voices uttering the same repeated words made its way along the street towards them, until the sentence, 'It's the Arms, there's been an explosion!' reached them.

'Gwilym's at the Arms!' Elizabeth shrieked, and ran off down the road, following many of Alexander Street's residents.

Panic filled Gwen's throat and she found it hard to swallow. 'Come on.' She took her husband's hand and followed on, her elbow still sore. 'Henry might be there too. He – he sometimes goes on a Saturday.'

Reaching the top of Jubilee Green, they saw smoke billowing up above the bushes of the gardens as they flowed down with the crowd, which was joined by more people from the adjoining streets.

Reaching the bottom of the gardens, the three of them almost rammed into the crowd there, which had come to a horrified standstill. Part of the back and side wall of the public house appeared to be missing, along with the garden wall, while a lot of men were either sprawled on the pavement and road, on their knees, or staggering to their feet.

'Gwen! Elizabeth!' called Anwen as she caught them up. 'Oh no, oh no, Idris was in there.' She let out a long wail of distress.

'Who's at home with the children?' said Elizabeth.

'Mamgu came in – in when I opened – the – the door. She knew Idris was here.'

'Gwen!' shouted another voice. She looked up to see her mother, just ahead of her father, running towards them.

'Let us through!' Albert shouted. 'Henry? Henry!'

Gwen and Tom followed him, along with Elizabeth who was shouting, 'Gwilym, where are you, Gwilym?'

Several others followed suit, looking for their loved ones. Behind her, Gwen was aware of a voice calling, 'Polly!' several times. She looked back to see Jim Coombes.

'Gwilym's here!' Tom called as they spotted him helping Twm Bach up. Idris and Hywel were struggling to help each other up.

'Oh Gwilym, thank God!' called Elizabeth, throwing her arms around him once Twm was steady on his feet.

Anwen called, 'Idris!' the same time as Albert shouted, 'Henry's here. He's all right.'

Gwen ran to her brother and hugged him. 'What happened, Henry? What on earth happened?'

'Dunno. We were all leaving when there was an explosion, from the back here.'

'That's the back of the public bar,' said Albert. 'Was there anyone left in there?'

'Only Steven, I think,' said Henry. 'He were at the other end.'

'I'll go and let Violet know I'm all right,' said Hywel. 'Then I'll be back straight away to help in any way I can.' He ran off up the road.

'Polly! Polly!' Jim kept on calling, frantically running around the road, inspecting those who'd been knocked over by the blast.

'Mr Coombes,' said Henry, running over to him. 'Polly was in the public house, but she and Mrs Moss had left the bar.'

'What about the rest of the staff?' said Idris. 'The live-in maid and the cook? And the gardener?'

'Not to mention the guests. Come on,' said Henry, 'we've got to get in and find them!'

'Don't be stupid, Henry,' Gwen called after him. 'It'll be dangerous.'

'All right now, stand back, all of you!' Sergeant Harries shouted at the gathered crowd, marching rapidly past them, backed by Constable Davies and a new recruit. Harries turned to the men who'd been leaving the Arms and their concerned families. 'And you lot too, out of the way.'

'But we've got to try, mun!' said Henry, walking backwards towards the front of the building. 'We can get in this way.'

'Henry!' Gwen hollered. 'It's too dangerous.'

'He's right,' said Tom. 'We need to see what we can do. Henry, wait up. We need a plan.'

Henry stopped and came back to stand nearby.

'No, Tom, you can't,' said Gwen, her heart racing. 'Please, you'll all get injured. Or worse, if there's another explosion.'

'Come away now, sir,' said the sergeant.

'Of course it's dangerous,' said Tom, 'but we can't leave people there.' He took a few steps away, towards the other men to call, 'Who else is coming in? We need to organise this for maximum efficiency.'

'I am!' yelled Twm Bach, marching towards him, brushing himself down. 'This was deliberate this was, I'd bet my boots on it. Whoever it was, we'll show them.'

He turned towards Henry's old battalion Pals, huddled together, watching. They'd grown in number as several who hadn't been in the Arms that evening joined them, including Daniel Williams.

'Come on, you lot,' Twm Bach continued. 'You've seen action. Show us what you're made of, and let's work at this together.'

'I don't think that's wise,' said Harries. 'I've called up Rhymney station. They're all dealing with an incident up at Bute Town at the moment, but I'm sure—'

'Oh shut up, mun!' Twm hollered. 'Between us we've been through a fatal pit explosion and a war to end all wars. And that fire at Mr Schenck's. Whatever arguments or fallings out there are between us, whenever there's a disaster the residents are always here to help.'

There was a cheer of agreement from the old Pals and the rest of the miners alike, echoed by the crowd behind.

'So, let's just get on with it!' Twm Bach punched his fist into the air.

Sergeant Harries lifted his helmet and scratched his head. 'I suppose the other police might be a while.'

'Right,' said Tom. 'Let's get ourselves into groups and decide who's going where.'

Several men started to come forward, but Gwen noticed that the old battalion held back.

Finally, Henry took several strides towards the old Pals, stamping down one foot, as if on parade. 'Mr Meredith and Twm Bach are right,' he said. 'We can't hide in the shadows anymore. We belong to a community here, and we're part of it, like we were part of our battalions. Come on now, men!' He spun around and marched away, not looking to see if anyone was complying. He stopped in front of Tom, stamping one foot down as before. He lifted his arm in salute. 'Reporting for duty, Lieutenant Meredith!'

To Gwen's surprise, all of the old battalion Pals got into line and followed on to where Henry and Daniel were standing with Idris, Gwilym, and the other miners who'd volunteered. Reaching their destination, they stood in several lines and saluted.

'Right,' said Tom. 'Let's get on with it.'

-

'There's shouting coming from up here,' called Henry as he, Idris and Twm reached the door further along the front of the building.

'You try and get through that entrance, and we'll see what we can do here,' Tom called back, standing at the main entrance on the corner, with Gwilym and Alun Lloyd.

Other groups had been put to work removing chunks of the ruined back wall around the garden area, with Daniel Williams in charge. Sergeant Harries, tutting and complaining under his breath, had nevertheless accepted that Tom's plan was the best chance of helping those trapped, until the police turned up from the other stations. He patrolled the street, keeping the crowd back.

Henry was about to turn the handle of the furthest door when the village fire engine was heard, roaring down the road, ringing its bell.

'Out of the way, everyone!' Sergeant Harries called, and the crowd parted.

When the fire engine had reached the top of Station Road and stopped, Phillips the Fire jumped out. 'What's to do, then?'

'Nothing needing water yet, Phillips,' Harries called. 'But you could help supervise the rubble moving.'

'Righty ho!'

Henry continued to turn the handle of the door and tried to push it open, but it was locked.

'Right, stand back,' said Idris. 'There's only one way to do this.' The others complied as he got close to the door and shouted, 'Move away if you're near the door.' He then administered several almighty kicks at the wood, near the handle, with one of his long legs. After doing this six times, the door flew open.

Henry entered hesitantly to find the panic-stricken faces of staff and guests, cowering to one side of the door.

'We couldn't find the key to get out,' said the cook. 'It's normally on the hook here.'

'You'd better get them clear, Henry,' said Idris. 'Twm Bach and I will see what we can find.'

The staff and guests ran out onto Gabriel Street, heading for where the police were keeping back the growing crowd.

'Hang on,' said Henry catching them up, 'where are Polly and Mrs Moss?'

'Oh Lord, I've no idea,' said the cook. She looked around at the maid and the gardener, both of whom shook their heads.

'Have any of you seen them?' he asked the guests.

But they hadn't either.

Henry felt his anxiety grow. Where could they be? And why hadn't they come out if they were able? So maybe they weren't able…

Tom came out of the corner door, shouting, 'The barman has been injured by some falling masonry. Could someone find a blanket please, so Gwilym and Hywel can carry him down to the hospital?'

'Does he know where Mrs Moss and Polly are?' Henry persisted, but before Tom could reply, there was another voice.

'Hold on a moment.' The crowd parted to let Dr Roberts through. 'I'm so sorry, but I was on a call up the end of Mafeking Terrace and we thought the explosion was thunder at first.' He stopped abruptly, taking in the damage down the side of the public house. 'Did you say Steven has been injured?'

'Yes, but we'd better bring him out before you examine him,' said Tom. 'The masonry is unsafe.'

'I'm not going to worry about that,' said the doctor rushing past Tom, into the building.

'But what about—' Henry tried again.

'Henry, Steven says that Mrs Moss and Polly went down to the cellar,' said Tom.

'What? Does that mean they're safe, or, or not? Surely they'd have appeared by now, hearing the noise, if they was safe.' He shuddered, a cold ripple passing from his head to his toes.

A woman ran over to Gwen, handing her a pile of blankets, before hurrying back to stand once more outside her house on Station Road. Gwen rushed the blankets over to her husband.

'I really don't know, Henry,' said Tom, taking one. He went back inside.

Idris and Twm Bach exited the door further up and came back towards Henry.

The gardener came forward. 'The entrance for the cellar's down between the stairs and the backroom, where they play games.'

'We got as far as that corridor,' said Idris, 'but the explosion, well, it seems to have taken the door down to the cellar out, and there was rubble in the way.'

Daniel Williams came up from the parties working by the back walls. 'Part of the back yard seems to have collapsed into a hole.'

'Well, the cellar extends out under the yard, I believe,' said the gardener.

Henry's vision blurred as the grim possibilities slammed into his mind. He felt like screaming, *Noooooo*, but held his nerve, conscious that he'd be no good if he fell apart.

Jim Coombes, who'd been swept behind the cordon, broke away, crying, 'Where's Polly, where's my gal? I want to join the search teams to find them.'

'It's better if you don't, being closely related to her,' said Sergeant Harries, walking over to them. 'If Mrs Moss and Mrs Smith are down there, you need to let the Rhymney police get on with it now. We don't want nobody else getting hurt.'

'Sergeant Harries is right,' said Gwen. 'You need to let them get on with it. Come on, let's get you all away from this danger.'

'But we don't know how long they'll be,' said Henry. 'If we wait for them, it might be, might be – too late!' He felt a fury bubbling up through the dread. 'I know you don't like Polly, Gwen, but—'

'That's not why I said it,' cried Gwen, her expression horrified.

'Isn't it?' said Henry. 'Had it in for her for a while, you have.' He ignored the sergeant's earlier advice and ran down to where the men were working.

'We need to get into that cellar,' said Daniel, 'before any more of it collapses onto Mrs Moss and Polly.'

Tom emerged once more, leading Gwilym and Hywel, who were transporting Steven on the blanket. Dr Roberts called, 'Would some of the women here accompany the staff and guests down to the hospital?'

Several women were allowed out from the crowd to help with this.

'Let's regroup and work on getting through to the cellar,' said Henry.

'No!' yelled Gwen. 'You've all done enough.'

'What's up?' said Tom, traipsing over.

Henry reiterated what had been said, his anger with Gwen obvious.

'We'd better get organised post-haste,' said Tom. 'Let me take those, we may need them.' He relieved Gwen of the other blankets, clutching them between his own arm and the artificial one.

'No!' Gwen shouted once more. 'It's too dangerous. And you can't manage with – with—'

'My one arm?' Tom finished. 'You've always encouraged me to do anything I want, Gwen, so now is not the time to doubt me.'

'I'm sorry, it's just—'

'I'm not going to use my lack of a real second arm as an excuse not to help here. We had situations like this in the war, digging out men buried in trenches that had been blown up. It's my duty.'

Gwen nodded limply, looking miserable.

'Right, let's gather everyone together again,' said Tom, 'and regroup to approach from different locations, including the stairs.'

'Enough of the garden wall has been removed,' said Daniel, 'so we'll be able to get in that way too.'

Henry went to follow Tom down, looking back briefly at Gwen, her eyes half-closed in pain, her hand over her mouth. When she saw him looking, she removed her hand to say, 'Good luck, Henry. I – I hope Polly's all right.'

Henry couldn't bring himself to reply, so nodded. With that, he carried on.

Chapter Thirty-One

Henry was with the team in the middle of the yard removing loose paving, shattered chairs and ruined tables. More men from the gathering crowd had joined them, standing in lines to transfer the wreckage along to the space on the road outside. The police from Rhymney still hadn't arrived, so Sergeant Harries had gone to phone up the station once again.

'How are you doing over there?' Tom called to the team working at the far end of the wide yard.

'Getting there slowly,' Daniel Williams called back. 'No signs yet of the cellar, just debris.'

'Polly! Mrs Moss!' Henry called from his position kneeling close to where the ground had collapsed.

'Be careful there, Henry,' said Tom. 'We don't want you falling in.'

Henry's reply was interrupted by a woman's voice screaming, 'Sioni, where's my Sioni?'

'Mrs Gower, get out of the way!' Sergeant Harries shouted, returning to the scene.

Henry looked up to see Connie standing where the garden wall had once been, getting in the way of those transferring the rubble to the road.

'My Sioni was in the Arms. Where is he? I can't see him nowhere.'

Henry's anger rose once again. An idea had been building in his mind the last hour, an idea that had grown into the monster of a possibility. He jostled past the men working there, until he reached Harries, who was trying to pull Connie away from the area.

'Yes, your Sioni was in the Arms all right,' said Henry, 'with John Bowen. But he left a while before the explosion happened. Funny that, like he knew.'

'You're a damned liar, you are,' she yelled. 'He's told me how you tried to accost him. I bet you knocked him out so he'd be in the explosion.'

Gwen appeared with Elizabeth and Anwen, shouting, 'Of course he didn't! That Sioni's a thug, and no mistake. He beat Henry up, not the other way round. That's why he had to take time off work.'

His parents must have told her all about it. Henry wished they hadn't, as that would only put her against Polly's family even more.

'That's a lie!' Connie yelled.

'No it isn't,' Henry had to admit.

'And of course,' said Gwen, 'Sioni's a fireman, so he has access to explosives. As does John Bowen! So where is he? Why isn't he here, helping, since he's undermanager? Mr Hopkins the manager is here.'

'I don't think we should be casting aspersions,' said Sergeant Harries.

'But she's right,' said Henry. 'Sioni had it in for Polly because of her accusations, and for me because I confronted him about accosting her.' And for the debt, which he wasn't going to admit to everyone here. 'Also Idris, Gwilym and Twm Bach for backing me up. And we were all in there tonight.'

'And he did have a good look round at us all before he left,' said Idris, coming up from the yard.

'Not to mention that Reg had it in for Nerys as well,' Gwen pointed out. 'And he'd been seen with Sioni, along with that Iolo Prosser. They're probably all in it together. You should be looking for them now, not hanging around here, looking on while others do the work.'

'There's no need for that, Mrs Meredith,' said Harries.

'But she's right, Sergeant,' said Elizabeth. 'And if they've got explosives, who knows what else they're up to?'

'And where are these so-called officers from Rhymney you've called on?' said Anwen. 'They must have finished at Bute Town by now.'

'Well, no, because there's been a major incident there.'

'My husband wouldn't do that!' cried Connie. 'You're all devils, just like Sioni said you were, thinking the worst of him.'

'Constable!' Harries called up to PC Davies. 'Remove Mrs Gower to behind the cordon, please.'

'But my Sioni, he might be buried here!'

'If he is, it's his own doing.' Henry ran back to where they were trying to make an entrance into the cellar.

Twm Bach waved his arm. 'Henry! I think I heard someone.'

Henry hunkered down beside him, listening. 'I can't hear nothing.'

'I'd swear there was a voice.'

Henry removed another chunk of concrete, passing it to Teilo, just behind him. 'Come on, let's keep removing this rubble.'

'Sergeant Harries!' Tom called from his patch. 'Over here.'

'Is it Polly?' Henry shouted.

'No,' Tom insisted. 'You stay where you are and keep going.'

Henry carried on but couldn't help glancing over to Tom every few seconds. What if it was Polly, or Mrs Moss, and he didn't want him to know? The men working with Tom gathered around a patch, looking down at it. When Harries reached them, he hunkered down and removed something. He stood, allowing a couple of the men there to remove more debris.

Finally, his stomach churning, Henry couldn't stand it any longer. He left his post and wound his way carefully around the rubble and the men working there. Arriving between Tom and the sergeant, he felt breathless, just managing to force out his, 'What is it?'

He looked down to see an arm. He looked around, but realised it wasn't attached to anything. He turned and was sick on the ground behind him.

-

'What's going on?' said Gwen, rising on her tiptoes to see what was happening. 'They seem to have found something.'

'Would you join the rest of the crowd, please, madam,' said Constable Davies, trying to guide the three women back up the road.

'We're not going nowhere while our husbands are there, in danger,' said Gwen.

'We can't be having all the wives down here.'

'Why not? Women are just as capable of helping.'

'Something's up,' said Elizabeth. 'A few of them are gathering near Tom.'

'I'm sure they'll come and tell you if there's anything to tell,' said Davies.

'Anwen, what's happening?' Enid called over from the crowd.

'It looks like they've found something – or someone,' Anwen called back up.

The crowd moved forward a little. Constable Davies ran back to the young recruit, seeing him struggle to persuade them back again.

'That got rid of him,' said Gwen, going a little closer to the wall.

Soon the rest of the crowd had surged forward, peacefully but determined. They gathered around, behind the women, the two constables having finally lost control.

-

'I told you to stay put, Henry,' said Tom.

'Who – who is it?'

'By the look of the coat sleeve, I'd say that was Iolo Prosser,' said Sergeant Harries. 'So I guess that answers the question of who's responsible.'

'But not the question of where he got the explosives,' said Tom.

Henry recovered himself. 'Sioni is a fireman in the pit, what has access to explosives.'

'So, we might find him here too?' said Tom.

'Or he may have simply passed them on to Prosser,' said Henry.

'That's jumping to a lot of conclusions there,' said Harries. 'Leave the police work to us, eh lads?'

'Sergeant, over here,' Alun Lloyd, leading another group, called over.

'I'm going back to digging this lot out,' said Henry, frustrated to the very limit that they'd made little progress finding Polly.

'Henry, I heard it again,' Twm Bach shrieked excitedly. 'A woman's voice, I swear.'

'I heard it too,' said Teilo.

Henry ran now, shouting, 'Idris, Gwilym, over here, quick.'

The men ran over. They all leaned forward, listening.

'There, did you hear it?' said Twm.

'Yes,' said Henry. 'It was someone calling for help. Definitely a woman. Come on, let's get this rubble cleared!'

They'd been removing the pieces slowly, carefully, for around five minutes when Tom appeared.

'We've found Reg Moss. What's left of him. Enough to be sure it's him.'

'Good riddance,' said Henry, unmoved, as he carried on with the job in hand. 'It'll save me the trouble of killing him myself, for what he's done.'

Not that he would have done. He'd had enough of the slaughter on the fields of France. To think he'd killed young

German soldiers in battles for doing what? Being pawns in the stupid games of selfish rulers. And all along there'd been bigger enemies here at home, in his own village.

'There's a gap here!' Idris cried.

Henry scrabbled along the ground to reach him. 'Hello?' he called through the hole. 'Is anyone there?'

'Help, help!' called a croaky voice, but only one. He sent up a small prayer that this wasn't significant.

'Hold on, we're coming to get you out,' he shouted back.

-

A whisper was travelling among the men working on the debris nearest to them. Gwen strained to hear what was being said.

'Did you catch that?' said Anwen.

'No, but something's happened,' said Gwen.

Elizabeth left them, heading towards Douglas Ramsay. When she returned, she said, 'They've found Iolo Prosser and Reg Moss, or rather, their bodies.'

Soon the news about Iolo and Reg had reached the crowd behind. It wasn't long before Connie came running forward again, shrieking, 'Sioni, where's my Sioni?'

Constable Davies managed to grab her arm before she made it onto the debris of the Arms' garden.

'People said he'd left,' Elizabeth pointed out.

'But your Polly hadn't,' said Anwen, accusingly. 'You don't seem to have any concern for her!'

'She's a lying harlot!' Connie screamed. 'And the Lord has punished her for what she's done. I knows me Bible. *Vengeance is mine, I will repay, says the Lord*, that's what it do say in Romans.'

'Then that should apply to your Sioni as well,' said Gwen, turning on her. 'For he were the one what did lend Henry money and then tried to extract a huge interest back, and then beat Henry up and stole his money for not paying.'

'Why haven't you reported this?' said Constable Davies as Elizabeth disappeared to talk to one of the men once more.

'Henry's only just told us. And what would you have done?'

'We can't do nothing if you don't tell us.'

Elizabeth ran back. 'They can hear someone shouting, under the ground. It must be Polly or Mrs Moss. Or hopefully, both.'

'But where's my Sioni?' sobbed Connie.

'Buried with those fiends Prosser and Moss, with any luck,' shouted another woman behind, before she surged forward, tying up her shawl. 'For he did lend my husband money too and did put a huge interest on, and now we're struggling each week to survive.'

'And my brother too,' called another woman. 'Told him it were twenty per cent interest at first, but now he's already paid back three times as much.'

Connie turned on the first woman, attempting to pummel her with her fists as she screamed, 'Liar, liar, liar!' The woman kicked out her foot and tripped Connie over.

'That's enough now,' said Davies, hurling Connie up from the ground.

'They're getting someone out!' A voice called over.

The crowd inched closer to the drama.

-

'Ow, ouch,' Nerys moaned as she was hauled up through the narrow channel that had been created.

'Sorry, Mrs Moss,' said Henry, holding one arm as Idris held the other. 'Not long now.'

He was desperate to ask about Polly, but knew they'd have to get Nerys up first, with her being in such a distressed state.

'One more pull,' said Idris.

'Just get me out,' she whined. 'Polly, Polly… ow!'

'What about Polly?' said Henry, barely able to get the words out with the tightening of his throat.

'Dunno. Unconscious maybe.'

Or worse. The thought did a loop around Henry's head. He needed to keep his nerve, imagine he was in the war, helping other men, put to one side that the woman he loved might be – no! 'Quicker we get you out, the quicker we'll find her,' said Henry, his voice hoarse. *The woman he loved*. It was the first time he'd used those actual words to himself, yet he knew it had been true for a while.

'There we go,' said Idris as Nerys's legs came through the gap and they sat her on the ground. He placed a blanket around her shoulders and called, 'Dr Roberts, over here!'

The doctor made his way over, giving her a quick examination. 'Can you walk?' Tom asked her.

'Yes, I can manage,' she said, limping.

'Mrs Owen, Mrs Hughes! Would you help Mrs Moss down to the hospital,' the doctor shouted over.

Elizabeth and Anwen came forward to take Nerys from Teilo and Douglas, then guided her around the rubble.

Henry was soon on the ground once more, with one of the miner's lamps that the manager, Aled Hopkins, had turned up with ten minutes before. He lowered it into the hole. 'Polly? Polly!'

The men around them became silent as they all listened for signs of life.

'If she's unconscious, she'll never hear us,' said Tom. 'We need to dig a bit more.'

'I'm not sure how much we'll be able to do before it all collapses,' said Idris. 'It's starting to crumble around the edge there.'

'We can't just leave her there,' said Henry, tempted to get into the hole and look for himself. He was slimmer than the landlady, so he could do it, then help her up, out of the gap they'd made. He knew they wouldn't let him, so he'd have to be quick if he was going to do it. But he'd need the lamp.

He stood, summoning the courage to carry out his plan. Breathing in, he was about to scramble into the hole when Twm Bach announced, 'A voice! I heard another voice! It must be Polly.'

Henry fell onto his stomach once more. 'Polly? Can you hear me?'

Nothing.

They continued to stay still and silent, their expressions frozen.

The top of Henry's nose filled up, like it always did when he was about to cry. Not here, please, he thought. He squeezed his eyes tight shut. *Let me be strong*, he prayed.

'Henry?' came a faint voice. 'Henry, is – is that you?'

'D'you hear that?' said Twm Bach, excited.

'Yes,' Henry called down the gap. 'Yes, we can hear you, Polly.'

The relief swamped him, making him feel weak. He just hoped with all his heart that she wasn't badly injured.

–

A terror gripped Polly as she came to into blackness. She'd been in the cellar. Was she trapped? She tried to stand but could only get so far. Instead, she walked along on all fours, trying to get somewhere, anywhere, that would offer her some chance of escape.

Perhaps if she called out? 'Help! Help me!'

She thought she heard a vague voice but couldn't be sure.

As she lowered her head in hopelessness, a definite voice came from a distance.

'Polly? Can you hear me?'

She scrambled forward once more. 'Henry? Henry, is – is that you?'

After another vague voice she heard, 'Yes... Yes, we can hear you, Polly.'

A dim light appeared up ahead and she went quicker.

'Can you see the light?' he called.

'Yes, I can see it.'

'Come towards it. We got Mrs Moss out, and we'll get you out.'

'I'm – I'm coming.'

Spotting the actual lamp now, she put her arms up. 'Can you see my hands?'

'Yes, yes,' he said. 'Can you lift them higher? We'll grab hold of you and get you up.'

Then she remembered the landlady had been with her. 'Where's Nerys?'

'She's already out. She's gone to the hospital for a check-up.'

With some relief, Polly lifted her arms, straining up as Henry and Idris reached down.

'Is there something you can step onto?' said Henry. 'So you're a bit higher up.'

'I'll see.' She explored with her foot. 'Yes, I think there's a small bump here, not much, but I'll try it.'

It was enough for them to be able to get a better hold of her hands as she stretched them up once more. Once they'd got her partway up, it was easier to get a grip on her and pull her free and onto the ground.

Dr Roberts was waiting, kneeling to check her over quickly. 'Could I have a couple of men to carry her to the hospital?'

Henry came forward, lifting her from the ground by himself, but he was struggling, and she could see he was bruised and scratched.

Idris came forward with a blanket. 'I'll give you a hand.'

They lay the blanket down and Polly sat on it. They took two corners each, lifted her up and started off towards the hospital.

'Was Nerys all right?' she asked.

'Yes, she walked to the hospital herself,' said Henry.

'Good. Is everyone else all right? What happened?' She dreaded the answer.

She noticed Idris and Henry look at each other.

'Yes, they're fine,' said Henry.

'There was an explosion,' said Idris.

Was this to do with Sioni, getting his own back on her?

'Polly!' came another voice as her father ran up beside her.

'Oh Dad, this was all my fault!' Polly closed her eyes and lay her head down as the tears fell.

–

Gwen watched as Henry carried Polly down Station Road, to the hospital on West Street. Constable Davies had just been sent up to Esther's house, to inform her that her lodgers wouldn't be returning. It was a wonder she wasn't here, among the crowd, making a fuss.

What a terrible night. The village never seemed to go for long without some major disaster occurring. They'd lost so many young men in the war. Then in the pit disaster five years back, they lost thirteen men. In the fire at the bookshop three years ago, the scout master, Cadoc Beadle, had perished. Two years back, her mother-in-law, who was then her employer, had run Delyth Bryce over and killed her, and then attempted suicide. Would fate ever leave them to peaceful lives?

She looked to where Tom was leaving the wrecked garden to walk over to her. Behind she could hear another fuss, turning to see Connie Gower once more quarrelling with the two women who'd accused Sioni of extorting money from their husbands. There was now a further woman there, and a man, both shouting at her.

'What's going on there?' said Tom, reaching her.

'It appears that Sioni Gower had a habit of being a moneylender, charging huge interest and putting it up all the time, not just with Henry.'

'And your father reckoned Iolo Prosser was connected, didn't he? And maybe Reg Moss.'

'Yes. It makes me more convinced that Sioni had something to do with this.' She pointed to the Arms. 'Poor Mrs Moss. After keeping the business going, and improving it by all accounts, she's got this to contend with.'

Sergeant Harries soon appeared from the wreckage, to where the dispute was now getting out of hand.

'That really is enough now, Mrs Gower, and all of you, otherwise you'll find yourself in Rhymney gaol. Ah, talking of which…'

A police motorvan could be heard driving down Gabriel Road, its bell ringing manically. As it approached, it became apparent that there was a police motorcar behind it.

'Sergeant, over here!' called Hywel from the destroyed garden wall.

'One moment, Mr Llewellyn… Everybody back,' Harries shouted to the crowd as the vehicles approached.

This time they complied, retreating to the pavements, leaving space at the top of Station Road.

'I'd better see what's happened,' said Tom, running across the road and leaving Gwen close to the argument, which was still raging.

Sergeant Harries guided the police vehicles in next to the fire engine and they came to a standstill. Soon, six policemen emerged from the two cars. Gwen recognised the plain-clothed man as Detective Inspector Strong, with his pencil moustache and bowler hat. He'd been responsible for arresting Gus Smith and her brother-in-law, three years before. The police gathered in for a rundown by the sergeant, but it wasn't long before Strong was looking over to where the dispute was taking place.

'Is Connie still going on?' said Anwen as she and Elizabeth re-joined Gwen.

'One moment, Sergeant,' said Inspector Strong, before marching over to Connie and her adversaries. 'Stop this immediately!' he demanded.

'Mind your own business, whoever you are,' Connie shrieked. She gave Strong a shove, which had him hurtling backwards a couple of steps.

'Uh oh,' said Elizabeth.

Connie went back to giving the nearest woman a piece of her mind. Strong, steadying himself, lunged at her, ramming her hand up her back.

'Get off me, you so-and-so!' she yelled. 'My Sioni'll give you what for when I tell him.'

'I'm Detective Inspector Strong of the Rhymney Constabulary, and I'll be more than happy to talk to him about it.'

'Oh, oh, good, then you can arrest this lot here, and them' – she pointed to Gwen's group – 'for saying my Sioni was responsible for assaulting my sister Polly, what's in the hospital now cos she were involved in the explosion. Ow, let go of me! And now they're all saying my Sioni's lent them money and overcharged on interest and—'

'You're not doing yourself any favours, Mrs Gower,' said Harries, bouncing up and down on his heels. 'For we'll be looking for him to have a word, as there's rumours that he were in with Reg and Iolo, who were the obvious perpetrators of this heinous act of violence.'

'And we'll start with questioning you,' said Strong. 'Constable, put this woman in the van.'

'What? No, you can't – ow – let me go,' Connie shouted.

But she was soon handcuffed and bundled into the back of the police motorvan. Meanwhile, the other arrivals from Rhymney were lined up as if on guard. Harries took Strong towards the bombed area.

Tom came towards them. 'Hywel has found some explosive that wasn't detonated. He's a fireman at the pit and he reckons that's where it came from.'

'Sioni was a fireman too,' Gwen called over. 'He could have got hold of it for Iolo and Reg.'

Strong turned, looking down his nose and flicking a hand in her direction. 'Leave this to us, madam.'

'I'm just saying,' Gwen stated huffily.

'My wife is right,' said Tom. 'And he was apparently in the public house earlier but left well before closing.'

'We'll give it some consideration.' He carried on to the site.

'Oh yes, it's worth consideration when it's a man what says it,' Gwen muttered through gritted teeth.

'Inspector Strong has never been known for his modern ways,' said Elizabeth. 'Here's PC Davies back.'

The constable went over to the police sergeant who'd come in from Rhymney. 'I've just been up Mrs Williams's home, where Prosser and Moss were lodging, and there doesn't seem to be anyone there. It's dark and locked up.'

'Could she have known what they were planning?'

Constable Davies shrugged.

'It seems odd that Esther would be out this time of night,' Anwen whispered to Elizabeth and Gwen.

'Maybe they told her to go away for a while,' said Elizabeth. 'Not wanting her to get wind of what they were up to. Is it likely she'd have kept quiet if she'd known, even being as she is?'

'Who knows with her?' said Gwen.

Inspector Strong and Sergeant Harries came back out shortly afterwards. Strong stood in the middle of the street, considering the throng. One of the constables he'd brought with him had fetched him a megaphone from the car.

'We will be cordoning off this area until the morning,' he announced, 'when we can have a better look in daylight, and we will be guarding it. Anyone who attempts to enter here, or the public house, will be arrested. You are all to go home now and stay there until the morning. When you men head to work tomorrow, you are to keep well clear of it.'

'And the women what work too,' muttered Gwen.

Strong walked away. The police standing around reiterated his command and people slowly made their way back to their houses. Some of the wives of the men helping remained, joining each other on the pavement outside the houses of Station Road.

'Come along now, ladies,' said Sergeant Harries, 'that includes you too.'

'But our husbands are here,' said Gwen.

'And they'll be sent home shortly too. Off you go now.'

Gwen didn't know what to say to persuade him, so instead said, 'All right.'

As she turned to walk up the road, the rest of the wives followed on.

Anwen shook her head. 'Poor Polly. I can't imagine she'll be able to work for a few days, after that shock. I wonder what long-term effect it'll have on her. Must be a bit like being buried in the mines in an explosion.'

'It must have been awful,' said Elizabeth. 'It makes me feel claustrophobic just thinking about it.'

Gwen resisted the temptation to say she deserved it, then realised, with much surprise, that she didn't even think that. She *did* feel sorry for Polly. Look at all the awful things that had happened to her, and she did nothing to help. In fact, quite the opposite. Even when Tom and Elizabeth had held no such resentment, and if anyone should, it was them. She felt awful about the whole situation now.

An idea came to her, about how to try to make it up to Polly. 'If she does miss some days of work, perhaps we could arrange for her to have a bit of pay anyway. So she's not short, like. Especially as the Arms will be closed. We have been doing better recently, and she has contributed some lovely work to that.'

She noticed Anwen and Elizabeth glance at each other, both with surprise in their faces.

'I think it's a wonderful idea,' said Anwen. 'I'm sure the others would agree. If you're sure?'

'Yes. It would be the right thing to do, after what she's been through.'

Anwen put her arm through Gwen's. 'All right. Let's do that then.'

'And when she returns, perhaps we could even offer her more hours?'

'We'll have a sit down with the others and have a talk about it.'

Gwen felt some of the stress she'd been feeling lately lift from her. Yes, it was definitely the right thing to do.

Chapter Thirty-Two

Polly had been determined to go to the chapel this morning, after she'd been discharged from the hospital following an overnight stay.

'Are you sure you're up to doing this?' said Delia as they set off from the house. 'You've not long got home.'

'Yes, I am up to it. Why shouldn't we go to our chapel, just because people choose to believe Connie's lies? I'm sick of letting people rule my life. After what happened to me last night, I really don't care what they think. And people will have seen Connie being arrested.'

Polly felt her old self re-emerging, or at least, part of it, the stubborn bit rather than the wanton bit, the piece of her that went after what she wanted, but without hurting someone else. *It's Henry you want*, she told herself. But she couldn't have him without hurting him and his family.

'But they're still looking for Sioni and think he could have some responsibility for the explosion, so they might blame us since he's in our family.'

'Let them!' she said. 'If they're stupid enough to think we'd have anything to do with it when I could have been seriously hurt, or worse, then they don't deserve our consideration.'

'That's the spirit, gal,' said her father, catching up, bouncing Herby in his arms as they walked along James Street.

'I dunno,' said Delia. 'People don't always think sensibly, do they?'

'Like I said—'

'I know, I know,' said Delia, not looking sure. 'Blimey, it looks even worse in daylight.' She pointed towards the McKenzie Arms as they approached it.

'Grandpa, what happen there?' Herby's eyes were wide as he pointed to the public house.

'Oh, um, there were an 'ole under the building, and it fell down.'

This explanation seemed to satisfy Herby, though he still stared at it, mesmerised.

Delia tutted. 'Gawd love us, I've no idea how Nerys Moss is going to fix that.'

'I thought that about the bookshop when they 'ad the fire,' said Jim. 'But that got fixed didn't it, wiv people's 'elp. I'm sure a lot of men'll be even keener to get the Arms fixed up again.'

Crossing over onto Jubilee Green, they noticed a small crowd gathering on the other side of the gardens.

'They're outside Esther's house by the looks of it,' said Delia. 'Wonder if she's in now.'

Coming up closer, they found Mabel standing with her mother, Rhonwen, who was holding little Lily's hand.

'What's goin' on 'ere then?' said Delia.

'Sergeant Harries fetched Christopher and Daniel, as they've got a key to Esther's house,' said Mabel. 'Harries and the constables are inside, looking for evidence. Christopher and Daniel are waiting outside.'

'So she's not back yet?' said Polly, spotting Esther's sons, looking glum by the front door.

'It would seem not. Or she's hiding away and not answering. Are you all right, Polly? Should you be out?'

'Yes, I'm fine, so don't worry.'

'I'm not bothered about hanging around here,' said Rhonwen, 'so I'll take Lily and Herby into the gardens if you like.'

'Thank you,' said Polly, 'that might be better.'

When they'd gone, Mabel said, 'Some people reckon Esther went away. There was some shouting heard a few days back, according to the neighbours.'

'They probably wanted her out of the way to plan their evil deed,' said Delia.

Polly shuddered, remembering the moment of the explosion, the blackness and confusion, and then nothing as she'd passed out from the shock. Waking up into the darkness had been frightening. She roused herself from the memory, unwilling to relive it. It gave her some appreciation of what Henry had been through.

'What's happened to your Connie now?' Mabel asked.

'She's still locked up, as far as we know,' said Polly.

'No, she was let out this morning,' came a voice behind. It was Miss Elizabeth. 'I saw her being brought back when I went for a walk, and the police searched her house while they were there. The next-door neighbour was looking out of the bedroom window and reckoned they found dynamite hidden in the coal store.'

'So it was him,' said Polly. 'And they've left Connie there on her own?'

'I think so,' said Elizabeth. 'Though I do wonder if she's safe.'

The same thing occurred to Polly. Even though her sister had been horrible to her, she was still her sister. It was too easy to be taken in by someone like Sioni.

'Oh she's safe, all right,' said Florrie, coming up behind. 'And shouting blue murder about how she's had a night of it because of that good-for-nothing husband of hers. I told her, I did, well it were you what made out what a saint he were, and then she says how he's no saint and how he'd been hiding dynamite in the coal bunker without her knowledge and how she could have been blown to smithereens.'

'She's changed her tune,' said a woman in the crowd.

'Oh aye,' Florrie continued. 'Then she has the cheek to say that first he molests her sister, and now this! I mean, it were her what spread it around that Polly had seduced *him*. Now it seems they made it up.'

'Just shows 'ow you shouldn't jump to conclusions,' said Delia.

'I never believed it in the first place,' said a woman who'd muttered insults at Polly in the grocer's one time.

'Nor me,' said another.

'Such hypocrites,' her father mumbled.

'Well, fank you for your support,' Delia called, somewhat mockingly. 'Now I fink we'd better go and see how our Connie is.'

'I'll stay put,' said Polly.

'I'm glad to see you out and about,' said Elizabeth. 'How is everyone else, do you know?'

'Steven's still in hospital with a broken arm and lots of cuts and bruises, but nothing what won't heal. Mrs Moss left the hospital just before me. She was angry more than anything else. And all the others are fine, just in shock.'

'What a relief!'

'Aye, I'm glad to hear that too,' said John Bowen, coming up behind with his wife.

'Such a shocking turn of events!' said Matilda.

'I didn't see you there last night,' Elizabeth said pointedly.

'Slept through it, would you believe?' said Bowen, shrugging and holding out a hand as if he couldn't believe it himself.

'So you don't know where Sioni Gower is? You left with him, and the police are looking for him.'

'I know, they've already questioned me.' He shook his head in disbelief. 'I went home as soon as I left the Arms last night and thought he had too. I'm frankly shocked that he'd be involved in the explosion.'

Matilda tutted. 'He was never a friend. He pestered John for a promotion.'

'Aye, he did that,' said John, shaking his head once more.

Polly glanced at Elizabeth, whose glance back told her she doubted the truth of what they'd said. There was no time to ponder it before Sergeant Harries stepped back outside, taking Daniel and Christopher to one side to speak to them. Christopher ran inside, despite the sergeant trying to stop him. Daniel followed on.

'What's going on?' called a voice from the crowd.

'Have you found anything, Sergeant?' said Elizabeth.

Harries bounced up and down on his heels a couple of times, his hands linked behind his back, before coming towards them and announcing, 'I need a volunteer to go down to the hospital, to ask them to fetch up a stretcher.'

'Is someone injured?' Polly asked.

Harries faltered, before announcing, 'We've found a woman's body. That's all I'm prepared to say.'

There were exclamations of shock and a murmur went around the crowd.

'I'll go.' Elizabeth turned and ran down the road.

'Thank you, Mrs Owen!' the sergeant called before heading back inside.

People started to turn away, heading to their various chapels and the parish church, shaking their heads and speaking in low tones.

'Let's fetch the kiddies and get to chapel,' said Polly. 'There's nothing we can do but pray for poor Daniel and Christopher.'

'So, you're coming today?' said Mabel.

'Oh yes, I'm coming.'

'Do you think it's Esther they've found?'

'I don't see who else it would be.' Polly sighed. 'What a dreadful turn of events.'

'Only got herself to blame, putting those two criminals up,' said an unsympathetic spectator as he tramped away.

'She was a one, sure enough,' said Mrs Brace the grocer. 'But she didn't deserve that. I'm so glad to see you up and about, Polly. I understand Nerys has been discharged too.'

'That's right,' said Polly. 'And thank you.'

Polly took Mabel's arm and they turned to go down the hill. There were several enquiries about how she felt, and her inevitable answer that she was fine.

'I wonder how quickly I'm going to get tired of that question from people and my reply that I'm fine,' Polly said to Mabel.

'It's good that people are asking though, isn't it?'

'Yes, yes it is.'

–

Polly was relieved when the service had come to an end, one in which Pastor Thomas had spoken passionately about shedding innocent blood, devising wicked plans, bearing false witness and sowing discord among brothers. He'd talked of the 'terrible incident' the night before, and how they'd found Esther Williams that morning.

So it had been Esther. The police must have come to tell the pastor just before the service had begun. Polly had felt like crying. Mrs Williams might have been a dreadful gossip, but to do away with her? The congregation had shuffled awkwardly during the pastor's sermon, when he'd mentioned how people were too ready to believe the wicked and spread lies that they hadn't questioned.

'Shall we collect Herby and go home?' her mother leaned towards her to ask now. 'Staying for tea might be pushing our luck.'

About to say yes, her determined spirit rose once more and she was surprised to hear herself saying, 'No. Why shouldn't we stop?'

'I agree,' said Jim. 'I'll go and fetch Herby. It was good of Mrs Thomas to say she'd keep a special eye on 'im during Sunday School.'

'I don't want to stop too long,' said Delia as Jim left. 'I think we should pop round to see Connie. Maybe ask her to come for Sunday dinner?'

Polly would rather not see Connie, but it also didn't seem right to leave her alone. 'All right. I'll get us some tea.'

'Not for me. I'm going to have a word with Rhonwen.'

Polly swallowed hard before setting off across the chapel and into the side room. Unlike before, when she'd got sideways glances and had caught mumbled insults, people smiled sympathetically as she went past. She was most surprised to see former members of the Pal's brigade not huddled together by themselves, but spread out among the rest of the congregation, chatting with people. Last night was a tragedy, but it had also been a turning point in bringing the community a little closer together once more.

Approaching the tea table, she saw Henry putting some sugar into a cup of tea. She gave herself a telling off as her stomach did a flip. He was not for her. She did want to thank him though, for helping her.

He looked up and smiled as he saw her approaching, just as she was waylaid by Anabel Thomas.

'Polly, your father's collected Herby, and I have to report that the other children were fine with him. Freddie was particularly happy to see him. I am so glad to see you and your family back. How are you? What an awful experience last night must have been for you.'

'Yes it was, but I'm glad to be doing something normal, and not wallowing in what could have happened.'

'That's a good way to look at it. I can't quite believe the news about Esther Williams.'

'There you are,' said Mabel, joining them. 'This lad's been looking for you.'

A skinny young man, about fourteen years old, stood slightly behind Mabel, screwing up his cap in his hands. Polly recognised him from the village but couldn't have named him.

'I've been asked to tell you that Sergeant Harries wants to talk with you outside. Out there.' He pointed towards the door in the tea room that took people onto the narrow road that linked Gabriel Street to Islwyn Street and was at the side of the chapel. 'He'd rather you were on your own.'

'Did he say what it was about?' Polly asked, her heart sinking at the thought of more trouble.

He shook his head. 'No.'

'Thank you.'

The lad nodded and hurried away.

'I hope it's not bad news,' said Anabel. 'I'll leave you to it.'

'Shall I come with you?' said Mabel.

'No, it seems to be private. I'll come back and tell you what it's about.'

She made her way through the crowd, passing Henry on the way. He was stirring a cup of tea and chatting to Idris and Gwilym. He didn't look like he was going anywhere soon, so she'd talk to him when she got back.

-

Out on the short street, she looked up and down, but couldn't see anyone. She walked to the bottom of the street, but only saw a few people leaving the chapel. Walking back up, she passed the door, and then the gate that led onto a tiny yard at the back of the building. The yard had a high wall. Perhaps the sergeant was on Islwyn Street.

Two steps past the gate, she felt an arm around her waist, before she was dragged through it and around the back of the chapel. She tried to scream, but a hand rammed itself onto her mouth, crushing it shut with fingernails that bit into the skin around her lips. There was a stench of stale alcohol, tobacco and sweat.

There were only two small, high windows on this side, and they lit a store cupboard at this end of the side room. No one would see her here.

'I'm going to crush the air out of you,' said the voice she knew was Sioni's. 'Yes, I'll suffocate the life out of you, the way I did Esther. Threatened to go to the police, she did, when she overheard our little plan. You can ask her when you see her, for you'll be joining her soon, in hell.'

His fingers left her face and slid around her neck so quickly, she had no time to scream. Soon her head was throbbing as she found herself unable to breathe.

–

Henry had been waiting to have a word with Polly, but twice he'd missed the opportunity. She'd gone out of the side door now, on her own.

Idris picked up a digestive biscuit. 'Polly seems to have recovered well.'

'Yes,' said Henry. 'I've been hoping to speak to her, to make sure, but she's gone again. I wonder why she used that door.'

'One of the pit lads what works with the horses was just speaking to her,' said Gwilym. 'I hope nothing else has happened.'

'Hold on, I'll have a word with Mabel.'

Henry left his tea on the table and went towards Polly's sister-in-law, where she was now talking to Jenny Richards. Idris and Gwilym followed him.

'Mabel, is Polly all right? I've been wanting to ask her, but she's just left.'

'One of the lads did tell her that Sergeant Harries wanted a word with her on the side street, alone. Maybe they've found Sioni Gower.'

Hywel, passing by with his stepson, stopped. 'Sergeant Harries is in the chapel, by the altar, talking to Pastor Thomas, if you want to speak to him.'

'That's odd,' said Idris.

Henry's brow creased. 'Something's not right.'

He twisted around and made for the side door, Idris and Gwilym following once more. Outside, they looked up and down the street, but she was nowhere to be seen. Neither was anybody else.

'Perhaps she's gone to find Har—' Idris started.

'Shhh,' said Gwilym. 'Do you hear that?'

It was like a muffled whine. 'Where's it coming from?' Henry whispered.

'Up here, I think,' said Gwilym.

They hurried quietly up the side street, Henry leading, until they came to the gate that led to a cramped, enclosed yard. The whine became louder for a split second, in which time Henry flew through the gate. Round the back of the chapel they found Sioni sitting on Polly, his hands around her neck, her legs flailing as she struggled to get air.

'Get away from her,' Henry roared as he threw his weight against him to knock him off her.

Sioni struggled to get up as Henry lifted Polly out of the way. Idris knocked Sioni to the ground, and he and Gwilym pinned him there as he battled with his fists and let out an almighty roar of anger.

'What on earth is going on out here?' said Mabel, running around. 'Oh my goodness!'

'Get Sergeant Harries and send a couple of the other men out here too.'

Mabel obeyed the order from Henry. He rubbed Polly's back as she coughed and half choked in an effort to catch her breath. Her neck was red and scratched, as was her mouth.

'That's it, Polly, deep breaths,' said Henry.

'You stupid cow!' Sioni hollered, all the while trying to escape Idris's and Gwilym's grip. 'Those bloody idiots, Reg and Iolo, couldn't even set the explosives like I showed them. And they was too late, as you'd all left. It was meant for Nerys, for Reg did want to repay her, but it were a bonus like, having you and Henry there. And you sods what think you can tackle me.' He looked up at Idris and Gwilym. 'I'll do a proper job myself next time, you see if I don't.'

'You can shut that up now,' said Idris. 'Prison is where you'll be going for a very long time, for several attempted murders at the public house and here. And attempted rape, of course.'

Alun Lloyd and Twm Bach tore around the corner in time to hear Polly say, 'And he strangled Esther Williams. He told me.'

'What!' said Twm Bach. 'That were you, were it, you beast.' He administered an almighty kick to Sioni's groin, causing him to grimace and double up.

'That's enough now, Twm Bach,' said Idris. 'You two get hold of a leg each.'

As they lifted a struggling Sioni, Sergeant Harries appeared, almost losing his helmet as he whirled around the corner. A string of people followed.

'That's, that's the boy what told me to come out here,' Polly struggled to say as she pointed at a lad with his mouth open in shock.

He stepped back, but Sergeant Harries grabbed hold of him.

'I didn't know he were gonna do that,' said the lad, shaking.

'You must have known it were Sioni Gower who we were looking for,' Harries roared.

'No, I didn't. I've only lived here a few months. I dunno many people. He just said he'd beat me up if I didn't run an errand.'

'You little runt,' Sioni shouted, attempting to kick out.

Harries pushed the lad away. 'I'll talk to you later. Somebody fetch Mrs Smith's parents. And Mabel,' said the sergeant, pointing at her, 'go and find the pastor for me. I need him to phone Rhymney station… And you' – he pointed at the young lad – 'do something useful and go and get Dr Roberts… You lot, carry Mr Gower into the side room.'

'I'll get you for this, Henry Austin,' Sioni screamed as he was carried away.

'I don't think so,' Henry called. 'And I think we'll call my debt cleared now, shall we?'

Chapter Thirty-Three

'You didn't need to come in, lovey,' said Nerys, spotting Polly in the dusty hallway of the McKenzie Arms.

The police had finally declared it safe to return to the public house the day before, five days after the incident, and already Nerys had workmen in, fixing the damage, determined to be closed for as little time as possible.

'I needed to do something, not sit at home, brooding.'

'Oh dear, your poor neck's still looking a bit red. The cut round your lips seems to have healed though.'

'My neck's a bit sore, but not too bad.'

'Well, if you're determined to do something, the glasses in what's left of the bar, those that weren't smashed in the explosion, need washing. There's a bucket to transport them to the scullery. And I've acquired some boxes to store them away in until everything's fixed. And the spirit bottles will need a wipe over and storing too. Then we'll have a go at cleaning up the dust and mess in the rooms what weren't damaged. We're lucky no one's stolen anything, but then, they've had a series of young constables on watch, day and night.'

Polly started on the task, thinking about her other job. Anwen had told her on the Sunday, when they'd brought her back into the chapel to be checked over by Dr Roberts, to take the week off to recover, and that they'd find her a bit of money to tide her over. Polly was grateful, but also afraid that Anwen was letting her down gently before sacking her.

Henry had hung around on the Sunday long enough to make sure she was all right, then had left the chapel. It wasn't like there was anything else he could do.

Nerys came in when Polly was halfway through washing the last bucket of glasses, picking up a tea towel to dry them.

'I hear they buried Esther yesterday, up at Rhymney,' said Nerys.

'Yes. Mrs Brace went. She said there were quite a few from the village.'

'They're burying the old sod next week,' Nerys said. 'Up at Bedwellty cemetery.'

'Reg?'

'Yes. What's left of him. I'm only going because my children are. I don't want no one from here to go, for he don't deserve it. At least they've got Sioni locked up. I knew they was up to something, those scoundrels. And that John Bowen was here with Sioni that night, yet they seem to think he had nothing to do with it.'

'Maybe Sioni was using him as an alibi.'

'Wouldn't have done him much good, since Matilda Bowen swears he were home by nine o'clock. That would have been, what, forty minutes before the explosion?'

'He might still have been involved in helping Sioni get hold of the explosive,' said Polly.

'Aye, but it don't sound like the police are considering that. So let's hope he weren't.'

Polly stopped a moment, her hands still submerged in the water. She was going to say what had been on her mind for a few days. 'I'm so sorry, Nerys. I can't help thinking that Sioni helped Reg and Iolo get the explosive so he could get his own back on me.'

'No, lovey, don't blame yourself. Reg was determined to get his own back on me for taking over the Arms and making sure his name was taken off the lease. He'd have got hold of the explosives somehow, whether Sioni had helped him or not. I guess you being in the bar was just a bonus for Sioni.'

'That was what Sioni said, but I still can't help feeling responsible.'

'Pah, men! Who needs 'em, eh? At least now I won't have to spend a packet of money on a divorce and go through all the hassle in the courts. Sorry if that sounds cold-hearted, but how else am I supposed to feel about a man who tried to kill me and so many others?'

'No, I understand.'

Nerys's problem with her erstwhile husband might be at an end, but she still had a husband in gaol. At least the problem of Sioni had been solved – for her at least, if not for Connie – but always there were other problems.

-

Gwen was by herself a few days later, stirring the cawl on the range, everything that had happened going around in her head. The mess with Henry and Polly was uppermost, and their involvement with the explosion at the public house. If Henry hadn't got involved with Polly, he'd never have been targeted by Sioni, who'd evidently waited for several people, including Henry, to be in the Arms before he'd given Reg and Iolo the explosives to plant.

But even as she thought this, she knew it wasn't entirely true. Henry had borrowed a lot of money from Sioni and had been expected to pay back a whole lot more, and the reason for that hadn't been Polly, but that grasping Amelia Bowen, who'd been a spoilt madam. If Polly hadn't borne Herbert Meredith's child, how would Gwen have felt about her as a partner for Henry? Even if they could ignore that Herby was Tom and Elizabeth's half-brother, there would always be the problem that Polly was married. Unless she divorced. She hadn't shown any signs of doing that so far.

Gwen was rubbing her forehead when she heard the front door close. She put the wooden spoon on the side of the range.

It was the right time for Tom to return from the newspaper office in Bargoed.

'Hello!' he called, half a minute before appearing in the kitchen with a briefcase. 'Is no one else home?'

'Elizabeth and Gwilym are up at the market garden.'

'He seems to help her out a lot now.'

'Yes, but then he did a lot of work on the allotments in the war, too.'

'So he did.' He came over and put his good arm around her, kissing her on the head. 'How has your day been?'

'Busy. We had another meeting, making decisions about the business.'

'Was Polly back at work this week?'

'Yes. She were working at Anwen's when we had the meeting.' She'd been sent to the front room as usual, but for a very different reason this time.

'Good. You're getting a lot more work now. I should think you could take Polly on for longer hours. She wouldn't have to work so much at the McKenzie Arms then.'

'It was one of the things I suggested today.'

'Really?' Tom looked doubtful.

The kettle was boiling. Gwen got a tea towel to pick it up and take it to the table, to pour over the tea leaves in the teapot there.

'Is Henry walking out with Polly again?' she asked.

'Not that I'm aware, but would it matter if he was?' He pulled a dining chair out and sat down. 'Look, I've been thinking about this since Henry came to see me, after the incident with my mother in the gardens.'

'Do we have to go over this again?'

'Yes, for the sake of Henry's happiness, I think we do. Why don't you have a sit down so we can talk about it, before Lizzie and Gwilym get back?'

'Let me finish making the tea first.' She could do with a cup, suspecting what was coming. She completed the task and sat down, leaning her arms on the table, the tea things set between them.

'For a start,' he said, 'I had lunch with my father today. I wanted to talk to him about paying some money towards Herby and Freddie.'

'Oh. When did you decide that?'

'This morning, on the train to work. He said that now Lizzie and I are off his hands, and he's earning a little more as manager of the Bargoed colliery, that he can afford a little something each month, until such time they might have a more permanent arrangement.'

'Meaning what?' asked Gwen.

'One or both might remarry at some point.'

'Right. What has this got to do with Henry's happiness?'

He crossed one leg over the other and linked his hands on his knee. 'Who knows, sometime in the future it might be possible for them to take up their relationship again. Gus Smith might pass on, leaving Polly free. It's happened for Nerys Moss.'

'Gus is only in gaol though, so it's hardly likely.'

'Fate's a funny thing.' He leant forward, taking her hand in his. 'The thing is, Gwen, we shouldn't deny Henry and Polly any happiness they might be able to have. My mother accepted Lizzie and Gwilym's relationship, after seeing the error of her ways. And, having accepted theirs, she had to accept ours. In fact, when I told her about it, she said you reminded her of herself as a young woman, full of life and confidence, and that she hoped you'd never lose it.'

'Did she? You never told me that before.' Gwen felt quite touched that her mother-in-law had said that about her.

'I know it's a different situation, but it's still to do with the happiness of two decent people. And I do think Polly is a decent person now, however flighty she might have been when she was younger.'

Yes, she was. Gwen knew that, though had always harked back to the old Polly, the silly piece who'd dressed in gaudy clothes and giggled, the self-centred hoyden who'd been a little mean to the younger children at school. Since having Herby and being abused by Gus, there were no signs of that Polly anymore. In fact, she seemed keen to help people and be useful. And really, not only should they act on the idea of giving her more hours, but she should also suggest that Polly sit in on the meetings. She'd no doubt have plenty of ideas from her time working for Mrs Bowen.

She stood up. 'I'm just going to pop round to my parents. I want a word with Henry.'

'You're not going to harass him about this, are you?'

'No, not at all. I'll be back for supper.'

She picked her jacket off the pegs in the hall and left via the front door. She had no idea what exactly she was going to say, but she'd think about it as she walked down there.

-

'It feels like autumn already,' said Polly's mother, tying her shawl in a knot at the front.

'Well, it is September tomorrow, love,' said Jim, flinging his cap on his head. He helped Herby off the dining chair and held his hand. 'You'll persuade your aunty Connie to come to supper, won't you, lad?'

'I tell her we have chicken, and she come cos she like chicken.'

'That's the spirit, lad.'

Polly's parents had been having problems getting Connie out of the house and were hoping her fondness for Herby would tempt her round for supper this evening. Polly had misgivings, using Herby like that, after Connie reporting her to the NSPCC, but she could understand her parents' concern.

'I'll get supper started while you're gone,' said Polly, looking forward to having the house to herself for a short time.

'Hopefully we won't be too long,' said Delia.

Polly bent to kiss Herby, who gave her a big wet kiss on her cheek in return. She rubbed at it and grinned as they went out the back way.

She hummed as she fried the chicken, browning it slowly before putting it on top of the vegetables she was about to put in the oven. She didn't get far before there was a hefty knock at the front door.

'Hhhur,' she sighed. 'It was too good to last.'

Having no idea who it might be, she pulled her pinny off and dropped it on the table. As she opened the front door, she was none the wiser about her visitor. It was a pinched-faced woman in a long, dark brown, pre-war coat and a hat that wouldn't have looked out of place at a funeral in 1910. Yet she couldn't have been more than ten years older than Polly.

'Can I help you?' she asked, hoping the woman had got the wrong house.

The visitor looked her up and down, her lips sticking out in disapproval. 'Are you Polly Smiff?' It was a London accent, similar to her parents'. She had maybe moved to Wales from the East End, like them.

'Y-yes, I am.' She froze, incapable of saying anything further. This woman had to be from the National Society for Prevention of Cruelty to Children, and she was judging her already.

'A bit more ordinary than I expected, though you're pretty enough, I suppose, in a dull kind of way.'

'I beg your pardon?' Who was she to pass comment on the way she looked? 'What's that got to do with anything?'

'I found out about you from Frances and Iris.'

Polly pulled her head back, looking at the woman askance. 'What have my mother-in-law and sister-in-law got to do with it?'

'They knows all about you, and now I do too.'

'Yes, they would know about me, since they used to live with me and Gus. And Vic, Iris's husband.'

'Yeah, and like I said, I knows about ya now too.'

'Who are you, then?'

'I'm Nellie Smiff.'

'Are you a relation of Gus's?'

The woman threw her head back and let out a piercing laugh. It took her a while to recover, after which she announced, 'You could say that.'

–

'Hello, Henry,' said Gwen, poking her head around the kitchen door. 'Mam said you was in here.'

Henry put a torn piece of paper as a bookmark in his novel and laid it on his lap. He was sitting in one of the armchairs by the range, so she sat in the opposite one.

'Yes, here I am.'

'How are your bruises?'

'They've almost gone now.'

'The scrapes on your face have healed nicely,' she said.

'Is this a medical visit?' he asked.

'No. I just wanted to check first.'

'First before what? That suggests you're here for another specific reason.' He looked weary, as if he didn't like the idea of what was coming.

'It's about Polly.'

'Hwww!' He closed his eyes and leant his head back. 'I've heard it all from you, Gwen, and I don't want to hear no more.'

'Well that's where you're wrong, Henry, because you haven't heard this, not from me.'

'So what is it this time, that it's not enough that she has a husband in prison and she now has a brother-in-law in one too?'

'No, that's—'

'Or how Sioni wouldn't have got the explosives if it hadn't been for wanting to get his own back on Polly?'

'I'm sure he'd still have—'

'Or another rant about how she's an embarrassment because of Herby being Tom's—'

'No! Will you give me a chance to speak, Henry!'

The scullery door opened, and Ruth looked around it. 'Is everything all right here?'

'Yes, fine, Mam,' Gwen said, rather too sharply. 'Sorry. I'm trying to get a word in edgeways, but Henry keeps interrupting.'

'Let her speak, *bach*,' said Ruth. 'Your da and I are popping over to the allotment to do a bit of work for half an hour or so. Mamgu's coming with us.'

'See you later,' said Henry.

'I don't want to hear you've had an argument when I get back.' Ruth closed the door.

Gwen chuckled.

'What's funny?' said Henry.

'You wouldn't think we were all grown up now,' said Gwen. 'She used to say that when we were kiddies, arguing over the paints, or the hoop.'

'They forget sometimes that we're adults. So, what is it you have to say?'

'First of all, Tom's persuaded his father to give Polly some money towards Herby, at least until she's in a better position. And to Jenny too.'

He sat forward, smiling. 'That'll help them both. It was good of Tom to speak up.'

'Of course, if either remarry, they'll be in a better position.'

'You forget, Polly is already married. That's one of the reasons we're not together.'

'Surely she'd get a divorce easily, with Gus's unreasonable behaviour.'

'It still costs to get a lawyer,' said Henry.

'Then maybe having a bit of extra money will help her sort that out.'

Henry looked at her and frowned. 'You've changed your tune.'

'All that's happened the last few days, and what Tom said, it's made me see we should all grab our chances of happiness, like I did with Tom, and Elizabeth did with Gwilym. And Violet with Hywel and Anwen with Idris, come to that. If we'd all given up because of the obstacles, we'd all be sitting alone, miserable, wondering what could have been.'

Henry leant forward. 'What are you saying, here?'

'I'm saying, go and tell her how you feel!'

'But she was the one what broke it up. I had a letter.'

'I know,' said Gwen, sorry for her part in that. 'But only because I made a fuss when my mother-in-law saw her. And you gave up too easily. She probably thought you didn't care enough to pursue it.'

'You think she thinks I don't care enough?'

'She might do. And she's only going to know otherwise if you tell her.' Gwen stood up, then pulled her brother up. 'Come on now, get your jacket and cap, and go and see her.'

'What if she's busy?'

'So, it's not important enough to chance that? Maybe you don't really care enough,' said Gwen, remembering from their youth that to get Henry to do something, you often had to tell him he couldn't.

'Of course I do! Right, I'll go then.' He stood up and headed to the hall.

'Good. No time like the present.'

–

'So, who exactly are you?' said Polly, trying not to get annoyed. This woman would try the patience of a saint.

'*I'm* Mrs Smiff.'

'Yes, you've told me that. Oh, you're a relation to Gus by marriage then?'

The woman laughed again.

'For heaven's sake, what's this all about?'

Polly had been concentrating so hard on this woman and this daft conversation, that she didn't notice Henry until he called, 'Are you all right there, Polly?'

She looked up to find that Gwen was also with him, just behind, as if marching him along. What on earth was this about now?

'I will be when this person here actually tells me what they're doing on my doorstep,' she said, 'instead of saying odd things and laughing.'

'I'm on your doorstep to tell you to leave Gus alone.'

'Leave him alone?' said Polly. 'I couldn't care less about him. He were an awful husband what was rude and abusive to me.'

'Ooh, you're a saucy piece!' said Nellie Smith. 'I've a good mind to give you a slap.'

'You'll have to deal with me if you try that,' said Henry.

'And me,' said Gwen. 'Who the blazes are you?'

Polly was pleasantly surprised to find Gwen sticking up for her but had no time to find out why before Nellie spoke again.

'I'm Nellie Smiff, Gus's wife! The real one, what he married eighteen years back. So you're nuffink but 'is fancy piece. And not so bleedin' fancy neither, by the looks of you.'

'Oh heavens, so you were already married to Gus, when he wed me?' said Polly, her hands flat against her cheeks in disbelief.

'Yeah. We was apart cos I'd left 'im for a while. Then I decided we should get back together, and I found his mum, Frances. It's 'er what told me he'd married you and moved to Wales, and that you was still 'ere, while he'd ended up in gaol. Daft as a brush she is, Frances, and seemed to fink it was all right to remarry if your wife left you. I ask yer! Went to see Gus, I did, in the gaol in Usk, and he were sorry and wants me back when he finally gets out. The kids'll be that pleased to see 'im, I'm sure, though they're nigh on adults now.'

'He has children?' said Gwen, her eyes wide.

'Bit of a shock for you, I'm sure,' said Nellie, grinning at Polly. 'See, he only wanted to marry you to get a job 'ere in the mines, and escape conscription, that's what he told me.' She looked smug revealing this information, folding her arms as if to imply that Polly would have to put up with it.

'Oh, that is marvellous news!' said Polly, clapping her hands together. 'I haven't had such good news in a long time.'

'What? You bein' funny or summat?' Nellie didn't look so sure of herself.

'No, not at all. I only married him to have a father for my son.'

'Just using 'im then. You're a bad lot.'

'You're one to talk,' said Henry. 'He used Polly to escape conscription. And an awful bully he were.'

Nellie looked around crossly. 'Look, I dunno who you two are, but I wish you'd bugger off. This has got nuffink to do wiv you.'

'Henry's right,' said Polly. 'He were despicable, always picking fights, always insulting me and pushing me around. And he turned out to be a thief and an arsonist. So you see, Mrs Nellie Smith, you're welcome to him, because now he has no hold over me and I can have nothing more to do with him.'

'Right, if that's your attitude, I'll be going back on the train to see Gus now. Then I'm going back to London, where Gus will come when he's freed in a coupla years. Not back 'ere.' She looked round the street and at the colliery ahead with a sneer. 'Don't say I didn't warn you. You keep away from Gus: he's mine!'

With that, she clomped away, clearly in a bad mood. Had Gus's wife hoped to upset her with this news, and get some satisfaction from that? Frances and Gus must have given her completely the wrong idea.

'I'll leave you to it,' said Gwen. 'And I'll make sure *Mrs Nellie Smith* goes to the train station. Oh, before I go, Polly, would you be able to do a few more hours in our sewing business? Maybe do Monday and Tuesday, nine to two o'clock as well. And perhaps we'll be able to offer even longer hours eventually.'

'Oh. Oh. I – yes, I'd like that. But I'd have to talk to Nerys first and give notice of my daytime hours. Thank you.'

'Wonderful! I'll leave you to it.'

When Gwen was out of earshot, Henry said, 'Two bits of good news for you! Especially that from Nellie Smith.'

'Why are you here, Henry? And why was Gwen so friendly?'

'She's had a change of heart. Reckons we should find happiness where we can.'

'Henry, thank goodness!' someone called from up the street.

Polly looked around and her insides shrivelled. Of all the times for her to show up. What on earth did she want?

Running none too daintily down the pavement was Amelia Bowen, clutching her hat, her less than immaculate hair coming down on one side. For all that, she was still attractive with her shiny red hair and pretty face with its green eyes. She ignored Polly, standing between her and Henry. His expression was a mixture of shock and… what? Pleasure? Concern?

'Amelia, what are you doing here?'

'Looking for you. I realised what a mistake I made. Maurice, he's, he's…' She started sobbing. After taking a tissue from her handbag and dabbing her eyes, she said, 'He wasn't the man I thought he was. Oh Henry, can you forgive me? I see now that you are ten times the man he is. You are so, so considerate.'

'It would be hard not to be more considerate than Maurice,' said Henry.

So that was that. Whatever possible hope she'd had regarding Henry – and Polly realised that, in her heart, she'd been hoping for another chance with him – she had only ever been second best to Amelia.

'Oh yes, yes!' Amelia flung her arms around him.

Polly went to go back into the house, until she saw Henry gently push Amelia away.

'It would also be hard not to be more considerate than you,' said Henry. 'You used me, you said as much yourself. You ran me down and you humiliated me. Now you want me back? What's happened? Has Maurice left you?'

Her expression, eyes downcast and mouth pouting a little, said it all.

'Go away, Amelia. I have no interest in any relationship with you,' he said. 'I don't even want to see you again, ever.'

Amelia, who'd gone a little pale, looked from Henry to Polly, as if she wasn't quite sure what had happened.

'I – I thought—'

'You thought I'd take you back, just like that? Then you thought wrong.'

She opened her mouth to speak, but must have thought better of it, instead turning on her heel and running off back down the street.

As the pair of them watched her, neither said a thing. It wasn't until she'd disappeared around the corner, Henry said, 'As I was saying, Gwen has had a change of heart. Reckons we should find happiness where we can.'

'I think you just had a chance to.'

'Huh! Not with Amelia. Not in a thousand years. What a lucky escape that was. But, if you're still interested, like.' He pressed his hands together, looking awkward.

'Oh. I think you should come inside, Henry.'

Yet again, they were interrupted as the middle-aged woman next door came out of her house and called, 'Yoo hoo, Polly! I've a letter for you.' She came towards them.

'A letter?'

'The postman must have put it through my door by mistake. I've not long got in, so I've only just seen it. Sorry about that.'

'That's all right. Thank you.'

The neighbour ran back inside, leaving Polly to stare at the envelope.

'Aren't you going to open it?' said Henry.

'It looks rather official. I'm afraid it might be from the NSPCC. Connie reported me as a bad mother.'

'I know, but she's hardly got a leg to stand on now.'

Polly looked at the letter for a few seconds, then turned it over and slid her finger along the seal. She quickly pulled the paper out and scanned it. As she did so, the fear dissolved, and she smiled.

'Sergeant Harries has told the NSPCC that the report made about me was false, so they're no longer investigating,' she said with a growing sense of calm.

'Good old Harries!' said Henry. 'He does get it right sometimes.'

She folded the letter back up and put it into the envelope, saying, 'I can't believe it. They say good news comes in threes.' Still holding the envelope, she cried, 'Oh Henry!' and threw her arms around his neck to hug him.

'So you've had a change of heart about what you said in your letter to me?'

'Yes, oh yes! With Sioni gone, and people realising I was telling the truth, and the NSPCC dropping the case, and not being married to Gus.' She took a deep breath. 'Oh my goodness!' She danced around, still holding onto Henry. 'I'm not married to Gus, I'm not married to Gus!' she sang.

Henry brought them to a standstill, stepping back but holding onto her arms and looking into her eyes. 'I came round to ask you to reconsider our relationship. Are you telling me, you agree?'

'Oh yes, Henry, yes, yes, yes! I know it'll still be awkward with Herby being Tom's and Elizabeth's brother, but, why shouldn't we be happy too?'

'I agree wholeheartedly.'

She lunged towards him, as he did the same, and they kissed, there and then, on her doorstep. She didn't care who went past and saw them; it would give her an opportunity to tell them her news.

When they parted once more, they saw Anwen and Idris going past, grinning.

'About time,' Anwen called.

Henry blushed, but Polly announced, 'Gus and me, we're not married. He were already married, see, before he met me.'

'Why, that is good news,' said Anwen.

'Make sure you tell everyone,' said Polly. 'I want the world to know: I'm not Polly Smith, I'm Polly Coombes!'

'Right you are.'

When they'd passed by, Polly said, 'You'd better come inside now, before the whole world sees us kissing.'

'But your family—'

'Have gone to Connie's. And I've been wanting to thank you for saving me after the explosion.'

'Saving you? Oh Polly, you saved me from years of depression and panic attacks. You made me see that life could be joyous again.'

She waved Henry in, then looked up and down the street, wondering if anyone else had seen them or overheard her news. Let them, she thought; she wasn't married to Gus anymore! She was free, free as a bird to marry somebody she really cared for and who cared for her.

Epilogue

11th November 1920

Polly watched as Henry took his place opposite Pastor Thomas and the various ministers from the church and chapels who were standing either side of the new war memorial on Gabriel Street. Henry was in the front line of three that consisted of Dorcalon's surviving soldiers from the Great War. In the row with him stood Tom Meredith, Daniel Williams, Teilo Brice, Alun Lloyd and Douglas Ramsay. The two lines behind consisted of twelve of the thirteen remaining survivors, and Elizabeth Owen, due to her stint as a VAD nurse in France.

Polly's brother, Maurice, who should have been there was absent, living in Aberfan with yet another woman, by all accounts.

Most of the inhabitants of Dorcalon gathered in behind the ex-soldiers. Polly was at the front of this throng, with her mother and father, who was carrying Herby. Her sister, Connie, now living with their parents too, had refused to come out.

Anwen and Idris were standing on the other side of them, along with their families. Next to them stood Hywel and Violet, with their three children.

Gwen stood on the other side of Polly with her parents, and further along was Gwilym with his family.

On the memorial, paid for by the collection at the August bank holiday events, were the names of the fifteen men lost in the war, including Violet's first husband, Charlie Jones.

The murmur of chatter faded as Pastor Thomas began to speak.

'We are gathered here together to remember the fallen heroes of a war to hopefully end all wars. Whatever our faiths or beliefs, today we are united in prayer, standing together in an effort to build a new world of hope and peace for us and the generations to come.'

The Silver Band struck up with the introduction to 'Abide with Me', and then the crowd began the first verse.

As she started to well up, Polly removed a handkerchief from her coat pocket and wiped her eyes. Gwen, sniffing back tears, placed her arm through Polly's. Henry's blond hair was visible up ahead. Her Henry, her love, a decent man in her life at last. They'd been through dark times, both of them, like so many others, but now those battles were over. And so she could start a new phase in her life, one of hope, happiness and love.

When the hymn came to an end, Pastor Thomas came forward once more to speak.

'At the going down of the sun and in the morning,
We will remember them.'

A letter from Francesca

So we've arrived at the end of the war in Dorcalon, but for many the conflict went on in some way or other. It must have been hard for a lot of the men to adjust to being home, after so many years abroad, whether they were in the trenches in France like my characters, or further afield. Many had injuries that would forever affect their lives.

The women, likewise, underwent huge changes in these years. Though many would have waited eagerly for their menfolk to arrive home, still there would have been adjustments after so long apart. Many of the women would have got used to running their own lives and, for some, earning their own money for the first time. Then there were those who had lost their husbands, sweethearts, sons and brothers.

Over a hundred years on, though not many who lived through that time remain alive, there are still a few around the world. As of 6th January 2022, the oldest person in the UK is Mary Walker, born in 1909. She would have been five when the war started. Furthermore, many of us still have a living-memory connection to those who survived those times. Though dead thirty-five years now, my great grandmother, who passed away when I was nearly thirty, was a young mother in the war. 'The Great War' seems such a long time ago in many ways, but in others it's very close to us all.

I'd like to send a big thank you to all the readers who've sent me lovely messages of support for the Wartime in the Valleys series. If you'd like to contact me to discuss the novels, or discover more about them, I'd love to chat to you on social media here:

Facebook: www.facebook.com/FrancescaCapaldiAuthor/
Twitter: @FCapaldiBurgess
Instagram: francesca.capaldi.burgess
Blog: www.writemindswriteplace.wordpress.com/

Best wishes,
Francesca xx

Acknowledgments

A big thank you, once more, to Keshini Naidoo at Hera Books for giving me the opportunity to tell another story in the *Wartime in the Valleys* series.

My grateful thanks go, as usual, to the friends who've been such a support during this time. Also, a shout-out to the wonderful organisations who've kept us writers in contact in various ways during times of lockdown, including the Romantic Novelists' Association, The Society of Women Writers and Journalists, and Swanwick Writers' Summer School.

Lastly, *diolch yn fawr* to the National Library of Wales for its fantastic online newspaper collection, which has been key in granting me a real insight into Welsh life during World War 1.